SAVAGE DOMINION

BOOK TWO
WYRMSHARD

SAVAGE DOMINION

BOOK TWO

WYRMSHARD

LUKE CHMILENKO

GD PENMAN

Wraithmarked

CREATIVE

Editor: Dominion Editing
Cover Illustration: Mansik YAM
Cover Design and Interior Layout: STK•Kreations

Trade paperback ISBN: 978-1-955252-05-8
Ebook ISBN: 978-1-955252-03-4

Worldwide Rights
1st Edition

Published by Wraithmarked Creative, LLC
www.wraithmarked.com

Since I popped up out of the soil of Amaranth like the biggest, ugliest mushroom you've ever seen, I've had exactly one girlfriend.

The paladin's blades shimmered in the twilight, moving so fast that it seemed the last scraps of sunlight could only barely catch them before they were gone.

There was no way that I could be that fast, that precise. Good thing I didn't need to be.

All it took was a blink and a grunt of effort and the great-sword that had knocked my other assailants on their asses shrunk and shifted, flowing like mercury around my body to form up again in a shield almost tall enough to reach my horns.

That beautiful dance smashed into the solid iron bulwark like a wave hitting the shore, and a grin split my face. "Didn't expect that, did you?"

Between the helm over her face and the bulk of the shield, I couldn't see my attacker's expression, but I was hoping it was a grumpy pout.

Back on Earth, I'd managed to square away a half-dozen girlfriends over the years, but I don't even know if they count any more, what with me being dead there and all. I kind of hope that they don't count. I was never the best boyfriend, even when I was trying my hardest. Which, on reflection, wasn't nearly often enough.

The smart play on her part would be side-stepping around the outside of my shield, so I lined up the little arming blade that I'd been left with after stripping off all the metal for my shield, pointing the thrusting tip towards that empty air and waiting. If she took the dumb side, the side with the sword on it, then I was still positioned in such a way that I'd be able to lash out and knock her back before she could press in close enough to do me any serious damage. It was a win-win.

She came over the top of the shield in one leaping bound, one foot touching off the top edge of it for extra height, slamming it down into the ground and wrecking my balance. That was a first.

Without the rote training for this kind of attack, I fell back on instinct, jerking up the arming blade to catch one of the descending shimmers of pointy murder. I turned it aside while the other still lanced forward, going for my throat.

Luck saved me then—the way it had a good too many times in the past. When I jerked my head around to see death coming, my horn hit the side of the thrusting blade, changing the destination of that razor-sharp point away from throat town and on a detour into empty air.

The full weight of my would-be stabber slammed into my face and chest then, but if she'd expected me to flinch, she was in for a shock. Having Alvaren pressed against my face was one of my favorite pastimes. I slammed my forehead into her with all the bunched muscles of my bullish neck and set her rolling back to a safer distance while I retrieved my shield from where it still stood wedged in the ground.

Even as I reached for it, it had started shrinking, the metal flowing away and reshaping. By the time I made contact with the handle, it had dwindled down into a hunk of metal no bigger than the cleaver in my other hand. A matching pair of cleavers. Two swords, just like her.

I feel like I'm entitled to a fresh start. So that makes my super-hot, blonde, Alvaren girlfriend my very first girlfriend. You might think that my very first girlfriend on this planet trying to slice my head off probably wasn't a good sign for the longevity of our relationship, but you'd be wrong. This was a massive step up from when I'd first met her.

Seren was back on her feet in some sort of elegant roll-backflip combo thing that bewildered me. She spun her blades and darted back in, hungry for first blood.

Even with the lighter cleavers, I was slower than her—sluggish-looking compared to the impossible grace of Alvaren—but I didn't need to be faster when I knew where every blow was going to fall. I'd been watching Alvaren fight since I first landed on Amaranth—or at least after I'd brought the species back from the special goblin-hell that their queen had dumped them in—and I knew their moves now.

Every one of them trained relentlessly for centuries to fight perfectly, but that perfection was a carbon copy of everyone else's. Once you could beat one of them, you could beat all of them.

It was really a shame I hadn't quite worked out how to beat a single one of them yet.

She came in hard and fast as always, not over-committing but pushing to see my limits. I had a better reach than her as my cleavers ran longer than the needle blades of hers despite their heft, and one of my arms was almost the size of her whole body. I just had to use that advantage, hold her back out of striking distance, and wear her down.

It might not have looked like it to the audience of gathered dvergar where they were lounging around the jungle clearing taking bets, but even though I was staggering and a bit beleaguered, I wasn't actually tiring. I couldn't. It was a faun thing. We didn't get tired.

I just had to outlast a swordswoman who'd been committing murder on a professional level since before the human race had crawled out of our caves back on Earth. Easy.

The first few strokes of her blade were coordinated, one razor edge chasing the other as she spun. Both chipped off one cleaver, leaving my other one free to sweep uselessly through the space where she'd stood. A moment too late.

She took to the air again, springing over that swing, spinning still and forcing me to duck or risk losing my face.

Touching down, she pounced back in at me. That would have been me dead again, but the flats of my cleavers were broad enough to serve as little shields when I swept them around. I turned the thrusts away, almost like I made them that way on purpose.

There was no time to make my own attack while that had her off balance. That was the thing you noticed with the Alvaren, the thing that made them look like they were so damned graceful. They weren't making one move and then making another once they'd done something. There was no stutter, no pause as one motion flowed into the next. It was all one move. Like everything that they were doing was a dance, and you were just in the middle of it. In the middle of a dance that nobody had taught you the steps to.

It looked like it was time to get down to business when she strode back in again, and the baying dvergar could tell too. They started hooting and hollering as the fight went from dramatic to methodical.

A thrust, a parry, a feint, a cut, a riposte.

Each of the alvaren's hands moved independently of the other. Each of them working me through a full fencing routine. Two full fencing routines at once. All things considered, I felt like I held up pretty well. Like I was dancing too. Moving back and forth across the packed dirt beneath our feet with some measure of competence that I didn't really feel like I'd earned.

Most of her feints were at my face, and most of her real strikes were at my body. Almost like she was scared to mess up my pretty face. That, or she wanted to make me extra distracted as I had to concentrate on not peeing myself every time a needle-sharp blade tip came at my eyeballs. Probably that.

I had strength on my side, though it probably wasn't that obvious given how fast she could recover. Every time I slapped one of her attacks wide with the flat of a cleaver, the force was almost enough to jerk the weapon out of her hand. I wasn't trying to win by overpowering her, but I wasn't trying to lose either. I was always going to be stronger than pretty much anything vaguely human-shaped, and acting like I wasn't wouldn't teach me how to fight better.

Her rhythm picked up once she'd rattled through a few of her attack routines until her hands were a blur. She kept me stepping back, running me in circles around the clearing, hoping I'd trip over a protruding rock or root like I'd done so many times before. It wasn't happening today. Not today.

When my moment came, I almost missed it. Both of her swords had lanced in at me from different directions, and I'd had to flip a cleaver in my left hand to catch the low thrust. If I'd been watching the swords, I probably would have missed it, but by then I'd won enough confidence to meet her eyes. I saw the moment of surprise when she realized that she'd over-committed.

I surged forward, slamming one arm down and one up, pinning her at the shoulders by the opposing forces knocking her blades out even wider.

We were face to face now as she lifted off the ground. I flicked my head as I reared back, hooking a horn under her helm and flinging it across the clearing. Her golden hair tumbled out and down her back, and her eyes narrowed to brace against the impact.

Across my shoulders and neck, those same colossal muscles I'd used to butt her across the clearing tensed once more, and then I hammered forward.

Her eyes closed, and her whole body tensed against the impact.

I placed a gentle kiss on her lips. Barely a brush of skin.

Victory!
Vitality increased to 19
Phalanx: Rank 8/10
128 Experience Gained

"Maulkin!" Seren's eyes snapped open, and a blue flush spread across her face as the dvergar began to roar with laughter around the edges of the clearing. This was better than I could have ever hoped for. I'd done worse than beat her. I'd embarrassed her. Oh, man. She was going to kick my ass all around this clearing when the morning came.

With a grin, I dropped her back to her feet. "Best two out of three?"

She retrieved her helm and tucked it under one arm, carefully avoiding the gaze of the dvergar who'd now moved on from cheering and jeering to exchanging money. After a losing streak of a month, the odds on me must have been really bad. If I'd had any idea that I might actually win a bout, I would have asked Mercy to put some gold on me.

"I believe that will be sufficient for today." Her eyes were still narrowed, and she spoke as stiffly as she didn't move. I didn't know if she genuinely didn't ache after these sessions or if she was just faking it, but I envied her. I'd be sore for the rest of the day. "You are much improved on the reckless ravening beast that I first encountered a moon back. Given a few more years training, perhaps you might make a passable foot-soldier."

I snorted with laughter. "I got you."

"You have come close enough to land a disabling blow. Once." She smiled at me frostily. "Once out of how many bouts?"

There was no way I was letting a little thing like a twenty-eight-day losing streak get me down now. This was a day for celebration. I'd finally won. All the training and practice and exercises and… everything I'd been devoting the last month of my life to, finally coming to fruition. "But you admit I got you?"

She strode to the edge of the clearing and attempted to hide the satisfaction on her face as the dvergar scattered out of her way. She called back over her shoulder, "There can be no denying that if we wish to see the Voidgod kissed, you are the Eternal for the job."

I stomped after her, giving my adoring fans a wave as I went.

About ninety percent of the crowd were scowling at me for taking easy money out of their pockets.

Our little dirt circle was way out in the jungle. Everything on this island was way out in the jungle, if you wanted to nitpick, but from the tower where we lived, this particular bit was way out. As we made our way back to the tower and the village grown up out of the ruins at its feet, it was like moving backward in time through my day. At the end of every day was the circle of mud where Seren kicked me around after every willing dvergar had tried their luck. Farther back there was this obstacle course.

Tree stumps jutted up at odd heights throughout the long half-empty channel of partially cleared forest we moved through next. For the first few weeks, I'd hated this bit, bouncing on the balls of my feet from one stump-top to the next, constantly on the verge of overbalancing, even when I was doing everything right. Did you know that Faun are top-heavy? As a species, we look like we've been skipping leg day for centuries, and the big honking horns on the sides of my head didn't help either.

After the second week, when it looked like I had the hang of it, Seren had recruited Mercy to shoot at me as I went. Arrows without heads that stung when they hit knocked me off balance, but they didn't actually do much damage. The problem wasn't that I was bad at getting out of the way, the problem was that Mercy was a really good shot. Seren knew that. The point wasn't for me to dodge, it was for me to keep balance while getting shot. Took me a while to work that one out.

With her languid, gliding strides, Seren had already passed through this whole section of the obstacle course by the time that I spotted her. Was this still part of my daily workout? I broke into a run.

Next was the acrobatics section of the course, meant to exhaust me before I could even get started on the balancing act. It never worked. There were climbing walls, and tunnels dug down under the roots of the forest—all the stuff that made outdoorsy people back on Earth salivate with excitement and people like me wonder what the point was.

Seren had informed me that the point was 'getting accustomed to my new body'. The same reason that she had me strip down and swim a mile along the coastline every other day before we started on this whole routine. Personally, I think she was just perving on me. Like when she had me lifting the weights we passed next.

We were just shy of the long, winding path back from our little corner of heaven to the village when I caught up to her and tackled her around the waist. I swept her off her feet and spun around and around, and she couldn't help but smile. Just a little—that tiny secret smile that she seemed to save just for me. I had to ruin the moment, of course. "If you'd prefer for me to spank you instead of kissing you next time I beat you, that can be arranged."

I didn't even see her drawing her sword before the tip of it flicked up to prick the underside of my chin. "Perhaps we should find a better use for that mouth of yours."

She was trying to be intimidating, but there was no stopping the grin that spread over my face now. "And what might that be?"

An arrow shot along the forest path and passed between our faces.

I dropped Seren, and we had both jerked back into combat readiness before we heard Mercy braying, "No making out in the forest! That's how you get woodlice."

I eased my reconstituted great-sword back into its baldric. "Mercy, I swear to the gods…"

"I was just coming to get you two. Dinner is ready, and Asher… well, it sounds like he might come out of the tower."

That was exciting enough news that I stopped bitching about how close I came to an eyebrow piercing. "Holy crap."

"I know, right! One of the dvergar he tricked into fetching and tidying in the library said that he was making noises all day. Like…

Eureka kind of noises."

I caught Seren by the hand and dragged her along as she was still trying to gather the exact words with which to eviscerate Mercy for shooting at us as a joke. "It occurs that thy compatriots are somewhat blasé about attempted murder. Perhaps because of how impermanent the state of death is for your kind."

"She wasn't trying to hit you." She was literally digging her heels in, so I stopped yanking on her arm in case it came off. Seren reached up and turned my face to her again, keeping my attention on her. Like I'd go all weak at the knees and dumb just because... Okay, actually, yeah she was that pretty.

"When arrows are loosed, there is always a danger. Danger she seems blind to, simply because it has no lasting meaning to either of you."

I didn't try to look away, but I did blink hard so I could get my thoughts back together. "Even if you somehow got hit, I'd heal you! Nothing to worry about."

Still, she cradled my cheek. "That arrow passed within an inch of my eye. You cannot raise the dead."

"Not yet." I gave her my patented cheeky grin again, but it completely failed to have the desired effect.

"Do you have no care for how my lifeblood is spent at all?" She cast her eyes down, and I realized that this wasn't just predictable bitterness about me beating her, making her switch to another avenue of attack. It was genuine worry. Genuine fear. Not of dying—I knew her too well to consider that she was scared of dying—but of dying to some stupid, pointless accident.

I groaned and felt like an asshole. "Alright. Alright. I'm sorry. You're right. I'll tell her off, okay?"

"And what of you? Will you stop treating your life as a game?"

"Why would I quit while I'm winning?"

This time the grin seemed to do the trick. She fell into step beside me, even letting me put an arm around her shoulders instead of shrugging it off. "When you first asked me if I would train you in the martial arts, when you expressed your desire to move beyond mere brute force and into the realm of actual craft, it had been my hope that you would approach the matter with some seriousness."

That actually brought me to a stop. "You don't think I've been taking it seriously?"

She gave me one of those sideways looks that meant I'd said something dumber than usual. "You have been positively… gleeful."

"It is fun!" I jostled her with my hip. "I'm meant to pretend it isn't fun?"

"The dvergar sparring partners that you bat around like a cat toys with a ball of yarn do not take kindly to your laughter, and nor do I."

I muffled a laugh, but not quickly enough to avoid a venomous glance. "So you're mad that I'm having a good time beating you?"

"Once. You have bested me once, and for that, I would allow a certain degree of satisfaction." Her shoulders slumped within her armor. "Frankly, that concerns me less than the 'good time' you seem to be having when I am besting you."

"If this is about the time I grabbed you by the… uh… chest when we were sparring…"

She slapped a hand over my mouth, blue tinging her cheeks. "That… matter… requires no further discussion. My concern is that it does not seem to irk you when you are defeated. No matter how badly I thwart your efforts, you seem untroubled."

"Well, yeah." I shrugged. "I'm learning. I don't expect to win every single time while I'm still learning."

"You are not… You are not a child in a classroom. You are a soldier, fighting a war against the most dangerous foe that this world has ever known. Against a multitude of enemies so powerful that they are thought by most to be legend, yet your attitude is that of a man without concerns."

We emerged from the forest into the village, and it was a proper dvergar village now. A month of non-stop construction work had transformed it from the abandoned ruins we'd found when we first landed on this island. The old outbuildings of Talon's Keep were still there beneath the wooden structures that had been built around them, but they served more as foundations than structures in themselves.

Everywhere that you turned your head there was industry. A great mound of dirt to the east marked the beginnings of the mine that would make this place a true home to the dvergar, but even that mound was not sitting idle. The soil was sifted for anything of value, then the dirt itself was used to build the raised plateaus of farmland over where the trees had been cleared back.

It had been generations since the dvergar grew food beneath the sun of the surface, maybe these ones never had, but Asher's never-ending book heap had filled them in on any of the technical details that they were missing.

The forges plumed smoke into the sky, staining the pale stone of the tower where it brushed by with soot. I'm sure Talon would have been pissed about us making a mess of his tower, but he was too dead to complain, and I kind of liked having the place a little bit messy. It made this place look lived-in. After seeing so much of Amaranth as a dead husk of a planet where civilization had dried up and blown away, some soot stains were a welcome reminder that we were still here.

I smiled down at Seren and placed another gentle kiss on her forehead. "Worrying isn't going to change anything. It isn't going to make me stronger. It isn't going to make the quest any less… big. It would just make me sad."

"I cannot for the life of me decipher whether you are a philosopher of great wisdom or an utter buffoon."

Mercy called over from the cookfire. "Oh, don't let him fool you. He's a moron."

"Love you too, Mercy!"

She turned back to the dvergar that always seemed to be clustered around her with a scowl. This time they were begrudgingly handing her money. I guess she'd been betting on me after all. Gambling seemed to be the only thing that the dvergar actually kept money for. Maybe it was different when they'd lived in their old city, but I hadn't seen much sign of it then either.

Gunhild ambled over to nudge me in the knee, smirking so hard I was worried she'd hurt herself. "Did you like to be winning for a change?"

I took one look at that smile and sighed. "You had money on me too?"

She let out a loud chortle, then leaned in closer to grumble, "You cost me dear, but it'll be giving me better odds when I be betting against you tomorrow, and I'll wager that little lass of yours has something to prove now."

Gunhild was right, of course. Even if Seren said she wasn't mad, I was going to get poked a lot tomorrow.

While she hadn't actually killed me yet, I'd spent the last of my Glory ahead of our first training session just in case she got carried away and I ended up popping back to life at my shrine over by the tower. I wasn't too dumb to admit that maybe Seren was right about me being a bit casual about dying, given that the worst consequences of her cutting my head off would be that I wouldn't have to walk so far to get back for dinner.

Around dinner time, I usually got jovial ribbing from whichever of the dvergar had volunteered to join in my training that day. After getting patted about with the flat of my sword for hours on end, the sight of Seren kicking my ass usually gave them some much-needed catharsis. Today a couple of them tried it with Seren and got treated to that same blank serial killer stare she used to give me every time I spoke. It stopped pretty promptly after that.

Even if Seren hadn't been her usual prickly self, things felt strange. Like the quiet before the storm. The news that Asher's endless research had finally borne fruit had spread much farther than just our ears. People kept spilling their stew because they were too busy staring at the door of the tower, just waiting for him to finally emerge. By the time that the bottles of post-dinner drinks were being cracked open, I was about ready to climb up the tower and drag him out by his tail myself.

I met Mercy's gaze across the fire, and she just shrugged. I looked to Seren, and she gave me a blank stare. It was possible that there would not be any smooching happening in the tower this evening. I had to acknowledge that possibility, even if I didn't like it.

Just when my patience was running out, I caught a glimpse of him coming down the stairs. I stood to go over and meet him, then thought better of it, sitting down again with enough force that the dvergar on the far end of the log bench popped up in the air. Oops.

It was a testament to how weird the energy was in the village that I was still on my first serving of stew, nudging it around in circles. Technically we didn't need to eat, as Eternals, but I was still in the habit from back on Earth. And when we didn't eat, the dvergar would get antsy. They were big on communal meals. Big on food as a love language. That was why some of the only things they'd saved from Khag Mhor before it crumbled into a pit in the ground were cooking pots and chests of spices. Anyway, they took it as a personal insult if you wouldn't eat with them. So we ate.

All of us except Asher, up in his tower. The Dvergar hadn't taken offense at that for some reason. I'd heard some of them talking about him when they thought I couldn't hear them. Consumed, was the word they used. Or maybe it was obsessed. The word didn't translate directly. My brain grasped the meaning, but I couldn't have said it in any other language than dvergar.

He had spent all this time in Talon's library, where he'd been sequestered for so long that I half-expected the color to have faded from his scales when he finally emerged, blinking, into the firelight. He still remembered how to speak at least. "Greetings to you, my friends."

Mercy just couldn't help herself. "Look who finally worked out how stairs work."

"My apologies for the long absence"—his head actually bobbed down like he was embarrassed, as though the rest of us hadn't been having a holiday while he did all the mental heavy lifting—"but I am sure that you shall find my investment of time paid off in full."

That perked me up in an instant. "You've found the location of the rest of the Shards?"

"Ah." His scaly snout pointed back down to the ground, and his tail swished. "No."

Mercy snapped her fingers. "But you've found a way to find them?"

"Also no."

I leapt to my feet in excitement. "You've found a spell to blow up the Voidgod?"

"Once more, that is a no."

Gunhild piped up. "You've found out where old Talon be hiding his liquor?"

Asher's tail was really lashing with irritation now. "I regret to say that I wasn't even looking for something along those lines."

Seren joined in the game. "Perchance thy has uncovered some great ancient secret that might prevent the restoration of the Voidgod?"

Asher trudged over and sank to his haunches beside the fire. "Alas, I cannot say that I have discovered any such thing."

"Guys, can we all stop guessing and let him tell us?" Mercy flopped back over the log bench like a puppet with cut strings. "Before we die of old age?"

I added my little contribution to the time-wasting. "We don't age."

Mercy's head popped back up to scowl at me. "But still, somehow, I can feel wrinkles appearing the longer that this drags on…"

Asher cut us off. "I have discovered the secret of the waystones."

The collected dvergar looked at him blankly, and I have to admit it took me a minute to catch up to what he was saying too. "The big floaty ring things?"

"The network that allowed instantaneous travel throughout Amaranth through arcane power, yes." He hadn't even groaned. I must have been losing my touch.

Seren asked, ever so politely, "Were you not meant to be researching the shards?"

"Even for a devoted researcher such as myself, there reaches a point when one must accept that a hundred corroborating sources are providing all that there is to be had." Asher slumped a little in the face of the question. It seemed to take a lot of effort to lift his head back up and meet our collective gaze. "From our earlier efforts, we have ascertained that the Great Wyrm Tsangaanax holds both his own and the dvergar shard, and the human shard has been passed down to the ruler of the Shattered Bastion. That left only the Faun shard to trace, and it seems that they have an oral tradition rather than a written one."

Mercy piped up, "So they spend all of their time down on their knees—"

Asher cut her off neatly. "Reciting tales of their history to one another."

"So what?" I was perplexed. "Nobody else ever listened in on storytime?"

"It would appear that the famously loathed and insular race of the Chagnar Faun were not inclined to share their sacred secret legendarium with any traveler who happened by." Asher scoffed. "I can find few references to the Faun at all in the collected records here—and almost always it is in the context of warfare being waged upon them so that areas they held might become… civilized."

There was a dull silence around the fire for a long moment, when we could all hear the crackle of the wood and the soft clunk of spoons in bowls. They were all waiting for me to launch into another rant about the poor misunderstood Faun, and I just couldn't bring myself to do it.

Did it suck that a whole race had been written off by the world of Amaranth? Of course, it did. Would shouting about it make a difference? Not right now.

When it became apparent that I was shutting up for the first time in living memory, Asher pushed on. "Perhaps I might direct your attention back to the fact that we can now be instantaneously transported anywhere in the world that is connected to our waystone network, potentially eliminating months of traveling time, and even permitting us a swift return to the field should we be defeated in combat."

"Never going to happen." I shared a grin with Seren and Mercy. Mercy hadn't joined us every day for training—most of her training time had been spent alone in the woods, hunting for the dvergar. Sneaking and shooting like she did best. It was all towards the same goal though. "That's what we've been doing while you've been reading. Practicing. Training. Honing our skills. The next time we run into a fight, there isn't going to be any of the old frantic slap and zap."

Asher clapped his scaly hands together. "Then let us put your training to good use at last."

Oh no. He meant right now. I wasn't ready. I wasn't ready yet. I hadn't worked out how to hide my little problem yet. "Do we even know where any of the floaty ring things lead though?"

"While it seems inevitable that some of the arcane nexus Talon bound into the chains have broken down over time, he left a full accounting of every place that the stones were raised. The coverage is not expansive, but nor did it stretch into those unknown areas where it is liable to have fallen into hostile hands. Several sites of interest to our quest are close by to the chain."

Mercy piped up with her own complaint, gods bless her. "What if there are broken stones in the chain? Does that mean we're all going to get turned into jelly if we try to go through?"

But Asher had an answer for that too. "It struck me that we could not be entirely certain of the extent to which the chain was intact, so I examined Talon's notation on the subject. It seems that you would simply be ejected from the last intact waystone."

"So it will just spit us out into the ocean?" I tried as hard as I could to make it sound like I was upset about the idea instead of excited about a giant magic waterslide.

"My expectation is that none of the waystones set out in the water will have been subjected to much in the way of interference, yet nonetheless, I do believe that it would be wise for us to send a single volunteer through first. That way, they might identify any trouble that may lay in wait on the other side of the stones."

All eyes turned to me then. I had no idea why I had this reputation for suicidal bravery, but he'd said volunteer, and I was not volunteering for a damn thing.

I wasn't volunteering to go out into the world and explore, maybe fight monsters, and unlock awesome new powers. I wasn't volunteering to ride the giant magic water slide. I wasn't volunteering for any of it. I wasn't signing up for anything except another month of chilling on a tropical island with my hot Alvaren girlfriend.

My last desperate attempt to dodge this bullet squeaked out of me while the collective stare of the whole village burrowed into the side of my head, judging me for not volunteering to shoot myself through the cannon and see where I landed. Dammit. Even I couldn't make it sound like that wasn't fun. "Do you know if this spell you've found even works?"

"The theoretical elements are all sound, but it shall only be through casting that we will be entirely certain of its success." He turned to stare at me, just like everyone else. "Once we have a volunteer to pass through the gate."

Once again, the sound of the crackling fire rose to fill the silence. Night birds called out among the trees, and high above us, the wild winds that Talon's storm-butterflies kicked up were whistling. Everyone was staring at me in annoyed silence.

Mercy was the one to break the silence. Predictably. "Okay, what the hell?"

"What?"

"Don't 'what' me! What you! What are you doing?"

"Nothing!"

"Exactly! Before we beat Talon, you were like… the fuel in the engine of this whole thing. You were raring to go, all day every day. Willing to do whatever you had to do to get out there and find the shards and beat the bad guys, and now… what? You just want to sit?"

"I've been busy. We've all been busy. We've been training!"

"Oh, bull. We didn't need training before, and we don't need it now. You just wanted an excuse to get sweaty with Seren all day."

Seren turned almost entirely blue but said nothing.

Meanwhile, I got angry on her behalf. "We got lucky! We're up against big scary things now. Tsangaanax made Talon into his bitch without even breaking a sweat, and that guy was a super-powerful wizard dude. We're trying to save the world; we can't just hope things are going to keep going our way."

Asher nodded approvingly at my sentiment, and that was when I knew for sure that I'd gone too far.

Mercy's jaw hung open. "Who the hell are you, and what have

you done with Maulkin?"

"Oh come on. Just because I think that we should spend a little time preparing instead of throwing ourselves headlong into trouble, you think that I've been pod-person-ed?" Try as I might, I just wasn't a good enough liar to convince anyone that I wanted the opposite of what I really wanted.

I wanted to get back out there. I wanted to go find the rest of the shards, slap them together, and then beat in Araphel's blank spooky face with it. I wanted that more than anything. But if things got rough out there, I had no idea how I was going to keep my dirty little secret.

Mercy was on her feet now, pointing an accusatory finger at me. "Maulkin would have been bouncing up and down on the spot if you told him he got to go through a magic portal that might dump him in the middle of the sea. Maulkin would think that was fun. Maulkin would have already made up three excuses for why he was the best choice to go."

The reasons were already on the tip of my tongue before she even said it. "I mean, with my stats, I would survive for longer if I got dumped in the sea, maybe long enough to swim to safety, and I don't really lose anything if I die since all my Glory is already invested. And I can remake my gear from nothing when I respawn."

Mercy grinned. "Starting to sound like Maulkin again…"

"But I just think that we should be cautious."

"By the gods." Seren gawked at me too, glad that attention was no longer pointed her way. "Did you truly just flinch when you said 'cautious'. Like it was a dirty word?"

"I… I…" Suddenly, the effort of lying to them all was too much for me. I was going mad sitting around here, knowing that somewhere out there Araphel was crawling back to life while I twiddled my thumbs. More than that though, I was so deeply bored. We had been doing the same thing for a month. Every day, getting up, exercising. Training. I felt like my brain was crawling up the insides of my skull. If it hadn't been for the variety of interesting things that Seren and I did in the bedroom we'd claimed up in the tower these past few weeks, I probably would have thrown myself in the sea and tried to swim to the Shattered Bastion by myself. With something like a sob, I broke down. "I want to get shot out the magic cannon into the sea."

Mercy grabbed me by the shoulders and cheered. "There's my big dumb guy!"

They were getting what they wanted. They were getting big dumb Maulkin throwing himself into trouble. They should have been satisfied, but Asher was still looking at me with a quizzical tilt to his head. He was suspicious. That same methodical brain that had been chipping through all the mysteries of Amaranth had just added why I was acting funny to his to-solve list. Great.

Okay, full disclosure. I might have done something really dumb. I make a lot of impulse decisions, and normally, they work out great. They're how I ended up as a big buff faun with a big choppy sword, spending the rest of my eternity on a bitching awesome dungeon crawl. They're how I got all my cool powers. They're also how I ended up with my dirty little secret.

Technically speaking, I wasn't a Lunar Eternal any more—at least, not just a Lunar Eternal. As I'd bound more and more shards of the Rusted Blade to my soul, it had started to change me. The moonlight inside me had started to dim. The glow in my eyes had faded until you could barely see it. I could almost pass for a normal Faun if nobody looked too closely at them. Most importantly, the mark on my soul that the gods had inscribed to say, "This guy is on team moon," had been vandalized with a little scribble that added, "and team Voidgod."

When I first landed on this rock, Asher, Mercy, and I were not besties. The fact that I was a Lunar Eternal while they were Solar ones... well, it was almost enough to put them at my throat right up front. Even as we've gotten to know each other, and they've come to recognize that I'm cool as hell, there have still been little moments where they didn't trust me, just because I serve the primordial pantheon of chaos instead of the prissy sunshine order like them.

By the end of our little quest to grab Talon's shard, I was pretty sure that all of that was behind us though. That they finally trusted me and recognized that Lunar and Solar Eternals could hold hands and frolic and junk. If they knew that I'd been signed up to the Voidgod softball team, that trust was going to evaporate pretty damned fast.

As if that little mark on my soul wasn't scary and confusing enough, the Pillars of Divinity which gave me all my godly powers had doubled in number, with every pretty sparkly pillar reflected with a dark counterpart. And that should have been that. That really should have been that. If I had just stopped then and there, I wouldn't have any problem keeping the dark pillars or my additional affiliation a secret from everyone else.

The problem was, some of those void powers sounded freaking awesome.

For every ability that let me create something or heal somebody in the Lunar Pillars, there was an equal and opposite reaction in the Void Pillars. My ability to build equipment out of raw materials with just a thought? What about disassembling the armor my enemies were wearing? Healing with a touch? What about draining the life out of somebody instead?

It was like somebody had taken all the awesome powers that the other baby godlings and I could tap into and then created the heavy metal version of them. I wanted them so bad.

So I made my stupid impulsive decision. When I had to sink the last of my Glory into something before going off to train with Seren for the first time, I ignored all the perfectly good, not-going-to-ruin-my-life options and went straight for those sweet, succulent void pillars.

Look, I never said I was smart. I've never even implied it. In fact, you could probably take a look at everything that I've ever said and done and sum it up as: "Damn, this guy is as dumb as a sack of rocks."

So I was more than a little uncomfortable about Asher's scrutiny, and I spent the rest of the evening sidling my way around the fire and doing my best to avoid getting sucked into a private conversation with him. Even though he might have had all the emotional insight of a coconut, he was also doggedly persistent when he thought that there might be an answer to one of his puzzles.

Luckily for me, I had a built-in excuse to go sidling away from the cookfire long before everyone was drunk and singing like usual. I caught Seren's eye across the fire and waggled my eyebrows at her. She didn't smile—those were still rare little treats that were usually reserved for in private—but she did give me a little nod of acknowledgment and slipped away from the conversation going on around her but never including her.

I stood up to follow her a moment later, telling everyone I was sleepy and needed my energy for being zapped through space and time by Asher come morning. They let me go without much resistance, even if they did usually enjoy watching me get drunk and abuse my Artifice powers for entertainment purposes.

At the tower entrance, Mercy was waiting with her arms crossed. "Took you long enough."

"Have you been waiting there this whole time?"

"No." She rose to her full height, trying to meet my gaze eye to eye and mostly managing eye to chin. "Just since I noticed you were trying not to talk to me or Asher."

She noticed that. Of course, she noticed that. "Well, you guys were being weird."

"No, don't do that." She strode in closer, and now we were seeing eye to nipple. "Don't try to turn this around on us. You are being weird. Really weird. And I'm used to your usual weird. Gods help me, sometimes I kind of like your usual weird. But this is a new weird. Weird even for you."

"Weirder than saying weird fifteen times in a row?"

She was close enough now that I had to squat a little bit to hear her hissing. "I can and will kick you directly in your boy parts."

I regretted squatting. That made her target so much easier to hit. "Just chill out! I didn't see you volunteering to get launched through Asher's magic catapult."

"Yeah, because if I did, that would be weird." She stomped back into the tower and sat down on the stone bench we'd made out of dead golem parts. "But you not volunteering? That is bizarre! From the second that we crawled out our graves, you've been in a mad panic to chase after the shards, and now you just want to kick back? What happened to you? What changed?"

"Nothing changed! Araphel still needs his ass kicked. I just"— Screwed up and absorbed too much of his evil essence and might be turning into a Voidgod myself—"thought we could all do with a little breather."

"So you really, really, just wanted to lounge around for a month with your new girlfriend?"

"Is that so hard to believe?" I pointed up the stairs after Seren. She was probably already up there, waiting for me. "She's really hot!"

"Okay, first of all, *ew*." She counted them off on her fingers. "Second, I am like ninety percent hotter than blondie brat, and I'm not an elf-supremacist psycho."

"So what, you're jealous?" I waggled my eyebrows at her. "You wanted some Maulkin for yourself?"

"And we're back to *ew*, again." She counted that on her fingers too. Was she counting every ew? "No, you are gross. You know you're gross. I just wanted to make it clear so that you know…"

I gave her an incredulous look. "That you're hotter than my girl-friend?"

"I am, but I'm only telling you that in a purely objective way that has nothing to do with wanting anything to do with your rhino-looking ass." She pointed her counting finger in accusation. "And don't think I didn't notice you skipping over the fact your sweet little Seren thinks we're all subhuman just because we don't have pointy ears like her."

"That isn't fair." I shifted uncomfortably. Mercy needed to stop being right on the money. It was getting annoying. "She's getting better."

She let out a completely mirthless laugh. "Yeah, she hardly even looks like she wants to spit on the dvergar anymore."

I slumped down onto the bench beside her so that I could keep my voice down. Those pointed ears on Seren weren't just for show, and sound echoed right up this tower. "She grew up surrounded by people like that. No contact with anyone else outside of that cult of alvaren greatness. Is it really that surprising that she believed the same stuff as everyone else she grew up with?"

"I had a racist grandma." Mercy rolled her eyes. "Didn't make me racist."

"So did I—goes with grandma territory, I guess?" Mercy looked ready to interrupt, but I talked over her little self-congratulation dance. "But I didn't grow up in crazy-elf-Nazi-land, and neither did you. She's doing better than she was. Okay? Sometimes she might fall back on… how she's been brought up, but that isn't her. It isn't all of her."

For a long moment, Mercy sat there in sullen silence, then, just when I was getting up to go upstairs and try to find some tiny sliver of joy in the evening, she stopped me with a boot stuck out in my path. "Don't think I didn't see what you did there, turning the conversation into something about her instead of telling me what is actually wrong with you. You know I don't like it when you keep secrets from me, Maulkin. And I don't like being lied to."

I stepped over her leg, and she raised the other one. "Who is lying to you?"

"This isn't over." She tried to lock her legs around my shin, but I jumped out and half-staggered over to the stairs as she called after me, "You're going to tell me what is going on."

I shouted back over my shoulder, "I've got no idea what you're talking about!"

"You're a bad liar."

The steps vanished beneath my stride, three at a time. "I must be an awful liar if I don't even know I'm lying."

As I rounded the corner and headed out of sight, she yelled, "I've got my eye on you."

I took a couple of steps back down the stairs, so she could see me from the waist down. Then I wiggled my hips. "On my rhino-looking ass?"

"Ew."

I wonder if she counted that one too.

CHAPTER 2

The sun rose, the dvergar got to work as noisily as ever, and I walked out to meet the whole gang over at the shore. The island was pretty thoroughly mapped by this point, both by the dvergar laying out their expansion plans and by me and the other Eternals hunting down what was left of the chameleon lizardman assassin beasties that were still running wild. In none of that mapping did any of us come across a big stone pillar and a floaty ring thing, making the one on the distant horizon, pointing back along the route we'd taken from Witchglass Overlook, into the one and only waystone relay that was feasibly accessible.

Asher worked out almost as soon as we arrived on the beach that it would have been easier to line up an angle on the floaty ring from one of the upper rooms in Talon's Keep, but none of us could be bothered wasting any more of the morning hiking back and forth through the sweltering forest. Instead, he set to work, checking and double-checking the incantation that would bring the ancient magic to life while the rest of us twiddled our thumbs.

Seren had come down to the beach to see me off in an uncharacteristic display of sentimentality, but the longer the delay stretched on, the more awkward having her standing around seemed. While I was here, she had something to focus her attention on. She'd been so delighted when I asked her to train me, and no small part of that was that it took her away from everyone else. When she was busy with me it was easy for her to ignore the fact that everyone else on the island kind of hated her.

In a weird way, kicking my ass every day had been helping her to fit in. For all their talk of being a peaceful people, the dvergar loved to watch a fight, and they particularly loved to watch some waif of a woman tossing around a giant of a man like he was an empty sack. She didn't have friends among the dvergar, but they had some respect for her skills—and maybe a bit of a fan club, watching her from afar.

Without me, she was going to be left lingering. There was work here for farmers and miners, for builders and planners, but warriors? There was no requirement for them. We'd seen to that when we cleared the island of anything that looked even vaguely hostile. I didn't even know if Mercy and Asher would talk to her when I was gone. I mean, Asher might ask her a relentless barrage of questions to try and get more information about whatever he was obsessing about at any given moment, but it wasn't the same as having a conversation with her like she was an actual person.

She gave me a chaste kiss on the cheek and then stepped back. "I shall be awaiting thy return with bated breath."

"Miss you too."

After cross-referencing three different scrolls and two books, Asher ushered me to stand between him and the floating ring poking up over the horizon. "Our set target is the Shattered Bastion, but if the spell should falter, do your best to discover nearby landmarks before you expire so that we can determine the reach of the undamaged waystones." I must have been looking a bit nervous because he tried to smile at me, showing rows of pointed teeth. Then he said the least comforting thing imaginable. "This should be entirely painless, so if you do experience any discomfort, please alert me as it may mean something has gone awry."

"Dude, you're about to lightning-bolt pea-shooter me across the world." When I laughed it had a manic edge to it. "That's a first for me. I don't know what it is meant to feel like."

Mercy grinned. "I hope it hurts like hell. Proper camel through the eye of a needle stuff. Squirting."

"Want to swap places?"

She scoffed. "And miss out on another riveting day of sunbathing?"

When I turned back to Asher for moral support, I realized he was already in the middle of casting. Oh crap. Glancing up at Seren, I saw her raising a hand to wave goodbye, then abruptly, she was gone.

Have you ever had every molecule of your body torn apart by wild magic and flung through the air? Do you have any idea what that feels like? Me neither. It all happened too fast for me to notice. One minute I was standing there on the beach, and the next I was just… somewhere else.

That somewhere else was a courtyard, of sorts. My arrival displaced the air with the sound of a tiny thunderclap, turning every head my way. The ring of the waystone set into the wall behind me also gave me a nice dramatic backlight as it glowed a dazzling green for a moment before fading back to grey.

The walls around the courtyard had been made from solid stone once upon a time. Not bricks but great sheets of rock dragged up into place and carved into the shape that was required. That had been once upon a time. Age and some terrible cataclysm had rent those walls, leaving the stone bubbled and melted at the edges of the damage. Somebody had patched the hole with clay brickwork now, but it stuck out enough that I noticed that wedge of terracotta before I noticed that there were a dozen armed men screaming all around me.

Humans. The first ones I'd seen since I landed on this rock. It was almost enough to bring a tear to my eye to see another human being. Mercy didn't count.

Bells started ringing up on the walls above us, and a cry echoed out through the castle beyond. "The enemy has breached the center yard!"

I spun around, looking for whatever enemy were bothering my

little human buddies, and then I realized who they were talking about. "Oh! Oh no. Guys, I'm not your enemy! I'm human too, or at least, I used to be. I mean. Let me start over…"

A crossbow bolt punched through my armor and embedded in my shoulder. Ow.

"Guys! I'm not here to fight you! I'm on your side."

Another crossbow bolt flitted down from the raised walkway along the patched wall. It would have hit me square in the face if I hadn't jerked to the side. I shouted a bit louder since they seemed to be hard of hearing. "Could you stop shooting at me? I'm on your side!"

The men who'd been down in the yard when I first arrived had drawn swords, axes, and shields. Some of them were fussing with armor straps, and others had run when I arrived, carrying the call of, "Breach!" throughout whatever building was beyond this little square.

That probably wasn't good news.

Up on the wall, more guards came pouring in, fully armored in the boiled leather and chainmail that seemed to cover everybody in this place. More crossbows were leveled at me. I had both my empty hands held up at this point, but that didn't seem to do anything to slow proceedings down.

The closest of the men down in the square seemed to find his courage, and he charged at me with his axe held high. After so long fighting Alvaren, he seemed almost comically slow, charging and roaring across the last few feet. I caught the axe under the head and jerked it out of his hands.

"Will you people just listen to me? I'm not here to fight you."

Fear was all I could see on the face of the man with no axe. No recognition of the words I was saying. No hint that he even understood, though I knew that with my Eternal's gift of speaking in tongues, he could understand every damn word. He scampered back out of reach in a panic, flinching away as if I was going to beat on him with his own axe. Instead, I dropped it on the ground and tried to lift my empty hands again.

"Guys, can you just stop for a minute? Who's in charge here?"

Despite their initial panic, the men up on the walls had fallen into their training now, the front rank dropping to one knee while those behind them lined up their shots, resting the hafts of the crossbows on their buddies' helms.

Oh crap.

The moment that the ex-axe-man was out of range, they unleashed their volley of bolts at me. A solid wall of spikey death, soaring through the air.

I got my shield formed just in time. It had barely hardened before the bolts hit it, the force of the impact sending me sliding back across the dirt yard. With a blink of my eyes, I shrunk the wall of raw iron back down into my sword and hefted it over my head.

It was bigger than any two of the guys who were now running at me, and I could actually see the moment that their brains processed what their eyes were telling them and panic set in. Their charge turned into a skid, and they tried to reverse direction, figuring out pretty fast that their little wooden shields weren't going to do much if I swung for them. Maybe now they'd listen. "Guys, I'm not here to fight anybody. I just want to…"

There were two entrances to the courtyard, one leading to another open-air area opposite the red scarred wall and the other opposite the waystone, sealed with a set of iron-studded doors that looked sturdy enough to stop even me from kicking my way through. Reinforcements streamed in through both of them, spilling out and forming into a right angle of battle lines. "Oh come on! Why does everybody in Amaranth want to stab first and ask questions later?"

Pikemen came up behind the first lines and thrust their big floppy spears out to rest on the flat tops of the front rank's kite shields. This was not looking promising either. They advanced on me, step by step, shrinking the width of their line by one body each time and closing the square smaller and smaller, driving me towards the corner of the outer wall, beneath the frantically reloading crossbowmen.

I was running out of room and running out of choices. If I didn't fight back in the next few seconds, I was going to turn into a shish-ka-Maulkin. So I did the only thing I could do. I fought back.

With one sweep of my great-sword, I turned aside the pikes that were thrusting at me, and before the ones to either side could start thrusting in at my flanks, I spun in a full circle, slamming the flat of the blade against the front ranks' shields.

There was a cacophonous gong, and the soldiers flew back into the ones behind them. The whole formation fell like dominos, and I leapt over them, going for the door. I needed to get out of here, get some distance, and maybe find somebody in the whole place who had a couple of brain cells and understood what it meant when I said: "I'm not here to murder you all. Please chill."

I headed through the doorway and into a corridor with the crowd of toppled soldiers braying at my back, plain stone walls stretching off as far as the eye could see, no tapestry or decoration or anything to make this place homey. Just rock. Even dvergar mines had more personality. There were doors off to either side of the corridor, but I could hear footsteps slapping along behind me, and I didn't fancy try-ing to fight in a solid stone tube that I was barely small enough to fit into. Another of the reinforced doors was up ahead, and I didn't like my odds of not smacking flat into it like a cartoon character.

For a couple of steps, my body stumbled as my consciousness swept out of it and along the corridor as far as my sphere of influence. I could feel the lock on the door as a staticky mass in my perception—some-thing too complex for my Rough Hewn Architecture to touch. Good thing it was nestled in a plain stone wall really. One little push of will loosened the wall's grip on the door, and it widened out enough that the deadbolt was now slotted into open air.

I banged through the now unlocked door and into another open-air square. There was no patch on the outer wall of this one, though some of the next building looked a bit piecemeal, and there were no archers standing guard up on the walkway. I figured they were the reinforcements that had come tearing in to shoot at me in the last open space. Great, no crossbow bolts. It was just a pity that was balanced out by there being even more soldiers standing around on my level of this one.

There was a split second to decide whether this lot might be more susceptible to pleading, flattery, and begging before I heard those slapping boots behind me closing the distance. No stopping.

Hunching up my shoulders and ducking down my head, I charged—not straight ahead to the next locked door but for the open archway to the side. For all I knew this place was a big circle, and chasing along through these walls was just going to take me back to the waystone courtyard. Time for a change of scenery.

The next courtyard in clearly hadn't started out life that way. The walls, where they stood, were still that same smooth stone, but it had started to vault up into a roof before the topside had been torn away. There were patches where you could still see the curve of it heading up before the melt swept the rest away. Most of the walls had gone the same way, ripped through by some great cataclysm and still on the waiting list for the shoddy brickwork patch-job that the outer wall had benefitted from.

If I ever got a whole second when folks weren't trying to murder me, I'd love to use Spirit Touch and work out what the hell had actually happened to this place. Guess that whole second was asking too much. While there was nobody hanging out in this room, there was a makeshift armory set up, a little camp fire burning in a soot-blackened corner, and a staff room for the guards out on the wall.

No time to think. Never any time to think. The shouts of my pursuers had been taken up by the crowd in the last courtyard, and they came stampeding after me. At least this place gave me some options. I reached out into my Sphere of Influence and felt all that raw stone, just waiting for some divine attention. The archway became a wall, and my closest pursuer slammed right into it, helmeted head smashing right through the thin layer of stone that I'd slapped over the gap.

For a moment I saw his face, all stubbly and grubby and full of rage, then I took off, surging my Potency for a great bounding leap out of the room, and landing with less grace than I might have hoped for on top of the most solid looking wall.

They knew the lay of the land, and I was scurrying through it like a rat in a maze. I needed some height, some perspective, somewhere that there weren't screaming dudes trying to murder my face off.

Staggering and almost tipping over into the next room, I got a glimpse of the scale of the place. The outer wall that I'd been running along the inside of was not some great circle. It was basically a straight line, stretching out for as far as the eye could see in both directions. It must have gone on for miles when it was first built, but now whole sections of it were just gone, and the parts that weren't looked the worse for wear. These rooms set back from the main wall must have once formed the living quarters and storerooms, but now the few that still had walls had lost their roof, and the few that had roofs seemed to be missing walls beneath. That same brutal melt had spread all across the place, bubbling away solid stone everywhere that it had touched.

From up here, it became clear that the big wall used to be at least twice the height it had been left. There were jagged spurs of stone still stretching up from it—all that remained of the upper floors. Wooden slats had been roped up onto them, and platforms had been balanced precariously as lookouts. Now that I'd spotted those, I could see the same wood everywhere. The clay bricks had been used to patch up holes where they'd been found, but the rickety wood structures were clinging to the old rock like a parasite. Out the back of some of the more solid-looking rooms in this row, there had been halls of that same shanty-town smacked together and lashed to the stone. I could even see stairways zig-zagging up to the top of the wall where the damage was worse and the big wall's internal structures had been melted shut.

I wish I'd spotted those sooner since soldiers were now boiling up them onto my level. No rest for the wicked. Why not give it one last try? "I'm really not here to fight you, guys! This is just a misunderstanding. We're on the same side!"

The first brave soldier made the jump off the stairs and onto the cross-hatch of wall-tops. She lost her shield in the jump but held onto that axe like it was her safety blanket. Half the size of me, she had twice as much space for her feet. What felt like a tightrope to me was just a narrow path to her, and if she fell, all her buddies down there would catch her. They would not be catching me. This was not a crowd-surfing situation. Some of them were already trying to get their pikes through the fragmented wall I'd made so that they could poke at me.

I held out my arms as wide as I dared, wobbling as I did. "You don't want to talk it out?"

She didn't want to talk it out.

Coming in hard and fast, she swept for my legs. She didn't need to kill me, just knock me off balance, and as I danced back out of reach of her hacking swings, she nearly managed it more than once.

Behind her, I could see more soldiers taking the risk and making the jump. A couple wiped out, slamming face down into the wall before vanishing back down out of sight, but enough of them stuck the landing that I was starting to get worried.

Where her attacks had failed to topple me, I nearly succeeded myself when half the weight of my sword shifted into a round shield for my other arm. My arms starting to windmill as I tried to get my balance back, and the soldier probably could have had me in that moment if I wasn't vigorously windmilling a sword through the space she'd have to run into to take her swing.

In a half-squat, I found my balance, then surged forward, slapping my shield into her with all the weight of a Maulkin in motion behind it.

By this point, I probably should have been trying to kill these people right back, but I still entertained the vague hope that they might realize I wasn't killing them and think to themselves, 'Hey, maybe he's a good guy, and we should sit down and talk to him about what he's here for instead of shooting at him and stuff."

When that soldier toppled over and fell the length of the wall to land directly on her head, that hope faded fast. Her neck snapped with a wetter sound than you'd have expected, juicy even before blood started to spread out around her and pool at the feet of her friends.

Peace had been a longshot anyway. Everything else on Amaranth had devoted itself to murdering me, why would the first humans I met be any different.

When the next soldier rushed in to take her place, I fell into the well-worn groove of my training. Slapping the thrust out and following it with a stab to the center of mass. A quick tug to retrieve my sword and then the shield was back up in position before the next one could approach. It was picture perfect; Seren would have been so proud—or at least she wouldn't have had some cutting remark about my performance for a change. I could do this all day, and if the folks with pikes and crossbows would have kindly thrown them away, I would have, picking off every soldier in the place one by one.

Since I wasn't living in a perfect world where folks line up politely to be brutalized, I had to move. Running along a wall that is about as wide as your feet is kind of hard to start doing, but it's a lot easier once you're moving. Once you're moving, I suppose that stopping is the next big worry, but I had no intention of ever doing that, so I put it out of my mind.

Somebody should have warned the soldiers that I wasn't stopping. It came as a surprise to them when I bodied them off the wall, slamming straight ahead with a shield that was about the same size as them, toppling them into the rooms on either side.

The rickety stairs were still packed full of soldiers that hadn't quite gotten their courage together yet, a press of bodies lower down with only a few semi-suicidal geniuses climbing up towards the top of the big wall so that gravity could help them instead of hauling them down. One made a leap right for me, misjudged it, and went straight down onto the pikes that were finally being angled up at me. He made it almost halfway down the long shafts of wood, screaming all the way until death took him.

At least that encouraged the rest of them not to try it.

With another great leap, I cleared the distance from the closest, half-melted wall and hit the stairs. They weren't built with something my size in mind.

They *really* weren't built for something my size, clad in full armor, to hammer into them like a cannonball. Wood splintered and showered down around me.

The soldiers on the level with me had leapt out to fall, preferring the certainty of making friends with the ground to the uncertain but probably gruesome fate that being there when I landed would have brought them. There were pretty good odds I would have made them into human pâté. Not on purpose, just on impact.

I had to scramble to catch onto something as the steps beneath my feet fell away. I thought for one awful moment that the whole stairway was going to drop, but I'd forgotten about the ramshackle construction. Even as the lower half crumbled apart, dropping the rest of the soldiers in a heap below, the parts lashed onto the top of the wall still held tight. It was a squeeze that sent bits of the stairs tumbling down each time I turned for the next zig-zag, but I used what was left of the stairs to mount the big wall.

The higher that I got, the more of the world I could see. Beyond the ruins of the big wall and the shantytown built up around it on this side, there were open expanses of grassland. Farms dug in with the same military precision as the other fortifications and palisades to supply the troops with fodder, fields with what looked a bit like horses, shacks dotted around to store the vital tools, and little farmhouses too. Over the horizon, I could see smoke rising from more camps or villages. This wasn't just a castle full of soldiers, there was a whole country behind it.

It made me wonder what could have been so scary that they built a wall this gigantic to keep it out before the obvious answer presented itself to me.

Araphel. It all came back to the Voidgod. Everything here came back to him and his war. This ancient wall must have been raised by the Eternals fighting him, to keep him or his forces out. The destruction that had been dealt, ripping this colossal structure apart, that must have been his response to it. The name of the Shattered Bastion made a whole lot more sense now.

Despite the many patches of wooden boards that the soldiers had tossed down, the top level of this little keep latched onto the back of the bastion was uneven and treacherous terrain. The stone was deceptively smooth where it had been melted away, but the bubbly bits were easier, with some decent traction. Switching back and forth between the two from step to step was probably what had me slipping the most.

I could see right along the length of the outer wall now I was up here. All the clustered crossbowmen were headed along the walkways towards me, and the noise in each of the courtyards told me that the folks down on the ground floor were doing the same.

All along the watchtowers, cries were going up, my location being crowed to everyone in earshot. The walls were not well manned—it would have been impossible to line the upper levels with enough bodies to cover the full length of the bastion—but between the crow's nest spotters and the mobile clusters of crossbowmen, they had a pretty efficient setup. I'd be sure to tell them how well they were running things when they were done murdering me for being here.

Bolts started to flit in my direction once more, but they flew wide or fell short. I ran for the outer wall as fast as my feet would carry me. By design, there shouldn't have been an easy way in or out on that side. All I had to do was hop down and then I was home free.

I was not prepared for the chasm.

Whatever melting destruction had taken so much of the bastion had actually been stoppered by it. I revised my opinion on how well it had been built and defended by the ancient Eternals. When you compared it to the destruction beyond the wall, it had held up amazingly well. There was a dead drop on the far side of the wall, plunging about three times as far as the land on the far side. The bastion reached all the way to the bottom, cracked and smashed but inexplicably still standing in the face of the cataclysm beyond. There were ashes laying down there, but beneath them was the same rough and bubbled stone that marked so much of the bastion. It was like all the topsoil had evaporated. Like everything beyond the wall had been sloughed away until only the sundered and pocked bedrock remained. The sight of it took my breath away.

In the abstract, I knew that Araphel was a bad guy, and scary powerful, but seeing just how much destruction he'd dealt to this place put it all in perspective. I was a big guy with a sword and a few tricks up his sleeve. He was a god.

A crossbow bolt grazed my shoulders, rattling the sea-serpent scales of my armor and bringing me back to the present. I spun to put the shield between me and the crossbowmen, then I took a moment to panic. With everyone else here, I'd have given us even odds of kicking the collective asses of this whole army, but on my own… I might come off a bit egotistical sometimes, that is the danger of admitting how awesome you are, but even I didn't think I could take on everyone in this kingdom and come out on top. Skilled or not, if they surrounded me, then eventually they'd chip through my health, even if it cost them a hundred lives to do it.

Another barrage of bolts rattled off my shield. They were close enough to aim properly now, which meant I needed to move. Charging them was probably my best bet. If I could put them out of commission fast then I only had to fight like… a hundred other guys hand to hand. I could do that.

My confidence might have taken a little shake after peering over the edge into the abyss, but I was still me. I could still win.

I lowered my shield to get a good look at them and realized with a start that they were retreating. They must have worked out I was coming for them next. But then I realized that the cries of alarm had stopped too. Everything had stopped, even the uproar in the lower levels. Some of the soldiers armed for close combat came pouring up out of the keeps on the walls, but they weren't making any effort to get across to this one. In fact, most of them seemed to be sheathing their weapons.

Maybe somebody had finally worked out that I had spent the whole time running away and telling them I didn't want to hurt them. Maybe whoever was the brains of this army had finally shown up to stop the body of it murdering me on reflex. I turned back to look the other way and understood the real reason for the hush.

At the far side of the keep roof, a woman strode forward. She was clad in the same mish-mash of armor as the other soldiers, but while they had moved in a drudge, she had the lithe elegance I'd come to associate with Seren. As she closed the distance, she tugged off her helm and tossed it aside, letting a long train of pleated black hair fall back from her sharp-featured face.

Maybe in the right circumstances, I'd have thought she was beautiful, but right now her skin was drawn tight over the bones beneath as her face contorted in rage. She half-shouted, half-screamed, "You!"

Orphia.

CHAPTER 3

I gave her as wide a smile as I dared. "Hi, Orphia, how have you been?"

"How have I been since you murdered me in cold blood?" She closed the distance between us, one step at a time, turning the glaive in her hands in a slow spinning figure of eight as she approached.

"Hey now, be fair. Asher was the one to zap you, and you were acting a bit psycho at the time."

She acted as though I hadn't said anything. That was a bit of a theme with her, only hearing what she wanted to hear. "How have I been? I have been filled with divine purpose—to unite this world against the second revelation. To seek the shards of the Rusted Blade and unite them as I will all the people of Amaranth under a single flag."

"Oh sweet." Maybe we weren't on the best terms, but that didn't mean we couldn't work towards the same goal. Maybe now that she'd realized that she had a divine purpose it had tamped down some of her psycho tendencies. Maybe a pig would fly by any minute now. "Did you find out where the Faun one is?"

She cocked her head to one side. "The only time that I have had to endure the company of that degenerate race has been when I am spitting them with my blade. As I mean to do with you."

"Uh, rude."

She tossed her glaive back and forth between her hands, making practice cuts that hummed in the air as she paced not towards me now, but in a slow circle, making me do the same or risk having her at my back. "The only pleasure that I shall take in this, other than seeing the look on your stupid face when I gut you, is that the others saw the light and saw you for the treacherous beast you were, abandoning you to your fate."

"Oh no, we're still friends. I just came through to scout out the lay of the land before the whole gang arrives." Her frown deepened as I said it, but it wasn't like she wasn't going to find out. "Yeah, they're doing great. Never been better. I'll tell them you were asking after them."

She snarled. "Tell them from your grave."

Leaping forward, she thrust her glaive at me so fast that I almost didn't see her move. It rang off the rim of my shield and got pushed wide as my arm jerked almost involuntarily at the sudden contact. Yet again I had fallen back on instinct instead of my training. Just like Seren kept warning me.

Orphia spun away, her blade sweeping around in an arc, covering her retreat. I wasn't chasing her. Instead, I was standing there, being perfectly civil. "I mean, that doesn't really make sense. You know I'm an eternal, the same as you. So you know that even if you do get lucky and stick me with that thing, I'm just going to come back again."

She came at me again, but I could actually see the moment that her Celerity Surge ended, and the blur of motion became possible to follow with the naked eye. I caught the first hack with my sword and flicked it away. She hissed as she retreated from me. "Scattered to the winds with no friends to carry you, no equipment to protect you, and no hope of finding either ever again."

She made another tentative thrust at me, but after a month, I could recognize a feint and just leaned back a little to keep it from scratching me. Still, she ranted on. "I should say that I am doing our treacherous kin a great service by cutting you down."

The next time she swung for me, I stepped in and caught her glaive just under the blade with the rim of my shield. She wrestled against me for a second, trying to pull it back and having no luck, wedging it even tighter. She might have been stronger than that skinny body of hers showed, but she wasn't stronger than me. "You haven't learned about shrines yet? I'm just going to pop up back at home if you kill me."

I tugged my shield down, and she staggered back. A blue flush crept up her neck and face as her aggravation mounted. I shrugged as though we were just talking. "You'll get my armor and sword I guess? That'll be annoying. There aren't that many sea-serpents around."

With a roar, she charged me, slamming the butt of her glaive into the ground to vault up in a graceful arc that landed her right on top of my upturned shield. She hammered the tip of her glaive down into it, then I felt her feet touch down. Her whole weight was bearing down on me as she ranted and stabbed down at me uselessly. "Why are you still chattering away? I will end you. Silence you for—"

With a flex of my arm, I flung her off, towards the drop. She had to drop her weapon and scrabbled for a grip on the treacherous melted stone or risk sliding right off into the abyss. I scoffed. "For like ten minutes until I get back here."

She dove into a roll, scooping up her glaive as she passed over it and coming up already lunging at me. Lightning coiled around her as she came on, dancing down her arms until it encircled her blade. Even as it hit my shield with a sound like a thunderclap, I could hear her screaming over the top of it. "Die!"

The weapon might have been stopped, but the lightning was not. It rushed into me through the metal conductor of the shield, wracking me with pain as it passed through every inch of me before grounding itself.

Smoke rose off my skin as I groaned. "Sorry, I don't know how to do that yet."

In the distance, I could hear her soldier buddies cheering her on, and I stopped wondering how she'd ended up here among them. She was a natural-born bully, and people like that always found a place, surrounded by others who reveled in it. People who'd stand back and cheer while somebody else got crispy fried, just because they thought that person was on the other team.

That smoke smelled delicious, though. Like bacon. No wonder every monster on this whole planet wanted to eat me. Orphia didn't speak, presumably overcome with how delicious I smelled, so I drew myself back up to my full height with a smirk. "The gloves are off then? We're using all our god powers?"

Her own smile at hurting me faded. The idea that I was holding back seemed to make her even angrier than the way I'd been dodging her so far. That whole thing about a woman scorned being mad as hell? That was her. She was the scorned woman. "What are you going to do, forge weapons at me?"

I let my sphere of influence sweep out over the roof. Everywhere that it had been scarred by the wild destruction that had swept over it was out of my reach—not like the things that were too complex for my simple grasp to manipulate but more like it just wasn't there. Like whatever had been done to it had robbed it of some essential element of realness. There were still streaks of untouched stone in amongst it that felt completely normal, but for the most part, it was like I was standing on nothing. Weird, but not really relevant. I wasn't slipping out of my body to build Orphia a condo. I was going to forge weapons at her.

She rushed in at me again, spinning her glaive in a spiral over-head, trying to hide where the attack would come from. While I was here, outside my body, it was like she was moving through molasses. Going this slow, I could see the moment my shield turned into a flow of liquid, and I watched it trace through the air in front of me and reform into a great-sword.

Snapping back to my body, I swung.

To her credit, she didn't let the fear show on her face as the blade's edge came for her, sweeping through every possible angle of attack in one lethal arc. All she did was drop to the floor and slide beneath it, sacrificing her own attack in exchange for her life. I stomped forward, trying to catch her while she was down, but she was too quick for me, tumbling to her feet just out of reach.

Holding a giant sword up all day just makes your arms sore. It is useless unless it is in motion. I didn't hesitate, heaving with all my strength to reverse my first swipe into an overhead cut that would split her in two before she could find her footing.

I would have got away with it too if it wasn't for those pesky Eternal powers.

Just as my sword would have hit her, she exploded into a cloud of mist. "Oh come on!"

Sweeping harmlessly through cloud-Orphia, my sword buried itself in the rippled stone below with a crack. Even as I hauled on it, the mist swept over me, then coalesced into her shape once more, not on the ground but up in the air. The metal screeched as I hauled it free and spun, but still, I was too slow. She hung in the air for a fraction of a second before gravity brought her and her glaive blade crashing down into me.

[629/890 Health]

Even with my armor, it bit deep into my shoulder. With all her weight and strength in the swing, the eel-scale just wasn't enough. Anyone else would have been split down to the crotch from a hit like that, but on me, it caught in my collarbone and stopped.

There was a lot of blood. More blood than I ever wanted to see coming out of me. More blood than I thought I even had in me. My arm on that side started to go cold and useless, but I wasn't letting it give up without a fight.

By force of spite alone, I lifted my hand and grabbed the shaft of the glaive.

Orphia stood over me where I'd fallen from the force of the blow, gloating, "On your knees before me, as befits your kind."

She twisted at the haft of her weapon, wiggling the blade, setting a fresh wash of blood loose down my chest and back but still not realizing that I had a grip on it.

I don't think she understood what was happening when I swung my great-sword for her one-handed. Like she couldn't understand how I still had the strength to do it. My guts had been hanging out, and I'd kept on swinging. In comparison, this was just a scratch.

But just because she didn't understand something, that didn't mean she was going to fall victim to it. She tried to haul her glaive clear and leap free, only to discover the death-grip I still had on it. That split second of hesitation was all it took for me to hit her.

[98 Damage]

The blow caught her in the hip. The rough-hewn blade was too blunt to cut through her leathers, but the impact was bone-crushing all the same. She folded around it and fell to the ground, screaming defiance at me as she skittered across the slippery stone.

Strength fled my arm now, and I had to drop my sword to reach over and pluck the glaive out of my flesh. My skin was thick, but beneath it, I was as soft, pink, and juicy as anyone else. I could have done without seeing that today too. I blinked my eyes shut against that sight, just long enough to activate the Primal power of Restoration and close the wound.

[890/890 Health]

The gap in my armor was still there, grey skin showing amidst the still-flesh blood, but the wound was gone. I set the glaive butt on the ground and used it to push myself back to my feet.

Orphia had recovered her feet as well, but she was limping badly, and I could hear a little crunchy noise each time she took a step. Guess she never learned how to heal herself. Dumbass. Still, you couldn't say she wasn't trying her hardest. She already had a dagger drawn from somewhere, and she was ready to throw down all over again.

I hefted her glaive in my hand and threw it.

She was already leaping to the side before she realized that it wasn't being thrown at her. It flew over the outer wall and down into the great abyss below. "You're done."

Back on her feet and wincing in pain, she started inching towards me. "This is not over until you lie dead at my feet."

"You've got no weapon. You've got no healing." I held out my hand to my side and with one little pulse of the Pillar of Artifice, I remade my sword in my hand from where it lay on the ground. "You're done, Orphia. Don't make me kill you again."

Her shoulders shook, and for one awful moment, I thought that she was crying. Screaming raving murderous Orphia was par for the course, but I had no idea how I would deal with a psycho who was also a crying girl. Lucky for me, she was laughing instead, wild-eyed and drooling a little as she cackled. Great look for her.

I was just starting to wonder what the hell she was laughing at when I heard the voice behind me say, "Nay, you are the one whose journey has come to its end, Moonstruck Beast."

Turning my back to Orphia seemed like a good recipe for a kidney stabbing, but I had to see who was there. I fully expected it to be an overconfident soldier boy, hoping to get some psycho smooches for standing up to the dude who'd kicked his boss's ass, but that wasn't it.

The man was middle-aged, with a full beard framing a creased face and long hair parted right down the middle, all shiny and golden blond to match his gold-filigreed armor. He looked completely human apart from the eyes, which blazed with a golden light. Another Eternal. Another Solar Eternal. Another Solar Eternal on Orphia's side. This day was going great so far.

One last time, I sheathed my sword and lifted up my now empty hands. "Listen, buddy, I'm not here to fight anyone. We're all on the same side here."

He did not approach, but he drew his own sword from where it hung on his belt. The moment he touched it, I felt like I couldn't take my eyes away from it, and when the shimmering silver of the sword was fully drawn it was almost hypnotic. I could feel it drawing me in. I wanted it. I wanted to hold it. Wanted to own it. Wanted it to run me right through if that was the only way to get close to it. That last thought was weird enough to shake me out of whatever trance the sword was putting me into, but I could still feel a tug towards it like magnetism.

Down by the golden hilt, there was one jagged section of the blade a completely different color. Dull and almost brown with age. That was what was drawing me in now. Not the pretty part that he flourished with obvious skill, but the ugly bit down at the root. The shard of the rusted blade that I'd come here looking for. I almost didn't notice when he spoke again. "Is that truly what you believe?"

I'd been so lost in my new fixation that I had to backtrack through the conversation in my head to catch myself back up to speed. On the same side. Do I believe that? Right. Okay. "Nobody wants the Voidgod to win, right?"

He stalked closer to me, looming large in my vision despite our height difference. Power seemed to radiate off him, an aura of danger and power. He hadn't arrived with the rest of us, which meant that he was one of the Eternals that had already been here for years or… centuries. How powerful could all of that time have made a man? "There are some who would say that the return of the Adversary would be entirely to the advantage of those who wish to spread dissent and chaos in the name of the pantheon of bedlam."

"Okay, but that isn't me." I waggled my empty hands in the air once more, just to make sure he could see how non-threatening I was. "I'm just trying to do the right thing and stop the bad guy. I'm not about spreading chaos or whatever."

"Master, do not heed his lies. Strike him down!" Orphia cried out from right behind me, and I nearly crapped myself. I had completely forgotten about her and her little knife in the combined presence of a shard and some sort of shiny golden demigod.

"Silence, child." The gold guy spoke softly to her—commanding but not overbearing. The voice of a man used to being obeyed. He lost all that softness when he turned his attention back to me. "Whatever you may believe of yourself, Chagnar, it is in your nature to spread chaos. It is what you are. Just as it is in our nature to stop you."

When he said that last bit, I was pretty sure the sword in his hand glinted menacingly.

My heel caught on a ridge in the melted roof, and I noticed that I was backing away from him. I don't respond well to fear. The old fight or flight thing? I don't have wings. The old rumble was back in my voice when I replied, "And nobody ever did the right thing when it didn't come naturally to them? Nobody ever thought about doing something bad and then didn't?"

He sprang forward so fast he blurred, the tip of his shiny sword hovering, perfectly controlled, just an inch from my neck. His bushy eyebrows drew down as he growled back, "You wish to bandy words with me, to speak of philosophy when the blood of my kinsmen is upon your hands?"

If he thought I was going to back off just because I had a sword to my throat, he didn't know me. "Your guys didn't give me much choice. From the minute I got here everybody has been trying to stab me."

"Because you're a monster," Orphia sniped from the sidelines.

I jabbed a finger at her face. "The man told you to shut up, Stabarella!"

His whiskers flicked, and I thought he might, just maybe, have had a smile on his face for a moment. "Though I do not care for his insolent tone, this Chagnar has the right of it, Orphia. Remain silent while your betters speak."

"Whoa! Hey now, I'm not better than anybody." Sometimes my mouth just goes on making noises whether I want to shut the hell up or not. "I mean, I'm better than her because she is a racist psycho, but I'm not like… inherently better than her."

This close I could see every line on his face. Eternals didn't age, so he'd been looking like this for as long as he'd been walking the world. If I hadn't spent a month trying to decipher the facial expressions of an ice queen Alvaren, then I probably wouldn't be able to read a single one of the expressions that passed over that stoic mask of his. As it was, when his eyebrows twitched up, I knew that he was surprised. "She is weak, and we are strong. In a world of untold savagery, might is the only law."

I disagreed with all of that, and my gut instinct was to tell him just how completely he was wrong, but on the other hand, he was the superpowered dude pointing a magic sword at me, so quibbling over this stuff didn't seem like my best bet for getting through the conversation with all my limbs attached. Maybe I'm smarter than I look? "So we're both strong. Does that mean we can talk, like adults, instead of waving our big swords around?"

He did not lower his sword. "You say to me that my bannermen struck at you from the moment of your discovery. Tell me how you came to be within the impregnable fortress of the Shattered Bastion."

"Oh." I shrugged. "I used the waystone."

The eyebrows twitched again, like agitated little caterpillars. Surprise. Again. "The waystones have not functioned since Talon went into decline, and you mean to tell me that some fresh-made Eternal has learned the secret of their use?"

"Well, yeah." He stared at me in disbelief. "Not me, obviously, but my buddy, Asher, worked it out. He's a real wiz at all that wizard stuff."

He let the sword ease down slowly to his side, and from the periphery of my vision, I could see Orphia's face drop at the same time, going from malicious delight when she thought I was going to die to dismay and then finally disgust when he slipped the blade back into its scabbard and that weird pull that it had on me faded away. "Then Orphia spoke truly. You travel with companions of the Solar Court?"

Okay, we were talking. Nobody was getting chopped up. This was good. This was what I wanted. Sure I still felt like I was walking a tightrope, but at least I was walking it in the right direction now. "They're not here with me now, but yeah."

He leaned in a little closer. "And they will vouch for your good conduct?"

"Asher will for sure." I grinned. "Maybe not Mercy—that kind of depends on what kind of mood she's in."

He returned my smile with a small and tentative one of his own. It was like he wasn't used to twisting his mouth that way. "Then I entreat you to send for them at once."

Orphia looked like she was about to puke. She darted forward, squealing, "Leofric! Those were the traitors who—"

He backhanded her so casually it took me a moment to spot what had happened. That big golden gauntlet of his cracked across her jaw and launched her across the rooftop to land in a heap. She did not spring up again the way she had when I knocked her down. She lay there. Beaten.

My hand was on the hilt of my sword before I told it to move, and I shifted to put myself between the two of them. "Hey, man, that is not cool."

"She is your enemy, even if you are not mine." His brows drew back down. "This creature would see you dead. She attempted to slay you but a moment ago. What madness makes you seek to defend her?"

I was kind of wondering that myself. What could be so impor-tant that I'd get in between Orphia and the righteous beatdown she deserved? Even as my brain tried to work it through, my mouth was already telling Leofric what my gut knew. "She's your girl, yeah? She's on your team? You can't treat your people that way."

He scoffed. "And so the chaos in your blood comes to the fore. It is the natural order that the strong should rule over the weak, and you would contest it?"

My hand was still up on the hilt of my great-sword where it poked up over my shoulder, and my knuckles were turning white. "If that means not slapping people around for no damn reason then yes, I'd contest it."

"She was disobedient. I told her to be silent and thrice she spoke. She knows the law of this land. She knew when she swore her fealty to me that I would not suffer insubordination." He said it like it was so obvious that I was an idiot for not getting it.

Maybe I was an idiot, but I still needed to make something clear. "If we're going to be working together, and you try that with Asher or Mercy… then I'll… I won't even have to do anything if you try that with Mercy. There wouldn't be enough of you left for me to hit."

"It strikes me that you still misunderstand your part in all this. We are not equals. I do not seek allies among the Eternals who walk Amaranth. I seek lords to set above the common man, that you might rule as the gods intended." He reached up and clapped his hands on my shoulders. "If you mean to serve the cause and wage war on the Adversary and all his servants, then I shall welcome you with open arms, but if you mean to subvert my great design in word or in deed then you are my enemy."

Oh, man. He was just as nutty as Orphia, but he had the power to back it up. I needed to grab his sword and get the hell out of here.

He didn't even give me a chance to answer before he bellowed, pushing me down. "Kneel before me, reject the heresy of the Lunar court, and swear fealty upon this sacred relic. The Lucis: symbol of my office, symbol of my divine right to dominion, and the mark of my righteousness."

Both sword and scabbard were hauled out of his belt, and he held it out level with my face. All I had to do was reach up and grab it.

After that, I just had to escape from the crazy powerful Eternal right in front of me, and all his minions, and get out of the castle that I was in the middle of that was full of his soldiers … and then the whole kingdom that he'd laid claim to beyond that … and then… Okay, I really needed a better plan than grab and run.

I reached up very carefully and laid my hands on the scabbard. I could feel the power of the shard thrumming inside it, pulsing just out of reach. Even through the scabbard and my gloves, I could feel it reaching out to me like it wanted to be with me. Like the pull I was feeling went both ways.

Opening my mouth, I did not have a clue what was going to come tumbling out. Luck saved me from whatever nonsense I was about to spout as suddenly, Leofric's head snapped around. A cry was going up from farther along the wall, and the soft sound of two little thunder-claps rolled over us, just like when I'd arrived through the waystone.

The whole gang was here.

CHAPTER 4

e had to run like hell to get there before fighting broke out, and even with a full-on sprint, it was only the sight of Leofric leaping down in all his golden finery to put himself between his men and Mercy's ready arrow that convinced his side to chill out for a second. "Those with the eyes to see would recognize that these are no invaders. They are Eternals, with blood of the same divine providence as I. They are our honored guests, not our foes, and though one may wear the form of the enemy, that does not mean that he himself is our foe. Set your arms aside and your minds to ease."

That might have worked just fine for all his soldiers, but Mercy retrained her arrow on his face before he'd even landed and showed no sign of aiming it anywhere else. After all our fond memories of Orphia, and the joys of meeting Talon, it was hard to trust other Eternals.

It was only when they spotted me clomping along the walkway on the outer wall waving my arms that they seemed to ease off a little, though I couldn't help but notice Mercy hadn't actually eased her bow back so much as temporarily adjusted her aim away from Leofric.

Asher, who I'd usually have considered the more coolheaded of the two, still held a roiling ball of flames between his claws and showed no sign of any plan to quench it. I suppose that given the length of time it took him to get a spell together, it was hardly surprising that he didn't want to put it down again until he was completely sure that he wouldn't need it.

Even so, it was kind of embarrassing that Leofric's buddies had dropped everything at the sight of him, and I had to clamber awkwardly down a ladder that was clearly built for toddlers to get back down to the courtyard and then jog over to whisper in Mercy's ear before she'd finally let the bowstring ease.

What Leofric didn't know was that I was whispering, "He is a complete psycho, but he's got the shard in his sword, and he thinks we all want to sign up to join his Eternal dream team."

Of course, even that brief moment of peace went to hell the moment that Orphia came into sight on top of the wall.

"Look out!" Mercy yelled as she shoved me aside to line up a kill-shot on the other woman. I was kind of impressed that she could even recognize Orphia after all this time, given that one side of her face was basically a giant bruise at this point after Leofric got slap-happy.

I lunged back into the way, knocking the shot wild so that it soared out over the wall instead of hitting Orphia head-on. Mercy kicked me. "What are you doing!?"

"You can't kill her," I said, regret dripping from every word. "She's with Leofric."

Mercy glanced from Eternal to Eternal with dismay. "Her? Really?"

I shrugged. "She saw him first I guess?"

"Couldn't he smell the crazy coming off her?" Mercy couldn't even bring herself to smirk with Orphia in sight. "I smelled it the minute I came through the portal."

Asher finally let his spell splutter and die between his hands, eyes still darting around the amassed soldiery. "I would imagine that he is accustomed to it."

I stepped in between the two of them and threw my arms around their shoulders before the sass got too far out of control. "I can't believe that you came through to rescue me so soon."

"It was decided by a vote to be more likely that you had forgotten our arrangements than that you had somehow been restrained by enemies and prevented from making your return to us." Asher really was feeling sassy today.

It felt like Leofric couldn't stand to not be the center of attention for a minute. He spread his arms wide, and in a booming voice, he started in with the sales pitch. "Welcome, my kinfolk, to the Shattered Bastion, the last standing stronghold of the first great crusade against the Adversary, and the holy place from which the next shall be waged."

That set off some rumbling among the crowds of soldiers still packed in all around us. I wasn't sure how I'd feel if my boss's cousins showed up and then he started telling everyone the end was nigh, but I doubted I would have taken it that well. Mercy's brows drew down. "You already knew Araphel is planning a comeback tour?"

"Not all of us are freshly made. Some have had time to see the workings of the Adversary still in play in this world. I have been warning of his return since time immemorial. From the very day he was slain, I set myself to prepare for his return and to proselytize to those who were doubtful of his survival. When young Orphia came to us, telling her tragic tale of betrayal and prophecy, I knew that the time must be nigh. Ever have I rallied the stout of heart to my banner, to man the Bastion and prepare to hold back the tides of darkness. Now it became clear to all why this was not mere vanity or paranoia but necessity."

My gods did that man love the sound of his own voice. I mean, holy crap. It was like a divinity all on its own, the sheer weight of his relentless boringness pounding down on you. I swear I was swaying on my feet by the time I replied, "I'm glad somebody is taking it seriously at least. Most of the folks we've met so far didn't even believe Araphel existed, let alone that he was coming back."

"You shall find only the faithful here. Faithful and armed for the coming battle in body and mind. I can think of few calls to arms with more potency than Orphia's warning. All the righteous of Amaranth have rallied to us."

A quick glance at the "righteous" massed around us made me

kind of dubious about their righteousness. They looked less like holy warriors and more like the desperate dregs who'd been drawn in by the promise of a roof over their head, food in their belly, and an opportunity to stab anybody that was wearing a different color uniform or looked different from them.

"I wouldn't believe everything she says." Mercy looked like she was pointing at Orphia for a second before I realized that her extended finger was the middle one and it was pointed straight up, not at the wall.

Leofric chuckled. "She said much the same of you, though in less kindly terms."

When he laughed, it felt like you were being washed over with warm water. Wrapped up in a big hug. Maybe his voice wasn't a power, but he was definitely radiating some sort of aura. Whatever else you wanted to say about him, he had presence.

I wanted to say a lot of other stuff about him, but I couldn't do that when he was standing right there.

"Come, my new kin, let us find you quarters and provide you with a lay of the land. There is much of this world that you cannot yet know. Secrets that only my experience has unraveled. Allow me the honor of sharing the wisdom of the ages with you."

That was one drastic change of tone from when he thought he had me at his mercy earlier. Suddenly, he was all buddy buddy, you're my blood brothers, let me tell you how pretty you are. Maybe it was because the others were Solar Eternals, and he genuinely thought that they were all on the same side. Maybe it was because they didn't look like Faun, and he was a racist dick-bag just like his loyal follower-slash-punching bag. Maybe he had undergone a drastic change in attitude as a result of personal growth and from now on he was going to set aside all that world domination stuff. Or maybe, and most likely in my estimations, now that there were three of us, he wasn't so sure that his ass wasn't the one that would get kicked if it came to a fight.

I think I'd probably have liked him better if he'd gone on being a megalomaniacal asshole. At least I could trust that. This new guy, trying to get on our good side, I had no idea what he wanted.

After seeing where the soldiers had been sleeping, I was expecting to be ushered into something similar, but instead, we looped around the wall with the waystone ring set in it and headed farther along the Bastion to another section that had been rebuilt from those red-bricks into something quite a bit more substantial.

Orphia trailed along behind us, far enough back that I didn't feel any worry about her stabbing us in the back any time soon. She was still limping, her face slowly swelling up as she scowled after me. As if I was the reason for all her suffering.

The whole time that we walked, Leofric gestured grandly about him, telling us of the repairs that they'd undertaken, and the battles that they'd waged to clear monsters from the ruins. Everything was a story with him, and it looked like he delighted in telling them, still in love with the sound of his own voice.

At least it saved the rest of us from having to do much of the conversational heavy lifting, freeing us up to have a good look around the place. There were a lot of people here. A lot more than I'd seen during my mad rush along the Bastion. The fact that they were spread thinly along a structure this massive didn't make their numbers any less.

The farms that were set back into the green pastures behind the wall couldn't possibly have been providing enough food for this many. For a standing army this big, the whole of the country beyond must have been funneling resources towards this one place.

I almost walked into the back of Leofric as he waved grandly at the little townhouse he had set aside for "honored guests."

"Awesome. Give us two minutes to find our beds, then we can go on the grand tour, right?" I smiled down at him as broadly as I dared. I really was not built for lying.

"By all means." All his flattery and grandiose storytelling had been directed towards the other two up until this point, so having to address me directly again, while still maintaining that degree of pleasantry, seemed to be a struggle for him. "It is my desire for you to feel comfortable here."

Inside the red-brick building that occupied what had once been a completely leveled section of the great wall, we found our quarters. The furnishings weren't exactly lavish, but they weren't bedrolls on the dirt floor like everyone else had to deal with either. The place was on two levels. It had timber floors that definitely weren't made of scrap wood like the other ramshackle parts that had been hammered together and tied to the side of the bastion. There was even furniture inside that wouldn't have looked too far out of place in the luxury of Talon's Keep. The top floor was divided up into bedrooms, which our escort of guards offered up to us as if they were the greatest gift we'd ever had bestowed on us. Mercy snorted when she saw the expectant look on her personal guide's face. "Dude, I've seen a bed before. It isn't that exciting."

That guy was scowling almost as much as Orphia as he skulked back downstairs.

I kicked the door shut behind him and turned to the other two. "Okay, here's the plan. We kill Leofric, grab the sword, and jump through the magic ring before all the minions pile on us."

Mercy and Asher looked at each other, then back to me. Mercy was the one to say what they were both, apparently, thinking. "Or we could just… not."

"What? The dude is a total psycho, just like Orphia. If you don't do exactly what he says then you're his enemy." I realized that my whole plan to not talk too loudly was falling apart rapidly, and I switched to a stage whisper. "He definitely needs to not be alive anymore."

"Maulkin, he's an eternal." Mercy rolled her eyes. "It isn't like he'd stay dead. And if we kill him then that is another enemy for life, chasing after us and trying to get his shard back, just like Briar by Moonlight and the Alvaren. Don't we have enough enemies already?"

Asher cocked his head to the side. "You do make an unfortunate habit of collecting nemeses wherever you go."

Mercy cocked her head the other way. "Nemesis-es?"

"Besides, it kind of looks like he's on our side, right? Out to beat the Voidgod?" She was doing that thing again, when she spoke really slowly, with a kind of sing-song voice. Like she was the presenter on some kids' TV show trying to teach me the names of colors. "Plus, he's got an army. An army could come in real handy. Maybe we just listen to his sales pitch."

I felt like I was running out of ammunition rapidly now that they'd decided to ignore the two very important reasons to murder him: that he had something we wanted, and that he was a dick. "He hit Orphia for talking back to him."

Mercy looked exasperated. "Good! You should have hit her too. With your sword. So she stopped looking at me. And breathing."

I turned to Asher, hoping for him to be the voice of reason, but while he usually trusted my gut, this time he seemed to be headed in an anti-gut direction. "I must admit that the prospect of harm coming to our onetime companion does not fill me with trepidation."

"I don't care that she got hit, I care that he…" Why wasn't I better at talking? If I could just explain to them what he'd been like up on the rooftop before they arrived then maybe they'd understand. I could picture it perfectly in my head, but I just couldn't get it into words. Instead, I finished up with a lame duck. "Listen, he's a bad guy. Okay?"

Mercy had sauntered over to press on the mattress and see how comfortable it was, not even pretending that she was actually listening to me anymore. "Sure. Okay. You don't like him. We get it."

"You don't get it!" I turned to Asher with desperation starting to creep into my voice. "He thinks he's better than everyone else. He thinks we should rule the world, just because we're Eternals."

Mercy flopped on the bed, then popped back up on her elbows to scoff. "Don't you spend half your time talking about how awesome we are?"

My mouth opened and shut a few times until I managed to blurt out, "That's just because the three of us are awesome people, not because we were born with powers… I think Seren's awesome too."

"I should not present Mercy with further evidence of your questionable judgment if I were you." Asher had leaned in close to whisper this in a conspiratorial way, but Mercy heard him and let out a harsh bark of laughter.

"So he thinks that we should be in charge. Why shouldn't we be?" She rocked back up onto her feet. "I'm not saying we're better than everyone we've met since we got here, but we were literally chosen by the gods to come down here and save the world."

"Yeah, save it"—I grumbled—"not crown ourselves kings of it."

"Queen. And I'd totally rock a crown."

Asher glanced over at her with something like a frown. It was hard to tell without eyebrows. "Mercy."

"Oh come on." She laughed. "I totally would!"

"The accessories involved, and how you would appear while wearing them, are not the matter in question." Asher sighed.

Mercy rolled her eyes and flopped back on the bed again, "Fine! So if it looks like he is going full-on world domination dictator we stop him, but that doesn't mean we can't get along for now."

"I don't like this." That was it. That was the best argument I could come up with.

"So don't like it." Mercy scoffed. "You think we liked it when you dragged us into all the messes we've been through so far? Maybe it is your turn."

Asher shrugged miserably when I looked to him for support. "Making use of the resources that Leofric has at his disposal to pursue our shared goals seems to be the most practical course, for now."

"Fine." I strode over and hauled Mercy up. "Fine! Let's go do the grand tour. See all the places he's going to hang the chopped-off bits of you when he decides you aren't being a good obedient slave."

"Oh my gods," Mercy groaned, going limp in my arms and making me carry her across the room. "You are so overdramatic."

"Bet you there is at least one dangling corpse." I dumped her on the floor in a heap, and she scrambled back up to standing.

Asher paused. "What would the stakes of this wager be?"

She didn't even have to think about it. "If I win, he has to stop making out with Seren in public."

If that was how she wanted to play it. "If I win, she has to start making out with Seren in public."

"Oh gross." She shoved me away. "Why are men like that?"

"What do you mean? I just want you two to start getting along." I waggled my eyebrows at her. "Everyone gets along better when they're making out."

Asher's tongue flicked out, tasting the air as he thought it through. "Does this mean that you wish for the three of us to 'make out'?"

Mercy and I both looked at each other in stunned silence for a second, both of us trying to fight back the laughter that was bubbling up inside us.

Mercy managed to pat him on the shoulder. "We get along just fine already."

"That is true," he conceded as I almost choked on the laugh still caught in my throat.

My list of priorities had shuffled. Killing the Voidgod had dropped to second place. Number one was now making sure that Asher never *ever* found out what making out was.

I headed downstairs and out the door as fast as I could get away from that conversation, and Leofric was waiting, with his arms spread wide. "It is my dearest hope that you find pleasant rest within the shelter of my walls."

"Yeah, the beds look great." I gave him an awkward thumbs-up. "Thanks for that."

"As Eternals, our lot in life is to wander where fate and duty take us. Very rarely has either taken me to places of great comfort. As such, I do my best to see to it that such things are available to us where I can. So that you might know that there is more than hardship in Amaranth."

Oh wow, the sales pitch was starting early. Stick with me, kid, and I'll give you the comfiest seats in the world.

When it became apparent that we weren't completely won over by the promise of pillows, he snapped his fingers, and an open-topped wagon drew up alongside us. The things I'd spotted earlier definitely were not horses. They had that same lanky build, but there was no question that the creature drawing this cart was not an herbivore.

Bestiary tickled at the back of my mind, providing me with the name of the critter. Chollima. They were carnivores alright, predatory pack-hunting horses with wide-open mouths packed to the brim with row after row of shark-like teeth, and they were blessed with the same tireless energy that empowered the Chagnar Faun. There was no fuzzy coat on their bare skin, no flowing manes either. Either one of them would have become clotted and matted because these things sweated blood while they ran.

Looking down I could see trails of that blood on the ground, spattered and dried out dozens of times over across the gravel-filled tracks running along the length of the wall. This must have been how they meant to reinforce and supply different areas if the Bastion did come under attack. Terrifying meat ponies to the rescue.

Out of some old habit, I reached out to pet the vaguely horsey thing on its muzzle and nearly lost a finger for my trouble before the driver got it under control. Mental note: do not try to pet the terrifying meat ponies.

"If you will climb aboard, we shall take in the full extent of the Shattered Bastion, much fallen from its former glory." I looked over at Mercy, fully intending on giving her a very meaningful look that meant "Please let me kill this asshole," but she was already hauling herself up onto a bench in the back.

With Asher, Leofric, and me packed in there beside her, it was… cozy. The three of them took up one side, and I had the other, with my back to the wall. That suited me fine. I'd rather keep my eyes on Leofric in case this was all just the set up for a stab in the back—and to see more of the kingdom beyond this one fortification that he was clearly so in love with.

I took a history class once upon a time, back when I thought college might have been a good idea, and there had been this one lecturer talking about what we thought of as the big wars, explaining that before the industrial revolution, you couldn't really get a battle going with as many people because there needed to be folk back at home doing the heavy lifting to keep the front-line folks supplied. She'd said that most medieval kingdoms could only support a tiny standing army because of the ratio of non-fighters required. I wished that I'd paid a bit more attention because I was damned if I could remember what that ratio was.

The main thing I felt certain of was that this human kingdom we'd landed on the angriest border of had to be pretty big to keep all these soldiers fed, armored, and housed—not to mention providing a steady supply of jerky for all the meat ponies.

So while Mercy and Asher ooh-ed and aaah-ed at the amazing architectural feats that somebody had melted behind me, I peered off towards those puffs of smoke on the horizon and tried to map them out in my head, working out just how many little villages were out there. How many people had to be living out there? Just living totally normal medieval farmer lives in Amaranth without any monsters stomping through, any mountains collapsing, or any of the other crazy crap that we'd been seeing since the moment that we first arrived. Maybe we just landed on the wrong side of the wall, and everything was nice over here?

I twisted around to take a look at the wall every so often when the other two made impressed noises. There was no denying that it was an impressive hunk of rock. Probably even more impressive if you didn't know how to reach out to the rock beneath your feet with your divine power and drag it up into a giant wall with pure will alone.

Beyond the little shacks that they'd erected as barracks, there was a fully functional smithy further along the line, a farrier, a fletcher, a butcher, and a baker. I looked for a candlestick maker, but Leofric explained that they burned torches soaked in oil as wax was prohibitively expensive.

Mercy was the only one who might have got the joke, and she didn't want it.

There was a whole city built into the long line of wall. Most of it latched on parasitically long after the original structure had been built and partially destroyed, but some of it burrowed right into the old Bastion's corpse. For instance, the butcher's had sides of meat dangling inside a hollowed-out section of the old wall where the devastation had eaten clean through and made a sort of natural-looking cave, complete with withered-looking stalactites of surviving stone for them to tie the meat upon.

I was so checked out by the end of the grand tour of the longest wall in the world that it took me a moment to understand Leofric was finally telling us something important. "…the most loyal servants of the adversary still raid against the Bastion, seeking both to tear down the memorial to those who defied him and to claim the lands beyond for their dark master."

I interrupted him before he could launch into his next soliloquy about some brave warrior or other who had bled to keep the monsters out. "Who are these loyal servants exactly? Because we haven't really bumped into any yet."

Leofric's mustache twitched again, irritated at the interruption but willing to indulge my apparently stupid question. "The natural allies of the dark one are the wicked Dvergar who first freed him from his stone prison, the void-spawn that he wrought from his own flesh to spread wickedness across all of creation, and of course, the uh…" He looked momentarily uncertain for the first time since I'd met him. "The Chagnar."

"You think the dvergar are evil?" Mercy said at the same time as I asked, "The Faun are attacking this place?"

I got the impression that old Leofric wasn't really ready for the questions and answers section of the tour yet, and he looked with regret as some landmark or other rolled by without his commentary. "While some Dvergar may have turned from their wicked path and embraced the gods, there is no denying that their sin was what brought the revelation upon us. Their demanding and seeking caused all of this. That is why they hide their faces now. They are riddled with shame—and rightfully so."

His tone went from conciliatory to barely restrained disgust when he turned to me. "As for the Chagnar, those vile beastmen have always been a thorn in the side of all that is good in this world. Only recently have they gathered the courage enough to launch forays against us here on the Bastion. Some dark power is uniting the disparate tribes of them under a single banner and rallying them against us. Against me."

"It is difficult to conceive of a good enough reason for any tribal society to throw themselves upon fortifications this substantial," Asher noted, forcing Leofric to concede a little ground again.

He did not like being questioned, but it seemed clear to me now that he was desperate enough for the help of the other two that he'd tolerate it, at least temporarily. It was a stark change from the way he'd treated me and Orphia. "Truth be told, there are folk tales passed among the peasantry that this land once belonged to the Chagnar, that it was their hunting ground before the revelation, and they seek to reclaim it. While I must denounce these tales as heresy, I cannot deny in my heart that there may be some seed of truth buried within them."

He shrugged and turned back to his great wall. "Who can truly say who owned this land in antiquity, in the unplumbed darkness before even Eternal memories reach?"

Mercy raised an eyebrow. "The faun, apparently."

"The faun…" He almost spat the name of that race before getting his temper back under control. "If we were to believe their lies, then every stretch of land was once their sacred hunting ground. They claim to be the firstborn of Amaranth, that all this world was once theirs before the Wyrm Wars. Were we to cede territory to them each time they claimed it was their heritage, we would have to live in the sea."

I resisted the urge to tell him to get in the sea as we trundled on in silence for another minute or so.

"So you're having some Faun troubles." Mercy had a speculative look on her face that I was instantly suspicious of. "You want us to go talk it out with them?"

"You cannot believe that the Chagnar can be reasoned with? That they would listen to the words of their most hated enemies? The moment that their sentries laid their eyes upon you, a swarm of the beast-men would be unleashed. You would be surrounded and slaughtered before a word slipped from your lips." There was the Leofric I knew and didn't love, barely concealed contempt reverberating underneath the surface level of politeness.

She nodded over at me, that same smug smile hovering on her lips. "What about him?"

My voice came out in a bass rumble. "What about me?"

Asher was studying me intently, head bobbing as the cart went over little bumps and lumps in the gravel road, grinding deeper and deeper into the well-worn ruts. "While it is true that they would identify Maulkin from a distance as one of their own kind, the moment that he was close enough the illusion would falter. Surely, from the moment that they perceive his ocular glow, it will be clear to them that he is an Eternal."

The voice of sanity had finally arrived in the building. "Exactly. Definitely wouldn't work."

"His eye glow is pretty dim." Mercy peered at me. "He might get away with it."

"Your serpentine companion has the right of it. Dim as his light may be, there is no mistaking the gaze of an eternal…" The wheels were turning under blondie's golden hair. Just like Mercy intended them to. I swear she was more dangerous with her mouth than she was with her bow. He paused for just a moment, then let his thoughts come tumbling out to ruin my day. "However, it is well known that the Chagnar worship the hideous gods of the Lunar courts. They might consider one of that pantheon's Eternals to be their natural ally—particularly if he came clad in the flesh of a Faun."

Mercy clapped her hands and sat back with a smug smile. "So just like that, problem solved. Maulkin can go in, find out what their deal is, and negotiate a cease-fire or whatever. Bring everyone to the table to work things out."

Leofric scoffed. "It is your belief that centuries of warfare can be brought to an end through conversation?"

"My boy Maulkin, here. He's super diplomatic." She leaned over to pat me on the shoulder, and I shrugged her off. She put her hand back, so I shrugged it off again. She did this three times before finally settling for slapping me on the knee instead. I couldn't move that out of the way in the cramped wagon. "I mean, he showed up here and made friends with you right off the bat. Right?"

"Indeed he did." Those wheels in his head weren't turning now, they were spinning so fast you could imagine smoke was going to start pouring out of Leo's ears any second now. "Why, if he were to engage the Chagnar leadership with that same diplomacy, then I could imagine that our conflict would be brought to an abrupt end."

Mercy clapped again. Aggressively. Right in front of my face. "Perfect."

We went over one last bump and then rolled to a stop back where we'd first started out. There was some drumming and barking of orders going on at the side of the road opposite the wall, but I was too busy seething at Mercy for signing me up to be this asshole's assassin. "Uh… do I get a say in all this?"

She laughed at that, and I honestly felt like hitting her. "Does this look like a democracy?"

Behind them, the rickety wood that I'd smashed down off the side of the Bastion as I climbed had been reconstructed into a hasty set of gallows. The upper beam of it was bowing under the weight of all the bodies.

A dozen men and women swung gently in the breeze. I spotted a few of the soldiers from down in the square when I'd first arrived up there, more than a few. I think he'd hung the whole square. I was pretty sure I recognized the crossbow-woman who'd clipped me in the shoulder too, spinning slowly at the end of the line.

For a moment, I couldn't even understand what I was looking at, then the reality of it sank in, and the awful logic behind it. This was Leofric's idea of an apology.

"No." It slipped out like a whisper. "No, it doesn't."

CHAPTER 5

After seeing the bodies, Mercy and Asher's faces went through some rapid contortions before they could get their opinions stuffed right back down to wherever they were bubbling up from. Orphia was up on the wall still, pretending to keep watch but glancing at us from the periphery of her vision each time that her head turned, a hint of a smile twisting at the side of her mouth. I had absolutely no doubt that she was the one that had organized the hanging gardens of the Bastion display for us. Just as I had no doubt that it was to make us act out. To start a fight.

Every part of me was screaming out to do just that. When I see evil, I hit it. That is what I do.

This right here, this was evil. I could feel the urge to draw my sword building up inside me like a scream. How many more of them would die if I reached for it? How many of them would throw themselves between me and Leofric, even when he did stuff like this to them?

Asher could see it on my face when he looked back to me, and Mercy didn't even have to look. She was already reaching down to grab my wrist. From a distance, it might have looked like she was in shock and seeking comfort. Orphia probably thought it was a sign that Mercy was weak.

She was holding onto me with all her strength, stopping me from reaching up and pulling this whole castle down on our heads. When Asher's eyes flicked down to observe that, he latched on to my other arm.

On the one hand, I appreciated the group hug, but on the other, I was kind of annoyed that they thought I wouldn't be able to control myself.

It wasn't like I was berserk. It wasn't like my blood was boiling, and that smug bastard was just a step away. It wasn't like I could rip him in half with my bare hands.

Asher was hanging horizontally off my arm by the time I noticed that I was reaching for my sword, and Mercy's arms were shaking with the effort of keeping my other hand pinned at my side. The look of blind panic on her face was enough to snap me out of it.

For a moment everything was quiet, then it was like all the sound of the world suddenly came back. Whatever dark place my thinking parts had wandered off to let go on their hold, and I was here again. Back in Amaranth, looking down at Leofric as he looked genuinely puzzled. "Those fools who would have done you harm have now left my service, and those who remain shall treat you with the proper respect."

Even now that the wave of fury had passed, I couldn't bring myself to say the words that he wanted, so it was poor Mercy who had to step forward and say, "Thank you."

The rest of our very civilized evening passed in a blur. Leofric seemed to sense that he'd made some misstep, even if he didn't know exactly what it was, so he made a great show of sitting us down with his troops for their evening meal, sharing his own much finer food with them freely. It probably would have been a grander gesture if we didn't know that Eternals didn't need to eat, but even with all his generosity, most of the gaunt men and women gathered around the fire ate little, too overwhelmed by the presence of Eternals in their midst to do much more than stare.

I hated it. I hated being put up on a pedestal by these people who'd clearly tried way harder than me to get to where they were, just because I was born into these powers. Mercy and Asher took it in stride. I suppose that Mercy got a good amount of this sort of fawning from her little Dvergar fan club back home, but all I could think about was the fact that somebody had made these people this way. Somebody had found them and taught them that they owed us awe.

All I had to do was look across the fire to know who that was. Leofric sat there with Orphia at his right hand. Her injuries had vanished sometime between our arrival back at this patch of wall and dinner, so that meant that either they had some wizard on staff with healing powers, which seemed unlikely given the lack of any indication that anyone nowadays could do magic, or, more likely, Leofric had some Primal healing powers like me.

That one made sense. It fitted in nicely with his benevolent holy overlord if he could lay hands on people and heal them. It was a handy miracle to whip out when you wanted to impress.

All that it had impressed on me was the fact that he could have healed her at any moment since the end of the fight, and instead, he left her limping around with half her face mashed in, to make a point. To remind her that he controlled everything, even her suffering. What a dick.

Mercy and Asher shared a few stories from our travels to widespread applause, but they were pretty careful to sidestep around any of the major events, like the Alvaren coming back, Talon's death, or us having a tidy little stack of Rusted Blade shards. It was nice that they were taking my warnings about Leofric being a bad guy a little bit seriously, even if they were still laughing at his jokes and drinking his beer. Okay, that was mostly Mercy. She made my drinking look like a healthy habit. Of course, with the poison resistance I'd developed from enough Dvergar parties, this stuff was like water to me anyway.

Despite the corpses of their companions swinging in the night breeze just downwind of us, the rest of the soldiers seemed to be close to ecstatic now that we'd arrived. None of them dared to say anything outright, but from the dark glances that they sent in Orphia's direction when she wasn't paying attention, I got the impression that she wasn't very well-liked by the folks under her command, and they were looking for us to take her place in whatever hierarchy Leofric had cobbled together.

Mercy getting blind drunk actually gave us the perfect excuse to duck out of the celebrations early. All the way back along to our rooms, she was belching out something like a marching rhythm. Even when she was sober she was like this, so it wasn't a huge surprise, but by the end of the walk to our quarters, I was carrying her over one shoulder as she sang something in Dvergar that it is probably for the best I don't translate. There were a lot of euphemisms, lots of things that were as hard as rock, and the soldiers escorting us were blushing. The downside of speaking in tongues. Everyone knew what we were singing.

Asher eased the door shut in the face of our escort with a lot of apologies about her behavior, and he looked genuinely surprised when he turned back to the room and realized she was standing for herself and stone-cold sober. He opened his mouth, but the finger she held pressed up to her lips silenced him before he gave the little deception away. We all snuck upstairs.

Mercy was the first to lay her cards on the table. "Okay, so maybe he is a bit of a bad guy."

Oh great, a concession. That was so helpful now that we were in the belly of the beast. "And you signed me up to be his assassin."

She at least had the good grace to look crestfallen. "Look, he's a bad guy, so maybe whoever is in charge of the Faun is a good guy? It makes sense, right?"

"I can't imagine the Faun leader is any worse than golden boy. But what about all the stuff about him being a servant of the Voidgod?"

"Pretty sure anyone that doesn't agree with old Leo is a servant of the Voidgod." Mercy scoffed. "Shine his shiny booties wrong? Must have been the Voidgod's fault."

Asher had watched all of this pass between the two of us in silence, his expression puzzled. "He does not seem to me to be better or worse than any other king. Perhaps the two of you simply hold all in Amaranth to a higher standard than you did your own rulers?"

That actually shut me up for a second as I thought it through.

Mercy rolled her eyes. "We didn't have kings, Asher. We had"—she slowed her roll for a moment as she tried to put it into words he might understand, glancing at me for support—"politicians?"

"People born with too much money, who told everyone else what to do," I grumbled. "Not much of a difference between that and a king, is there?"

In the rarest of rare moments, Mercy shut up. She stood there and made no noise, and Asher and I both had enough time to take a breath. Eventually, I was the one who broke the silence. "Look, if it was up to me, I'd just hit him a lot and take his sword, but you think there is a better way to do this, and I trust you. Just tell me what to do. Tell me how to be sneaky or make friends with assholes or whatever."

"Okay, well stop calling him an asshole, to start with." She was trying not to laugh, but it was escaping in little snorts.

"Never going to stop calling him an asshole. Step two?"

"Laugh at his jokes. Smile." She forced her own face into a grimace. "Act like you think he's right. Even if he isn't right. *Especially* if he isn't right."

Asher's head cocked to one side. "May I ask where you learned all this subterfuge?"

"Have you ever dated a man?"

I'm sure that was meant to be some sort of feminist mic drop moment for her, but I'm a big believer in honesty. "Yup. I mean, I didn't find out it was a date until the end, but yeah."

The wind was taken right out of Mercy's sails, and I almost felt bad for her. Almost. Then Asher piped up, "Will it be necessary for Maulkin to 'make out' with Leofric if we recognize it as the best way to assure others of friendship?"

Just like that, the grimace grin was back on Mercy's face.

I backed away from her slowly. "I would really like to not."

"No, no…" she said. "I like where this is going."

Holding up my hands in defeat, I tried not to shudder at the image of Leo making smoochy faces. "Okay… how about we never speak about making out ever again."

Mercy raised an eyebrow. "So the bet…"

"What bet? I don't remember any bet." I backpedaled my way to the door. "Let's go to sleep. I've got to suck up to fantasy-land Mussolini tomorrow."

Asher was still standing there, head tilted to one side. "I do not understand that reference."

Mercy snorted. "I'm surprised Maulkin understood that reference."

"We had the history channel." Then I added, "Shut up."

I left the two of them to it. Even through the closed door, I could hear Mercy groaning as she tried to explain world history to a lizard-man from another dimension. I was almost to the door of the other room when I felt the ping of my Lifesense. There was someone on the other side of the door, standing in the other room, waiting to catch us alone. A trap. I knew it.

With a pulse of will, the great-sword on my back shifted and slithered into a pair of cleavers in my hands. If Leo and his minions wanted to get the drop on me, then they were going to have to do better. I kicked into the room and closed the distance before Orphia could even draw her sword. Both cleaver blades scissored into position around her scrawny neck before she could even squeak.

It would be so easy just to keep on moving. Just to let the blades snip together and feel all my worries fading away. Leo couldn't fault me for it. He'd already slapped Orphia around for chasing after me without permission. He'd probably thank me. This was probably the in that we needed. He obviously wanted Eternals in his camp. If he was suddenly missing one and needed a replacement, surely that just opened up more opportunities for us.

But she was still a person, even if she was Orphia, and I didn't need to kill her to stop her from killing me. So I didn't.

"What do you want?"

I eased the blades apart enough for her to speak without doing herself an injury. "I want you gone."

"Yeah." I rolled my eyes at her. "You made that abundantly clear."

"You are the spawn of chaos, and you have corrupted those who should have been brother and sister to me. You are—"

At some point that night I wanted to get to bed, which meant cutting her off before she could launch into her usual screed. "Can we skip the insults and rambling and get to the point. You didn't need to sneak in here to tell me I'm the worst. I've heard it all before."

Her eyes had narrowed to slits, and the bones in her face seemed to jut out, stripping all over her natural Alvaren beauty away and leaving the stark truth of her madness on clear display. "You are not going to corrupt Lord Leofric. You are not going to turn him from his divine purpose. I will not let you."

I eased the blades back from her neck, then shrugged once I was sure it wasn't going to cause catastrophic bleeding. "I don't want to? We all want to beat Araphel? Yeah? Nobody wants to beat him more than me."

"You cannot win me over. You cannot trick me. I am not going to be deceived by honeyed words. I know you for what you are." Maybe I shouldn't have taken the swords from her neck so soon. She was looking more and more axe crazy with every passing moment. "But… Leofric has not hardened his heart enough to do what must be done. He has forbidden me from dispatching you, thinking that you might convert to the cause of righteousness."

"Great. So you decided to sneak in here to tell me you aren't going to sneak in here and murder me. Much appreciated. Get out." I stepped to the side and pointed to the door.

"I do not sneak. This is my domain, and I travel freely within…" She started off snarling, then somehow managed to get herself under control. "No. I will not be distracted into bandying words with you again. I have come here to tell you the truth and hope that it might make its way through that thick skull of yours. Leofric will not succumb to your wiles. He will see you for what you are. He will know you as his enemy. When that time comes, there shall be nothing that you can do to stand up against his power. He will destroy you utterly. Banish you to the darkest corners of the world…"

I yawned. "Uh-huh."

"All of this is certain to come to pass, but I wish to spare my lord the heartbreak of your betrayal." She closed the distance that I'd put between us, urgency vibrating through her. "Leave now. Nobody will stop you. Nobody will pursue you. Just pick a direction and walk. There is nothing keeping you here."

"My friends are here."

"If you cared for these 'friends' at all, you would not doom them by continuing your association." She was close enough now that those big golden eyes of hers were bathing my face in radiance. With a little bit of smugness, I realized that even though her face had been hand carved by the gods themselves, she wasn't as pretty as homegrown Seren. "They are Solar Eternals, the avatars of all that is righteous in this broken world, and your very presence taints them."

I stared her down. "I'm not going anywhere."

"Then I have wasted my kindness on a beast that cannot comprehend it. Hardly surprising."

"Been great catching up with you, but now it is bedtime." Piece by piece, I took my armor apart and set the hunks of metal and adjoining eel-skin down. "Are you getting out, or are you getting naked?"

The look on her face in that moment almost made having to deal with her again worthwhile. "Disgusting."

"Don't knock it until you've tried it." She backed out of the room, reaching for the door but never quite managing to tear her scowl away from me. I yelled after her as she retreated for the stairs, "Once you go Faun, there's no moving on!"

When I glanced around, Mercy was standing there gawking at me, with Asher doing his best not to do the same behind her. "Orphia popped in. Wants me to die, go away, or both."

"So she hasn't changed much?" Mercy smirked. I kept forgetting how much Mercy hated her.

"She's got a nasty crush on lovely lord Leo, but otherwise, she's the same crazy bitch as always."

"It is most unfortunate that she cannot be reasoned with." Asher sighed. "It would be helpful to us to have another ally in the quest."

"She wants to be friends with you guys. You guys are shiny golden boys and girls like her and Leo." I sulked back to my room. "It is just me that she hates."

Asher didn't seem to catch my tone, turning to Mercy with a curious tilt to his head. "Perhaps she might be more amenable to reason once Maulkin has departed on his mission, come morning."

"Uh, pretty sure I don't want to be friends with her," Mercy said, glancing my way. "She sucks."

Maybe she thought she was giving me moral support, but I was grumpy, and Asher wasn't a good verbal punching bag. "So I've got to play pretend, but you don't? How is that fair?"

"Orphia doesn't matter," Mercy called through. "Leo though, he's old, right? He's badass? And he's got a shard already."

I popped back out into the hallway, just itching for a real fight. "I could take him."

"Could you?" Asher's stare was boring into me. But he wasn't trying to provoke me. I knew him too well for that. He didn't expect any sort of emotional response to anything he said and seemed constantly amazed when the rest of us had our little outbursts. He genuinely wanted to know the answer, and I couldn't lie to him, even in as foul a mood as I was in, because he'd base his decisions on the stupid things that we said.

I groaned for a long, long time, then finally admitted, "Well… the three of us could for sure."

He nodded at that. "Then that shall be our course of action should all other opportunities fail."

"Ugh." I stomped back through to the other room. "I'm going to sleep."

Mercy stomped right after me, although she had the good grace to spin on her heel so she couldn't see me continuing to undress. "Asher bunks with you."

I threw a stretch of legging at her. "Asher steals the blanket!"

She yelled back over her shoulder, "There are two beds in here!"

"Maulkin has been known to produce quite tremendous sounds with his nose while he is sleeping." Asher poked his nose around the door. "Perhaps it would be for the best if I just—"

"Nope." Mercy shoved him in. "No cold lizard feet in my bed." She slammed the door shut. "Goodnight."

CHAPTER 6

hen morning came about, I had not gotten a ton of sleep. I wasn't grumpy about that since this new body of mine apparently didn't need sleep to function perfectly, but the long dark stretch of the night had been filled with thoughts that just wouldn't stop niggling at me. Weirdly, I spent more time worrying that Seren was lonely back home than I did about the whole spy and assassination mission that I was heading off on. Or the whole fortress full of people that had been trying to murder me earlier in the day. Or the super-powerful ancient eternal who might decide I was a heretic in need of burning at any moment. Or the dark god of destruction that could talk to me if I touched the magic sword bits I'd collected. Or...

It was amazing I didn't spend more time worrying, let's be real.

I had expected there to be some pomp and ceremony when it was time for me to head out into the blighted lands beyond the Bastion, but it seemed that whatever dramatic scene I was picturing was not going to happen. If there had ever been big old gates in the big old wall, then they'd been part of the smashed-up parts that had been patched over. When anyone on this side of the Bastion wanted to go down into the Ashlands, they did it by rope. Even a lift would have been nice, but our boy Leo thought that anything that might aid and abet enemies trying to surmount the wall was a bad idea, and honestly, he was probably right.

Abseiling down the Bastion to land ass-first in the ash wasn't my idea of a good time, but given all the falling from high places I'd been doing recently, I was mostly just happy about how strong the rope felt.

Asher and Mercy had come to see me off, of course. As had Leo and Orphia, though I couldn't help but think their waving was definitely a lot less enthusiastic. Leo, who did not appreciate being called Leo, informed me of the direction where his scouts assumed that the Faun were massing, and Orphia gave me a glare like I was trying to steal her man. Then away I went down the rope.

From what Leo's scouts had reported back, and from the number of scouting missions to certain areas that had just not come back at all, it sounded like there was a ridge a few days out that was my best bet. Which meant hiking. Walking through this big pile of dust. Strolling. I love hiking so much. It is my favorite thing. Dying halfway through a hike definitely wasn't a welcome relief from the living hell of hiking. Nope, not at all…

I just had to keep putting one foot in front of the other and remember I was on an epic fantasy adventure, not walking for no good reason. As long as it was an epic fantasy adventure, the bit of my brain that was screaming about how boring hiking was would shut the hell up.

The shifting ash beneath my feet did not make the journey easier. Every step forward, I'd slip half a step back while I was going up the slopes, and on the way down them, it was a constant struggle to get my feet unstuck quickly enough that I didn't tip over and land on my face. Between the horns and the shoulders for days, I was pretty top-heavy, and this place was giving my sense of balance a real workout. It almost made me miss Seren's stumps in the jungle. At least they stayed more or less in the same place instead of moving around underneath me. On the other hand, when I slipped out here I didn't get a stump to the crotch and a disapproving Seren stare.

There was not a whole lot in the way of scenery. The ashes had banked up into dunes, and slowly but surely, the Bastion slipped down under the horizon behind me, leaving me with nothing to look at but yet more ash dunes in every direction. I had my footprints behind me and the sun in the sky to keep me right as far as directions went, but a gust of wind wiped my tracks clean, and the sun was dipping down towards the horizon before I knew it.

I'd been walking all day, and the only thing that had changed were that some of the lumps under the ashes were slightly bigger than some of the other lumps. Were they just piles of ash? Was there still some solid land underneath that was making them hump up like that? Did I actually care, or was I just so bored looking at heaps of ash that I was inventing things to think about?

It was the last one. I was going crazy. Just shutting my eyes and stretching out my sphere of influence could have told me exactly what was under the ash, but the sun was down before it finally occurred to me to try it.

As it turned out, there was nothing under the ashes, or at least there was nothing that my Artifice could sense. It was like the scarred parts of the Bastion—completely absent from my extrasensory perception. On the one hand, it was kind of novel being able to wander around without the imperceptible presence of all the world pressing in around me, on the other hand, it meant that Artifice was basically useless out here. I'd be able to remake what I'd brought with me, but everything else was inert.

My initial plan to slap together a quick cottage for the night was ruined, and I didn't actually need to stop, thanks to the whole Faun never getting tired thing, so I just kept on plodding on. And on. And on. The stars filled up the sky, and I did not know them.

I wasn't an astronomer or an astrologer—or whichever one it was that looked at the stars through a telescope instead of telling people the stars were why they kept having bad days—but I'd gotten familiar enough with the stars in the sky through my years back on Earth. These ones were wrong. I didn't even know enough to say how they were wrong—they were still up there, twinkling away like they were meant to in every direction that I looked—but I couldn't recognize a single constellation.

This was why traveling with other people was better. On my own, I had too much time to get sappy and weird about stuff that didn't really matter. When the sun was up, I didn't care that this was a different planet from the one I grew up on, so why was I getting all misty-eyed thinking about good old Earth now? Earth wasn't that great. It didn't even have dragons. Or hot elf girls. Amaranth was definitely better. Sure everything was trying to kill me, but so was everything on Earth. The stuff here was just more up-front about it, and I had a chance to fight back.

All day long as I'd been hiking, something had been itching at the back of my brain. Something that I knew that was important about now. Something about this place that I'd learned sometime since I arrived here on Amaranth that was on the tip of my tongue. Well, the tip of my brain. Something about the Ashen Wastes? Something that one of my new skills had popped into my brain fully formed without me actually learning it. What was it?

I could see just fine in the dark, and there wasn't a whole lot to see, but I had been keeping my eyes peeled for any hint of the Faun. From what I'd been told by the dude who thought they were all evil and out to get him, they claimed this whole place as their territory and patrolled regularly. I had not made a good impression when I came crashing and smashing into the Bastion, but so long as I didn't screw up too badly, the Faun might actually like me. So long as I got a word out before they shot at me and I had to kill them right back.

So I listened as hard as I could for anything but the silky sound of shifting ash. I stared over the top of every dune as I mounted it. I even caught myself sniffing the air, hoping for some campfire smoke. That last one was a mistake—I got a nose full of drifting ash and started sneezing. Not little delicate snuffles either, those big, booming dad sneezes that made you think the guy who was sneezing might actually turn inside out. The dudes manning the walls of the Bastion probably heard me. Guess I wasn't getting the drop on any Faun out here.

I was straining all the regular senses so hard that I didn't even catch the blip on my Lifesense until it was too late. At the same moment that I noticed something alive down underneath the ashes, it was bursting up out at me.

Back in Witchglass Overlook, a chompy little worm had latched on and chewed a chunk out of me. This thing was that thing's big brother. And by big, I mean about a hundred times as big. This thing was as wide around as me, and I couldn't even guess how long the slick red body, coated with clumped ash, actually was.

I only got a brief glimpse of that body writhing up out of the ground before the plume of ash it had thrown up blocked all vision. If I was a standard-issue Eternal, I probably would have been screwed, but Lifesense took over when I had to clamp my eyes shut against the shower of grit, lighting the thing up in glowing green, every channel of life-force flowing through the thing shining.

Training with Seren paid off again. My sword was in my hands and swinging before I even knew the thing was coming at me.

[66 Damage]

My rough-hewn blade might have struggled against armor plates, but this thing was all squish. It bit into the meat, and I watched as every channel of life-force that it crossed blinked out. It wasn't a killing blow, but it was enough to hurt.

The Dhole reared back, hissing and spraying me with that same viscous ichor that coated its body, letting it slip easily through the ashes. Thanks, Bestiary skill. Shame you didn't help out before the thing was already trying to eat me.

The cloud it had thrown up when it first emerged was blown clear by the thing's breath, and now I got a glimpse of the big angry sphincter it called a face, lined all around with barbed and hooked lamprey teeth. Even with a gash cut right across it, making the lower half loll open and leak, I did not want to go in there.

"Wow, you are one ugly dude."

The insult probably didn't make it attack me again, but it probably didn't help.

Lashing forward with all those teeth rippling out towards me, I had to appreciate how straightforward the Dhole was being. It was kind of like a batting cage. It threw its weight forward and met my sword's edge once more.

Was I the smartest guy in Amaranth? No. The fastest? Nope. The prettiest? Probably not. Was I strong enough to smack a charging Dhole in the face and make it stop? Hell, yes.

The whole body doubled up behind what I'm charitably calling its head, a six-car pileup of worm, rucking up in a heap like it had just run headlong into a solid object. There were moments when I questioned my choices since arriving on Amaranth, but this was not one of them.

"Did I just make you even uglier?"

The maw of the Dhole was gaping even more now, crisscrossed by my two blows, all four quarters of it flapping open, curling back like flower petals. It stank like old blood inside that ruined mouth. Rust and rot. I grinned. "You want some more?"

I shouldn't have gotten smug. Pride comes before a giant worm vomits up dozens of its writhing babies in your face.

They latched onto me before I even knew what had hit me. They were Khorkhoi, like the one that had chomped me back in Witchglass Overlook, but with none of the lethargy that lying in wait for years had instilled in that one. Like their big daddy had burrowed through the ash, these little charmers started digging into my flesh. They were slowed just enough by my armor that I wasn't turned to swiss cheese on the spot—all of them except the one that latched onto my forehead.

I grabbed it by the tail, but it was slick and slippery, flapping about and twisting in my grip as it ate my face. In the end, I gave up trying to pull it off and just squeezed as hard as I could. It burst like overripe fruit in my hand, red sludge bursting between my fingers. Still, the head went on chewing until it finally realized it was dead and dropped off.

That one worm trying to eat my brain was enough of a distraction that it had given the rest of them time to wriggle their way into the gaps of my armor, squeezing in and chomping everywhere they could reach.

Pain assailed me from every side, nipping, buzzing teeth digging into me, grating over my ribs, and burrowing down into my muscles.

[621/890 Health]

I was not dying like this.

With a roar, I split my sword into cleavers and set about myself, hacking one worm in half after another. They were pinned in place by their own hold on my flesh, and while I couldn't swing at them with all my strength in their awkward positions, I could hit them hard enough to make them pop. One by one, the little chomping jaws stopped, and the dead worms' heads slipped back out of me, surrounded by a fresh wash of my blood.

Wiping blood and worm guts from my eyes, I turned to give Daddy Dhole a sneer.

It wasn't there.

Two tons of worm didn't just vanish. Stretching out my Lifesense to its limits, I caught the last hint of a tail vanishing out of range. It ran away. The giant murder worm ran away. I threw my cleavers down in disgust. It had stolen my kill! I mean, sure, it had saved itself from inevitable death, but worms weren't meant to be smart. They were worms. Bestiary had not said anything about them being smart. I couldn't believe that after bleeding all over the place and getting gnawed on by babies I wasn't even going to get—

My grumbles stopped when I felt the ash beneath me shaking. Maybe we weren't done yet. A quick flex of Artifice reformed my great-sword in my hands, and I waited, stretching out my senses to their limit.

Deep down beneath me, just where the ash gave away to the null I guessed was stone that I couldn't touch, I caught a hint of movement. The dhole brushed the edge of my sphere of influence for just a moment, then it was gone. Then again on the other side. It was circling underneath me. Faster and faster. The ash that had been packed so solid beneath me just a moment before seemed to soften, then it began to twist. My feet sank in, then my shins. I tried to fling myself clear of the sinkhole the Dhole was making, but I had nothing solid to kick off, and I ended up just flopping over into an ever-deepening pool of ash and sank like a stone.

The ash closed over my head with that same soft hissing I'd been hearing all day, and those alien stars went out. The Ashen Wastes gently reset itself as if I'd never been there.

I couldn't breathe, and I couldn't see. Everything was black. Despite that, I could still feel myself sinking down, deeper and deeper into the ash. Anywhere else in the world all it would have taken was a quick burst of Artifice to launch myself back to the surface, but here in this dead place, I was powerless.

Down into that deep dark nothingness, I went on sinking until the reach of my sphere of influence was extended out far enough to encompass the Dhole's circuit. It was slowing now, whatever senses let it track the movement of prey on the surface had told it that the trap had snapped shut on me. It made one last slow circuit before wiggling my way. Could worms gloat? The languid swish through the ash felt pretty smug to me.

It should have known better. I was going to puke my babies on its face. Okay maybe I wasn't going to literally do that … but something with the same vibe.

Vibrations in the ash would have warned me it was coming, even if my Lifesense didn't have it lit up—the only thing in the dead darkness. It took all my willpower to stop struggling, to stay still and play dead. If it really waited until I'd suffocated then it was out of luck. My body was going to blink out of existence when I respawned, and it was going to go hungry. But if I could get it to come for me now, it might still get a taste of me, and I might still have a chance.

My lungs burned in my chest. I could feel my health ticking down with every passing moment. Death was coming for me—a lot quicker than that sneaking, nervous Dhole. Maybe he wasn't hungry. Maybe he was leaving me down here for later. Joke was on him, all he'd get to eat was half-chewed eel-skin armor. Not that he deserved any better. Kill stealing jerk.

Just when I thought I was doomed to pop back up in Tropical Dvergar Town, the Dhole decided it was snack time. It came on in a mad rush, tattered mouth flopping open in anticipation just before it reached me where the ash held my feeble mortal frame completely immobile.

Even with my potency surged, it felt like I was moving through molasses, so slow there was no chance I could actually deal any sort of damage with the swing of my sword. Good thing damage wasn't the goal. As the mouth flopped open, my sword came around, not slicing anything but wedging those jaws wide open.

I clung to the blunt back side of the cleaver blade as the impact of the Dhole against it rocked me. The ash that had encased me vanished down the thing's throat, but I stuck there in its craw like a chicken bone, gasping in the foul and fetid air. All around me the vibrant red flesh pulsed and flexed as it tried to close those wretched teeth into me, but it couldn't. It could contract at the sides, but the top and bottom couldn't. It couldn't snap shut and puncture me.

The big angry hose was not pleased with this, and it bucked and rolled, trying to dislodge me. More ash billowed in through its open mouth and covered both me and the Khorkhoi that were slithering out the ducts in between its teeth. I was a big guy; I could take a little bit of ash plastered onto me. The teeny Khorkhoi couldn't. The ash and drool and blood all mingled into a paste as thick as concrete, trapping the baby murder worms where they lay.

More and more ash came flowing in, choking the Dhole, setting it retching, hissing, and pulsing all around me as it tried to dislodge it and me. It wasn't built to travel down here with its mouth open. It needed open air, just as surely as I did. It had to go up.

We burst through the surface, and my roars of laughter rolled out over the dunes. The worm had done exactly what I wanted it to. Now it just had to do one more thing like I wanted. It had to die.

I leapt clear of the mouth, tumbling back to my feet on the dunes and leaving the sword in place for now. The Dhole was flinging itself back and forth, tossing up huge clouds of dust but making no attempt to dip back under the surface. It would have choked itself out if it had.

Once I had my breath back and the Dhole was lying limp on its side, half-exhausted and half-choked, it was time for a killing blow. I crept up on it, nice and slow, but even as careful as I was coming, it felt the vibrations through the ground and started flopping around like a beached fish all over again.

Guess there wasn't going to be an easy way to do this. I gave up on stealth and just walked right up to the thing, ducking under a couple of wild flails it made in my general direction. When I was close enough to lay a hand on its rubbery hide, it was time. I called my sword back to me, deconstructing it from inside the thing's mouth and into my hands in one smooth flow of liquid metal.

I took a breath to get my balance, then I swung.

Even with a sword as big as mine, and all my strength behind it, it wasn't enough to take the Dhole's head off. It was enough to cut more than halfway through, but I had to elbow into the oozing wound to bring the blade down, again and again, before finally, I was all the way through, and the hissing abruptly stopped.

Legendary Foe Defeated!
165 Experience Gained
150 Glory Gained

Silence again. Just my ragged breathing, the distant stars, and the smooth drifting of the dunes.

I'd won, but that didn't mean I was any less screwed. With all of the chaos, the burrowing underground, the bull-ride inside the Dhole, and my less than stellar sense of direction at the best of times, I was now completely turned around.

When the sun came up, I'd remember which side of me it was on when I set off in the morning and have a vague idea of the right way to go, even if I might have been sidetracked by miles by this point. I had no idea how far the Dhole dragged me around before surfacing. Yeah, this sucked.

I spun around on the spot a few times, hoping I might catch a glimpse of something familiar. I even looked at the sky and tried to remember what the stars had looked like when I was headed the right way. It was hopeless. They were a random collection of dots in the sky. How were they meant to tell me anything?

Should I wait until morning, all alone with my thoughts? Maybe roaming in a random direction was a better idea. If I got lucky, some other wildlife might pop up and try to murder me.

I almost did it too, but then I heard a nagging voice in my head that sounded like Mercy calling me a dumbass. There was a little snip-pet of Seren, commenting on my lack of patience, too. Why couldn't Asher be my conscience. He would never dunk on me like this.

The dead Dhole was the only landmark for miles, and it was also the only thing resembling furniture, so I clambered up on top of its squishy body and lay down, sinking in an inch as it expelled liquids and gasses that I really did not want to think about. A quick brush over it with my Artifice revealed nothing of value. The only solid bones in the whole thing were the teeth, and even they were too small to be much use, unless I really wanted to patch up my poor, battered eel armor with lots of spikes all over it. As much as that would look badass, and it would look so very badass, I would end up stabbing myself about nine hundred times a day, and nobody has time for that.

That reminded me to use Restoration on myself. It was definitely more useful when you were in a group since everybody seemed to have their own cooldown timer before they could be healed again with the power. Good thing I had all night to wait out that timer and heal myself until I was pristine and factory fresh again.

Sinking another inch into the Dhole, I let out a long sigh. I was glad that my hair had finally grown in, but that did mean that it could soak up all the lovely fluids that I seemed to encounter on a daily basis. Back at Talon's Keep, I got my every-other-daily swim to shuck off the worst of the grime, but out here in the middle of nowhere… let's just say you don't appreciate modern plumbing until it is gone.

So there I was, lying on a stinky cushion, staring up at the stars, with nothing to do for hours and hours and hours. Nothing to occupy my thoughts. No sign of any living thing for miles. I couldn't sleep, obviously—there might have been more Dholes just waiting to pop up and make me their midnight snack—so I was just lying there. Bored.

I don't do well with bored. Give me life-threatening monster attacks over bored anytime. When I am bored, I make trouble for myself. Back home, the amount of trouble I could make was pretty limited, but here in Amaranth, with all the powers of a demigod, I could do some real damage. Which was why after about a half-hour, I had the shards of the rusted blade out of the pockets inside my armor, and I was trying to fit them together like a jigsaw puzzle.

Some bits slipped together perfectly, but others didn't seem to go together at all. I was definitely missing the hilt piece, which I guessed was welded into Leo's sword. The Alvaren piece was the tip, and Talon's piece attached just beneath it, still sharp along its edge. That meant that the Faun piece that was completely missing from history and the two bits that Tsangaanax had hoarded were other lengths of the blade. Put back together, I guessed it would be a longsword for anyone else but a short-sword for me. That wasn't ideal, but judging from Leo's Lucis, I could always strap some more metal onto the thing to make it bigger without it losing too much mojo.

Mercy and Asher hadn't really spoken about it, but I think we were all kind of assuming that I was going to be the one swinging the Rusted Blade around once we got it back together. Neither of them had shown any inclination to get up close and personal with the monsters, and while the image of Mercy shooting a sword out of her bow was always going to bring a smile to my face, it probably wasn't super practical. This was going to be my burden. I was going to have to be the one to kill the Voidgod. Maybe if Leo hadn't been a complete nut I might have handed the quest over to him, but he was, so I couldn't.

Unfastening the clips that I'd added to keep them firmly in place, I pulled off my gloves and let the night air breeze between my fingers. Sweaty palms. Gross. I almost wiped them off on myself before I remembered my current slimy state.

Almost without a thought, I picked up the shards again. One in each bare hand.

"So we have found our courage again?"

Araphel's voice didn't come from the shards in my hand. It didn't echo to me from a great distance through Psychometry, the way that most of the ghosts that power showed me. He boomed in my head like his mouth had snapped open on the inside of my skull, and he was yelling every word.

My mouth was dry when I answered, "What do you want, Araphel?"

"You are the one who communes with me. Surely, the real question is what you want."

It took me a moment to get over that reverberation in my poor brain. There was something uniquely unpleasant about Araphel's voice. You know how really good music can make you feel like your soul is getting bigger? His voice did the opposite.

I didn't even have to think about my answer. "I want to kill you."

"Yet, I do not wish to be killed." That awful voice was easing now like he was trying to dial it back and make himself more palatable. It wasn't better, it was just a different kind of suffering to listen to him. It set my teeth on edge. I lay there with my eyes clamped shut so I wouldn't have to see him as well as hear him. The idea of him looming over me as I lay here was just too much to bear. *"So let us seek a compromise."*

"What? I only kill you a little bit, and then we call it quits?" I probably shouldn't have snorted with laughter in the figurative face of the Voidgod, but nobody has ever said I was smart.

"Abandon your quest. Keep the shards far from one another." The more he tried to ingratiate himself to me, the more it made my stomach heave and my head ache—like nails on a chalkboard, except the chalkboard was the inside of my skull. *"Keep them as trophies or cast them in the sea for all that I care, but do not let them all come together."*

It took some effort to ease my grip on the shards enough that they weren't drawing blood from my palms anymore. Touching most things with Psychometry bombarded me with images and sounds from the whole history of the object, but the presence of Araphel was so overpowering that nothing else got through. I'd never know who struck the blow that felled him. I'd never know who forged the sword. I'd never know whose hands each of the shards had passed through. All of that was gone. Replaced by him. His looming, aching, presence. Just like the Bastion and this desert and everything else, it was tainted so thoroughly by the touch of the Voidgod that it would never be anything but his leftovers again.

I took a deep breath. I really wasn't holding up my end of the conversation here. "So what's in it for me?"

"Your court shall reign supreme over what is left of this world. Those you call kin shall survive my coming. You shall survive it. This is a greater charity than any I have ever offered." He really thought he was making me a good offer here. Like I cared about team moon getting the scraps of the planet when he was done chewing on it. My friends not dying would be nice, but if they were willing to stand back and watch everyone else in the world drop dead to save themselves, I wouldn't have wanted to call them my friends.

There was nothing that he could offer me. There was no compromise that would be enough. For this world to survive, Araphel couldn't.

I licked my lips. "How about this. I put this sword back together, then I lift up your tail and shove it right up your shiny black—"

There was no restraint now. No subtle inveigling his way into my brain. His voice hit me like a sledgehammer. *"I am a god."*

"You're a dick!" I roared back into the empty night. "You wrecked this world. You'll wreck it even more when you come back. There are people trying to live here, and you just—"

Araphel pummeled me with his voice. Every word nailed into my brain, sharp and cruel and agonizing. *"You will do as I command, or I shall—"*

It took all my will to growl out, "Hanging up now."

Then I let the shards fall from my hands to splat on the worm below.

I groaned all the way back up into a sitting position, then I put my head in my hands like I could crush the ache behind my eyes into submission. I even gave my horns a few gentle rubs to see if that would help. It didn't. Just felt weird.

Pulling my gloves back on made me wince with pain from where the shards had dug in. Even the places they hadn't broken the skin looked rust red, leaving perfect impressions of them on both my hands. Once they were fastened back into place, I stowed everything back away where it belonged and flopped back all over again.

That had been stupid, even by my usual standards, and my usual standards were right down there with eating the silica gel pack in my bag of jerky and buying things from infomercials. Antagonizing the dude who already wanted to destroy the world. Good job, Maulkin. Good job. Although, maybe it wasn't actually the real living Voidgod who I'd just threatened to prod in the rear. Maybe it was just the echo that was still attached to the shards. Maybe this wasn't going to have terrible repercussions later. Yeah, I was just bugging a ghost. Not a god of destruction. Maybe.

I lay back and stared at the sky again. All those stars, yet the black between them was still there—and so much bigger than any one of them. The sun, the moon, they were just tiny blips in the universe in comparison to the spaces between. The void. It seemed to stare back at me. All that darkness pressing down, unstoppable. Endless. I blinked. Maybe brain-to-brain contact with ancient evil gods wasn't good for me. I didn't usually get this weird while stargazing. Not without tequila.

There was anxiety gnawing at my guts as the implacable darkness stared down at me, and it was almost enough to make me pick up the shards again, to try and talk Araphel down from the thing he was born to do. The thing that he desperately wanted to do more than anything. To offer him some real compromise that we both might accept. I knew it wouldn't work. Just like I knew I couldn't trust Leofric or any of the gods we'd met so far. They were all cut from the same megalomaniacal cloth. They'd all do whatever they had to, say whatever they had to, so that their team won. Even if it cost the lives of everyone on Amaranth.

The sensation of the fear, dangling in my guts like a lead weight, made me stop and wonder. I do stupid things without thinking them through. That is the complete opposite of anxiety. This was not my anxiety. Someone had put it in me. Araphel had put it in me.

Once I knew that it wasn't mine, it was easy enough to ignore it, and it fizzled away to nothing almost immediately, but that had come from him. Touching the shards had let him sneak those feelings into me without me even noticing. I needed to be even more careful to keep my gloves on.

But here was the thing that stuck with me. He had to have gotten that anxiety from somewhere. He had to know what it felt like to be able to inflict it on someone else. He had to have the recipe. And what's more, despite being the all-powerful dark god of evil or whatever, he'd come to me, and he'd tried to cut a deal. He was running scared. He was scared that I was going to put the sword back together. He was scared that I was going to kick his ass.

He was right to be scared I was going to kick his ass because I was going to kick his ass.

CHAPTER 7

What was left of the night dragged on, and I made a less than graceful dismount of my worm-corpse-bed when some smaller critters came up from beneath the ash and started chowing down on it. I guess that there wasn't a lot of food on the go in a desolate wasteland devoid of all life. Who'd have thought?

I got back to a safe distance and watched the show, fully expecting another worm to pop out and treat me as an appetizer for the banquet, but no matter how ready I was to rumble … well, they weren't. Even when the whole ash desert beneath the Dhole carcass was writhing and heaving with competing carrion eaters, not one of them even looked my way. Not that they could look since they didn't have eyes.

Don't get me wrong, I was ready for a fight. After getting my brain tickled by Araphel, I was ready to fight just about anyone, but I didn't feel the need to slap the crap out of some worms that were just trying to get some dinner—as long as that dinner wasn't me. Over the course of what felt like an hour, they noisily and messily devoured the Dhole while I watched, and when the ash finally stopped heaving, all that was left was a damp patch in the ash. That had filled up some more time at least. Kind of like watching a nature documentary but squishier.

Then it was back to standing around, waiting for the sun to glow on one of the horizons so I could get going again.

There was barely even the first hint of light when I took off running. All of yesterday's halfhearted attempts at stealth were forgotten in my joy. I didn't care that I was slipping and sliding over the dunes. I finally had something to do. I was free to run, to move, to live.

Beneath me, I caught hints and glimmers of Dholes and Khorkhoi of all sizes, all diving deeper as I passed. Maybe they really were smarter than I might have expected, or maybe I was still crusted with Dhole blood and that distinct aroma was warding them off.

As the day broke fully and the sun started to creep up into the sky, I was startled to find that there was stone beneath me again—not just the dull numb null of the stuff that the Voidgod's powers had washed over, but real workable stone below that. Ridges and rises. A whole topography buried beneath the ash and destruction. Hints and clues about the world that had been before Araphel got his claws into it. Maybe this had been a mountain; maybe it had just gotten lucky and whatever had been unleashed on this land had bounded over this patch by luck.

It wasn't until later as I came upon ridge after ridge that a picture started to form. They were the outer edges of a crater, but a crater not caused by one big bang, but by an explosion that kept happening, over and over and over, spreading out farther and farther with each repetition. I was heading towards the epicenter. That was where Leofric had sent me. To the heart of all this destruction.

The ridges came closer and closer together the nearer I got to that center, bucking higher and higher beneath the ash until some broke the surface. It was null stone that I couldn't touch with Artifice at first, but then more and more pronounced peaks and spikes with cores of rock that still felt alive and workable to my senses appeared. Past midday, the ash began to give away beneath my feet to solid-feeling stone that my Artifice couldn't sense. What ash there was seemed to be there courtesy of the wind instead of being resident. There was still plenty of it stacked up against the foot of the stone spurs I now found myself passing between, but it wasn't everywhere.

At some point, the flat of the desert gave way to an uphill climb—gentle at first, then growing steeper—and soon the circular ridges that had been thrown up became real impediments to progress, and I had to go wandering along them to find the places where they had been crumbled, or where they were slung low enough that I could make the jump over them.

It was only when I had to use Potency Surge to leap over a particularly high one that I finally noticed that I wasn't alone anymore. I landed heavily with a stumble in what looked like a vegetable patch cultivated in the ashy soil that had gathered behind the high ridge, and there was a Faun just standing there, staring back at me. From the armor and the spears, I was guessing that she wasn't a farmer. From the stricken look on her face, I was guessing that she hadn't expected me to jump over that wall in one bound.

"Uh. Hi."

To her credit, the surprise didn't stop her long, and she was already hefting that spear up to take her shot before the words were even out my mouth, and I started having flashbacks to my arrival at the fort on the other side of the ash.

"No, no, no. Don't javelin me." I held my empty hands right up in the air. "Don't throw. I'm here to talk. I'm just here to talk."

"What kind of trick is this?" There was a frantic edge to her bass voice, but at least she wasn't impaling me. "Why do you wear our skin? Why do you speak our tongue?"

"No trick! This is my own skin. But I'm not a Faun. I'm an Eternal." I started talking even faster to get through the rest before she had time to throw anything. "And I'm telling you that now because I don't want you to think I'm trying to lie about that in any way. I'm being honest. So please don't shoot at me."

The flinty tip of the spear was still pointed at me, her arm still cocked back, missile ready to launch. There was a growl in her voice that brought all the hairs on the back of my neck to attention. "You come from the camp of the adversary."

"Oh no. That's just where I landed." I took a half-step forward before I realized my mistake and threw my arms right back up again. I really did not want to have to fight Faun. "I'm not on that gold-plated prick's side. I swear."

Her eyes narrowed, the hump of her nose wrinkling. "You are one of his creatures."

"I'm really not." Was this paranoia, or did Leo actually have creatures? I really hoped he didn't have creatures. Creatures and a whole army and a pair of Eternals felt like a lot of work, even for me.

"He has carved you into the shape of the Firstborn, but you are not." Her dark lips curled back from teeth that she had sharpened to points. That looked cool as hell. She had the body that Seren's mind would have fit into perfectly. Her horns looked like they'd been filed sharper too. Everything about her was honed for wicked violence, and I was kind of into it?

I dragged my gaze back to her eyes. The pupils were like a goat's—a sideways figure of eight. This was the first time I was seeing a Faun in real life with all the details. It was weirdly exciting. Like meeting your long-lost family and making contact with an alien species all rolled into one. If your long-lost alien cousin was a buff warrior lady that wanted to step on you. "I already told you, I'm an Eternal, not a Faun."

"Like him."

"No, not like him. I'm a Lunar Eternal." I pointed to my face, then jerked my hand back up before she could throw. "Check the eyes. Moonlight, right?"

She took a cautious step forward to examine me. Those golden eyes darting up and down, side to side, taking in every inch of me. Shame I was covered in bug guts really. "Another trick."

"Okay, here's the deal. Nothing I say is going to convince you I'm not a secret monster, right?" Her eyes narrowed, but she nodded along with me. "So why don't you take me to somebody who can tell for sure? You've got to have a wizard or something lying around. Right?"

She slowly eased her spear down from where she had been holding it steady above her head, ready to launch, all of this time. Her knuckles were still white where she gripped it. "Koschei would know for sure."

I lowered my hands too, just as slowly. "Great, let's go see Koschei."

She backed away from me slowly, letting me step out of the vegetable patch and onto the ragged stone once again. I gestured to her. "Uh, lead on."

Once more, that voice of hers made the hair all over my body stand on end. "When Koschei declares you an abomination, I shall be there to spit you."

I grinned at her. "And when he says I'm his new best friend, I shall be very polite to you because, hopefully, we'll be friends too."

She spat into the ash pile by my feet.

"Am I meant to spit back? Is this a Faun greeting thing?"

"No." She didn't seem amused. Oh well. I can't win everyone over with my sparkling personality. I had to drown Seren twice and knock her out once before she was my girlfriend. Maybe if I was aiming for a casual friendship with this Faun lady, I'd only need to do a little light maiming.

She jerked her head away from my admiring stare. Her hair was braided back with beads of ivory dotting each thread, spaced out so that they didn't bump together and make a noise. She had to jerk her head again before I worked out she wasn't just waving her hair around, she was gesturing for me to walk ahead of her.

"Alright, enjoy the view." I put an extra wiggle in my hips as I walked away. Asher would have sighed, Seren would have rolled her eyes, and Mercy would have shot me in the butt-cheek. This Faun said nothing at all. Not a peep. It was a bit disappointing.

We followed around the curve of the next raised crest just a short distance until she stopped behind me. "In."

I looked at the barren wall of stone beside me. "Uh? How?"

She spat again. "You are not Chagnar."

"Already covered that."

With a little huff of disdain, she launched herself past me, running sideways up the wall. If Faun had anti-gravity powers all this time, I was genuinely mad that nobody had told me about them. She got to the crest of the stone and spun on her heel to look back down at me. I was tall, apparently tall even for Faun, but she was looking down on me like I was an ant from up on that wall.

I moved closer in to the wall of ruined stone, studying it carefully with my eyes since my other senses told me nothing, but it was only when I was almost beside it and looking along that I saw the footholds she'd used. Clotted with ash, and barely wide enough to fit a fingertip, let alone a foot. I couldn't tell if they'd been carved in and then obscured, or if this was just the formation of the bristling upshot stone and she could somehow recognize it without a second glance. Maybe she was just so used to traveling this terrain that it was natural to her.

It certainly wasn't natural to me, but that didn't mean I was giving up without even trying. Taking a deep breath, I broke into a run, angling my broad body out from the wall so that my feet would hit it instead of my shoulders. I made a little jump once I was up to speed, and my foot skidded down the stone until it jarred for just a moment against a ledge before slipping off. It was enough. I pushed off from there, slamming my next foot down even higher, scraping over flat stone until my heel caught on another protruding edge then I was off again.

I almost made it. Well no, I didn't. I made it about a quarter of the way up before my top-heavy body veered out, my legs pumped in the open air for one moment, then gravity caught up to me, and I ate dirt.

The Faun on top of the wall toppled over too. Falling back out of sight beyond the ridge for just long enough for me to think she'd been attacked before her booming laughter rolled down over me. Great. The roars of laughter turned to wheezing and gasping, then back to a fresh set of whoops when she dragged herself back up to the ridge and saw me clambering to my feet.

She was struggling for breath by the time I was trying to line up for another run at it. Wheezing out, "I am an Eternal, warrior of the gods, and… I…" She couldn't even finish her mocking for laughing so hard. She just slapped one of her hands down on the ridge and cackled.

"Yeah, yeah. Laugh it up."

This time I didn't hesitate. I didn't second guess or worry about brushing my shoulder or my horns on the wall. It wasn't like they could make things go worse than the first time around. I really thought that I was going to make it, right up until the moment that my foot came down on a smooth patch of wall, and I started to fall. I twisted out, away from the wall, so I'd at least have a chance of landing on my feet, but before I'd dropped an inch, I jerked to a halt.

The lady Faun had a grip on my horns, down by the base where they met my skull, and she was hauling with all her strength. It wasn't going to be enough. I was a big guy. I appreciated the effort, but it wasn't going to work. "Just drop me."

"We do not have all day."

I dangled there like a weird puppet, trying to dig my heels into the wall and get some traction, but it didn't seem to be helping much. "I'm too heavy. Just drop me."

Another hand latched onto my horns, then another, and another. A guttural voice growled out, "We do not lift alone."

They lifted me up over the wall by my head, spinning me around and hauling me in, and a few things became apparent in quick succession. The first was that Faun in general seemed to be a lot stealthier than me. There was a full patrol's worth of spear-toting watchers arrayed around the concentric rings of the crater. The second was that while I was big for a Faun, I certainly was not the biggest Faun around. One of the big fellas who had a hold on my horns made me look like the before picture in a weight lifting supplement advert. The guy that got sand kicked in his face by the bully.

I eyed them all, massive and bristling with weaponry, and finally had some idea of why Leo's little posse was so scared of these guys. "Uh, thanks."

The five gathered Faun looked around at each other and shrugged together. A Mexican wave of indifference. One of the other women was looking me up and down in a way that I've got to describe as predatory. She was bigger than me too, her horns curving up to points above her head and making her look even taller. She nudged the first lady Faun with her elbow. "Want help?"

The first lady Faun, who'd nearly busted a gut laughing at me, glanced at me and snorted. "Do not need it."

More shrugging followed, then without a backward glance, they all spread out back to their posts, dark hair, grey skin, and dusty armor blending with the spikes and whorls of the stone all about us. Even after watching them take up their positions again, I struggled to pick them out after I'd glanced away. They could teach Mercy a thing or two about sneaking.

The next time we came to a ring grown too high, Lady Faun gave me a disdainful look. "This time?"

I did my best not to pout as I gave her a nod. She mountain goated her way up the invisible footholds, and I Surged my Potency again, leaping clean over it and landing in another vegetable patch with a squelch. So much for my grand entrance.

Those muddy patches were everywhere now that I looked back down over the concentric plateaus—everywhere enough ash and dirt had been heaped up. The Faun were living here, making a home for themselves in this most inhospitable place, and that meant growing crops. It meant guarding it against invasion. I thought I was going to find some campsite in the middle of the ash desert, and instead, it seemed like I was strolling into the Faun version of a town.

Getting closer to the apex of all the ancient explosions that made this place, more and more of the natural surroundings leapt up in the lea of the rocky outcroppings. Here and there I could see trees growing up out of still-living soil, their branches laden with woven baskets and drying Khorkhoi remains. There were Faun here too, hulking like me, but not in the way that the Lady Faun was. She was like a stallion rearing up for battle while the other Faun I saw were more like pack horses, trudging along. We were all noble animals in our own way, and I'm sure any one of us could have given a human a good kicking, but there was still a world of difference between the folks I'd seen out manning the battlements and the normal people just getting on with their lives.

Everywhere I went in this world, I kept finding them. People just trying to live their lives without powers or training or magic or destiny giving them what they needed to stand up for themselves against Amaranth. I didn't know if this place had always been so violent and dangerous or if that was all Araphel's doing, but I did know that he wasn't trying to make it better. If he came back, it would be like this place all over again, explosions on top of explosions, and all these people that had nothing to do with anything were the ones who'd catch it.

"Are you remembering all that you see, spy?"

I jerked around to find those pointy teeth of my guide bared at me. "Not a spy. Really not a spy. I've just… I've never met Faun before. This is all exciting stuff for me, seeing how you live."

"This is not how we live." She spat again. "This is how we survive. This is what we are brought down to."

Wow, I'd just stamped right on a sore subject there. "I heard somebody say that the land on the other side of the wall used to belong to you?"

Her voice was getting louder now, her tone going from the grim declarations and mockery she'd been sharing with me so far into something else. It was like she was reciting an old story that she knew word for word. "All Amaranth was our hunting ground. Now we are driven from fertile lands to this… dust."

An age-bent old woman ambled by us with a basket of crops on her back, shaking her horned head from side to side. "Shame. Shame."

Like a rumble, it echoed out from the mouths of all the Faun in earshot. "Shame. Shame. Shame."

She was roaring as we walked through the town, bellowing at the top of her lungs, and every head turned to face us. Every mouth hung open to join the chant. "This world was made for us, then came the wyrm with their fire, then came the pale ones with their chains, the underfolk and their living dark. Eternals and humans. Enemies all. Every one of them took and took until we had nothing but these last scraps of dust."

I could feel their misery pulsing against my skin. Shaking the stone beneath our feet. "Shame. Shame. Shame."

"We are the firstborn. Greatest of hunters. Greatest of warriors"— her voice faltered to a droning whisper—"and what we did not offer in our kindness they stole in their treachery."

"Shame."

The whole settlement had fallen silent. We were near to the epicenter now, of that I had no doubt. Skins had been strung up over the branches of the more plentiful trees here, stretched over bones to make something like tents or lean-to shelters. Not for the folks to sleep under, I had no idea where the people here slept, but to protect the few crafts that were being undertaken from the worst of the elements. There were no cooking fires that I could see, though in some places a puff of smoke might escape from out one of the haphazard tents.

If we were anywhere else, I would have built them houses. I would have made this place into somewhere safe for them to live without fear of wind whipping through with a storm of ash. But here, so close to whatever catastrophe had struck, the only thing that my Artifice could touch was what they had brought here with them. Even the trees felt dead to my Lifesense.

I cleared my throat and blathered through the awkward silence. "Thanks for the history lesson."

"There are no others who will speak our truth." She wouldn't even look me in the eye as she said it. "Even when our truth is shame, we keep it."

"You don't have anything to be ashamed of."

"So say our cowards—the ones who would have us forget what we were. What we are." When she turned back to me, those golden eyes burned as bright as any Eternal's, filled with passion and rage. "The brave have the courage to face the truth. We are meant for more than this. We are due more than this."

"You are." I held up my empty hands again, just giving her a little reminder that I was not in any way fighting her. "You deserve better."

She was still staring at me with the same deranged intensity. "Amaranth belongs to the Faun."

"No arguments here."

She looked me up and down with contempt once more. "You would say anything to save your own hide."

"My hide is fine either way. There's nothing you or anybody else can do to me that's going to stick. That's what the whole Eternal part of the name is about. Everlasting." I shrugged and lowered my hands. Force of habit was a hell of a thing, and I'd spent one lifetime trying not to die. It was kind of difficult to let go of that. "I think you're right. It is messed up that you have to live out here in ash-ville when there are plenty of much nicer places that you could be hanging out."

Her lips slowly edged back down over her teeth. "Truly?"

"Yeah, I mean, the other side of that wall had a lot of nice green spaces where you could hunt things that aren't worms, and if you go far enough past Leo's little cargo-cult, you'll get to even more empty spaces. You don't have to stay here, you know that right?"

"You would have us abandon this place?" The hump of her nose wrinkled up in an instant. Her hand flung up to the spear slung over her shoulder. "Leave it untended so that our enemies can lay claim to it?"

I put my hands over my eyes and groaned. I was so tired of everyone looking for an excuse to stab me. "Can I just talk to Koschei please?"

Silence still filled up the village after the shame chanting, but when I said that name, that silence took on a whole new aspect. Oppressive.

It broke with a roar. "Who seeks Koschei?"

The biggest Faun I'd ever seen was standing at the top of the next, final crest. He carried an axe in each hand that could have felled a tree with one swing. He was dressed up in the shiniest armor I'd seen all day. Not just pretty, but better crafted than any other Faun's too. This guy was clearly the boss.

"Hi, yes. Me. Maulkin. I'm the one who seeks Koschei… Is that you?"

He burst out laughing. Literally doubling over. Dropping his axes and slapping his knees. "He thinks I am Koschei?!"

Even the grumpiest of all Faun standing beside me with her hand on her spear couldn't hold back a chortle. I sighed.

Another giant of a Faun came lumbering into sight on the ridge, a hammer with a head as big as my whole torso balanced on one shoulder and his other hand slapping the axe-guy on the back as he roared with the same laughter. "I am Koschei!"

The old woman with the crops called over her shoulder. "I'm Koschei."

"You're hilarious." It was my turn to scowl, apparently. "That's what you are."

Another lady-Faun lurched up over the crest cackling so hard she could barely wheeze out, "Do not listen to them. I'm Koschei!"

I turned back to the woman that had led me this far. "So is Koschei actually a real person, or was this all just the setup for a really unfunny skit?"

The two absolutely gigantic Faun up on the crest stumbled apart, and I fully expected to see yet another beast of a Faun pop up between them to declare himself, but instead, it was a Dvergar.

He came up to the shins of the titans around him, was dressed in furs and scraps that wouldn't have looked out of place on a beggar, and whatever beard he'd had was shaved clean away, along with his eyebrows and hair. But what he did have, was a pair of eyes shining moonlight down at me. Oh.

"Come up, little moon runt. Best we get to speaking."

CHAPTER 8

"Do you know where you've come wandering to?" Koschei spun on his heel to face me once we were past all the looming Faun warlords and inside the cave he'd claimed as his own. Since he came up to about crotch height, I had to make an extremely abrupt stop or become a lot more intimately acquainted with him than I'd planned to.

I teetered on my tiptoes for a moment before rocking back on my heels. "Very rarely."

He reached out and patted the wall. The stone was still dead to my other senses, but by the light of my eyes, I could pick out the wild whorls and spikes patterning all over it. The same force that had created the ridges outside had scarred this cavern. Koschei wandered deeper as he spoke, running his fingers across the bumps and humps with a more than passing familiarity. "This is the place where it happened. The one who did it turned to ash. The land he walked turned to ash. Everything, wiped away with the death blow. Take a walk any way but to the Bastion and you see the wastes. Nothing but the wastes. On and on, as far as the sea. Not the half a world they said would die with him, but enough. Too much."

It stopped me in my tracks when I realized what he was telling me. "This is where Araphel…"

"Where he fell." Koschei nodded his little bald head deeper into the darkness. "Where the hero of Amaranth fell. Where the world stopped dying." He let out a little sigh. "Or started dying slower."

Now instead of stomping along as usual, I tried to keep my clumsy footsteps from echoing. Like I might disturb all the history that was piled up here if I made too much racket. I followed the little Eternal farther and farther from the dwindling daylight until only we would have been able to see, and only our special glowing vision let us pick our way forward.

Beneath the earth, the tunnel bloomed out into a cavern. Nothing grandiose, but big enough that I had to strain to see the opposite side in the darkness. At the very center of that empty sphere, there was a black mark on the stone, broken up only by the paler silhouettes of a sword, broken into fragments. I couldn't help myself. I stepped down to them and bent to look. My two shards were there among the rest of the pale marks. Perfectly outlined. He was either telling the truth, or he had put way too much planning into this lie.

I wet my lips and felt like I was verging on doing something blasphemous when I finally spoke up. "Why are you here?"

"Am I here to steal past glory, like gold clod on his wall? Am I basking in memories of better times?" Koschei cackled. His voice had none of the gruffness I'd come to associate with the Dvergar and their rumbling language. It was musical. Almost comedically high-pitched. Like he was a little Eastern European leprechaun. "You know why I'm here. You can feel it, same as I feel it."

He had his hand on the wall again like he was savoring the texture. I tugged off one of my gloves and pressed my bare hand to the floor. Aether told me nothing. There was no rush of ghosts. It was null. Just like my Sphere of Influence. "The dead zone?"

"Not all our gifts are useless here but enough of them. The rest are numbed." He plopped down to sit cross-legged beside me. "The void god's greatest gift, robbing us of ours."

If this whole place was invisible to the gods and anyone wandering around with god powers, that meant we were hidden too. "So it is camouflage? You're hiding here from other Eternals?"

"You met Leofric? He set you after me? Vengeance burns brighter as the ages turn. When there is no end to the cycle, it is not quenched with any amount of blood. He kills me. I kill him. He raises his armies, I put them down. It does not stop. So long as I live, he will hate me. So long as he lives, I will stop him."

Up until this point, I'd assumed that everything Leofric had told me was a lie, but now I realized with a start that one part was true at least. "Oh, so you really are rallying all the Faun against him?"

"If I could, I'd rally all the world against him. But this world, his kind, his masters, and his servants, they've had the run of it too long. Amaranth is poisoned against us."

I knew this place was a mess, but I didn't know the Solar Court had done any of it. "What?"

"They call us beasts of chaos. That we run wild and do as we please no matter the walls they build to keep us in. What is the word for that? Not chaos. Freedom." He reached out and turned my head by the horns until I was looking at him, so I could see nothing but the glow of his eyes in the dark. "Araphel left Amaranth so scared that they handed it all away to Leofric and his ilk, to kings and laws and their precious order, because then, when the bad came, it was not their own fault. They found their freedom in subservience. Weak. Cowardly."

He gripped tighter to my horns when I tried to pull back, one of his tiny hands on each side of my head, pinning me in place with a strength that his tiny body should have been incapable of. I could feel his Aether flare and mine shining to life inside me in response. In the blinding light of his eyes, I could see everything he was describing, playing out like shadow puppets in front of the moon.

"In the time before there was balance. Sun and moon could fight, but neither one of us could win because we're evenly matched in power. Then the Voidgod came. Hasn't been a Lunar Eternal since me. Not until you." The ancient battlefields shimmered and danced before me. Glorious battles between titans and gods in mortal skins. What we

Eternals were meant to be. Living in this world, and waging battles for supremacy, but protecting the people here too. Felling the wyrms when they came burning. Breaking the chains of magic that bound the Faun.

"The sun-gods kept pouring their servants in. Pouring more of their will in. Locking more and more of the world in cages. Everything numbered and quantified and trapped. Trapped in this terrible stasis for all eternity. The world cannot heal, it cannot grow, it cannot change. And it is not because of some long-dead Voidgod. It is because of them."

I could see it now. The words of my being, inscribed by some bureaucrat's pen in the dark court of the Heavens. The rules of the world being set in stone and all the possibilities that had been dwindling. The grand pillar of divinity at the heart of each god fragmented and filed away in separate columns. The great tangled web of carefully constructed order that had completely swallowed up the whole of Amaranth, pinning everyone and everything in place.

His expression was startled when I surged my Potency to tear free of his grasp and the overpowering weight of his stare. My breath came ragged, and my body shook. I wanted to kill him then and there for pushing his thoughts into my head, for trying to force me to be like him. Instead, I told him the most devastating thing I could manage. "Leofric would have done that if he could have."

Already tiny, he seemed to shrink even further when I said that. He couldn't meet my furious gaze. "You needed to understand."

"I understood fine without you trying to force yourself into my skull." I staggered to my feet, stumbling under the weight of the assault. The swirl of ghosts and memories were still drifting around this dark cavern like long-dead dust. "I understood Leofric fine when he made his pitch and tried to win me over to his cause, too."

He scrambled to his feet, those tiny hands clenching into tiny fists. I'd felt the strength in him. He could probably punch a Faun to death without much sweat. "Then you have chosen to serve him?"

"No. Of course, I didn't." I put my hands over my eyes, trying to rub away the afterimages of his blazing eyes. "You're both idiots."

His flighty little pixie voice went flat. "What?"

"You are both idiots." It came out in a roar, echoing back on me just as loud. I didn't care. After what he just pulled, I was allowed to shout. "You're so caught up in fighting each other that you've forgotten about what really matters."

He was shouting back as if volume was what his argument needed after he'd already broadcast it at full volume right into my skull. "He wants to put the world in chains!"

I turned away from him. Looking at him made my blood boil. If I started swinging then every Faun up outside the cave was going to come running, and I was going to have to kill them all. I didn't want to kill them all. Like it or not, they were my people. "And you want everyone to be free to do anything they want whenever they want to. I got it. That's fine. You two can go on duking it out for all eternity. I've got more important things to deal with."

"What could be more important than freedom? It is our very purpose for being?" He caught me by the wrist and spun me around, trying to meet my gaze, that hazy glow of Aether still dancing all around him. His spirit, just waiting to force itself in me again. To make me feel how he felt. To make me nothing more than an extension of his will. "What could be more important than freeing the world from bondage? More important than casting down a tyrant?"

"Araphel is coming back."

That took the wind out of his sails real quick. "What?"

"You're camped out here of all places, and you don't even know?" I groaned and slumped back down to the ground. "He's coming back."

There was a desperate edge in Koschei's voice now. He fell to his knees as I sat, all his attempts at brain-blasting me into submission forgotten in an instant as blind panic took over. "He cannot come back. He was defeated. He died."

"How many times have you died and come back? What about Leo? We aren't even full gods, and we manage it. You think Araphel can't?"

All the quiet presence that Koschei had cultivated crumbled as he scrabbled for straws. "But it makes no sense. Why would he be coming back now of all times? Now, after so long?"

I shrugged. "I don't know. I don't know much at all. The prophecies said it is soon. And there have been enough weird coincidences for me to start believing in those prophecies."

"I do not believe it." He drew himself back up to his feet, level with my face again. His voice cracked. "Not yet."

What could I say to that? I didn't believe it either, not after the White Prophet told us it was so. Not even after I'd laid hands on the first of the shards after picking a random direction to walk in. Even now I struggled to believe that the fate of this whole world was somehow my responsibility. But here I was, taking responsibility for it anyway.

Maybe this second life was meant to counter-balance last time around when I couldn't even be trusted with the survival of a potted plant. Maybe I had delusions of grandeur just because I'd literally been chosen by the gods to save the world. Maybe it was because I'd spent my whole first lifetime as a background character in other people's stories, and this time around I had the opportunity to actually make a difference in the world. So I sat there in silence while he tried to wrap his head around it, pretending that I knew for certain that what I was telling him was true, when only Asher completely believed it.

Koschei's voice had lost all its charm now. It was a somber drone when he said, "Even if it is true then… What can we do in the face of such malice? What can be done to stop him?"

I pointed past him to the stained rock in the middle of the chamber. "The same thing that stopped him last time."

"The Rusted Blade?" His laugh came like a sob. "It is gone. Sundered into—"

He froze when he looked up and saw the pieces of metal in my hands. He didn't doubt what his senses were telling him. He didn't think that it was some sort of trick. Some things were too fundamentally real for even the most deluded demagogue to turn away from. The shards… this place… they felt more real than the rest of Amaranth, so steeped in history that the memories we couldn't touch with our Aether weighed down on it.

"You have two shards. How did you? … How could you? …" Even now he was struggling against the overwhelming reality that we all faced. He reached for what he knew—the structure of this world that he claimed to want overthrown. "You are scarcely more than a newborn. How could you have two shards?"

"Those coincidences I was talking about? These landed in my lap. More or less." I brought the two pieces together in front of his eyes. It was as if I wasn't there anymore. Just him and the metal. There was a real danger in letting him know I had these shards. Every wannabe dictator on Amaranth probably wanted what Leofric had, and I'd just flashed two of them to somebody who was already at the brainwashing strangers phase of his own descent into madness. But at the end of the day, despite what he'd done, my gut still told me that Koschei was one of the good guys. He seemed to genuinely care about the Faun at least—even if he cared about beating Leofric more. Besides, he had something I needed more than safety. "I know where all the rest are, except for one. The one that the Faun were given."

His brows drew down, and he blinked hard enough that the sexy lumps of old metal in my hands lost their hold on him. I was guessing I'd just trampled right on top of another touchy subject.

When the Faun were feeling passionate, there was a growl in

their voice that you could feel vibrating your skeleton. When Koschei was angry, it was more like a pissed-off Chihuahua. "We were given nothing. We fought Araphel the same as everyone else once his true nature was revealed. We bested him, and we were entitled to our share of the bounty."

I hopped on the hype train, hoping that it might stop at useful information junction. I asked excitedly, "So where is it?"

"Hidden. Gone beyond the reach of all who would use the shard against us." He was so proud of himself, grinning away while my hands closed into fists around the shards. "Gone somewhere Leofric can never go to seek it."

I picked my words as carefully as I could. "Which is where exactly?"

"The Faun worship their dead. The memory of them, the spirits that I call up, is the greatest service I do for my horned kin. It is why the chieftains heed me. I speak for their dead."

I'll admit that I was starting to lose patience a little bit when I interrupted him. "Yeah, I've got Aether powers too. What's your point?"

"With the Pillar of Aether, it was possible for me to bind a physical object to the spirit of—"

I clapped my hands, shaking him out of his reverie. "Soulbinding, yup. Done it twice. Skip to the good bit."

He paused for just a moment to scowl at me before he launched into storytime all over again. It was something else he had in common with Leo—they both loved the sound of their own voices. "Long ago, there was a great hero among the Faun." Koschei stared off into the darkness, those same images that he'd been beaming into my head playing before his eyes. His memories of time so long past that I couldn't even wrap my head around it. "Gorgafel. A warrior beyond all others. A match for the Voidspawn, for Eternals, the greatest of their kind. To him was passed the shard, and to him I bound it, so that even in death, he would be its guardian."

From the sounds of it, I was finally going to get the big undead fight I'd spent so much time psyching myself up for when I first discovered Aether. I was already giddy with anticipation. There was going to be a dungeon, with skeletons wandering around, and maybe the entrance would be in the shape of a skull, and you had to walk in through the mouth. I was so ready. "So where's the grave I've got to desecrate?"

Koschei looked at my obvious glee with reproach and no small amount of pity. "I did not bind it to his flesh. I bound it to his spirit. He has passed from this world into the realm of the dead, and he has taken the shard with him where none can follow."

What did that even mean? "So…"

"It is beyond your reach, Eternal. Beyond both of us, and Leofric's quest to assemble the blade and rally all to his side too. Amaranth is our prison. Even in death, we cannot escape it."

I pressed the heels of my hands into my eyes so that they didn't explode out of my head from all the pressure in my skull. There was a scream of rage trapped inside me, and I had to block every exit or there was no way of knowing where it would come blasting out. When I trusted myself to speak, all that I managed was a rumbling groan. "That is the opposite of helpful. You get that, right?"

"We could not have known that Araphel might someday return." Koschei was already mounting a defense. "I was doing what I must to protect the Faun. You have seen how the Solar Court's chosen people have treated them. You bear their flesh; you know their burden. I had to do what I could to keep them from harm."

Trusting my eyeballs to stay put, I lowered my hands and gave him a baleful stare. "And instead you doomed the world. Good job."

He was fidgeting, angry at me for questioning his decisions, or angry with himself for making them. "The Faun—"

I wasn't letting him use them as an excuse. Not when it was so blindingly obvious that all he cared about was keeping the Faun shard out of Leofric's hands at any cost. Did he actually care for them at all, or were they just the ideal excuse? "The Faun could be living in some beautiful green forest with plenty of food and freedom to roam, but you dragged them here to the dead end of nowhere so that you could hide from Leofric. So you could plan your little wars against him and prove once and for all that your team is the biggest and toughest. Exceptional work, buddy. Really looking out for them."

"If they do not fight back, then the whole world will be taken from them. Would you have them roll over and die?" Was he talking about the Faun or himself? If all he knew was endless war, of course, the promise of peace felt like imminent death.

"Have you taken a look outside lately? Do you know how little of Amaranth is still populated by anything other than monsters? We built a whole new island kingdom last month. We roamed across empty plains full of game and giant mushroom monsters and…" I could barely look at him. I had to swallow down my disgust. "Whatever parts of Amaranth aren't overrun by monsters are empty. You've had your eyes locked on Leofric for so long that you didn't even notice that?"

He piped up immediately with another excuse. "The desolation—"

"Is here. Not everywhere."

He seemed more and more frail with every passing moment. How could he have lived all these thousands of years with nobody calling him on his shit. Was he like Leofric, so sure that he was right that he couldn't even hear reason. "The Bastion—"

"Stands between you and the stuff that Leofric built. Not the whole world. You could have walked around it. You could have built boats and sailed off along the coast, out to sea, or anywhere else. You could have strolled back out of the Ashen Wastes in whatever direction you first strolled into them, and you would have found somewhere empty for your people to live. But you only cared about beating Leofric."

Up until that moment, I could tell he had still been trying to play the wise old mentor, but now I'd pushed too far, and his rage reared up. Anger at being questioned. Anger at dooming the Faun to this misery. Anger that should have been turned directly back on himself. This was all his doing. Spittle flecked his lips as he snarled out, "Do you have a clever answer for everything, stripling? Do you know more than all who came before you? Or am I just such a simpering old buffoon that you find it easy to make light of me. The soul of the Faun is that of a warrior. You ask that I take them from the war that they were promised? It would destroy them as surely as any battle. Worse, it would break them."

"Those old ladies outside, drying out bits of worm and scraping in the dirt to feed everyone, they've got your warrior spirit?" I didn't mean to laugh in his face, but it just kind of came out. "They'd be sad if they didn't have to camp out in a desert?"

He drew himself up to his full height and unleashed another wave of Aether spirits, prying at the edges of my senses, trying to force their way into my mind and make me see things his way. I caught a glimpse of his legendary Faun hero for just a moment, a shadow of him standing proud and massive between me and the moonlight. Koschei's voice echoed down to me as I was at the bottom of a well. "The spirit of the Faun…"

It wasn't going to work this time. I knew the trick now. With a heave of my own Aether, the moonlight peeled away from me, leaving me back in the dark of the cave. I crossed the distance to Koschei in a scramble, wrath pulsing just under my skin as I snarled, "The Faun would survive without you interfering. They might even find that they like not being at war with everyone all the time. I know even I could do with a break from it once in a while, and I think fighting is fun."

Koschei might not have fallen off his high horse, but he stumbled back away from me quick enough. "You…" I braced myself for the abuse to come, but instead, he let out the saddest little laugh I'd ever heard. "You've given me much to think on."

Well, fair was fair. If he could put up with me being the voice of reason, I could do the same for him. "Listen, I know that you're right about Leofric. I know he wants to be king of the world, and I know that he's going to be a nightmare to get rid of once he gets any sort of foot on that ladder. I'm not saying you're crazy—I get it, he's bad news—I'm just saying that we need to get our priorities in order. We need to save the world before we fight over who gets to run it."

He looked at me for the first time with anything resembling respect. "And Leofric is willing to set our conflict aside for this noble goal?"

The sound that came out of my face is best described as a blart. A blart of laughter that I couldn't stop before it escaped. "You think I'd trust Leo enough to tell him any of this stuff? He's a psycho."

"So you expect me to make concessions to him without any in return?" He settled back on his haunches, frowning. "Without even giving him any indication of why I have joined my strength to his?"

"Buddy, I don't expect anything." I threw up my hands. "All I know is that I need his shard for this whole thing to work, same as I need the Faun one."

"I have already told you that our shard is beyond your reach." Koschei at least had the good grace to look ashamed about it. "Your plan has fallen at the first hurdle."

To my surprise, the initial rage screaming had faded away to something else bubbling away in the back of my head. I was going to have to sit down and have a good stare at the character sheet in my head to be certain, but there was something about the way the Psychopomp power was phrased that made me think it might be good for more than just perma-killing stuff that was meant to resurrect. "I've still got some ideas about that."

"Ideas?"

"Chernghast has given me some gnarly powers that I might be able to use to get around that whole death thing. I'm actually wondering if maybe this is why he has given me them."

That seemed to finally have him gobsmacked—even more than the whole end of the world deal. He rocked back off his haunches to land with a thump on his bony backside. "Your patron."

He didn't need to hear about the whole deal with my mixed-up god-court allegiance stuff right now, so I just nodded knowingly. "So yeah, let's just focus on getting Leo's shard for now."

"You have given me much to think on. But I am an old man, set in my ways." He crossed his legs as if it had been his plan all along to sit around on the floor of this cave for the rest of the day. For all I knew, this was how he spent all his time. I'd spent the last month doing obstacle courses and getting slapped around by a sexy elf, so I really wasn't in the right place to judge anyone's lifestyle choices. "Give me some time to think. Let me come to some ideas of my own."

I really wanted to just leave him there to think it through. To come up with some cunning plan that would wrest the Lucis from Leofric's grasp without me having to fight the dude, and Orphia, and his army. Time wasn't on my side though. "I can't hang around too long. There are other Eternals back over in Leo's camp. My friends. People who care more about this mission than anything else. I can't leave them there forever. It's only a matter of time before Leo says something extra-stupid and Mercy shoots him. Or she shoots Orphia on principle. Or—"

"He has two other Eternals at his beck and call?" Every time that I thought Koschei was done being surprised by things, he had some new, disgruntled expression ready to show me.

"Well, he's got one. And I've got two. And you've got uh… you." I counted them on my fingers. "Hold up. Am I winning?"

"I am surprised that Leofric is willing to entertain any Lunar Eternal in his court." Koschei was watching me carefully now like he thought I was up to something. Great. "He was always of the opinion that we were monsters in mortal flesh."

"Oh yeah, he still feels that way. So does Orphia. She's his loyal little minion now. But Mercy and Asher, they're uh…" My brain stalled out for a minute as I tried to come up with a way to describe our relationship in a way that this old grumpy Eternal would understand. "They're on my side. Definitely. No question. Even if they are Solar Eternals."

A sweat had broken out on his forehead. He did not look pleased with this news. He did not look even slightly pleased with this news. "Three fresh-born Solars for the one of you…"

I stopped his descent into panic with a wave of my hands in front of his face. "Yes, but only one of them is a bag of dicks like Leo. We've got them outnumbered."

"The true nature will out." He sank back down into himself, brows drawing down, eye-lights dimming with his mood. "The tyrant in their blood will always come to the fore."

"Oh come on. They think we're all wild animals. You think they're all slave-masters in training. Isn't it possible that we're all just people?"

His squeaky comedy voice came out in a low growl. "You have not seen what I have seen."

"And you haven't seen what I've seen. They're my friends."

"Millenia of experience outweighs your… opinions." He spat the word like it was dirty. "They will betray you. Bind you. Make you subservient to them. You are not the first to try courting favor with the enemy. Through the Revelation, many of us fought side by side, but in the end, it always turns out the same."

This was getting out of conversation territory and heading into that big dark patch on the map labeled *here be ranting*. "It doesn't need to be perfect, and it doesn't have to last forever, we just need to hold together long enough to beat Araphel."

For what felt like forever, he just sat there in silence, brows drawn down, and thoughts so far away he couldn't even see me on the horizon anymore. I was starting to suspect that he'd genuinely forgotten I was in the room when he grumbled, "Give me time to ponder all this. Go speak with my people. Our people. Learn who they are before you tell me how they should live and die. You owe them that much."

He seemed to think that the conversation was over. I didn't really feel like arguing about whether or not we could go on arguing, and the prospect of getting to know some Faun was tempting, so I started walking back to the surface, pausing at the entrance to the cavern for just a moment. "So, uh, they were concerned about me being a monster or something? Should I just tell them you said I'm not and hope they trust me?"

He blinked, then said with absolute conviction, "If you'd lied to me, you'd never have left this cave."

It would have been laughable if I hadn't already been manhandled and brain blasted by him in the course of a normal chat. Whatever aura of power was hanging around Leofric was here too. All the centuries spent gathering glory and climbing towards godhood had made him more than the spindly frame that he inhabited. While Leo did his best to cultivate an imposing image, Koschei seemed to do all he could to keep his strength a secret, only for it to come spilling out. There was no denying what he was.

The walk down into the heart of the Wastes had been quick, but climbing back up to daylight seemed to take ages. That conversation could have gone better. I kept feeling like I should have lied to Koschei, or at least told him the truth about different things. Maybe his intrusive Aether brain probing stuff would have told him that I wasn't being honest with him, but I couldn't help but feel like I'd screwed up somehow.

I emerged from the cave with my head still repeating the conversation back and forth to myself, only to come face to face with the tip of the Lady Faun's spear. Caught unawares, instinct kicked in, and I slapped it away, hard enough that the shaft of the thing broke in two. Oops.

Beyond her, the chieftains were still gathered, eating and chatting among themselves. At the sight of me, the air filled with roars of laughter. "The runt returns!"

Lady Faun did not look happy with me as she scrambled to get the top half of her spear out of the ash-bank by the cave entrance where it had been embedded. Sheepish, I tramped over to join her. "Sorry."

She snarled at me. "This spear survived a hundred hunts."

There wasn't much I could do here in the middle of this tainted place, but the spear wasn't made from the same null material as the ash and the stone. Artifice washed out through the void I could feel all around me and practically leapt to the broken pieces. Putting it back together was as easy as breathing.

It didn't occur to me until the laughter abruptly stopped and everyone was staring at me that it might have been the wrong move.

Lady Faun had dropped the spear like it was something poisonous and half the chieftains had leapt to their feet, reaching for weapons.

She hissed, "How did you…"

"I told you I was an Eternal. Doesn't anybody listen?" I reached out with Artifice again, not changing the spear but hefting it back up into her hands.

She caught it, but she was backing away from me with fear in her eyes. "Koschei cannot—"

I cut that off with a shake of my head. "We're different."

"I see that." Her expression went from scared to something else as her gaze traveled up and down me, interested in me in some way that was just this side of predatory.

"He told me to spend time with you all. Get to know you." I was feeling a bit like a side of meat, the way she was staring and licking her pointed teeth. "So, do you want to show me the ropes?"

The chieftains had settled back into their chatter, but they were eyeing me in a way that was a lot less friendly than Lady Faun. She laughed. "Ropes?"

Right. Yes. Different planet, different lingo. I tried again, "What is a day in the life of a Faun like?"

Her grin grew even wider. "We hunt."

CHAPTER 9

The Lady Faun was called Mhirka, and she was not a big fan of people asking her questions. She didn't bother introducing anyone else as we moved through the camp, and it took a fair bit of badgering before she'd even tell me her name.

I was gradually realizing as we moved out through the circles of stone that this was not anything like the campsite I'd imagined when I first set out. There were hundreds of Faun here. Most of them were working on the haphazard farms in the inner rings, closest to the apex of the desolation, right where I'd expect everything to die the most. Apparently, whatever roots and tubers they'd planted were tougher than the touch of the god of destruction. I could not imagine them tasting good, but maybe evil potatoes were better than regular ones?

There were more stretched-skin tents as we moved farther from the epicenter. Way more than I'd seen on the far side. We headed away from the Bastion, farther from the prying eyes of Leofric and his minions. It made sense that they'd stack up over here.

All the chiefs started to make more sense too. This wasn't just one clan of Faun. The sparse clothes and armor that they wore were different from one to the next, but I'd see repetitions in color and theme, patterns of scars carved into the bare grey skin, standing up like ridges. Some wore traces of fur, bleached to white or harvested from some snowbound beast. I never seemed to spot the same Faun twice, but they were perpetually in motion. I kept moving my estimates up. There had to be more than a thousand Faun. There were as many of these glorious grey giants as the puny men that Leofric's wall had to show for itself.

We wove through the camp, following some path that I didn't know, not heading dead away from Leofric's lands now but lulling over to one side. I tried to ask why, but Mhirka just snapped, "Shallows!" which was as informative as hell.

The rings crumbled more and more as we headed this way, and when I started to feel living stone that my Artifice could reach in the upturned ridges we passed, I took a second look at what had seemed like the same destruction as surrounded us at the first glance. This was not the same. The walls of stone had been brought down, not by the great explosions when the Voidgod died, but by hammer strikes and effort. No Artifice, just violence. The Faun had beaten the stone into submission, creating a great smooth ramp, disguised as the same chaos that surrounded it.

Why this bit and not any other bit? I couldn't say. Maybe this bit had just pissed them off.

The dead desert of ash stretched out from the foot of the ramp, and I had to bite back a sigh. I'd had enough of this place to last me a lifetime already. It was only then, when I glanced back up the ramp, that I spotted a half-dozen more Faun trailing along behind us, bristling with spears and jostling each other for position. "Uh, how big is this thing we're hunting?"

"Khorkhoi are small but fast. You must be ready for them. They spring from the ashes. Listen for them. Your ears will serve better than your eyes."

"Little red worm dudes. Yeah, I've met them before…" I glanced back over my shoulder again. "So why do we need so many people?"

She glanced sideways at me. "Protection."

"You don't need any…" I spoke louder so that the Faun trailing behind could definitely hear me. "I'm not going to hurt you."

"They are for you. From me."

I didn't laugh. That was good. I got the impression that if I laughed she might have stabbed me in the gizzard, and I don't even know what a gizzard is. I always picture it as some sort of lizard in my belly? Anyway, good for me, not laughing. "I don't need protecting."

She still wouldn't look at me, and I couldn't work out why. It was like she was embarrassed about something. "You are a new male, a warrior, joining with our clans. There may be… competition for you among the chieftains, among the women. They want to make sure I do not stake a claim unfairly."

None of that made sense to me for a surprisingly long time until finally, the penny dropped, and I couldn't look at her either. They were chaperones to make sure we didn't get freaky while we were meant to be hunting worms. That was a whole other thing that would never have crossed my mind. I felt like my brain had stalled out. "Oh. Oh! Okay. Wow. I mean, you are like… eight foot of pure gorgeous, and anybody would be crazy to say no—"

"I have no interest in…" She tried to interrupt me as I rambled, but there was no way that I was going to stop with only one foot jammed in my mouth. Oh no. My mouth was running now, and no force in this world could make it stop. I certainly couldn't.

"…But… uh I'm seeing someone right now, and we haven't talked about whether or not we're seeing each other exclusively yet, and I'd really have to talk to her about that before I could even think about—"

She turned to face me head-on and shouted with all sincerity, "You disgust me!"

"Oh thank the gods." I deflated a bit.

Thankfully, she wasn't actually paying attention to me as I tried to pull myself back together. She'd dropped down into a crouch, and she was patting at the ash. Desperate for the distraction, I squatted down too. "What is it? Worm-sign?"

She arched a brow. "Worm sign?"

I sighed. "Can you tell where the worm is?"

She pointed. "Beneath the ash."

"I… I thought you could track it."

"They leave no tracks." She cocked her head to the side. "They are under the ash."

"I… right." Somehow I had traveled to another world, become buff, slayed giant monsters, landed a hot Alvaren girlfriend, and I was even worse at talking to girls than when I'd been a couch lump. Damned if I was going to stop trying though. "So how do we find some worms for dinner then?"

Her patting on the packed ash had become rhythmic now—a steady rat-a-tat-tat—the sound reverberating down into the ash. "We do not. They find us."

She went on drumming, and I went on waiting. Now that I understood how it worked, I felt like a bit of an idiot. Like we were going to go stalking over the dunes and catch a worm napping in the sunshine.

Time stretched on, and I tried to join in with the drumming, only to catch a slap on my hand between beats. "Steady. Like rainfall. You have no rhythm."

So then I was back to hanging around, waiting for worms to show up. I started to wonder if maybe this was an elaborate prank. Hazing the new guy. It seemed in character for the Faun I'd met so far. I mean… it was funny, but I had too much other stuff to be getting on with to appreciate being sent to the store for a skyhook or plaid paint or whatever. Hunting the worm even sounded like a made-up job. I stared down at Mhirka, trying to work out if there was a smirk hiding behind her fixed expression of concentration. If it was there, I couldn't see it, but then again, her face had been a source of confusion to me since the moment I'd met her. Sexy confusion. Language was translated for me, but expressions on these inhuman faces were inscrutable. I think that's what inscrutable means anyway.

The longer that I waited, the more that my brain started to pester me. What was I going to do? I didn't even know why I was here, except to try and make Leofric happy. Something that I personally could not care less about. Actually no, I did care. Anything that made Leo happy was probably a bad thing. The thought of kicking puppies was probably the only thing that got him up in the morning.

What was the best-case scenario here? The Faun attacked the wall for me and all died? Or killed all the soldiers on the other side? There would be too much blood on my hands either way. All because two Eternals had been having a tiff for a millennium or two.

I didn't like being stuck in a position where I had to choose who lives and dies. That was why when I was a kid and my parents asked if I wanted to be a doctor, I proceeded to be academically disappointing for the rest of my life.

It had been fine here in Amaranth up until now because most of the time when I was deciding people should die, they either wanted to, or they had signed up for it by attacking me first. I didn't have to think about it. I didn't have to try and balance it in my head. This was different. As far as I could see, the only ones that deserved a hasty chopping up in all of this were Leo and Koschei.

A khorkhoi leapt out of the ground and latched onto my ass before I even noticed the tell-tale puff of ash. "Oh, come on."

I reached for my sword, but more of them were already bursting up out of the ground as flesh torpedoes launched directly at the center of mass. One by one they latched on, chewing and chewing through my poor, battered armor. It didn't seem fair that I got wormed when Mhirka was the one doing all the drumming, but I guess when you see a big hunk of man meat like me, it only makes sense to assume it is the buffet.

With a flex of Artifice, I split my great-sword into a pair of cleavers and set to work. Lopping off heads and hoping that would stop them chewing. It did, eventually, when the dumb-ass worm realized that it was missing everything below its neck. But by then there were more coming, and I had no time to think.

Fencing with Seren had honed my reflexes, but nothing could prepare me for a wall of chompy worms all coming at me all at once. If I had a moment to think, I could have made a shield, but the time it took me would have let another dozen of the little nippers latch on. So my blades spun figures of eight, catching them as they came. Some I struck as they went for me, and others splatted against the broad flats of the blades. A few made it through, but not enough, and there were moments when the leaping worms stuttered or slowed, and I could lop the lucky ones free of my flesh before they got much more than a mouthful.

Mhirka stood well back of all this with a smile on her face, not even pretending that she was going to help. If a stray khorkhoi got past me she might step forward to end its wiggles with a thrust of her spear, but she seemed content to let me bear the brunt of wormaggedon.

Gradually, the storm slowed until it was just a gentle patter of worm on iron. Until, finally even that stopped, and there was no sound but the leaking of worm juices into the ash, and the breeze drifting the dunes.

There were still a few detached heads chomping into me as I wiped my blades clean on my thighs. Something wriggled between my teeth, and I spat out a worm giblet. No idea how that got in there. I couldn't recall biting any worms. Maybe a bit just flew in while I was screaming abuse at the worms. Who knows? "Thanks for all the help."

Mhirka was pacing back and forth, skewering worm bodies on her spear for ease of transportation, making one giant worm kebab. Gross. "This is the way of the Chagnar Faun. Our enemies send monsters to feast on our flesh, and we make them our dinner." She hammered her spear down, again and again. "This is the way of the Chagnar Faun, snatching life from the jaws of death. You are not Faun. You are soft.

Weak. You seek the easiest path in all things."

I watched her angrily stabbing the stuff I'd already killed, brushed some more heads off my shoulders, and then actually thought about what she was saying instead of getting angry about it. There was no point getting mad. She was right. I wasn't a Faun. I liked them, they seemed like fun people to hang out with, but I was an Eternal, and pretending otherwise would have made us both less than we were.

Blinking my eyes so I could escape the limits of my chunky man-flesh and use Artifice, I transformed my cleavers into an iron pike, swayed for a moment, then started skewering the worms by my feet, haphazardly at first, then building up speed. Once I was sure that the anger from her commentary was all gone, I asked. "Who told you that everything has to be hard?"

She brandished her stick of slimy meat. "This is our way. To face the harshest challenges and emerge stronger for it."

Still, something niggled at the back of my mind. Koschei had brought them here, but somehow, they were happy with it. It made no sense. Even the dvergar had bitched and moaned about their tropical paradise because it was different. People didn't just accept stuff like perpetual misery and deserts of flesh-eating worms. "But why though?"

"Why must the bird fly?" She drew back the first of her spears and reached for another, now surrounded by meat and dripping with slime. "This is our nature."

I snapped my fingers. "Kiwis."

Oh, there was no confusion about her facial expression now. That was definitely contempt. 100% pure sneer. "What nonsense do you speak now?

"Kiwis are a bird. They grew up on an island with no predators, so they don't fly." I wiggled on the spot, kiwi impersonation spot on—shame she'd never seen one. "They just waddle around, looking chill and chubby."

Contempt had twisted into confusion. "You have some point in this?"

I kept on skewering bugs for dinner, getting more and more vigorous as my temper frayed. "Birds fly because they're forced to. Fish swim because it's the only way to get around in water. You keep surrounding people with deserts and death, they're going to think that is all that there is."

She spat into the ash. "We have no need for the soft comforts of other lands. We are strong."

"Because all the ones who aren't die." I didn't know that for certain until I said it out loud, but it was the only thing that made sense really. The logical extreme of their obsession with individuality and personal power above all else.

She beat a fist against her chest, smearing gore and worm-sludge. "They are not Chagnar. They are not strong."

"So even if they could cure diseases, plan better hunts... even though they could make you a spear that flies straighter than any you can make yourself, if they can't use it, then they deserve to die?" She had to understand how wrong this all was when I spelled it out to her. She had to.

She didn't. "That is our way."

I was scrabbling for figurative straws as I chased a tricky bit of worm around in circles with my spear-tip. "And all the old grey women I saw back at camp, they deserve to die too?"

She drew herself up to her full height and stared back across the ash towards the stony spines of home. "If they have not got the strength to stand, they should fall."

"Yeah, that's insane." Oops didn't mean to say that bit out loud. Oh well, I was committed now. "And I'd bet anything you like that all this survival of the fittest crap comes from Koschei."

The tip of her worm-loaded spear swung to point at me, fury

etched into her face, her shoulders aligned with the spear. Every part of her was tensed for the lunge. "It is our creed. Despite all that the Faun have endured, still we survive."

She looked genuinely surprised when I didn't fade back from the threat. Hell, I was surprised at the fire in my voice when I shouted back, "You deserve to do more than survive! You deserve to thrive! If you had just a little patch of real land, your farmers could feed everyone without having to scrape in the dirt! You could hunt real animals instead of worm meat!"

She didn't attack, but she didn't falter either. "We have been driven here by our enemies. Driven to the edge of—"

I cut that nonsense off dead in its tracks. "What enemies?"

She swung her spear out, flicking bug juice in an arc, pointing out at everywhere but here. "All the people of this world loathe us, they would see us—"

"There are no people." She pulled up short, stunned that I'd interrupted her again. "Almost everywhere I've been in this world is empty. There are monsters all over the place, sure, but big tough Chagnar Faun like you could clear them out in like a day, tops. The only one who has driven you anywhere is… you. All of you, following Koschei. Obeying him like good little slaves."

She flung down the spear and charged me then. I dropped my own and caught her hands before they could lock on my neck. She roared in my face, "Chagnar bow to no one!"

She pushed against me, and I could see the moment of surprise when there was no give. I had been buffing up my potency since the minute I landed on this rock. Fingers interlinked, she was the one to give ground as I surged back in against her. Her feet skidded in the wet ash. "Then why are you doing what he tells you?"

With a twist of her wrists and her hips, all my bulk was turned against me. I lost my footing, almost tumbling to the dirt. If it hadn't have been for my grip on her hands, I probably would have gone down. Even so I was down on one knee as she growled down to me. "The strongest lead. This is our way."

I didn't know I was grinning until I saw my face reflected in her eyes. No wonder she was pissed off. "So if I kicked his ass, you'd all do what I say?"

She pushed down on me until my wrists were twisting back, and I let her drive me down until I was almost sitting. She snarled. "Koschei is beyond you."

Then I flopped back, letting her weight and mine carry us both over in a clumsy roll. One moment she was standing over me, the next she was laid out on the ash with her narrow waist trapped between my knees and her arms pinned down.

"Keep underestimating me." I leaned in close enough that I could feel her frantic breath heaving on my face—so close that I could see her figure of eight pupils widening in excitement. "I dare you."

She did not try to buck me off, laying perfectly still beneath me as I clambered back to my feet and collected our spears of bugs, hefting them up onto one shoulder and setting off back towards camp.

Sometime between me getting up and me holding out her spears to her, she had found her footing once more, but I was very deliberately not paying attention. My blood was thumping in my ears, and I dreaded to think what might happen if she came at me again. I had kept my temper under a short leash since I'd almost killed Seren. I didn't like what this rage in my gut could make my body do without even consulting my brain. The funny thing was, I was never an angry guy before I died. Maybe it was some flaw or feature of this new body. Maybe it was something to do with being a lunar eternal, beast of chaos and all that jazz. Maybe now that I had enough power, I could feel the desire to change things for the better burning in me.

She took her spears without a word, and if our little entourage of observers had anything to say about us wrestling in the dust, they kept it to themselves. Given what I'd seen of the Faun so far, maybe wrestling was another normal bit of conversation for them. Regardless, they beat a retreat ahead of us, and we came back to the settlement, if you could even call it that, before the sun had dipped down beneath the highest upshots of stone.

Mission accomplished on all counts. There was plenty of bug for folks to eat, and I had learned what I needed to know to understand the Faun. Even if it was stuff I'd have preferred to go my whole life never knowing.

Mhirka parted ways with me as soon as she could, still keeping herself to herself. We dumped our worm-load into a basket of her clan, then that was the end of it. The prickling anger that had kept me painfully aware of her presence all the way back across the dunes abated as she shuffled off into the crowd. I wanted to follow her, but I also wanted to stay as far away from her as possible. I had no idea what might happen the next time we met, and the longer I didn't have to work it out, the happier I'd be.

So I wandered on my own for a little while as the sun crept lower and the winds whipping across from the barren expanse beyond the stones turned chill. I saw everything in the place through new eyes now. The reluctance to share any task, making each farmer seek out their own little patch of dirt, every bent-backed old Faun shrinking with age to set up their own stew pot. Even the scouts I passed on my way back in were all alone, all peering out in the same direction when one of them could have done the job of three if they'd just talk. The endless clashing colors of all the clans came to make more sense too. Each one was more of an extended family than any sort of communal culture. Only one thing was holding them all together here in this hell, and that was Koschei.

It all came back to him. Every thought that I had, every plan that

I tried to concoct, it was him or Leo in the center of it. Now I'm not claiming that I'm a genius or above-average intelligence… or of average intelligence, but when all of your plans hinge on the whims of one person, you start thinking about going to see that one person. I headed towards Koschei's cave in the middle of the settlement, shouldering past the chieftains that moved to block my way without even noticing them loom over me. It was posturing, and I didn't have the time or the patience for it. Surging strength, I could have thrown them off the crest. As it was, I just pushed through them as unobtrusively as I could muster.

There were some comments about my diminutive size, which were honestly pretty brave coming from people with crotches at punching height, but I paid them no attention. Why would I bother arguing with the monkey when the organ grinder was right down that tunnel?

Once more my journey into the depths of the earth seemed to take so much longer than it had when Koschei was bouncing along ahead of me, and this time I worked out why. Even though I didn't rely on them the way that I did my eyes and ears, my other senses were deadened down here. I couldn't feel the materials I was walking over with Artifice. I couldn't sense the pulse of life outside beyond the stone. Even the gentle cushioning layer of the memories embedded in the stone was missing when my Aether flared up. It was like I was drifting through empty space even though I could feel the gravel crunching underfoot, and it left me disorientated.

When I came out into the room where it happened, it took me by surprise. It shouldn't have. It was the same distance I'd walked to reach it the first time around, but somehow, it was a shock when I stepped out into the open space.

For his part, Koschei seemed unsurprised. He was still sitting cross-legged and glowing like a beacon of Aether. I didn't know if he was communing with the ancestors or just having a good dig around this area trying to sense the history despite the null zone. All I knew was that his mind was elsewhere.

I poked him with my toe.

He went on glowing and smiling beatifically like a tiny buddha. Not super useful when I needed to talk to him. And I did need to talk to him. I needed to see if what I'd said earlier had changed his mind in any way—if his mind even could be changed after so many centuries in the same rut.

I poked him again.

His eyes snapped open, and moonlight flooded the chamber. I didn't crap myself, but it was a near thing. "You have returned to me."

"Yup. I'm back." I tried not to groan as I said it.

"And you have lived among my people for a day, walked their path, learned their ways, come to understand why they live as they choose to live."

Tactful. I had to be tactful. What would Mercy say? Actually, no, that was a bad standard for tactful. What would Asher say? Nope… actually he is no good at talking to people either. Oh gods, if I was the one who was good at talking, we were all screwed. I couldn't even get pizza places to throw in free garlic bread when it said on the menu that they gave you free garlic bread. I grumbled out, "Far as I can tell, they live the way you tell them to."

If I'd hoped he might have let that little prod go by without comment, then I was dreaming. "Oh, they may heed my counsel, but there is no denying that the vital strength of the Chagnar is unmatched among mortal races. They compete, and they strive for greatness. They live and breathe it."

Once again the blood started to beat in my ears. When I thought about what he had done to these people. Not only dragging them out here as the culmination of his centuries of manipulation, but embedding his twisted ideas about right and wrong in them to the point that they thought what he told them was their own culture. It came out in a growl. "We can do the philosophy argument later. I want to know what you've decided."

He raised a hairless brow. "Do you mean, will I cast aside my duties to the Faun just because you have been convinced by some charlatan that you have some great destiny and history is being unwritten?"

I had to un-grit my teeth to try and push through. "I mean, are you going to talk about peace, at least long enough for us to stop the apocalypse?"

He looked entirely too smug when he answered me. "No."

"No." I echoed it back to him.

"I do not know how Leofric has turned your mind or what new powers he has unlocked since last we crossed paths. I do not know how he has created this illusion of a White Prophet in your memories or contorted reality to make you believe that the Alvaren walk the world once more. I do not know how he had poisoned your spirit so that all of these obvious contrivances might be believed true, but I do know that I cannot walk into a trap and leave the Chagnar without their most stalwart defender." So, apparently, he'd had a good rummage around in my brain with his Aether powers. My brain meat had been violated. I couldn't really bring myself to be upset, let alone surprised.

He turned his glowing gaze off towards the Bastion, as though he could see clear through the solid stone and all the intervening distance to where Asher, Mercy, Orphia, and Leofric were probably having another really awkward dinner party right now—assuming that Mercy hadn't already started kicking teeth out of people's heads. I wished that I was there with them, instead of down here in this dark hole.

They were on Koschei's mind too. "How could I abandon my people when the enemy is massing beyond the wall. Four Eternals bound to the path of the tyrant. One of them of an age and power with me. Three more, newborn but full of boundless potential. It is far too great a threat to allow to fester. We must lance this boil before it can corrupt the whole world."

"Thanks for clearing that up. You're going to ignore everything I said to you, and everything that you plucked out of my memory without asking, except the bits that fit in with what you've already decided, and then you're going to pretend that I'm crazy instead of accepting that things are changing. Cool. That makes things easier."

I pointed my spear at him.

CHAPTER 10

His eyes did not widen now. All the surprise that he'd made a great show of earlier was absent. "So the assassin finally reveals his true nature. When trickery did not avail him, he turned to—"

"Shove story-time up your scrawny ass." He actually seemed shocked that someone had interrupted him. "There are no Faun around to believe the trash you're trying to spin into gold anyway."

He rose slowly to his feet, coming up to about my knees, but radiating such power in the close confines of the cave that it overwhelmed me. His voice beat in on me from every side, the power of his Aether hammering at all my senses. "First, you tried to sway me from my course with lies, and now you seek my end. Well, I must tell you that it shall not come at your hands, you mewling whelp. I've outlived stars in the sky while you've yet to reach the span of a single lifetime."

He knew everything about me. He was digging around in my skull even now. He knew everything that I had to say before I said it. I said it anyway. "I'm not working with Leofric. I'm not some—" Pain lanced through my head as he probed deeper, forcing every word to come out true in a great wild rush. "I didn't come here to kill you, but you've rigged the whole of Faun civilization up so that the only ones that people will listen to are the strongest. You've made it so that when Araphel comes back, they'll go running back to him with open arms. I've got to put an end to all that, right now. But because of your stupid 'might makes right' setup, if I want the Faun to listen to me, I've got to beat you."

"And what shall you tell them to do, in this imaginary world where you could best me." He whispered it into my ear, and I spun to see nothing there amidst the maelstrom of Aether.

Actually talking was becoming more and more difficult. All my senses had been dulled down by this place, and suddenly, being exposed to all his dazzling Aether was like ripping off a blindfold and staring straight into the sun. I could feel my brain vibrating inside my skull, and still, he poured out more and more. The weight of his power, of his will, was pressing in on me from every direction. Crushing me. "I'll tell them to go find somewhere that the living is easy. I'd tell them to farm and frolic and fornicate and do all the other f things that people are meant to do to be happy and healthy."

I had no idea where he was now. The swirling ghosts of his memories intermingled with my own, throwing up glimpses of the places we'd been like I was seeing them through a hall of mirrors. The bloody forest with giant mushrooms traipsing through. Some barren wasteland covered in purple scrub with the great stone tablets of some ancient civilization ground down to gravel. The Alvaren city, trapped beneath the earth. The battlefield that this place had once been, sun blotted from the sky by the wings of Voidspawn beasts. When Koschei spoke, his voice beat at me from every direction, louder than anything I'd ever heard. "You would make weaklings of them."

"I'd give them their lives back, to do what they wanted with them." It came out like a whimper instead of a roar. He was getting in my head. He was making me believe that I was powerless compared to him. When there was a display like this going on, it was hard not to be shocked by the disparity in power between us. The first blow hadn't even been struck, and I already felt like I was dying. "You're meant to be all about freedom, don't you want that for them?"

He hammered the difference between us into me like the nails of a coffin. "Only the strong are truly free. All others must bend to their might."

How could I hope to fight back against him? He had thousands of years to grow in power, and I'd been here for the blink of an eye. I'd spent more time dicking around in the jungle with Seren than I had actually doing anything important. All the glory I'd fought so hard for was nothing compared to his. I was nothing, and he was everything, and I should just get down on my knees right now and grovel for forgiveness.

He was strong. I was weak. He was so close to being a god, and I was so close to being dirt.

I might as well just give up now. I might as well just lie down and let him kill me. If he thought that was what was best, I should just obey him. He was so much more than me, so he must be right. The strong ruled the weak. That was the way of the world. That had always been the way. Everywhere.

But when I opened my mouth, the words that came were not the abject submission that I was compelled to offer. Instead, I rumbled out, "You sound like Leofric."

I guess that wasn't what he wanted to hear. There was a moment, just a brief moment, where I could grab a breath before he came pounding back in on me with all his power and the crushing certainty that he was better than me in every single way. My own feeble Aether power flared up in that breath, but it just wasn't up to the task of holding him off, not when he was bringing it all to bear. I had no idea what his pillar of Aether looked like, but if it was smaller than a redwood, I'd be extremely surprised.

The spear had fallen from my hands at some point, and I couldn't even see where it had landed. Not that I'd need a weapon to throw myself at his mercy and beg for forgiveness like a worthless idiot like me should.

He'd pushed me too far. That last pulse of emotion was tinged with his irritation—both at me talking back to him and my continuing to resist. He was angry at me for not realizing how worthless I was.

The joke was on him. I always knew what I was worth. I had always known, even back when I spent my life slobbing around in front of a television doing nothing, that I was awesome.

I closed my eyes and slipped out of my body. It was even scarier out here than it had been inside. At least in my body, I'd had the dull sensation of stone beneath my feet to ground me, even if my Artifice insisted that it wasn't there. Without the anchor of flesh, all the spirits that Koschei was invoking against me became visible and terrifying, sweeping in and out of my head, one after the other. All that effort to charge in and make me feel like crap.

Shame that there was nobody home.

He'd realize in a moment that I was gone, but for now, I could think clearly without being bombarded. I still couldn't see where he was through the frankly ridiculous number of spirits he'd called up to flood the room, but my senses did latch onto one solid thing in all of the swirling chaos. The solid iron spear I'd carried in with me.

It was an anchor back to reality. Solid metal. Rough-hewn by my shoddy Artifice skills. Pointy at one end. Long. Otherwise unremarkable. Useless where it was lying.

A simple flex of my will made it a sword once more, and another tug brought it back to my hands through the swirl of incorporeal abuse, clearing the ghosts away for just a moment.

I had to drop back into my body to catch the sword, and all at once, I was bombarded again. Koschei was upping the intensity of his brain-crushing, pouring all his power out in Aether, summoning up every spirit he had at his disposal and launching it into me with the clear message that I was worthless. I was less than him, less than everyone.

I had a sword in my hands, but what use was a sword against that power, against that crushing knowledge that I was useless and worthless and pitiful. It couldn't cut the certainty out of my head.

But, thanks to Psychometry, it could cut the summoned spirits that were putting that certainty there. With heavy limbs, burdened with the knowledge that it was pointless to fight back, I swung.

The first swing was as useless as he made me think it was going to be, awkward and clumsy like I'd never held a sword before. The tip struck the stone in front of me, and I nearly lost my grip. Another wave of despair took me. Why was I even trying? I was nothing. I was scum. I was a rat.

Anger boiled up inside my gut. I was a rat that had been backed into a corner. This time when my sword came up it sang, whistling through the air, first up, then around. Practicing the perfect defense that Seren had been forcing me to drill through day after day, every angle of attack blocked and parried with each sweeping rotation of the blade. Everywhere it struck a spirit, that spirit fragmented into the same nothingness. I wasn't nothing. They were nothing. They weren't even alive.

Still, the torrent came on and on, dread and fear and loathing turned aside with a slash. Self-pity skewered through when it tried to lunge at me from behind. There was no end to all the spirits that Koschei could summon, but there was no end to my dance either. The leaden weight of my inferiority melted away as my muscles began to burn.

My blade moved faster and faster, this great iron slab spinning like a ballet dancer around me, guided by my strength, by my certainty in my own skill. Practice had made perfect. Not one of the ghosts made it to me unscathed, and the few that came limping in were garbled and mangled, bearing tiny broken fragments of the thoughts that they were meant to convey.

I was weaker than Koschei. That was all the first one to drift over me managed to whisper, and I almost laughed out loud. Of course, I was weaker than him. Everything was weaker than a demi-god with thousands of years to build himself up, what did that matter?

I was younger than him; he knew better than me. Everyone I'd ever met thought they knew better than me, why would I start believing them now?

I could not defeat Koschei. If that was true, then why was he so scared of fighting me that he'd rather blast me with a million ghosts than actually try his luck?

Koschei kept on going, dumping more and more of them on me, trying to wear me down, and entirely forgetting the first thing that I had learned about this Faun body of mine. It did not tire. Faun are relentless. The longer this went on, the more of his resources he burned through, whereas me? I could do this all night, and every swing just got better and better.

The certainty that he had put into me crumbled in the face of my questions. The doubts that he was trying to put into me were coming from him. He was the one who was afraid. He was the one that didn't know how this was going to end. I was a giant horny god of death, and he was a little goblin hiding in a cave, and he expected me to cower before him?

I was breathing hard, but not too hard to bark out a laugh. "It isn't working, old man."

He was completely justified in blasting me at that point.

[703/890 Health]

A blinding ray of azure light cut through the swirl of ghosts and hit me square in the chest. Ice spread out from it, crackling across my armor and skin, the chill sinking down into me, bringing the frantic hammering of my heart to an abrupt stop.

Still, the cold spread, even as I stood there dead on my feet. I couldn't breathe; I couldn't move. One shot had been all that it took to end me. All this time, he'd just been toying with me.

I fell to my knees with no strength to keep my weight up, and the swirl of spirits departed, Koschei brushing them away with a flick of his wrist. "You were never my match, and you were a fool to think you might be."

Still, the ice spread, creeping up my neck, down my waist, encasing me in a crackling crystalline shell, sapping the warmth of life from my dying body wherever it went.

Confidence returning to him, Koschei strolled in closer. "You could have served a purpose. You could have fought by my side, but instead, this is what you choose?"

Deep within my chest, my heart thumped. The cold had not stopped it, just slowed it to such a crawl that I barely had the strength to stay conscious. Something must have shown on my face because Koschei tutted. "Did you think me an old doddering fool? Ready to cast you back out into the world to gather strength and attack me again when I least expect it? Do you think that you are the first Eternal that I have defeated in all my years? The first of my opponent's pieces that I have taken from the board?"

The ice had me coated up to the chin and was down past my knees, spreading across the floor and pinning me in place in a big solid chunk of frozen water. It was cool down here, even before the ice he'd summoned. With a lurch, I understood what he had planned. I was going to be an icicle for the rest of eternity. Trapped like some fossil, but awake and aware of it the whole time.

Hell, no.

Two pillars within me flared to life, Primal and Ascension. The strength flooded back through my body as Restoration undid the damage of the ice-blast, and then it doubled up as I surged my potency.

Like the big buff man I was, I flexed right out of the ice.

It burst out from around me in a shower of chunks, spritzing

Koschei and giving me the moment I needed to fall forward and scoop my sword up in my hands. He was surprised, but he wasn't taken by surprise. His hands were surrounded in a nimbus of that same azure light, his stance the casual combat readiness I could see in Seren before we sparred. Loose and limber.

I struck. Sweeping my sword up from the floor and into a wild thrust that might have gotten lucky. It didn't. He slapped the flat of the blade aside, leaving a frosty handprint, and he had his other hand clawed and reaching for me as I stumbled forward.

No, thank you. Once in the icebox was quite enough for one day.

He might have knocked the thrust wide, but I had already been aiming down as well as forward thanks to the height difference. It didn't take much of a twist to make my blade jam down into the stone floor, jarring me to a halt and sending an ache all the way up to my shoulders.

His hand couldn't quite reach me as it swiped by.

Before he could recover and lunge at me, I staggered back. I had reach on my side … unless he decided to blast me again. Which he probably would if he had any sense.

He blasted me again.

This time I knew what was coming, and I managed to get my sword around into the path of the ray before it could strike. It reflected neatly off the pocked and ugly side of the great cleaver blade and traced a thin line of frost up the wall to the side of him.

I worked out I could angle it at him the same moment he did, so even as I struggled to twist my sword against the torrent of freezing energy he was squirting out his fist like a firehose, he abruptly cut it off.

We began to circle each other, waiting for our opportunity. Still, he seemed intent on boring me to death with speeches instead of actually fighting. "You have some tricks, I cannot deny that, but they will not avail you against true power."

I growled back. "You didn't dig deep enough in my head when you had the chance."

He sneered. "You would invite me back in?"

I gave my sword a turn in my hands, trying to get some feeling back after my time as a popsicle. "How about I share my secrets the old-fashioned way?"

He laughed in my face and hammered his fists together, sending a wave of freezing air out through the room that crusted my eyelashes with frost and made the floor slick and slippery. "You have no secrets. I have seen it all. All as I might have expected from a tag-along lackey of the Solar Court."

Another clap of his hands and another arctic breeze swept through. He didn't even need to fight me really. He could just keep chilling me down until I was useless. Restoration and Potency Surge wouldn't be recharged for ages. I'd be a big cartoon ice-cube with horns sticking out long before then.

"You saw what you expected to see, but you didn't see everything. You didn't see the things that your Aether couldn't touch."

He scoffed. "There is no power in this world that could hide the whole of you from my sight."

I swung for him, and he slipped around me with almost casual ease, darting in to slap at my leg and making me dance out of reach, puffs of my breath drifting between us. All these years building up that tiny body of his, there was no limit to his speed. To his strength. Good thing that I'd intrigued him enough that he was still playing with me. "Araphel could do it."

"No being still living in this world could do it." He rolled his eyes, moonlight strobing over the cave roof. "Unless your deranged tale of the Voidgod returning from the dead involves him appearing right behind me at this moment, I do not think that I have anything to worry about."

He tried for another blast at me, the startlingly bright blue ricocheting off my blade right back at him and making him dodge aside. I tried to rush in, but the impact of the beam attack had knocked me back on my heels, so I lost the precious fraction of a second when he was off-balance, and he was ready before I could get near enough to swing.

We circled again as my poor, battered brain tried to come up with a plan. I let my mouth run in the meantime. "The only person that I could trust with my secret is somebody who is about to die. Someone I know is going to take it to their grave."

He rushed in, almost jovial as he swept by my clumsy parry and punched into my ribs. It sent a sharp shot of pain and chill up through me. Something cracked when he hit me, but I couldn't say if it was bone breaking or ice forming inside me.

He gloated as I stumbled away, gasping for breath. "Then you could not have chosen more poorly. As you know all too well. I am Eternal."

I let the pain and exhaustion show, letting my sword droop down until I was leaning on it. One lung was frosted shut inside me, and the other was working double time and still struggling. The chill was slowing my heart again, but it was still thrumming away thanks to all the adrenaline rushing through me.

When I turned my head back up, he had closed the distance between us and was readying another blow. "So was Talon. Right up until the moment he wasn't."

He froze in place as if all that Creation energy had been turned back on him. "Archmage Talon?"

"He had the shard soul-bound to him." I pushed myself back up to my full height as he gawked at me. "There was only one way to break that bond."

His eyes widened as he read the truth of my words on my face. "No."

I took a step forward, leaving my sword standing wedged in the stone behind me. I stalked after Koschei as it was his turn to step back. "I already told you Chernghast gave me the power."

"Chernghast could not." Spittle flew from his lips as his rage and confusion bubbled out. He was an old man, set in his ways, that was what he'd said. He couldn't even comprehend a world different from what he already knew. Just the thought of it made him angry. "No god of the Solar or Lunar court can end the life of an Eternal. Their nature is as ours. They are beings of creation. The only god who could grant such a gift would be…"

"Araphel."

I reached for the dark pillar inside me, not to use it, just to taste it. To touch it. To let the darkness within me show in my eyes. I could not see the eyes in my own head, of course, but I could see every detail that the darkness had hidden from me before springing into sharp contrast—things that I'd had to rely on my eyes' weak glow to illuminate before.

Koschei could see it. He saw the light in my eyes die and the darkness fill them. That same impossible darkness, so devoid of light that it hurt to look right at it. I had him off balance before, confused and angry, but now I had him afraid.

"No. You cannot be. He… he is dead. He could not make Eternals. There are… It is impossible. Impossible!" As if he could punch my existence away, he swung at me with all his might. It struck me in the gut, full force. I made no attempt to get out the way. I made no attempt to stop it. Something inside my muscled torso popped under the pressure of the blow, and agony spread throughout me.

[626/890 Health]

I accepted that blow as my due. I accepted the pain in exchange for what it gave me. What did it give me? It gave me a firm grasp on the little bastard's wrist.

He tried to pull it back, to rip himself free of my grasp, but I had been through this before, and I followed along with him instead of trying to hold him still. It didn't matter where he went now. It didn't matter that the chill of the aura around his hand was freezing us together or burning at my skin as it spread out from the point of impact. All that mattered was that I had him.

With a flex of Artifice, my sword leapt to my hand. I held it upright, the tip almost touching the cavern's roof, and took a steadying breath.

Koschei whimpered. "You can't."

But I could. And I did.

He twisted away from it and flailed with all his might, so the first blow was clumsy, at an odd angle. It deflected from his face and clipped over his shoulder before going wide. His Vitality was so high that a single sword blow couldn't break his skin. That was fine. Like I said before, Faun bodies don't tire.

In a flurry of motion too fast for my eyes to follow, he started pummeling me with his free hand, each strike launching an icicle spike deep into my flesh, over and over. Chill spread through me, but the rage burning at my core never spluttered.

I hefted the sword again and slammed it right down on his shoulder this time. The skin parted beneath his robe, and blood began to flow. Anyone else would have lost their arm to that first hit. Anyone else would have been lucky. They wouldn't have had to feel the second, third, and fourth hits that it took to dig down through his millennia-old flesh and slip that limb free of the torso in a gory spray.

The scent of blood filled my nose as I brought my sword up and down. Up and down. Methodical. Like a butcher at the block. Up and down. Up and down. Skin and robe. Blood and muscle. Gristle and bone.

Somewhere in the middle of my butchery, he began to scream, cursing me in every language of Amaranth, shrieking in pain, and demanding I stop. Demanding the Faun come running to his rescue. We were too deep in the cave for anyone to hear.

I didn't have a magic ray gun, lightning bolts shooting out of eyes, or brain molesting ghosts at my disposal. That wasn't the kind of Eternal that I was. All I had was my sword. So that was what I used.

With his arm off, there were no more counter-attacks. No more attempts to freeze me, or hit me, or fight back at all. Koschei stared down at it lying in a pool of his blood like he couldn't believe this was happening. His voice was a mousey squeak. "What have you done?"

Most people lose an arm and that is the end of the fight, but not my boy Koschei. He had too much Vitality for grievous bodily harm to faze him. Too much of the nebulous "Health" for the fact that half of his torso was a raw open wound after my clumsy attacks to let him die.

So I did what I had to do to kill him. I kept on swinging.

To give the man credit, he kept on trying to pull away from me, even as I beat him and beat him. When one of his legs fell away at the hip, he still went on struggling, lifting the other one up to push against me. That made it even more awkward to whack him, and it finally gave him the leverage he needed to bring his full strength to bear against me. Down two limbs, and he still bowed me over with a tug.

The frantic terror seemed to leave him the moment that he realized that he still had power. He was a real mess, but despite the chunks missing out of his face and his whole right side being fairly meatloaf-y at this point, his eyes narrowed as he worked out his next move.

I couldn't give him time to think. If it came down to thinking, I was going to lose.

Spirits started coiling around us again. He was going for another brain gouge. Well, I wasn't giving him the opportunity. We'd been fighting down here for what felt like an hour, so I wasn't surprised to find my Pillar of Ascension glowing away at full power again. I surged my strength, and for one wonderful moment, I was strong enough to stand up straight despite him straining against me. I used that wonderful moment to spin on the spot and throw the little bastard as hard as I could.

Koschei spun end over end across the cave, twisting himself around so he could land limb side down and scuttle off like the weirdest crab you've ever seen. Not on my watch.

Blood fell in a splatter as my sword flowed out of its solid state and reformed in the same worm-hunting spear I'd carried worms back to town with earlier. It wasn't pretty or elegant, but it was solid in my hand as I drew back my arm and launched it after Koschei.

He saw it coming, of course he saw it coming, and he twisted again in the air to avoid it, but his maimed body was hideously off balance, and my surged Potency had it flying so fast that it took even me by surprise.

Ever seen a pinned butterfly? That was Koschei.

Blood bubbled out of his mouth with the latest scream. The spirits that had been called up wisped away into nothingness as he lost concentration. I had him.

Even with a spike through his chest, an arm and a leg missing, lumps of his flesh scattered across the floor, and more blood sprayed about than I thought that his little body could ever have held, he still went on struggling. As for me? I was starting to feel every one of the injuries he'd inflicted on me. The icicles in my stomach had started to melt, and my own various fluids were running down, mixed with that water. I staggered as dizziness swept over me, and the jolt knocked one of the ice spikes right out of me. Wouldn't have thought that would hurt more than it going in to start with, but it did.

While I could use Restoration time and time again, I couldn't use it on myself again so soon. If I wanted to lay hands on Koschei and try to stitch him back into shape, the Pillar would allow it, but using it on the same person repeatedly was against the rules somehow. I'd have to wait it out a little longer, feeling my own health score dripping lower and lower with every patter of gore on the floor.

I reminded myself that it didn't matter—that dying wasn't the end for me, the way I was going to make it the end for him—but it still felt bad. It hurt, and it felt like… dying. I'd already died too many times to want to experience it again. At least two times too many.

It felt like a marathon just walking over to the far wall with all my injuries, and through it all I could still see Koschei wriggling and twisting, trying to push himself away from the wall and along the spear so that he could get down and go on the offensive all over again. The spear was longer than his arm and his leg, so all he actually managed to do was push himself off the wall, at which point the weight of his big head full of profound thoughts flipped him to dangle upside down.

He reached for the spear haft with his one remaining hand and started pulling himself along, his hands so slippery with his own blood that he could barely get any traction.

The light of my eyes was dimming. I had to grab onto the end of the spear to keep my balance by the time I reached him, and I had to hold onto it to keep my balance as I kicked him in the head, sending him slithering back to hit the wall once more.

I spat out a mouthful of my own blood to mix with all of his. "You're tough. I'll give you that."

Koschei didn't deign to answer me. I was pretty sick of the sound of his voice by that point anyway. A twist of my wrist and a touch of Artifice snapped half the length off the spear, and I reformed it into a cleaver.

A hideous mewling sound filled the cave, echoing back and forth. Koschei grabbed for me, but I stepped around to the side with no arm, and he couldn't spin himself around before I caught him by the top of his bald head and held him still for the last cut.

"Goodbye, old man."

That would have been a killer one-liner before I chopped his head clean off, but reality wasn't that pretty. My first strike rebounded from what should have been soft tissue in his neck, hardened through all his years of advancement into something tougher than it had any right to be. So I had to chop at it again and again and again.

There was no sense of victory by the time that I was done. No sense of anything except disgust, as layer after layer of flesh was parted by my hacking. This was ugly work, but someone had to do it. I concentrated on my *Psychopomp* gift, and I cut.

With a hollow thump, the head fell to the floor.

New Skill Discovered! [Aether Resistance]
New Skill Discovered! [Spirit Strike]
New Skill Discovered! [Elemental Fist]
New Skill Discovered! [Ascendant Cognition]
Legendary Foe Defeated!
Celerity increased to 22
Piety increased to 8
Polearm: Rank 2/10
Aether Resistance: Rank 4/10
430 Experience Gained
7000 Glory Gained
Tier of Glory Ascended!
Tier of Glory Ascended!

I followed after the dropped head, flopping down beside what was left of Koschei with a groan that seemed to fill up the sudden silence. There was still some dripping as what was left of the old Eternal's blood drained from his hanging corpse, but after the cacophony of violence that had been filling this place up for what felt like hours, it was positively soothing.

"Well… that sucked."

CHAPTER 11

Normally, I beat up a monster, and afterwards I felt great, but Koschei was on my team, technically. Normally, I would have had Mercy and Asher there to cheer me on and talk about how awesome I was or what an idiot I was. Both were fun, honestly. But here, alone in the dark, covered in blood and hurting all over, I did not feel awesome.

I tried to remind myself that it was worth it. "Two tiers in one go. That's the good stuff."

My body was a real mess, but so long as I stayed still, my health was holding steady.

[142/890 Health]

Wow, that was even worse than I'd expected. As soon as Restoration came back up I was using it. If Asher was here, I probably would have let him use the nasty burny healing spell he had on me—the one that felt like pouring lava in your wounds. That was how bad my current state was.

The silence stretched out again. Nope. None of that. I reached out to turn Koschei's head around to face me. The light in his eyes was out. His flesh was still here instead of fading away. He was really dead. "Man, I wish you weren't a big bag of dicks like Leo. I really could have used some help with the whole end of the world thing."

I wobbled the head from side to side and put on a squeaky voice. "I'm sorry, Maulkin, maybe the next Eternal you meet won't need murdering."

"Well, I don't know about that, buddy." I sighed. "I mean, first there was Talon, then there was Leo, now there's you. I'm starting to think every Eternal on the whole planet might be an asshole."

"Not all of them!" The head lolled onto the side after that wiggle, and I had to prop it back up again.

"Yes, all of them." I spun him in a slow circle with a finger in the middle of his forehead. "I guess all the decent ones gave up, ran away, or got minced up and turned into abominations. I think that's where the abominations came from anyway…"

Koschei squeaked, "Maybe I could have told you if you hadn't chopped my head off."

I flicked him on the nose. "Well, maybe you could have just told me useful stuff instead of being a dick."

Staring down at the dead face of Koschei, I giggled a little bit to myself. Then laughing hurt, so I stopped. "Okay, talking to a severed head, probably not a good sign."

"Probably not," Koschei replied, so I turned him around to face away.

I had time to kill, so I might as well make the most of it and do some of the fiddly admin stuff that came along with being a demigod. I closed my eyes and cast my attention to the glowing Pillars of Divinity within me.

Taking care to ignore the temptation of the Void Pillars and all the cool new stuff they might be hiding within them, I immediately poured some of my hard-won Glory into Aether. Part of that decision was because I'd just learned that you could basically throw ghosts at somebody as an attack like Koschei had been bombarding me with, but mostly it was housekeeping. I needed to power up my Soul Bonding so that I could latch it onto the next Shard that came into my possession and make sure we never lost it. There was a little trickle of worry about that whole plan since I kept getting more and more Void flavored with every shard I harnessed to my soul, but unless somebody came up with a better solution, I was sticking with it. Even if we did come up with a better plan, an extra soul bond would give me the chance to bring along a weapon or some armor every time I died. That would be helpful as hell. Maybe even some amazing magical artifact if we ever found any. I assumed that Amaranth had amazing magical artifacts that weren't just rusty bits of an old sword. Probably.

My crappy gear was definitely starting to weigh on my mind. Not just the lack of wondrous magic objects, but the diminishing returns on the bare minimum stuff I'd scraped together. Every monster I ran into was able to chomp right through the can to the delicious Maulkin spam inside. And hitting Koschei over and over while my useless blunt sword barely made a dent in him? That was just depressing.

New equipment was definitely in order. Artifice was probably the pillar I used the most often, but I'd invested the least amount of Glory into it. That didn't seem right. Plus, I had a whole swathe of skills in it that would level up when I empowered the Pillar. Sure pouring some glory into Primal might have unlocked some new healing powers and gotten me out of the jam I was in right this second, but getting better armor and weapons might make the difference between ending a fight untouched and having all these holes poked in me all over again. Look at me, delaying gratification like a big smart boy. Mercy would be so proud.

At the end of the day, the changes I was making to myself were permanent. I couldn't just go chasing after whatever shiny new thing I fancied each time that I grew in power. Tempting as that might have been. I dumped the rest of my Glory into Artifice, then gave myself a look over.

Maulkin – Chagnar Faun of the Lunar and Void Court –
9th Tier of Glory
Statistics:
   HP: 522/1270
   Devotion: 240/240
Attributes:
   Potency: 47
   Celerity: 22
   Vitality: 19
   Piety: 8

Well, that took care of the worries about bleeding to death down here on the floor of some dank cave. I still wasn't better off proportionally, but as the increased Tiers of Glory refined my spirit into something more godlike, my body seemed to follow in its footsteps. That was probably one of the things that bugged me the most about the whole investing a whole tier's worth of glory into a void pillar thing. Not that I had marked my soul eternally with evil or whatever, but that I hadn't got the sweet health bump. I mean, sure, the Void and all its powers are antithetical to all life, but couldn't it have given me a little health increase anyway? I was probably lucky it hadn't taken health away, to be honest.

With the increased power in my Pillars, I should have unlocked a whole swathe of new divine skills or divinities or whatever they were called, and after hoarding experience from most of my training with Seren as well as the last few days, I had over a thousand points to spend buying new cool tricks.

A glance confirmed that Rough Hewn Weapons, Armor, and Architecture had evolved into Inferior Weapons, Armor, and Architecture which… uh… still didn't feel great, to be honest, but it was an improvement. Improving Artifice had also extended my Sphere of Influence even further than it had reached before. The whole cave was inside it now—a bit of the tunnel too. I couldn't feel any of them because of the Voidgod's malign influence on this place, but once I got somewhere alive, I was going to have a great time. I might even be able to help the Dvergar with their mining back at home, hauling out some ores from hard-to-reach places. No wait, that sounded too much like a job. Never mind. Maybe I could just tell them where to dig for the good stuff.

Aether was up to three tiers now, so there was a lot of new stuff unlocked in there, but so much of it was kind of… obtuse? Like, yeah sure Astral Projecting out of my body might be handy sometimes, but you know what was always good? Hitting stuff harder. Trapping unbound spirits and crystalizing them into a material that could be used to forge magic gear? Okay, yeah, that one did sound cool, but it looked like the actual crafting stuff came further up the Aether ladder, and I was in no hurry to climb it since I spent more of my time trying not to use Aether than actually using it. The only one I definitely wanted was Spirit Strike. After being on the receiving end of a ghost-slap to the brain, there was no way I could let it pass, so pop, there went three hundred of my hard-earned experience points.

Ascension skills were pretty scarce, apart from the Surge ones. I seemed to unlock new Divinities in that tree when I'd maxed out the normal skill equivalent. So, I had Ascendant Brutality and not much else. I was really good at hitting things hard. Woo. Go me. Ascendant Cognition was there, greyed out, and I had no idea what those words meant together until I dipped my attention into it and realized it was about refining my brain into something more… godly. Shame I hadn't invested enough Glory in Ascension to use it.

I toyed with the idea of Celerity Surge, both so I could jog back to the Bastion faster, and so I could surprise the crap out of Orphia the next time she tried to do her own superspeed trick. That would have been really funny, but it didn't suit the way that I fought. I was not big on running away from my problems or dodging all that much if I was being honest. Most of the time if I dodged out of the way, it meant that whoever was standing behind me would get whacked instead. If I did that and Mercy got hurt, I would never hear the end of it. Literally never. She was going to live forever, and even three thousand years from now I could imagine she'd still be dunking on me for that one time I ducked and she got a club to the face.

Vitality Surge seemed like a better option. Being able to shrug off blows like Koschei had would be much more helpful for my career as a meat shield. Yeah, that felt right. I sank another three hundred in.

That left me enough for one more Divinity. One more uber-powerful god-tier move that I could use to turn the tide of a battle. I couldn't think of one.

The siren call of all the Divinities in the Void Pillar I'd unlocked was hard to ignore, but I was pretty sure that using any of them was going to draw attention. I'd already splurged experience there just after we beat Talon, and I hadn't even dared to try out that power yet, even when I'd been all alone in the desert, just in case somehow somebody spotted me and immediately sounded all the Voidgod alarms.

Nobody knew how much experience I had except me. Nobody needed to know if I kept on buying guilty little secret powers. Yet somehow, I still felt ashamed when I shuffled over to the list of them and started looking through. While all the other words glowed with moonlight in my mind, these ones were so black that they stood out even in the darkness of my inner self. Wow, that sounded super goth.

Then I sat there staring at them and dithered for so long that Restoration ticked back to life.

I'd save my experience for later. It wasn't a big deal. There might be some helpful skill I wanted to grab on the fly—like that time I'd learned sailing.

I slipped back into my body and triggered Restoration before I'd even opened my eyes. The ice had all melted away by now, so the wounds were wide open for the stitching. They prickled as they closed, but that was nothing compared to the weird sensation of whatever sweetmeats Koschei had popped when he gut-punched me re-inflating inside me. The noise that I made when I felt that was not dignified.

Finally, I opened my eyes.

There was a spear leveled at my face. I could have done without that. Mhirka was the one holding it. I could have done without that too. Arrayed behind her, taking up the whole of this cramped little cave, were the gathered chieftains of every Faun clan. They were looming, colossal things so large it was hard for me to even read them as Faun instead of some sort of lumbering ogres. They had to bow their heads to stop their horns sticking in the pitted roof, and I realized with a start that most of the pits in the roof were probably from their previous visits. All of them were staring at me.

"Good morning."

Tears rimmed Mhirka's eyes. She had not touched dead Koschei, but it was pretty obvious what had happened to him since I was down here covered in his blood.

She thrust her spear for my throat, and I only just had time to Surge Vitality before it struck home and killed me. As it was it jabbed in, hard as a finger would have prodded a human throat, making me cough and gag. "Hey! Knock it off."

She looked from me to the spear with dread and confusion. She knew it was sharp; she'd been killing bugs with it just a few hours back.

The chieftains were not so quick to act. One of them laid a hand on Mhirka's shoulder to draw her back, and she shrugged it off violently but seemed to take the hint. She didn't try to stab me again.

My voice came out strangled until I spluttered a little more. "The strongest one is in charge, right? That's how this all works?"

I could see the betrayal on Mhirka's face contending with her dread and hatred. What a mix. She looked like most of the women I'd ever been on a blind date with. There was sure to be some guilt in there, like she had been the one to give me the idea to kill their beloved pet Eternal. As if he hadn't made that decision for himself thousands of years back when he decided to make them into slaves.

I looked past Mhirka to the gathered giants. "I killed him. I was stronger. So, the way that she tells it, that makes me the boss now, right?"

"Koschei did not rule us," Giant hammer chief rumbled. "He was not Chagnar."

"But you listened to him. He was your advisor, and the advisor of the one that came before you, and all the other ones before that too, right? He spoke to the ancestors?"

They were looking around at each other, the full magnitude of what I'd done just sinking in. I might have accidentally just killed their whole religion as well as the little tyrant that had perched himself on top of it. Oops.

Through her tears, Mhirka snarled, "He spoke for our dead. He told us their will."

"Okay…" Well, I'd already come this far, might as well go the distance and get murdered by the angry mob. Time for the moment of truth. "That was a lie."

That seemed to hit them even harder than the realization I'd cut them all off from their ancestors, rippling out through the room. Some of them paled. Some of them flushed with rage. Color-changing Faun. Great.

I wet my lips, tasting my own blood, and then I pressed on. "He was telling you what he wanted you to do, what he wanted you to be. Maybe he really was listening to your ancestors, maybe not, but the Chagnar who went before, they didn't want you to come here. They don't want you to suffer."

Double-axe chief had both of his axes in his hands. Maybe he didn't have anywhere else to put them. Maybe he hadn't come down here to chop me into chunks. He roared, "They were Chagnar, they would have wanted us to–"

I didn't need to shout for my words to cut him off dead. "To be weak?"

Every Faun in the cave bristled when I said that—all of them except Mhirka. She was staring down at the cave floor, some long rusted machinery between her ears rattling slowly to life. That was fighting talk. I'd just insulted them all. This was going to end in a mess. I could already tell.

"You don't make a people strong by culling their numbers. You don't make them strong by taking them into the desert and starving them. If the Faun want to be strong again, a force to be reckoned with in this world, they need to change." I said it all in a rush so that they couldn't shout me down before the end, but I needn't have bothered. They were all staring at me in abject silence.

The tallest of the Faun pushed forward through the crowd—a woman bent almost double to keep the curled horns on her head off the roof. She had to twist her neck to glare at me. "Who are you to tell us that we must change? Our ways have been the same since the stars first shone on Amaranth. We have always been here."

"Who am I? I'm the guy who just walked in here, fresh off the boat, and beat the most powerful Eternal in your camp."

That seemed to shut them up all over again. They might not like what I was saying, and they might not have liked me, but under their own stupid system, they had to listen to me because I'd killed the guy that they listened to before. There was no denying it, I still had the cleaver lying beside my hand.

No wonder they'd signed up with the Voidgod when all you had to do to get them on your side was be the biggest bully on the block.

"Now maybe Koschei made it all up. Maybe he told you this was the way your people had always lived so that he could make you behave the way he wanted you to. But let's say that he was telling the truth. You've all done things the same since the dawn of time?" I took a deep breath. Every time I suggested that Koschei was a filthy liar, they seemed to get upset about it. Oh well. "Maybe you have, maybe Koschei just kept you doing the same things you'd always done, but the world hasn't stayed the same. If you want to survive in the world we're living in now, then you need to change."

Mhirka didn't look up from the bloodstains on the floor. She was working through all this at her own pace. Hearing my words, but thinking about other stuff, she mumbled, "The ancestors spoke through him."

I had my suspicions about that. "Yeah? Did it look something like this?"

When I used Spirit Strike it wasn't nearly as impressive as the perfect storm of spirits that Koschei had been able to invoke. All I mustered was a pathetic little wisp, shooting out from my forehead to whack into Mhirka's. It didn't carry fear or doubt or anything like it. Just my horrible certainty that he'd been lying to them all along.

She raised a hand to touch the spot on her head where the spooky little puff had hit her. All of the other Faun were gawking at me. If I had to guess, then I'd say that was exactly what it had looked like when the ancestors spoke through him.

She looked at me without hate in her eyes, possibly for the first time since I'd met her. "How did you? … What did you? …"

I pushed my Aether again, and another little white whisper of a thought sprang out of my head and shot out, past Mhirka to pass invisibly through double-axe guy's thick skull. Koschei lied. That same whisper. Again and again and again I pushed that thought out, feeling some reserve of power I'd never touched before draining with each one I unleashed. It didn't leave me feeling dumber or weaker or anything like that, just kind of hollow inside. Maybe that was what Asher felt like after doing one of his big spells. I'd have to ask him one of these days. Either way, when I blinked my eyes shut after bombarding the whole room's worth of chieftains with tiny ghosts, I could see that my *Devotion* was down to 32 from the healthy 240 it usually sat at.

I took a deep breath to steady myself, and then I spoke again. "Either you can believe that I speak for the ancestors now, or you can believe that Koschei was just using his powers to trick you all this time. I don't care which, so long as you listen to me."

Maybe cheering was too much to hope for after everything else that had happened today, but I'd kind of hoped that they'd all stop looking quite so desolate. No reason to feel bad about Koschei being dead. He was a dick. Although I suppose that now they were all feeling bad because they'd mindlessly obeyed someone who was using them for his own ends for millennia. Oops.

Finally, the giant hammer guy sank down onto one knee and asked me. "What would you have us do?"

At least I had an easy answer to that one. "Go away. Find somewhere pretty and green where the hunting is good, the land is fertile, and the Faun can become strong again. Build homes. Make babies. Teach them things. When life stops being a struggle, it doesn't mean that you're going to get weaker, it means that you are winning. That you're stronger. Like lifting a big weight gets easier the more you do it."

You would think that I'd told them all to go and throw themselves off a cliff from the sour expressions.

Mhirka piped up again, still desperately trying to cling to her anger. I couldn't blame her for that; it must have felt like someone had pulled the rug out from under her feet about now. "You would have us abandon this sacred place?"

"Who is it sacred to? It is a lump of dead rock in the middle of a dead desert made when some evil thing died thousands of years before you were even born." I pushed myself slowly to my feet and was quietly pleased that my legs didn't give out after all the massive blood loss. Restoration really was awesome. I definitely needed to upgrade Primal again soon. "It's a gravestone for a monster that didn't deserve one. Why are you even here?"

"The enemy," the tall woman said to her own feet. "The Gilded Charlatan."

Two-axe guy joined in. "He lurks behind the great wall, just waiting for us to show weakness."

"So let him lurk! He's been lurking since… always!" I shrugged. "Who cares if he takes this place?"

Mhirka snarled at me, baring all those filed teeth at me again. Why did I find that kind of hot? Was it because I had a Faun body, or did I need therapy? "Do you care nothing for the ways of our people?"

"Not when they're stupid ways." I shrugged, and the ruined scraps of armor still clinging to my shoulder tumbled off to land with a thump. Desperately in need of an upgrade. "Not when they're making the Chagnar Faun weak."

Bulky hammer man barked, "Why do you care if the Faun are strong?"

"You think I choose this body for a joke? The Faun are the best thing about this crappy planet." That drew some smiles from the gathered crowd. Flattery will get you anywhere, apparently. "If I can get you guys fighting fit again, then just imagine what you could accomplish."

Mhirka's eyes narrowed when I said "fighting fit." She leapt on it. "You would make us your soldiers, your slaves?"

I laughed in her face. All these years, the Faun had been peons to some lying little Eternal, and now that someone was finally telling the truth, she was scared that it just meant the mask was going to be pulled off. "I'm not going to make you anything. As soon as this conversation is done, I'm out of here. I've got my own stuff going on."

The tall woman reached out a hand to me, then snatched it back as if she'd just realized what she was doing. "You would rob us of even your guidance?"

"Guys, I don't have any guidance. I don't have any wisdom. I'm an idiot. But even an idiot can see that what you guys are doing out here isn't making you happy or strong, or… anything. I mean, you're eating worms. You can't tell me those taste good."

There was some rumbled laughter, though none of the chieftains seemed willing to admit it was coming from them. Eventually, hammer man admitted, "They are… foul."

"You don't need an Eternal to tell you how to live your lives. You don't need the ghosts of dead people bossing you around either. You're the Chagnar Faun. You're the biggest badasses in all of Amaranth. You know how to hunt, how to fight, how to do all the things it takes to be awesome." I pointed up the tunnel and let out an excited shout. "So go be awesome!"

They did. They took off. The press of bodies down here in the cave thinned, and I turned away from them to get myself ready for the hike back across the ashes. I retrieved the spear and the cleaver, mashing them back together into a great-sword so I could slot it back into the baldric the Dvergar had made me. Then I scooped up Koschei's head under one arm and turned to leave. He was going to be a lot more useful to me now than he'd ever been in life. Plus, he was an excellent conversationalist. That would make the long journey feel shorter.

Mhirka was still standing there when I turned around. "Uh… hi. Did you not buy the whole, go be awesome, thing?"

She was perfectly still, looking not at me but at the headless body that had now tumbled to lie on the ground. "Why have you done this?"

"Because you people deserve better than to be toys for some stuck up"—I fumbled through a half-dozen different words for extremely short people in my head, but I was pretty sure they were all slurs so I finally just said—"Eternal."

"You say that you do not want us. That you will not lead us. You mean to abandon us when we need guidance the most." She stared at me as I made a show of checking I had all my things together. I wasn't planning on coming back this way ever again, so leaving something behind was a no-no.

I shrugged as I went past her. "You need to lead yourselves. As you're super fond of saying, I'm no Chagnar. Find your own way."

"If you are not Chagnar, you are prey." She said prey like it was the tastiest word she'd ever had in her mouth. "Why would prey want us strong, when we will turn that strength against you?"

I crouched down in the center of the mess that I'd made of this place. Blood and ice-melt had pooled down in the middle of the room, and I had to wipe it away with the flat of my hand before I could see the marks that the shards had left, still scarred into the world. "Maybe I want a good fight if it comes to that? Maybe I'm a little bit Chagnar after all?"

She was staring at me so hard I was starting to get self-conscious. Maybe I had a hunk of Koschei in my hair. Eventually, when I wasn't saying anything else, she squatted down beside me and looked at the marks as if she might decipher some meaning in them. "What are you keeping from us?"

I debated telling her nothing or spinning her a lie, but at the end of the day, that would make me no better than Koschei. She lived in this world, so she deserved to know the truth about what was going to happen to it. Everyone deserved to know. "Araphel. He's coming back."

There was no sudden gasp, no fainting away. She spoke with the same dubious contempt she'd treated everything I'd said to her from the start. "The Voidgod was slain."

I shoved off my knees to get back to standing. Some of the holes in my side were going to take another round of healing before I was back on top form, and I really didn't fancy another wrestling match. "Why does nobody get the whole Eternal concept? Gods can't die. Whatever's stopped him coming back before now is going to stop working, then we've got Voidgod all over the place again."

"So, you came to plead that we do not join him?" She sneered at me.

"Uh no. I came to see if Koschei would help fight him. Turns out he was more interested in his own games."

She cast a glance to the dead man again. "You do not want the Faun to fight for you?"

"No offense, but you guys look like you're about one bad day away from dead. Maybe once you've recovered a little you might want to join in the Voidgod ass-whooping but... I'm not asking for anything." I gave Koschei's head a little wiggle. "You've had enough of Eternals making demands."

She nodded at that, slowly rising to her full height and scowling at me with all her might. "Our paths shall cross again."

I smiled at that. "I hope so."

She was not smiling. She was extremely not-smiling. "It may mean your death."

"Won't be the first." I shrugged. "Probably won't be the last either."

She walked me out, but we didn't have anything more to say to each other after that. She had a whole new world-view to work out, and I'd just killed the closest thing to an ally I might have found in the whole world. Neither of us was feeling chatty. When she slipped away, I didn't hear her go.

The whole settlement was in disarray as I strolled out. Tents were being broken down, materials gathered up into bundles, and gardens being uprooted for whatever bounty they could offer before the long walk out of the desert. I took it all in without interfering. None of the Faun looked all that happy to be leaving, even though it would be to an easier, happier life. I suppose that they didn't know that yet, just that the place they'd called home was being snatched away from them yet again.

At least leaving the Faun settlement was easier than coming in. All I had to do was fall down off the stepped levels until I reached the bottom. If there were still sentries posted in the deep shadows that the moonlight cast, then I couldn't see them—which was kind of the point I suppose.

I gave the whole thing one last long look, then I set off towards the distant horizon. Couldn't keep my adoring fans waiting after all, and there was no way that I wasn't going to be Leofric's new best buddy after chopping the head off his oldest enemy and killing him permanently. I was expecting a parade.

CHAPTER 12

There was no parade when I got back to the Bastion. There wasn't even a rope.

There had been no worm attack on my way back, and I was profoundly disappointed because I'd been looking forward to seeing if my new level of Artifice could find something useful in the giant monster corpse that I could use. I supposed that I might even have been able to refine the teeth into some patches for my armor since it was in a pretty bad state, eel-skin sloughing off to leave my skin exposed underneath.

Either they hadn't expected me to come back so quickly, or they hadn't expected me to come back at all. I shouted for a little bit, but the wall was high enough that I wasn't sure anyone up there would actually be able to hear me. Which was just great. Or maybe they'd turned on Asher and Mercy the second I was out of sight, and now they planned to leave me out here to be worm food. Also, a distinct possibility.

Regardless of what I was going to find on the other side of that wall, I still needed to get onto the other side, so I made a little spike on the pommel of my sword, wedged Koschei's head on it, then started to climb the desolate stone.

Pocked and scarred by the explosion that had ruined this place, I found it easier than I'd expected to find hand and footholds, and the fact that Faun don't get tired really helped out with the whole climbing thing. I mean, I wasn't going to be rocking up any mountains any time soon, but here on this big flat wall peppered with holes big enough to hook my hands in, it was pretty manageable. I wasn't even out of breath, which was lucky because I was still in the middle of an in-depth conversation with Koschei about my relationship problems. "…I don't even know if she even likes me? You know? I beat her in a fight, then threatened to kill her, then saved her life, and then I gave her some swords, and that is like some ceremonial thing with the Alvaren I guess? Like, the king gives his knights a sword or something? So maybe she just thinks I'm her duty?"

"I don't know, man, that sounds like a weird situation."

Surging my Potency, I leapt up the wall in great bounds, hammering my hands into the walls and making new cracks to pry into where there weren't already hand-holds. "I know, right? I mean she was the one who invited me to… take it to the next level or whatever, but did she actually want to, or was it just what she thought she had to do? Like… am I her job?"

"No wonder this is messing with your head, brother." Koschei nodded along involuntarily with my movements. "Sounds like you need to sit down and have a talk with her about your feelings."

I turned around and yelled in his face, "You shut the hell up, severed head. I am a man, damnit! I will never willingly sit down and talk about my feelings. Never!"

"I'm just saying that maybe if you told her that you were worried about all this, you might be able to sort it out." The next stretch of wall was thoroughly riddled with holes, so when the potency surge faded, it wasn't so difficult to slip back into the old climbing rhythm again. I was still only about a quarter of the way up the wall after that surge. It was mid-morning by the time that I got to the foot of the Bastion, but this climb might take up the rest of the day.

"But what if she turns around and I'm right, and she's only banging me out of duty. That would suck."

Koschei's mouth flapped open and shut now as rigor mortis faded. "Plus, you wouldn't be able to grab any more elf ass."

"And that would be terrible!" I yelped. "Do you have any idea how hot she is?"

"Hey, man, you don't have to tell me. I might not have a body, but I've still got eyes, you know?"

I took a hand away from the wall to grab hold of his face. "You keep your eyes to yourself, Koschei. That's my girl."

Between the pinch of my fingers, his mouth opened. "Or maybe she isn't. Maybe she's just doing booty duty."

I turned my attention back to the wall. The higher I got, the rarer the fingerholds were, and the more I was having to launch myself up to grab onto them. For a while I ended up moving sideways instead of up, just searching for something I could use.

With a sigh, I looked back to Koschei. "Plus, she's still got that whole Alvaren supremacy thing going on. I am not a big fan of that. She thinks that she's better than everyone else in the world, just because she's got those pointy ears. I've tried talking to her about it, and sometimes I think she gets it, but then the next time I look around, she's got that look on her face like the dvergar are worms or something."

"Oh yeah, man, that is nasty." His head bobbed forward until the mouth was right behind my ear. "You should probably break up with her."

I turned to look him in the eye. "Are you just saying that because you want to date her?"

"Hey, man, I'm just a severed head. What am I going to do with her?"

That was a fair point. I turned my attention back to the task at hand for now. The handholds were getting smaller and smaller until sometimes I was supporting my full weight with just my fingers hooked into a tiny gap. It was a good thing my Potency was so high. If you'd asked Asher to climb this thing, he would not have made it past... well.... the ash desert, probably.

Potency surge had ticked back into action, so I took advantage launching myself up onto the bare expanse of stone above me and hammering in my fists. For as long as the surge lasted, I moved up in leaps and bounds, but the moment that it faltered, I was going to be stuck unless I got past this smooth bit.

With one final grunt of effort as the surge died, I launched myself like a crossbow bolt up the length of the wall, air whistling in my ears. Then I saw it. The level of the ground on the other side, where an industrious tree root had pushed its way between the pale stone to dangle before my eyes. I grabbed onto it with both hands and hung out there while I worked out my next move. I glanced back to see Koschei staring. Then I groaned. "Oh gods, I'm actually going to have to talk to her about all this. Like a mature adult or something."

"Better you than me, man." His head lolled from side to side, mockingly as I swung from the root. "If you try to break up with her, you're probably going to end up my height."

"I hadn't even thought about that. What if she goes stabby crazy on me?"

"Wouldn't be the first time," Koschei pointed out, all too accurately.

I let myself hang limply from the root for a second, then I started to pull myself up again. There was a patch of brickwork up above me. The recent repairs were missing the pockmarked holes I was used to, but that made up for it with gaps where mortar was meant to have been put in. They'd laid it from the other side and never had any way to check how it looked out here. "Oh, man, it would really suck if she murdered me."

I cleared the bricks in no time at all, even as Koschei said, "You'd get better."

"I mean like"—I waved a hand back and forth as I searched for another handhold—"emotionally."

Koschei lolled to the side. "Oh yeah, that would sting."

"Who the hell are you talking to?" Mercy was peering down at me over the top of the wall.

I was so happy to see her I nearly lost my grip. "Mercy!"

She shouted back. "Maulkin!"

Leaning back and peering, I could see her head and shoulders poking out over the battlements. She seemed to be alone. "Asher?"

She shrugged. "Nope."

My fingers started to slip, and I had to press myself back against the wall rapidly. "Rope?"

"Oh, yeah. One sec."

The second passed, along with a good few more. "Any day now."

"I'm tying it to something so your fat ass doesn't pull me off the wall. Shut up."

The rope dropped down, and the coil of it whacked against me, still unrolling as it went on its merry way down the wall. I really should not have looked down. My hands were shaky when I grabbed a hold and gave it a tug to make sure it would take my weight. Thankfully, it did. From there it was as simple as going hand over hand up the rest of the distance, strolling up the side of the Bastion like it was a day in the park. I even had enough breath to banter properly again. "Aww, even after all this time you're still thinking about my ass."

Mercy was out of sight, but I could hear her when she made a little snort. "Thinking about cutting this rope and dropping you on your ass."

"Wouldn't want to damage my good side."

"At least we both agree that face is a mess."

My mess had just popped up over the side of the wall as she said it, and I could see that she was smiling. Aww, she really did miss me. There was nobody else around. A few of the guards were scattered farther along, but they seemed to be keeping their distance. Given what I'd done to them when I first arrived, I couldn't really fault them. Although I wasn't sure why they'd be hiding from Mercy since she was on their team—or at least wearing their team colors in her eyes.

I gave her a smile in return, and her expression slipped back to its usual snarky smirk like it was more comfortable for her than letting me see her genuinely happy. I'd never ask her about her last life since she seemed so intent on avoiding the subject, but I wondered sometimes what had happened to make her this way. I shook the thought out of my head and stretched my arms out. Even if they didn't get tired, it still wasn't exactly comfortable climbing all that time. "Did I miss any excitement?"

She rolled her eyes. "Not unless you think watching some smug prick stroking his own ego non-stop for days at a time is exciting."

"Asher isn't all bad."

She coughed instead of laughing. "Leo. He's a real piece of work. Just like you said."

"Did he give you the whole speech about not being equals? He's king, and you can be his underlings, all that real charming stuff?"

Her eyes flitted to the guards, checking they were out of earshot before she dunked on their boss too hard. "I think you got the abridged version. Our one wasn't that straightforward, and it lasted for... actually, he might still be in the middle of it. I got bored and snuck out to check for you."

"Because you missed me so bad." I put an arm around her shoulders.

She shrugged it off. "Even you are better than listening to another minute of 'oh I've lived a billion years, so you should all think that I'm terribly interesting.' I swear I've never met anyone so in love with themselves."

Looking out across the verdant green land beyond the Bastion, it was hard not to compare it to how the Faun had been living, scraping in the dust and desperately trying to stay alive. "So, you get that he's the bad guy now, yeah?"

"I never thought he wasn't." Mercy shrugged. "I just hoped we might be able to… use him I guess."

I grinned down at her. "Well, mission accomplished. He's going to be our best buddy from here on out."

Her eyebrows shot up into the mop of her white fringe in surprise. "You got the Faun to give up?"

I reached back and plucked Koschei from his perch with a squelch, holding him out to her with a flourish. "Better."

She did not look happy. Why didn't she look happy? Very carefully, Mercy asked. "Why have you got a head?"

"I always said that the only way to get—"

She cut me off with the kind of glare that could probably kill small mammals or knock birds out of the sky. "If you make a joke right now, I'm going to scream. Why do you have a head?"

I wobbled him from side to side, jovially. "This handsome chap is Koschei. He was the Eternal pulling the strings on all the Faun."

"You went in there and killed him?" That omnipresent smirk had faded, and I was starting to get really worried that I'd screwed up. "Just like Leofric wanted?"

"I thought that was what you wanted me to do?" I didn't mean to make it sound like I was mad at her, but damn it, I was. She'd told me to go and make Leo happy, and now I'd done it she was flipping out at me like I'd been the one to do something wrong.

She thumped me in the shoulder, sending me staggering back a step towards the edge. "What the hell?"

"You wanted me to buddy up with Leo." I waved Koschei's head at her. "This guy is like his nemesis. Leo's going to love it."

"What had happened to you? You were the guy that made us go help some random caravan because it was getting attacked by Svart. You were the guy that made us stop and help everybody we met. If there had been a kitten stuck up a tree, you probably would have been right up there trying to get it down. How do you get from that to murdering somebody just because it is convenient?"

There were whole sections of this conversation that I felt like I'd missed. It was like she was talking in code, and I didn't know how to translate it. This was not an uncommon experience for me. "I… what?"

"I thought you were a good guy, Maulkin. Even when I saw you go nuts at Seren and do what you did to her, I thought… he just lost his temper. It could happen to anyone." She was looking at me like I'd sprouted another head. Like this was some terrible revelation. "But this is… this was calculated. You killed somebody… A good guy wouldn't do something like this."

"I'm pretty sure we've been killing people since we got here."

She was physically backing away from me now, unwilling or unable to look me in the eye. "People that were trying to kill us, or people trying to hurt innocent people, not just somebody who… got in the way. What is wrong with you?"

"What's wrong with me? What's wrong with you?!" The anger boiled up my throat unbidden. I didn't want to do any of this. I didn't want to kill an old Eternal just because it was what was required. If we'd just grabbed the sword and run like hell back at the start, then none of this would have happened. "You're the one who told me to be best buddies with the gold-plated prick. Did you think that we could get there with our hands clean? He is a bad guy. Bad guys like bad things."

"I thought you could…" Her face twisted in something like pain. "I thought you knew the difference between right and wrong. I thought that if it got to the point where you had to decide if you'd do something bad to get on his good side then you'd stop, or we'd trick him or… I guess that was expecting too much of you."

She was backing away faster now, turning and stalking off along the wall. "Mercy…"

"I don't want to talk about this. I don't…" Her voice went deathly quiet. "I don't know if I want to talk to you at all. I need to think about all this."

Still, I called after her, "Mercy!?"

She stormed away along the wall, almost crashing right into Leofric as he leapt casually from a courtyard to stand beside her. She did not meet his gaze, but she seemed to shrink away from him unwittingly. I'd never seen her afraid of anything. Or at least, I'd never seen her afraid enough to back down from anything. What had he done while I was gone?

He spread his arms wide as he approached me, sunlight glinting off all his golden everything. The same feline smile slunk across his face as before he sent me off. "And so my wayward son returns."

"Leofric." I shoved all my feelings back down into a little box and battened it shut as fast as possible, frantically trying to remember how you were meant to talk like a normal person. "Hi. How are you?"

"What is that between your paws, oh wretched beast of chaos." He said the words like they were a joke, but I could tell that they were real words he would have used to describe me if I hadn't been there. Rude enough to amuse him, but polite enough that I couldn't object. Real class act. He had barely looked at me before his eyes were drawn down to Koschei.

I tossed the head over, and he caught it without a hint of effort. "Maybe you recognize him."

He looked bemused as he lifted the severed head up to face level, but it didn't last. His hands shook as he lowered it again. "Koschei? But how can this be?"

Tempting as it was to brag about how I'd managed to bag an Eternal that was so much older and more powerful than me, I wasn't really in the mood after Mercy had been such a downer about it. Besides, this was the moment when everything could go really really wrong for me and old Leo here. "There was a whole lot of chopping involved."

"He was an eternal, just as we are. When he was slain, his flesh should have faded to be reborn. How did you…" He trailed off in wonderment.

"Oh, he is extra-dead. Permanently dead. No longer alive. Benefits of having a Lunar Eternal on your team I guess."

Now he was either going to love me or freak out and kill me. It could go either way, depending on whether or not he knew that perma-killing Eternals was a power that only the Voidgod had at his disposal. There was a bit of a gamble involved, but I felt confident in my choice to wave the severed head around. Koschei had been a Lunar Eternal like me. He had known the limits of what we could do. For all his age, it seemed to me that Leo had never bothered to learn about us.

"You…" His voice was ragged with emotion. I stood frozen in place, gut gurgling with dread as I imagined how the next moment was going to go. A tiny teardrop slipped from his sunbeam eye and trickled down his cheek. "You have given me a great gift this day. The greatest gift. Since the dawn of time, that vicious haunted pygmy was a thorn in my side, and now, finally, I am free of him."

He hoisted Koschei's head up and roared with laughter and delight. I felt a bit queasy.

Excited and chatty in a way that I'd never expected to see him, Leofric went on, "I had thought that through our combined efforts that he might have been contained or driven off for long enough to prevent him from aiding his dark master when the Voidgod returned, but this… this is a boon beyond all others. You cannot know how long I have… I spoke in jest before, but you are my son now in truth, bound by a tie deeper than blood. You are my most beloved servant."

With a sigh, he dropped Koschei's head like it was trash and crushed it under his shiny golden boot until it popped. Then he took a hold of my shoulders. Ugh, this was so awkward. "Uh, thanks… dad?"

He blinked away the tears from his eyes and slapped me on the shoulder with enough force that it set my bones rattling. "You shall be the Warmaster of this great legion when we march upon the Voidgod. All that I have, all that I am, shall be bent to your purpose."

It had all been worth it. Killing Koschei. Fighting through worms and deserts and scattering the Faun to the four corners of the map. If it got us the help we needed, then it didn't matter if Mercy sulked about it. We were trying to save the world. The universe really—if you bought into the whole thing about all other places being a reflection of Amaranth. That was important. Really important. The most important thing that anyone had ever done, ever. So, if I had to do a few things that made me feel crappy along the way, then that is what I'd do. "That is awesome. That… that's exactly what I need. Araphel is coming, and we need to pull together everyone so that we can stop him before it is too late."

"My armies are yours. You shall speak as if with my voice." He put his arm around my back, aiming for the shoulders, but he was not quite tall enough to reach without twisting weirdly. "All that you need to is command it, and men will spit themselves upon their own blades."

I let him lead me along the outer wall, glancing out over the desert beyond and wondering if I might catch a glimpse of any of the Faun as they got to go and live free at last. "Well, hopefully we won't need to do much of that."

"It matters not that they do. It matters only that they will." He squeezed my back as if it was my shoulder, grabbing a handful of muscle through my armor. It wasn't sore exactly, just weird. "Such is their loyalty to my cause. To our cause."

"Uh, good. I guess." I still felt like I was walking a tightrope every time I spoke to him. Just waiting for me to blurt out the wrong thing and kick off a war.

Why couldn't Mercy have stayed here? Even if she was mad at me, she was still better at handling social situation stuff. I mean, she had her own Dvergar fan club within two minutes of arriving in their city. She could have had Leo eating out her hand. Unless she decided to slap him with it. Which she probably would. Okay, maybe she wouldn't be all that useful, but I still felt like I'd been abandoned in a lion's cage.

He dragged me on, forcing me to pick up my pace as we cleared the length of the giant wall in great strides. "Come now, I am sure that you cannot wait to see Orphia's face when she learns that you have surpassed her and supplanted her in my affections after mere days."

"Okay. Yes." I couldn't help but grin. "That actually sounds like a lot of fun."

"Glorious. Come with me, my son, and witness the next mighty weapon to be added to our arsenal."

Immediately, the dread came back. What had they been up to in my absence? I had vague ideas that Mercy might have had the knowhow to teach them how to build a cannon or something, but I knew that she wouldn't have done it. Whatever Leo had found to parade in front of me was going to be something local. Something dramatic probably, judging from the spring in his step as he led me along to see it. Sure, some of that was definitely about the decapitated Koschei, but he'd been in a good mood before we'd even bumped into each other today. And if he was in a good mood, then that almost certainly meant that something really bad was about to happen.

"Imagine if you will, an army that has no need for a supply line behind it. Troop positions that can be reinforced in an instant from anywhere else that soldiers are stationed. How can the Voidgod stand against us, when our forces can be anywhere at any time? When we can strike with all the haste of lightning? Retreat before the adversary can blink?"

It felt like he'd been preparing that speech for a while, so I nodded along with him politely until I abruptly realized what the hell he was talking about. "You're talking about the waygates."

"Of course!" He chuckled. It was a weird thing, even knowing that he was a real dick, when every time that he was pleased, I felt it. I felt happy that I'd pleased him. Like he radiated warmth. Like I was his loyal pet. It was more insidious than the Spirit Strikes that Koschei had unleashed but no less oppressive. "The other great bounty that you and your companions have brought to the cause."

The Waygate came into sight, down in its courtyard. As did Asher, finally. At least I knew why he hadn't shown up to greet me. Why would he come and help his dearest friend up a wall when there was maths he could be doing. He glanced up as some sunlight deflected off Leofric's armor and hit him in the face, met my eyes for an instant, then he was back to work. What a nerd.

A nerd, surrounded by Leo's soldiers on all sides, none of them looking all that friendly. If they hated me for looking different, I dreaded to think how they'd been treating him. "You do know that only Asher can use them?"

"For now." Leofric's radiating happiness seemed to ratchet up another notch, glowing all around him as he released my shoulder and made a heroic leap down into the center of the packed dirt square. I jumped down myself, but it wasn't nearly as pretty. I thumped down and staggered forward until he caught me, trying not to laugh as he hauled me back upright. Like you'd laugh when the cat fell off the table. "He assures me that the principles are simple enough for any lay-mage to acquire the spells needed to activate them. It was designed as a system of transit all across Amaranth, after all, not meant only for the elite geniuses of Talon's academies."

I glanced around at the gathered soldiery. None of them had impressive beards or robes. Mostly they looked tired and dirty. The few beards that were around looked less flowing and more like they'd just forgotten to shave for a few days. "I didn't know you had uh lay-mages."

Orphia stepped out of the shadow of the building I'd made my mad-dash escape through. She was not radiating joy. She was squirting out the opposite feeling. Not in the literal way that Leo was, just being her usual joy and delight to be around. She was scowling like if she looked angry enough about my new relationship with Leo, he might change his mind and murder me instead. She was really barking up the wrong tree.

Leofric paid her no mind. Eyes only for Asher. "What we do not have, we can make. There are some among the troops who can wield some measure of the power arcane. It will be a simple task to forge them into the tools that we require."

"So…" I didn't have a damn thing to say about forging people into tools that wasn't going to end in me calling him a tool. "What's the plan for today?"

"Brother Asher means to make a demonstration, I believe. To pass through the gate to whence you originated and then to return to us bearing some token of that place." He glanced at me, amused. It was so bizarre to be on this side of the inner circle, getting treated to all the good vibes I could stomach. It wasn't hard to see why people like Orphia would end up so desperate to fit in and be part of his gang. He had charisma. Charm. Just like every bully that had ever kicked me in the ass in school before I had my growth spurt and started kicking back. Everyone wanted to be on the bully's good side, to be part of the joke, instead of the butt of it. "I believe that he suggested bringing through a book from Talon's library, though I have my suspicions that it is only because he finds the company of my men to be less than intellectually stimulating."

I couldn't help but genuinely smile at that. "Dude loves a good book."

Mercy stepped out from amidst the gathered swarm of troops, slipping through them like she was a gust of air. When she decided to start talking to me again, I was really going to have to ask her how she did it. Everywhere we went, she didn't just fit in, she fit in so well she could slip through unnoticed. Maybe it was something to do with all her stealth skills, but I had a suspicion it was just her. Just like Seren was naturally graceful, and Asher was naturally snout-first in a book, Mercy blended in.

True to her word, she couldn't even look at me. The fact that Leo had slung an arm around me again probably didn't help. She stepped up beside Asher and started talking in a low, urgent tone. I couldn't pick out the words, but from the way that he stilled in his scribbling, I had a pretty good idea of what was up. He didn't look at me either as if by looking at me he'd be betraying what Mercy was whispering away to him. He very deliberately went back to writing.

Finally letting me out of that vice-like hug, Leofric turned to the crowd that had surreptitiously gathered around the top of the walls, waiting for the magic show. "The time has come for the tide of war to turn my friends. No longer must we cling to our fortifications and hope. Now the fight can be taken to the enemy, wherever they reside. In a moment, our dear friend Asher shall stride a thousand leagues in a single step, and soon, each and every one of you shall do the same."

A ragged cheer went up, but Leo didn't falter in his speechmaking. "From the safety of this great bastion, we shall be able to reach everywhere that the waystones are built, from the island paradise of Talon's Keep to the Dverbal Hinterlands and even to the Serpent's Gate. Everywhere that chaos has spread, we shall bring stability and peace as easily as stepping from our doorstep!"

The cheer was a bit more coordinated this time around, and it must have been loud enough for Leo to be satisfied. That's right, the supposed savior of the universe had the same ego as a children's entertainer, unwilling to move on until he got the clap he thought he was entitled to. The sooner we got away from this psycho the better.

He turned to Asher with a wide smile. "Brother Asher, have you had enough time to make your preparations?"

Asher glanced to me for less than a moment, but his deliberately expressionless face immediately set suspicion prickling up the back of my neck. It was hard to get a read on a lizard face at the best of times, and more often than not I was relying on the tilt of his head, the speed of his blinking, even the flick of his tongue to determine what he was feeling when he wasn't outright telling me. Right now, that deliberate stillness told me nothing. Which was a message in itself. He didn't want me to know what he was thinking. He gave a precise bow to Leofric, then raised his arms like a conductor, preparing to cast his spell.

If it hadn't have been for Mercy, I would have had no idea what was about to happen, Asher was the absolute master of the poker face. I never wanted to gamble against him. Mercy, on the other hand, she wore her heart on her sleeve, which was just as gruesome to look at as the metaphor implies. All the betrayal and hate and sorrow she was feeling welled up on her face as she met my eyes, and for one awful moment, I thought she might actually cry.

When it looked like he was about halfway into the elaborate casting, Asher flung his arms back at the waystone. All of the gathered crackling and half-formed magic leapt away from him in a rush, flooding the ring and making it blaze with light.

Mercy leapt through with one last, almost apologetic glance at me. Oh, that was not a good sign. She had stepped right on my nuts without feeling the need to apologize before. Asher flung himself backward once she was through, and the magic crackled out to catch him, whipping him away in a blaze of white-hot light into the ring and beyond.

I'd barely taken a step forward when the light died, and suddenly, I was all alone here, surrounded by enemies again. All eyes turned to me now that the magic show had gone sideways, and I had absolutely no rabbits to pull out of hats. "Uh."

Leofric's hand drifted down to his belt, to the Lucis hanging by his side, radiating power even sheathed. He growled, "What is the meaning of this?"

Orphia did not look confused by this turn of events. She looked delighted. She had already hefted her glaive ready to charge in at me. All she had needed was an excuse, and Mercy abandoning ship was exactly the right excuse. I didn't have a Solar to vouch for me anymore. Something that Leo had not specifically commanded had just happened, and control freak that he was, now he was going to have a tantrum about it.

Before he could even start, I turned to Leofric with my hands held up. Look how harmless I am. "I am as surprised as you."

"You don't look surprised," Orphia sniped as she crept in closer.

I pointed a finger-gun at her face. "Zip it, Stabarella!"

When I glanced back, it was like looking right into the sun. All of Leofric's attention was focused on me. All the light pouring from his eyes was on my face as he studied me. "She is correct, you do not seem at all taken aback that your allies have left you behind."

My voice nearly squeaked. Pretty hard to do when you've normally got the bass sound of tectonic plates humping. "Mercy. She's just a bit... flighty. Maybe she decided she just had to hop back and see some of her friends, or—"

"Or this was all a contrived attempt to gain my trust that has now faltered, and they mean to return in force when we least expect it." Leofric had turned to face me now, the crowds of soldiers scattering back while still trying to keep him in sight. Not because they were scared for the safety of their glorious leader but because they wanted to see the fireworks.

"Dude, we are nowhere near that organized."

His hand still hovered by his hip, fingers flexing. I didn't know what it would feel like if I got hit with that sword. None of the other shards actually did anything at the moment, but I figured that Leo's was different since it had been reforged. There was definitely some divine power stuck in those hunks of metal, and I dreaded to think what it could do if it was unleashed on my body. Maybe if I was lucky, it would only hurt as much as being hit with a sword. Which is a lot. "Perhaps that is why you were left behind in the retreat, this lack of organization."

I couldn't take my eyes off the sword on his hip. Orphia could have been doing the fandango beside me and I wouldn't have even noticed. All my attention was on him. "Leo, listen. We're on the same side here. We all want Araphel stopped. There is no need for you to do anything… hasty.

He sighed. "I should have known that any gift as grand as the one you presented me would come with a dagger for my back in the other hand."

"No." I rocked back on my heels, hands still right up in the air, empty. Look how harmless I am. You wouldn't hit a Faun with no weapons, would you? "No. That isn't—"

"Be silent, traitor."

My eyes darted to her for an instant, just reminding myself where she was. Too close. In striking distance already. "Orphia, if I wanted your opinion… Nope, sorry, that would never happen."

She didn't matter. She wouldn't do anything if I had Leofric on my side. I just had to remind him that we were on the same side. "Listen, Leo. I don't know why Mercy did that, but it doesn't change anything. I'm still here, I'm still your Warmaster. We can still take the fight to the Voidgod, yeah?"

There was a flush in his face that I didn't understand until his brows furrowed down. Here came that tantrum. "You have stolen the most vital armament of our crusade. Snatching the promise of the waystones from us on the eve of our triumphant march."

I let out a nervous laugh. "Asher will come back any minute now. I'm sure he will. He's probably just going to pick up a book, just like you planned."

"They are gone."

"They have abandoned you," Orphia added with unbridled joy.

I couldn't even argue with her. That was exactly what they had done. My only friends in the world, gone. Me, all alone in a castle full of enemies. Two Eternals ready to murder my stupid face off. Mercy's plan had really screwed me over.

It was time to go back to my plan.

CHAPTER 13

Plan A. My original plan had been super simple, just like me. Hit the bad guys. Take their stuff. It was the kind of genius planning that had got us this far in our quest to unite the shards and save the world. It was direct and to the point.

Of course, that plan hadn't really accounted for something like Leo, bubbling over with barely contained power and rage. Maybe I could have taken him in a fight if it was just the two of us, maybe I could have sprouted wings out my ass and taken off, but it wasn't going to be a fair fight. The moment that Orphia had the chance she was going to stab me in the back and keep on stabbing until there was nothing left. You could always rely on her that way, she was consistent.

Which left me with Plan B. Take their stuff and run away.

Easier said than done.

If I wanted the Lucis, I was going to have to pry it from Leo's cold, dead hands. I'll admit that was the kind of plan that normally would have given me warm fuzzy feelings, but right now, it wasn't practical.

We both went for the sword at the same time, and he would easily have beaten me to it—since he was so much faster, and it was attached to him—if it wasn't for that handy new trick that I'd picked up out in the desert. I hammered my Spirit Strike into his grimacing face, carrying only one thought. One word. Fumble.

Everyone makes mistakes, even thousand-year-old demi-gods. He yanked on the hilt of the Lucis, making it leap out of the scabbard, then for one brief glorious moment he lost his grip on it, and my big clumsy fingers wrapped around the soft leather. I hip-checked him as I yanked it free.

Quest: Return of the Voidgod
  Acquire Rusted Blade Shards: 3/6 Complete
  400 Glory Gained

I would have had more luck trying to smack the Bastion down with my ass. All that happened when I crashed into him was good old Newton's laws kicking in with the equal and opposite reaction, bouncing me off him and out of reach of his grasping gauntlet.

It had all happened so quickly, I barely even realized that it had worked before Leo was coming at me again. Seren's training kicked in. I spun away from those grabby gauntlets, bringing the Lucis around me in a circle to knock any attempted lunge away. It clipped off the side of Orphia's glaive as she tried to thrust it home, turning the blade aside and putting me inside her reach.

She started to backpedal still flailing the glaive around, trying to bring it to bear against me and doing nothing but forcing Leo to stay out of reach. Her eyes weren't on me anyway, they were locked on the sword. The symbol of Leo's power, in my hand. That had to sting the old ego a little bit.

Leo finally got it together enough to shout, "Stop."

The impact of the word washed over me, and I could feel my movements still involuntarily. That was the true power of that supernatural charisma of his. Just a word, and everyone froze like statues. Orphia was paralyzed, wide open to attack but infinitely more worried about pissing off her master than getting a blade through her gut. I hammered my fist into her instead, folding her around the punch and knocking her aside so I could get to the door.

This time, I knew the way out. If I could get up on the ramparts and grab a rope, I could drop down into the Ashlands and run like hell. Maybe hook back up with the Faun if I was lucky. My brain still hadn't fully wrapped itself around Mercy and Asher abandoning me to my death. That was the kind of thing that took some processing, and I did not have time right now to be getting weepy.

My shoulder took the door off its hinges, and I went on running, Lucis trailing behind me, Leo sprinting after me without a moment's delay. He was close enough that I couldn't hear for the clatter of his armor. Close enough that I could feel his fingertips brushing over the blade of the Lucis until I yanked it up in front of me. The door at the far end of the tunnel was shut, and in the time it took me to get through it, he would be on me.

Good thing we were in the heart of the wall now, not up on the surface where the Voidgod's death explosion had screwed everything up. Artifice washed out through the solid stone, and with a laugh, I slammed it shut behind me.

Leo hit the new wall with a clang and a roar of fury, but he was too damned late. I smashed through the door at the far end and was out into the courtyard before he could backtrack or, more likely given his temperament, smash his way through.

There was still good stone down beneath the packed dirt of the next courtyard, and when I reached for it and hauled it up beneath my feet, I was launched like a rocket into the air, soaring over the guards milling about beneath me and landing with a grunt and a roll on the next shattered rooftop.

The laugh that had escaped me when I shut a building in Leo's face had carried on, and I caught myself giggling away all the way to the side of the wall. There was no rope on this one, but it would be simple enough to bound along to the next one before Leo got his act together.

Or at least it should have been, but just as I was turning away from the uproar from the square I'd just added some striking stone pillars to, I caught a flash of movement in the periphery of my vision. If I didn't already have the Lucis in hand and moving, Orphia would have spitted me on the spot. As it was I turned it away just in time, yet again.

Every time she didn't manage to stab me, she looked genuinely surprised. You would think she'd be getting used to failure by now. "Oh, will you go away."

The blade sang by my head as she made a half-hearted swipe, and I had to duck. This close, I could see she had a crazed look on her face, not the usual narrowing with rage, but googly-eyed deranged bliss at the thought of my impending death. "You shall fall, and Leofric shall delight in none more than me."

"You were so weird when we first got here." I parried her next thrust, too slow to follow up on it. She was testing me, not trying for a kill. "How did you manage to get even weirder?"

"This world is hell, and we are here to suffer, to be refined by that suffering into living gods." She spoke as if it was any sort of explanation instead of yet more insane rambling. Maybe there was just something about being Alvaren-shaped that made you absolutely bug-nut crazy. Did the elegant skulls squish their brains?

She came in at me again, not the playful jabs that I'd been parrying but a real onslaught that I had to backpedal away from rapidly to avoid becoming Swiss cheese. I was just lucky she didn't have enough sense to circle around me and put my back to the drop, or I'd have been forced right off.

Why wasn't she smart enough to do that? I mean, she wasn't a genius or anything, but it wouldn't have been hard.

The Lucis was so light in my hand that it felt like I wasn't holding anything at all, and it had me clumsy and off-balance. If I wanted to waggle a fly-swat around then that's what I would have made. I couldn't use my strength with this thing for fear of the flimsy blade snapping in two. And the reach on the thing was less than the length of my arm. If Orphia had any Potency to speak of, the slaps I was using to turn her attacks aside would have been useless.

It was time for an upgrade.

The metal of my great-sword flowed around me in a wash that startled Orphia out of her latest attack and put her on the defensive. I hadn't been sure if this would work, what with the Lucis being super fancy and magical, but apparently, slapping a whole load of metal on top of it didn't interfere all that much. I'd have to fiddle with the grip of the thing later to get it properly comfortable in my hands, but for now, I had a decent giant cleaver to wave around.

So I waved it. Two great sweeping cuts left to right, then back again, sent Orphia scampering back out of reach. On her heels, she had the moment she needed to think. She gathered lightning around her glaive blade as she waited for an opportunity to unleash it on me, but I was not falling for that one again. I wasn't giving her a shield as a nice big target.

The air stank of ozone, and my hair stood on end each time that it swept by, but still, she couldn't make contact. I wasn't letting her hit me with that big pointy taser again. Once was enough for one lifetime, thank you very much. I danced back out of reach, hopping back in to make swift cuts and keep her from gaining too much ground when I could, still getting used to the weight of the rebuilt Lucis.

Even now, with the combined weight of the original sword and my own big chunky boy, it felt lighter in my hand than it should have, flowing through the motions I was trying to make with such ease that it threw me completely off balance. Maybe this was the super-power of having a chunk of Rusted Blade in your sword. Maybe if I ever actually hit someone with it, rainbows would come shooting out. At this rate, I was never going to find out.

The brief sweet window with no Leofric in my life was at an end. He hopped clean across the courtyard that I'd remodeled in a single bound to land by Orphia's side.

"You come into my home…"

He raised an empty hand, and a stream of luminous green lanced out from the palm. Not a zappy ray like I'd been expecting, but a continual squirt of liquid. Where it struck the stone, it ate through it. Where it clipped my pauldron before I had the chance to dodge away, it began to melt away to nothing. I had to pulse Artifice to toss my armor off before the acid ate through to flesh.

Still, Leofric roared. "You slaughter my people! …"

He lashed his hand across, and the line of acid struck off the ground and splashed up at me in a wave. I had to strain Artifice to yank stone up through the dead material on top of the Bastion to intercept it before it washed over me. Even the stone wasn't enough. The moment that the acid hit it, the whole lopsided wall I'd just managed to drag up started melting away. When it smoked away, Leo was still there, with both hands upraised and some new thrum of Primal energy gathering between them. "You steal my most prized artifact…"

When he snapped his hands apart, a Khorkhoi the same size as me leapt out of the green glow, launched at me like somebody loaded it into a worm cannon and lit the fuse. I caught it on the edge of the Lucis, splitting it in half, its own momentum doing all the cutting work for me until it toppled into two parts at my feet.

When I looked up from it, Leo was there. Right there in front of me. He'd moved so fast I didn't even see it happen. His face was a rictus of fury. "And then you dare to strike me?!"

I dared to strike him again. Whipping the sword up, still covered in worm guts, to bury it in his crotch. He sidestepped it with the same disinterest that he did everything as if I hadn't almost made him sing soprano, and his fist caught me square in the chest.

There had been no wind up, no indication that a blow was even coming. One second he was standing there, the next I was hit.

Surprise took the air out of my lungs as much as the impact. The pain arrived after I'd skidded back a few feet over the ruined rooftop. Whatever got popped and healed earlier was still tender, and the broken ribs jabbing down into it were not making things better for it. There was a visible dent in my chest when I looked down, and worse yet, that same acid he'd been spraying around willy-nilly was splattered right in there, burning away at me.

It wasn't the worst pain I'd ever experienced, but it was right up there with demon-spider-god poison.

He must have enjoyed the look of horror on my face when I glanced up because he didn't immediately punch my whole head off. Instead, he crossed his arms and smiled. The acid was eating out from the point of impact. Sizzling away my skin, my bones, my everything.

Orphia took her chance while I was distracted by impending death and swung for me, the flat of her blade hitting the side of my head and discharging with a thunderclap.

Everything went black.

If it had just been the glaive smack, I probably would have been out for the count, but the lightning racked down through my body, lighting up every nerve with agony on its way to earth. If my heart had stopped beating, that zapped it back into action.

Every massive muscle in my body contracted as the storm passed through, and I was in mid-air by the time I snapped awake again. That helped with springing back to my feet but not much. Most of the muscles I'd usually use for sitting up were gone, eaten away by Leo's acid. I was well on my way to having the flattest tummy on Amaranth, and I couldn't do a single sit-up. I pulsed Restoration through my body, and it was almost immediately overwhelmed by the sheer power disparity of the Primal acid arrayed against it. No sooner did something heal than it was eaten away again, giving me all the pain of having it eaten away again too.

Still, I managed to twist and stumble to my feet, lashing out with Artifice to throw up a wall between me and the murderous smug expressions on Leo and Orphia's faces. It didn't work quite right. I fumbled it, and instead of hauling up stone from beneath the Void-touched rock, I just shot out random spurs of stone from where the wall was still alive to my senses. They crisscrossed and jutted out at weird angles and did nothing to stop Leo taking careful aim with his palm and readying another blast of lethal acid.

My body was in ruins, and only grim determination was keeping the Lucis in my hand, but none of that did anything to dim my divine gifts. This time I made the same mistake again, on purpose: reaching with Artifice, not to put a barrier between us, but to hit them with the up-thrust of stone.

Where the rock burst up into Leo's godly flesh it stopped dead, but my girl Orphia hadn't been buffing herself up nearly as thoroughly. When the rock pushed at her, she flew, one spike taking her in the thigh and launching her sideways, another hooking under her armpit to spin her around, and another just jabbing her in the back for some extra height.

I'd hoped that getting whacked with all that rock might have thrown Leo's aim off, but the spray of acid caught me square in the back all the same. There was nothing in this world or any other like a chemical burn for its pure pain potential, and I am not ashamed to say that when it washed in a searing line from my hip to my face that I screamed like a tiny baby that had just pooped itself. I mean it was high-pitched, and it was grating; I was having a real bad time.

The acid that poured into the hollow where my torso used to be just sped up the destruction of whatever internal organs I still had left. The popped thing from earlier was just straight up gone now, along with all the wibbly sausage-looking coils that I'd been trying to hold in as I ran. The ribs that had been crushed in had fallen to melt into paste on the stone. When I looked down, I could see spine glistening in the sunlight of Leofric's gaze.

[42/1270 Health]

Leofric brushed aside the stone around him like cobwebs and began to advance once more, not even bothering to part the stone when he could walk right through it. My back was to the empty sky, and I had nowhere left to run.

Dying didn't scare me. I knew it wasn't the end. I knew that I'd be able to come back again and again until whatever I was up against was ground to dust. But I hated defeat. No, actually that wasn't true, I could roll with losing a few times, I just hated losing to this asshole. Leo strode towards me in his shiny golden armor, acid and poison dripping from his fingertips as he closed in on me, and I knew, I just knew he was going to try to make this as slow and painful as it possibly could be. He was going to revel in it. I'd shown him up. I'd done the things that he could never do, and now he was going to hurt me to make himself feel better about it. Well, screw that, I was nobody's punching bag.

My legs were done for, lost to my senses and possibly detached by this point. It didn't matter, I still had two strong arms attached to a body that was a hell of a lot lighter than I was used to, I flipped over to drag my raw dangling ribs and guts across the ragged stone. Oh, that hurt a lot.

I was trailing a smear of Maulkin slime behind me like a snail as I dragged myself closer and closer to the edge of the wall. Leofric sounded like he was yawning. "I do not wish to climb down to retrieve my stolen property. Stop him."

I was so lost in becoming sauce that I hadn't even noticed Orphia make her crunchy landing, or whenever she'd climbed over the top of my little stone fence to stand beside me, sneering. I looked up at her, blood and liquidized organs dribbling down my chin, and despite it all, I still pitied her for what she'd become.

Her face was twisted in a mask of delight as she swung her glaive blade for my face.

If she'd just stabbed me, I would have been done, but Orphia, she hated my face, she absolutely had to go for the flashy face smash. Plus, I'm sure she wanted to do something impressive in front of her new sugar daddy.

I surged Vitality and caught the blade in my teeth.

One side of my face already hung open from the acid, and the glaive cut into the other, opening up a wider grin than Faun faces were ever meant to have, but the top of my head did not pop off like she'd wanted. I surged Potency too and bit clean through the metal as Orphia gawked at me.

More blood poured from my ruined mess of a face, but through it all my laughter gurgled. Even now she couldn't beat me. Even now, I was better than her.

She tried to jerk her shattered glaive back, but I caught hold of the haft, and we had a little wrestle until finally she worked out that she could brace the back end on the rock and haul it straight up until my weight worked against me.

I was hefted into the air for just a moment, one eye still functioning well enough to see the ash dunes spread out before me, and I used every last drop of my surged Potency to fling myself forward. I didn't know how much of me was still attached by that point, but I guess there was still enough to belly-flop off a cliff.

The wind whipped by me, whistling, and the world spun end over end. I closed my eyes before I saw the ground leaping up to meet me, and I turned all that was left of my focus inward, lighting up the Pillar of Aether in a blinding column of moonlight.

Then everything went dark.

[0/1270 Health]

It had been a while since the last time that I died. I hadn't actually done it since I first arrived on Amaranth despite the best efforts of literally every living thing I'd met. Which meant that I wasn't actually all that sure what would happen next. The pain stopped. So that was nice.

I kind of figured that I'd just open my eyes and be in my shiny new fresh-built body. Apparently, it didn't work like that. At least, not immediately.

My other senses, the ones that weren't tied to my body, slowly came back to life, and I could see my upper body lying there at the bottom of the wall. My legs lay a distance further along, having finally snapped off in the breeze as I fell. My face was almost all bare skull thanks to the ever-advancing acid. Even that bone was perforated and crumbling, adding to the ashes piled up at the base of the wall.

"Could have done without seeing that."

I didn't currently have a stomach, so I couldn't feel sick, but watching my body like that made me uncomfortable in a whole load of other ways. Thankfully, I didn't have to watch long.

Death was by my side, like he'd been there all along and I just hadn't noticed before now. He swept one sleeve of his robes through the air, a glint of bone protruding past the edge of the rough black fabric. My body was wiped away by the motion. Now you see it, now you don't.

"Thanks."

Death inclined his head towards me in a little nod. Then abruptly, I felt a tug like a big elastic band had just been attached around my middle. It was the same sensation I felt when my awareness lingered in a part of my Sphere of Influence that my body was moving away from. Like I was off-center. The only difference was, this wasn't my dumb meat staggering away from me as I tried to do some Artifice work. This time the body I was meant to be attached to was half a world away.

I managed to yelp out, "Bye!" to Death before the world started whipping by.

With no body, I didn't have to worry about hitting anything in between me and my destination, but that didn't mean seeing it all fly by me at supersonic speeds wasn't a little bit disconcerting. I zoomed through the Bastion and was soaring over the kingdom beyond before I had time to recognize a thing, then there were fields and forests and ruins and cities and a massive ravine. Rivers and ponds. Swamps thick and buzzing. More desolate muddy nothing with some great beasts loping about, half-hollowed mountains, grass, water, all flying by so fast I couldn't comprehend the details. The ocean lingered a little longer, then I was back to Talon's Keep, to my Shrine. To my body.

I sank gratefully into my flesh as it formed, sighing like an exhausted man flopping into bed. A base need was driving me to nestle inside it where I belonged, my poor spirit rubbed raw by exposure to the world outside. Hermit crabs. That was what it reminded me of. Eternals were hermit crabs, and bodies were shells.

One staggering step forward was all I managed before I was slammed off my feet. I had a sword in hand, but my armor was gone, and this thing was inside my defenses already, grappling with me as it bore me to the ground, pinning me for just an instant before it reared back to strike, and my brain caught up. Seren smiled down at me before hammering a kiss home.

CHAPTER 14

The kissing went on for quite some time, and I really wasn't complaining. After the day that I'd just suffered through, I had earned some smoochy time.

She eventually jerked back as though something had stung her, which wasn't impossible since we were all camped out in the jungle. From the blue blush that chased over her face, I realized that it was just propriety. The dvergar working around us weren't staring, but there was no way that they'd missed us making out. "You have returned."

With some effort, I hoisted myself back up to sitting. The body still felt like it was settling in. Like all the wires hadn't been fully connected yet. Or like it was a new shoe that still pinched a little. "I have!"

She put a foot on my shoulder and pushed me back down, scowling. "You were defeated."

"Well, I got what I wanted, and they didn't, so I'm going to call it a win." I shrugged, and her knee wobbled up and down. "Even if I had to die to get it."

Her eyes fell on the Lucis, now returned to its normal shape and size since I'd left all my metal and other gear behind. I was kind of surprised that I'd gotten the whole thing. When I used Soulbond on it during my plummet, I'd been expecting just to nab the shard. Getting a handy sword in the deal was great. "You have successfully recovered another fragment of the weapon?"

"Yup, we're halfway there." I held the sword out, and she gingerly took it from my grasp to study it more closely. "Two more stops on the quest express and we'll be ready for Araphel."

She took a couple of practice swings with the blade, learning its balance, smiling softly at the craftsmanship. "And once more you have left powerful enemies in thy wake, baying for your blood and planning to obliterate you and all you hold dear."

I smiled at her again, sheepishly. "You know me so well."

She let the sword droop to her side and pinched the bridge of her nose. "Perhaps just once, you might actually destroy an enemy instead of allowing grudges against you to fester?"

"Hey, I did kill one super-powered grudge-bearing dude." I made my way back to my feet, still unsteady, like a little baby horse. "One out of two ain't bad."

When her hand fell away, she was glowering at me. "Then you may spend half of the night in my bed and the other half on the cold stone floor contemplating your actions."

"Can I take you down onto the floor with me?"

She had flushed blue again, but before she could give me an answer, her head snapped around. "Your kin have returned."

You could hear them before you could see them, emerging from the forest in the middle of what I'd normally have called a raging argument, except only one of them was yelling. Mercy, predictably enough, was bellowing at the top of her lungs, while Asher spoke so softly it made me wonder if Mercy even heard him over the noise of her stamping feet.

"…Killed somebody for no reason at all. You can't trust someone that murders people to make their life easier. That's like trusting a shark, or Seren. It is crazy…"

If Seren was insulted by the comparison, she didn't show it. Amoral apex predator from the dawn of time seemed like a pretty apt description for her if you took out the fishy bits.

Asher stopped dead in his tracks at the sight of me. Was he relieved to see me? Upset? Give me something, lizard face. Anything.

It took Mercy a moment to notice him frozen in the middle of a soothing rebuttal and spin around, but when she did, there was no hiding her expression. Pure dismay. Like I'd just hauled down my trousers and taken a dump in her breakfast cereal.

I've got to be honest, I was a little bit pissed at them. So I waved, smiling wide, although not as wide as Orphia had made me. "Welcome home, guys! How was your trip?"

Mercy's frozen expression told me nothing, but Asher was ever a creature of good manners. "Our traversal of the arcane network proceeded as well as could be expected given the demand for hasty recalculations. How went your own… journey?"

I advanced on them, still grinning so hard I worried my teeth might crack. "Oh you know, I was doused in acid, attacked by a giant worm, had half my face hacked off and my brain electrocuted, lost both my legs, and fell off a mile-high wall. You know. The usual."

Mercy sniped back immediately, "Oh no. Did your new besties not like it when we took their teleporter away?"

Asher bent almost double in a bow. "I beg your forgiveness, I did not know what was intended when Mercy informed me that we had to depart. It is only since my arrival here, and her subsequent interruptions of my attempts to re-open the waystone network, that I came to understand it was her intention to abandon you."

All of the training really had paid off. I had an arm out to catch Seren before she'd even drawn her swords. "No! No! We are not attacking each other. We are on the same side. We just need to talk."

Seren struggled in my arms. If I hadn't spent a month learning all the ins and outs of the way she could twist and turn then she would have broken free, but now all I had to do was hoist her up onto my shoulder so she lost her traction as she roared, "She left you there to die?!"

Okay, kind of hard to argue with that when a) they left me and b) I died, but I tried to play it down anyway. "Technically yes, but it is all just a misunderstanding."

"A misunderstanding?" Mercy barked. "Oh, so you didn't just murder some guy to win a psycho's trust?"

She really wasn't making it easier to stop Seren killing her, and honestly, my temper was a tad frayed after getting six colors of crap kicked, chopped, and melted out of me. When I snapped back, it was a roar that sent the closest Dvergar running for cover. "He was cuckoo for coconuts too! They're all crazy, all the old Eternals! They've all been fighting each other so long that they can't understand a world where there is anything other than fighting each other."

Now that I was angry, it seemed to make things easier for her, like she'd been off balance before and having someone to fight against was putting her back on an even keel. "How convenient for you."

I tossed Seren back down onto her feet and stormed over to Mercy myself, that same cold rage gripping the base of my guts and creeping up into my chest, softening my roar into a bitter whisper. "You know what would have been convenient? If he hadn't been. If he would have listened to a single word I was saying to him instead of jumping to the worst possible conclusion just like you are doing right now."

"Aww"—she pouted—"did he not want to be best friends either?"

"Are you serious right now," The rage flared in the face of her mockery. Mercy making a joke at my expense was usually how she showed she cared, but now all my feelings were getting twisted up. "After what you just pulled?"

She shrugged as if a horned giant wasn't looming over her. "What do you care? You got what you wanted from the start anyway. Or is that not golden boy's sword I see in Seren's hand."

Seren snapped back. "You shall soon see it run through you, vexatious wretch."

I let a little laughter rumble out despite myself. Despite everything. "Hey, hey, let's not call people names, even if they are hilarious old timey names."

Seren scowled at me now. "From the beginning this one has treated you without respect. From the beginning she has questioned your choices, fought your every decision. I do not understand why you have not cast her out."

"Because we're friends." All the anger washed out of me when I told the truth of it, leaving behind a sad ache.

Good thing Seren had enough anger for all of us put together. "She left you to die. This is not the action of an ally, let alone kin."

This was never going to be fixed if one of us didn't try to reach out to the other, and since Mercy clearly wasn't done being petty, I decided I had to be the bigger man. Figuratively, as well as literally. I reached out my empty hand to her. "Friends make mistakes."

She looked at my hand as if it was the turd I'd dropped in the cornflakes. "Murder isn't a mistake."

Asher finally spoke up. "Mercy, it cannot have escaped your notice that violence has often been the only solution to the problems that this world faces."

"He killed another Eternal and paraded his severed head around like it was a trophy. He has gone so far off the deep end I don't even know how to…" she trailed off with a look on her face like she'd now taken a spoonful of the cereal.

"What? You thought Leo was just going to believe me when I told him I'd killed someone who can't die?" She glared at me, but I was sick of being treated like this. "You think he'd just take it on trust? I needed to show him something, and Koschei's head was already off."

Before Mercy could come snarling back at me, Asher held up his hands, then very carefully asked, "Maulkin, tell us why his death was a necessity."

Finally, I was getting a chance to tell my side of it instead of the version that Mercy had just imagined up. "He was using the Faun, he'd been their… I don't know, their pope or something, for as long as any of them could remember. They were all dancing to his tune, living out in the middle of nowhere, eating worms to survive when they could have settled anywhere in the world. I tried to convince him we had bigger problems. I tried to… He used his powers, he looked inside my mind, he saw everything that had happened, and he still didn't believe me. He thought it was a trick or a trap or something. He tried to freeze me in a block of ice so I could never come back and bother him again."

Asher bobbed his head along to the rhythm of my words, then he turned to Mercy, "Then it does seem that his death was justified."

She pointed an accusatory finger. "Of course, Maulkin thinks it is justified. He's the one that did it!"

"Oh, like you would have done anything different if you'd been there instead of me." I didn't mean to roll my eyes, honestly. Maybe if they had still been glowing like the others it wouldn't have been so obvious, but they were dimmer now than they'd ever been.

"Of course I would have. I would have left!" Mercy almost cleared the distance to hit me before Asher's hand on her shoulder brought her to a halt. It was a good thing he was there. Seren was standing sullen and silent by my side, and if this turned physical, I didn't like Mercy's chances. Not against the two of us. "If the Faun want to eat worms, that's their business. You can't just stroll in and kill anybody that you don't like!"

"We kill monsters! All the time!" Okay, maybe I roared a little bit. Oops.

She yelled just as loud back at me. "Yeah, because they're monsters, not people!"

I pointed vaguely in the direction of where I thought the Bastion was, but it was a barely educated guess. "Leo, Orphia, all their lot, they think the Faun are monsters. Inyoka too. Some of them even think Dvergar are monsters. They definitely think that a Lunar Eternal is a monster. So tell me, where is the line?"

"Oh I'm right there with them now. You are a monster. I don't know if you've done something to yourself by attaching lumps of Rusted Blade to your soul, or if you were always like this and just… hiding it, but I've had enough!" The last words came out as a scream.

How long had this been building up before I killed somebody out of sight and gave her the excuse to melt down? Orphia had thought the worst about me from the get-go, and Mercy had hated her so completely at first sight that it almost seemed like we'd ended up on the same side by default. Had she been watching me out of the side of her eye all this time, just waiting for me to show my true colors.

Back on the boat when I'd lost my cool and Seren had nearly… When I did what I did, Mercy had been the one to come see me, to ask me how I was feeling. Was that all just a prelude to this? Had she been looking then for the same excuse to hate me that she'd found now?

She turned to Asher with a quiver in her voice after all the yelling. "We're leaving. There are still three shards out there that we need to find if we want to stop all this Voidgod stuff. No point sitting around."

I sighed. "You need me."

"No!" she snapped back. "We don't!"

Asher spoke softly, consolingly, "Mercy."

I cut her off before she could storm away. "I know where the Faun shard is."

Her eyes narrowed. "Then tell us. Prove you aren't the monster we think you are. Tell us where it is."

"Mercy." Asher was a little louder now, but not loud enough to get past all the self-righteousness she'd stuffed in her ears.

I crossed my arms. "Nowhere you can go without me."

"Oh save the cryptic messiah crap for somebody that is buying it." She went for her bow. I'd been expecting it throughout the whole argument, but there was still some part of me that had hoped she wouldn't actually draw a weapon on me. That our friendship still meant that much to her. "Tell us where it is!"

"Mercy!" Asher's shout stopped her dead in her tracks.

She turned on him, snarling, "What?!"

"We must stay together." His arms sank to his sides.

It was her turn to have the wind taken out of her sails. "Are you kidding me? You're taking his side?"

Asher was unflappable. "There are no sides. We all serve the same purpose. We all seek the Voidgod's end."

"He is killing people!" She was yelling in his face, but Asher didn't even blink. Did he even have eyelids?

He cocked his head to one side. "If that is so, how many more would he kill without our presence enforcing restraint."

Her face and her resolve crumpled into confusion again. "What?"

Asher strode between us like he was giving a lecture to some students, claw pointed up as he pontificated. "Let us assume that your supposition is true, that your erstwhile friend has fallen to some evil and murderous urges, who in this world could better prevent him from acting upon those impulses than us?"

Mercy looked disgusted. "You want us to be his jailers? His keepers?"

"We seek the Voidgod's end. Whatever else you might think of Maulkin, there is no denying that he has strength that has carried us through conflict and strife many times before." He spun to face Mercy. "Would you let him run loose to do what harm he may or set a harness upon him and turn him once more towards our goal?"

It took me a second to scrape back through all the memories of my past life to understand exactly where I'd seen someone behaving like him before, then High School loomed its ugly head and I remembered. He thought he was in a debating contest. He thought he could win this by throwing logic at her.

As a person who's first and only resort in a debate was talking about the size of the other dude's mother, I decided to keep my mouth shut and let him do his thing. Wasn't like he could screw things up more than I'd already managed just by living.

Mercy seemed to be at a loss for a moment. She'd been ready for a screaming argument about whether or not I'd gone bad, not a reasoned debate based on the idea that what she was saying was right. Eventually, she said, "How are we meant to trust him?"

Asher looked at me to see if I was going to start yelling, but I gave him a tight-lipped smile. Oops, Mercy didn't like that. Her scowl drew down so low the tiny sun in each of her eyes looked like it was setting upside down. And she was back to yelling again. "How are we ever meant to trust him again when he does stuff like this?"

"Trust is earned with time." Asher strode between us, breaking Mercy's glower. That was why he kept walking back and forth. He thought that we were like Siamese fighting fish, and if we couldn't see each other we'd knock it off. "Perhaps as our journey continues, you shall find evidence in his actions that Maulkin can be relied upon once more. But if we part ways, how could that reconciliation ever take place."

Mercy shot that down without pause for breath. "So I'm just meant to forget that he's gone off the deep end?"

"You are meant to weigh all his actions and judge him on their merit." Asher kept speaking softer and softer, the angrier that Mercy got. This time even I had to lean in a little bit to catch everything.

She glanced from me to Seren with a sneer. "Sounds like a good way to get stabbed in the back."

"Then Maulkin shall march at the front, as he ever has." Asher said it as though it was the most obvious thing in the world, taking her literally in that way that he sometimes did, when you couldn't be sure if he actually didn't understand you or if it was some kind of joke.

Mercy nodded to Seren. "And his stabby little sex toy?"

Seren already had the Lucis in hand before all of this started, and she'd drawn her other sword from her belt as she leapt forward. I had nothing. No weapons, no armor, no plan. I had to surge Potency and launch myself after her if I wanted Mercy to survive the next seconds.

I caught the back of her belt and yanked her back down to earth, and the blades swished harmlessly through the empty space in front of Mercy's face. Two inches further and she'd have had a free nose-job. With a sound like a wounded animal, Seren spun at me, grip reversing on the Lucis and the tip driving back for my chest. She wouldn't really kill me. I was sure of that. 90% sure. Mostly sure. Oh crap, she was stabbing me.

Already bleeding, I stumbled to the side as a line opened up across the rags that had been draped over my new body, and the lower half of them fluttered away on the breeze. If she hadn't been hitting me with the same move every time I got behind her in training for the past month, I'd have been spitted.

There was nothing for me to fight back with, so I reached out with Artifice. My senses flooded after so long in the desert and the Bastion where so much had been void-touched and inert. Life bloomed everywhere around us, stone and sand and dirt were heaped in layers beneath our feet, and the boundary fence was in easy reach too. None of which would make me a damned weapon.

Seren charged for Mercy once more, swords drawn back in lethal symmetry, the tips would end their course on the far side of her body, and Mercy was still just standing there. She'd gone for her bow again, she'd started to get her feet under her, but nobody could move as fast as the Alvaren. Their bodies moved at the speed of thought, obeying without any of the indecision or reaction time delays us mere mortals suffered through.

Stone leapt up between them. Not a solid wall, because I didn't have enough stone in ready reach close to the surface, but interlocking bars of the stuff shooting up at odd angles, just like I'd hauled out of the Bastion roof. Back then I'd been facing somebody so strong the rock had crumbled at his touch, here I just had Seren to contend with.

The rock latticed around her swords as they thrust, knocking them off angle until more sprouts of stone could lock them in place. She abandoned them, leapt back, and was ready to go up over the top of the makeshift shield I'd thrown up when I caught her around the waist and bore her down to the ground.

She squirmed and writhed to get out from under me, using every trick she'd ever shown me in the brief wrestling sessions that had preceded weapons training. She was nimble and experienced and could work leverage I didn't even know existed, but she was also small. Compared to me, most people were. My weight crushed down onto her and knocked the wind from her lungs. Even still she bunched up her legs beneath me and kicked up, launching me end over end through the air.

Throughout all of this, Asher was still just standing there chatting away. "Seren has always chosen her own course but heeded Maulkin's council. So long as he does not degenerate openly into conniving villainy, I suspect that she will be restrained from violence."

With her momentary freedom, Seren had sprung back to her feet and was darting forward once more. I caught her heel just before it slipped out of reach, and she fell, twisting around as she did to hammer her other foot into my face. That was downright rude.

She tried for another kick, and I flung myself forward, relying on my weight to carry me through again. Her booted toes scraped over my ribs, but there was flesh on those ribs again, so even though it hurt, it still felt like a dawdle compared to the last beating I'd taken.

She was sullen and silent as I crawled up the length of her and collapsed with a hand over her mouth. The cold fury seemed to have left her, judging by the playful way she bit into my palm. Then finally, I managed to get a word in. "If this is going to work, I need you to not kill Mercy."

I carefully moved my hand to let her speak her piece, and I tried not to enjoy it too much when her cool breath washed over my face. "Are you deafened to the insult that she has done me? Do you have no care? Does honor demand no satisfaction?"

"Seren…" I had no idea how we were getting out of this one with everyone alive. "She is going to apologize, then we're all going to get along, just like before."

Mercy had stepped around the lattice of stone, which I noticed was already crumbling to pieces. Not surprising, given how hastily it had been put together. She sneered at the two of us entangled on the ground. "The hell I am."

Asher was examining the stonework like it was the most interesting thing going on. "Mercy, it seems the only course that will not end in bloodshed."

"I don't care." She nocked an arrow. "I can take her."

I had eased off Seren a bit, and she used that extra space to squirt out from under me like a torpedo, throwing herself into a roll that ended with her on her feet and her hands back on the hilts of the swords locked in the crumbling stone. "Rank arrogance as befits such churlish bespawler." She whipped them out of the dissolving rocks and spun them over her hands. "Let my blades give answer, and we shall see how the snoutband fares."

I couldn't help myself. Obviously, I couldn't help myself. Nobody would want to make this situation worse than it already was. I snorted. "Wow, really rolling out the old timey insults today."

She leveled the tip of the Lucis at me, but it couldn't have cut me nearly as deeply as the pain in her eyes. "You make mockery of me too?!"

Clambering to my feet, I held up my hands in supplication, shaking my heavy head from side to side, just in case I wasn't being clear enough when I said, "No. Of course not. She shouldn't have said… any of the stuff she said. I'm sorry. And she's going to say sorry too."

Mercy sniffed. "I'm really not."

"For…" I had been doing a good job keeping my own temper under control up until now. I was willing to kick back and let logic boy do his thing. Following him through to whatever solution he came up with that would let us all work together again, but now I was finding the prospect of Seren hacking Mercy up more and more appealing. "Mercy could you just think for a second before you talk. Are you that desperate to die?"

Wind began to coil around her, not taking form around the arrow thrumming on her bowstring but lingering. Getting ready. Mercy's brows drew down. "I can take her!"

I had to close my eyes so that the hate I could feel building up inside me didn't shine out. This was Mercy. She was my friend. Sometimes friends had little fights. She wasn't the enemy. I kept telling myself, over and over. She was my friend. When my mouth moved, my voice came out so low it set what was left of the stone lattice shaking. "No. You can't. You can't take me either. You definitely can't take both of us. Maybe Asher weighs in for you, maybe he doesn't, but either way, you die. Over nothing."

She twisted to line up her arrow on me instead of Seren. That was good news. I could take the hit and bounce back. Seren would just die. Mercy snarled, "So what? I'll just come back again!"

I spread out my empty hands in a sweeping gesture. "Where? You can't think we'd leave your shrine intact. How does losing everything help you?"

Her eyes narrowed as she hissed back, "At least I'd be away from you."

Tempers were running high. Maybe me and Mercy had never been friends, maybe all the little secrets I'd been keeping had shown through and finally tipped her off that something wasn't right about me. I didn't know which. All I knew was that I didn't want whatever we had together to end like this. "Mercy, I know you don't believe me, but it doesn't matter. We all need each other. This thing we're doing, it is bigger than any one of us. We need to see it through."

"I know that. You think I don't know that. You think that you're the only one worrying about the whole world ending when you could have stopped it?"

I could see the weight of it on her shoulders for the first time. I'd been blundering through this whole world like I was having a great time, Asher had been so lost in the joy of learning about everything and everywhere that this was like a holiday for him too. Mercy was the only one who hadn't been delighted to land here. She wouldn't talk about her life before, except the little sparse hints that we'd managed to cobble together. Maybe she'd been happy there. Maybe this place was hell for her.

There was no point trying to mend burning bridges right now. "I don't need you to be my friend if you don't want to be, I just need for us to move on from this. To keep moving forward. Otherwise, the bad guy wins."

"Oh now you're a believer in this big magical quest that we've all been dumped in the middle of." She scoffed, but the arrow aimed at my head slowly lowered, first to my heart, then to my crotch. It lingered there for considerably more time than it really needed to before she pointed it down and eased off the pressure on the string. "You used to be even more skeptical than me about it. What a convenient change of heart."

"Yeah, I am a believer actually." I was as surprised to say it as she was to hear it. "I believe in what we're doing. I believe that it matters."

"So what, you had an epiphany? A miraculous vision?" Every word was dripping with so much sarcasm I was surprised it didn't look like Leo's acid spray. "Did one of the gods drop in and tell you that we should believe everything the pasty lizard told us?"

I had really been hoping to hold off on any more revelations or arguments for one night, but I didn't want to hold anything back and get accused of being a liar later. Not when I already had so many different things that I really didn't want them to know about. "Kind of."

Asher's head tilted to the side as I said that like I was an interesting specimen under his microscope. "Has some event occurred to allay your suspicions? I must admit that your newfound faith is something of a surprise to me also."

Time to just spit it out. Get it out in the open. Stop worrying about one of the many dirty little secrets that had been keeping me up at night. It even sounded ridiculous to me when I said it. "I saw Araphel."

"What?" Seren head snapped around. It kind of made sense that she'd be the one to freak out about the prospect of the Voidgod already being back, what with having lived through the first Revelation and all the fun that brought.

I gave her a little smile, meant as a comfort, but she went on staring like I'd just transformed into a giant jellybean. "My spirit touch, it lets me see the history of things, and the Rusted Blade…"

"You saw the means by which he was slain?" Asher was almost tripping over his own feet to get to me in his excitement. In a hoarse whisper, he asked, "You know how he means to return?"

"No, it is more like… his ghost is still haunting the sword bits." Seren dropped the Lucis and then took a step away from it for good measure. "He… he spoke to me."

"Well, now some of the psycho killer stuff makes a bit more sense! How long have you been having casual chats with the god of dark and evil?" While Asher had scampered over like a happy little puppy,

Mercy stalked towards me like a big cat with prey in sight.

"I've only done it twice since we got Talon's shard!" I wasn't sure why I felt like I had to defend myself. I suppose that it was guilt. I'd known from the first moment I heard Araphel that they'd want to know all about it. I should have told them. Just like I knew that right at that moment I should have been telling them everything. Throwing myself on Mercy's mercy. The truth was, "It scared the hell out of me the first time it happened."

She was easing tension back into her bowstring. Slow, like I wouldn't notice her doing it. Like I couldn't see her gathering the elemental power she used for her big blast shots around her too. "So what did the Voidgod's ghost say?"

Man if she was mad before, she really wasn't going to like this. "He offered me a deal."

"I knew it!" Guess I was wrong. She didn't look mad, she looked delighted. Vindicated. "I knew something was up. You got all black-veiny when you strapped the shard into your soul, and your eyes went out and… I knew you'd turned evil because of the Voidgod."

I pressed on with my story. She wasn't actively trying to murder me, so the more of it I could get out before the fighting started, the better it would be for me. "He promised me that if I kept all the shards apart, if I threw them in the sea or buried them for him, then when he came back, he'd let us live. He'd… give us a part of the world that was safe and ours."

"So you just handed him the universe so that you could be comfortable?!" She looked at me with such contempt I could almost feel myself shrinking. "What the hell is wrong with you?"

The proud booming voice of mine that made stone shake and monsters flinch was whittled down to a whisper by the time that I answered her. "I said no."

"Oh yeah, right." She strode off, throwing her hands in the air.

"Oh my gods, this explains everything. All the time you suddenly didn't want to hunt shards any more, when you were so content to just lounge around with your new girlfriend. You gave up. You kept us here while Araphel came back. I can't believe that you…"

Asher had been looking at me curiously throughout all of her ranting and raving, but now he spoke up. "Mercy, he has just stolen a third shard."

She glanced back over her shoulder. "So?"

"Why would he have collected another fragment of the weapon if he meant to keep them separated?" Asher looked from her to me and back. "Even if you fear that we cannot trust his words, his actions speak louder."

At least one person believed in me. "I told him to shove his deal up his ass. He wouldn't be offering little people like us a deal if he wasn't running scared. If we can get the sword, we can kick his ass."

"That's great, super, but why are we only just hearing about all this now? If you've been chatting it up with the Voidgod and it is all good news, why not tell us all this?" She came back at me, all accusatory fingers and snarls. I was getting real tired of looking at her snarling. She was much prettier when she smiled. Although if I'd said that, I had pretty good odds of my next words being, "Ow, I have an arrow in my face."

"When, Mercy? When was I meant to have told you? You wouldn't stand still and listen to me for a second back at the Shattered Bastion."

She threw back her head and laughed, but it wasn't anything like the barks of amusement that a particularly good jibe would draw out of her. It was bitter. "Oh so you just happened to have this convenient catch-up with the Voidgod in between murdering Eternals in the desert."

"Even if I'd had the chance, why would I tell you anything when you're just looking for an excuse not to trust me?"

She let go of both arrow and bow to shove me. She wasn't strong enough to actually move me from the spot, but I rocked back on my heels as she yelled in my face. "Oh I see, you've been keeping everything a secret because I'd be angry at you for keeping secrets! That makes so much sense!"

Seren's voice came slithering into the conversation. She had no expression on her carefully trained face, but her words held a chill. "He owes an uppity retainer no explanation."

Asher's eyes widened, and I had to shout to be heard over the explosion of rage from Mercy. "Whoa! Slow it down there."

She was going for Seren now, and I had to throw myself between them to keep them from each other's throats. Mercy roared, "What the hell does that mean?"

"I forget what a laggard you are." Just one of Seren's eyebrows raised, but on that placid face it spoke volumes. "I say that you have ideas above your station."

Mercy's mouth fell open. "My station?"

Seren wasn't throwing herself up against me like Mercy was, she was too refined for that. Instead, she leaned back a little before making her jibes. "You are but a servant of Maulkin, and it would behoove you to treat him with the respect that he is due."

"You think that he's my boss?" Mercy let out another bark of bitter laughter. I really could have done without catching it right in the face.

When Seren looked Mercy up and down, you just knew that she didn't like what she was seeing. It was the classic high school mean girl contempt look, as performed by an immortal warrior from the dawn of time. "Ever has he been your leader, guiding your course, yet you expect him to explain every choice that he makes? To share his every thought and secret at your command? What soft lives you must have lived, so far from the fields of battle that you have never learned that obedience is a retainer's first and last duty. That immediacy supplants contemplation. It matters not why we are commanded, only that we obey."

It actually succeeded in shutting Mercy up for a whole second. Her mouth hung open, and finally, she turned to look at me and yell, "What the hell?"

Meanwhile, I could hear Asher powering up for another lecture behind me. "I believe that you may have fundamentally misunderstood our triumvirate, placing us within the hierarchical structures to which you are more accustomed… you see—"

I said, "Everyone, shut up."

To my surprise, they actually did.

I let the peace hold for just one blissful moment, then I spoiled it all by speaking. "We could talk ourselves around and around in circles all day. All that matters is, we're all on the same side, we all want Araphel dead, and we need to put the sword back together to kill him. Right?"

Asher nodded carefully. "That is correct."

"I suppose so." Mercy shrugged.

Seren remained silent, still glowering at Mercy as though her gaze alone might carve a hole through her.

I nudged her. "Right?"

She could hardly make her big speech about obedience to Team Maulkin and then argue with me in front of everyone. Still, she didn't look pleased when she nodded. "As you say."

I blew out a little sigh of relief. It wasn't much, but it was a start. "So what we need to do now is move forward. I know where to find the next shard. I know how to get us there. All we need to do is settle all this crap down enough that we can go get it. So"—I swallowed hard to keep my emotions in check but did what needed to be done—"Mercy, I am sorry I kept secrets from you. Doesn't matter why I did it. Doesn't matter how long I did it. I shouldn't have. Now do you have something to say to Seren?"

"Fine! Whatever! Sorry, I said you were a pointy-eared blow-up doll." She did not sound very sorry. "It isn't like me saying sorry is going to stop her from cutting my head off the next time I turn around."

The fact that she'd said the words would probably be enough for Seren. She was a lot less interested in how people felt than who was dominant to who in any given situation. Just saying the words was the concession that she needed. Life among the rigid structures of Alvaren society had made Seren weird, but once you understood that weird, it was surprisingly easy to work with.

So I turned away to address Mercy's concern. "It doesn't need to. Seren won't be coming with us where we're going next."

"You mean to abandon me again? So soon?" Apparently, I'd looked away too soon. If I'd had a second without scrapping and arguing, I might have been able to break that news to Seren a little more gently, but right now, I was feeling the pressure.

At least Mercy had the good grace to wait while I got slapped with some girlfriend disappointment. "I'm sorry, Seren, but even if you could make the trip with us, there's no way you could make the trip back. I need you to hold out here just a little bit longer. Keep the dvergar safe, keep the tower protected. Will you do that for me?"

She said nothing for a long while as though she was weighing up her options. She looked me in the eyes, saw my sincerity, and wilted ever so slightly. "I had best be rewarded in abundance with delights both carnal and more lasting."

Mercy couldn't stop herself. "Ha! She just said your carnal delights didn't last long enough."

I chased her off with a bellow. "Can we have a moment here? Please? One moment without the peanut gallery chiming in?"

Asher bowed. "I cannot make any promises for Mercy, but I shall attempt to restrain myself from commenting upon your wooing."

Seren didn't smile really. Smiling was probably considered a sign of weakness where she came from—living a happy life did not rank high on the Alvaren priority lists—but there was still an air of amusement about her when I turned back to meet her gaze. "Is this wooing? Am I to be wooed?"

"I'm hoping you're already a little bit wooed." I leaned in close enough that our lips were almost brushing, then something else slipped out. "I missed you."

She jerked back from me as if she'd been stung. That was weakness again. I was showing weakness by admitting that I'd thought about her when we were apart. I was admitting that she was a weak spot that my enemies could use to get at me. Alvaren society wasn't all back stabbing all the time, but there had been periods in its history when assassination of friends and lovers was a common way of conveying displeasure with certain politicians choices, and of course, Seren had lived through those periods of history. To her mind, I'd just painted a target on her back with my words. A target that was made so much more dangerous by my unwillingness to kill everyone that opposed or threatened me.

Sure, only Asher and Mercy might have heard me say it, but in Seren's mind, they were competitors, struggling to ascend to my position of leadership. That was why she hated public displays of affection. That was why she slapped her hand over my mouth every time I tried to tell her how I felt about her. I barely had my act together when it came to talking to human girls, adding in a whole different culture on a whole different planet was not making me any smoother.

The only thing I had going for me was that Seren had basically signed herself up to follow me in a very permanent way after I'd given her those swords. She wouldn't be going anywhere, even if I did screw up constantly. I suppose that is the benefit of us both living forever—plenty of time to work out what the other person likes and start getting things right. Either that or plenty of time for the petty grudges and arguments to spiral out of control because her unbreakable honor was going to force her to stick with me forever—whether she wanted to or not.

I shook the thought away before I could spiral back down into the blind panic I felt every time I thought about having a relationship conversation, turning back to business. "So Koschei knew where the Faun shard has gone. He didn't want anyone grabbing it and using it against him, so he soul bonded it to some big buff Faun called Gorgafel."

Asher nodded along with that. "Then it seems that we must hunt this Gorgafel and separate him from his burden."

I rubbed the back of my neck. "Well, uh… funny story about that. He's dead already. He died ages ago."

Mercy knew something was up. Her scowl was back full force. "So we just have to find—"

"His soul in the afterlife."

"What." Mercy's reply was entirely flat.

CHAPTER 15

There had been a lot of shouting after that. A whole lot of shouting. From everybody. I may also have shouted a little bit. None of them were entirely on board with my plan to kill ourselves. Or rather, Mercy was very much on board with the plan for me to kill myself, but not so much the bit when I'd have to kill them if they wanted to come along. She also had absolutely no intention of letting me out of her sight since she remained convinced that I was going to run off and start doing evil and wicked things the second that her back was turned.

I didn't really plan on going to the land of the dead and kicking ghost puppies, but even Asher seemed concerned about how badly cosmic balances could be knocked off by somebody blundering about. He didn't think I was bad, just dumb as a sack of spanners, so that was comforting.

It was definitely better than Mercy's not-so-subtle suggestions that this was just me trying to murder them all without giving them a chance to fight back. It was good to know that there were some things she thought about me that even she wasn't comfortable outright saying, but it still kind of stung.

Seren was extremely opposed to the whole idea. She was pretty convinced that if we died and I used my Psychopomp powers to send us to the underworld or heaven or whatever, it was going to be a one-way trip.

In the end, we had made no progress, it was long after sunset, and even though I didn't physically get tired or need sleep, I was still tired of arguing. I slunk off into the tower with Seren, Asher returned to his beloved library, and Mercy went off to find her Dvergar fan club.

Catching up with Seren that evening was definitely the highlight of the day, even if I still had the same nasty doubts niggling the whole time we were jiggling. She didn't actually make me sleep on the floor when she was done with me, which was nice, but I suspected that it was because she was annoyed past the point of that sort of playful banter.

It was physically possible for me to sleep, even if I didn't technically need to, but that night I couldn't. My brain was too full of stuff. There is a reason that I prefer not to use it too much, otherwise it always ends up like that, loud and clattering around in my skull when I just want a bit of peace.

No matter what the others said, my plan was the only one that could work, so the arguing was pointless. I think we were all just spoiling for a fight if we were being honest—not that I was quite ready to be honest. Mercy already thought that I was a monster just because I had seen the Voidgod. If she ever found out that my Court was changing, there wouldn't be a discussion. Hell, even the ever calm Asher would turn on me in a second.

Lying there, listening to her breathe, I wondered which way Seren would go if it came out. I didn't even know if she liked me most days, let alone loved me enough to put up with me being... what I was. The fact I was a Lunar Eternal had been enough to make most folks hate me on sight. I dreaded to think what this latest development was going to do to my popularity.

The way that everyone on Amaranth spoke about Void-touched creatures, they were basically the worst thing that could possibly exist. Worse than the abominations and the monsters that covered the place. It was probably the only thing that the whole world agreed on. Now I was one of them. Maybe I wasn't some servant of Araphel or a mindless beast, but the words Void Court were scribbled onto my soul.

Maybe, if our little gang survived the secret coming out, they'd eventually realize that I hadn't chosen any of this. I didn't choose team moon or team void or anything. This was all stuff that had been done to me. Sure, some of it was caused by me making bad decisions, but most of them had been made because we were backed into a corner, not because I just loved being bad.

After about an hour of staring lovingly at Seren while she slept, she hit me. Not hard, but hard enough for me to get the message. I rolled out of bed and lumbered off to find something to do with myself.

First, I pestered Asher in the library, where I got him to admit that my plan was the only one that might possibly work despite all the frantic research he'd been doing into bodily resurrecting Gorgafel. Apparently, it wasn't possible, even for the old Eternals that had top-level Primal powers at their fingertips, but that didn't mean that Asher was willing to stop banging his head against the figurative brick wall just yet.

If we had infinite time, I might have just let him. We could have started making our plans to go and find Tsangaanax and his hoard of shards first and then doubled back to the Land of the Dead one later once we'd worked out how to haul it back to the world of the living, but the idea of just hanging around didn't sit right with me. Mercy had been so right about how weird I was acting taking my month-long training break. Sure it was paying off dividends now that we were fighting tougher enemies, but the whole tortoise and the hare thing never really made sense to me. The moral of the story had never quite worked. Going slow only won you the race if the other side decided to take a nap before winning. Araphel was probably pretty well rested after several thousand years.

This shard was in our reach today, so we needed to grab it.

Down at the bottom of the tower, I set to work crafting myself some new gear. The Dvergar were more than happy for me to take the ore and wood that they'd set aside in exchange for me using Artifice to bang things together for them too, so through the night I worked, making Mercy a new bow, making myself a new sword and a new set of armor, then wandering over to my shrine and making a few adjustments so that when I came back from the dead again I'd drop right into them. I was pretty proud of that idea—and the fact that it might come in handy if Mercy decided to murder me for no good reason was purely coincidental.

I guess Mercy was having trouble sleeping too since I spotted her stalking around the ramparts of the new wall that the Dvergar had thrown up to protect them from what was left of the local wildlife after we'd spent a full month attacking anything vaguely dangerous. I don't think they'd fully wrapped their heads around the idea that they were on an isolated island rather than bang in the middle of a million different monster territories. The biggest thing left out here were the dog-sized frogs, and from what I'd heard Gunhild grumbling, some of the younger Dvergar were now licking them recreationally.

With all her amazing stealth skills, I didn't hear her drop down from the wall, circle around, or come creeping up behind me, but I knew that she was there because I knew her. She'd seen me near the shrines, she'd remembered the threats of breaking hers earlier in the day, and she was coming to see what I'd done.

I held up her new bow.

Was I trying to buy back her friendship with the shiny new bow and armor I'd made her? Of course not. She was a grown-ass woman who wasn't going to be won over with shiny things. Did I want her to have the best gear possible because we were still on the same team, even if she kind of hated me and might use this shiny new bow and arrows to give my body some extra holes that I never asked for? Absolutely.

She snatched it out of my hand without a word. I called over my shoulder, "You're welcome."

She snapped back, "Go suck a Svart."

"I mean, the Alvaren were Svart, so technically…"

She rushed at me, leaping up to clamp a hand over my mouth. Hooking her legs around my waist to keep herself in position. "Nope. No. Stop. Do not want to hear about your sex life. Ever."

I stared at her for a second until she moved her hand.

"I'm just saying that…" The hand slapped back into place with more force than was probably needed.

She was laughing despite herself. "Don't say another word."

I held up my thumb, and she scowled at it as if trying to work out what the gesture was implying, then she dropped back down to standing and seemed to remember all of a sudden that we weren't meant to be friends anymore. She waggled the bow at me. "This doesn't change anything."

"It wasn't meant to." Shrugging my shoulders, I turned back to the rest of the ore stacked up by the smelters. It would take the dvergar days to work through what I could do in minutes. They were going to wake up tomorrow to a real treat.

"You understand why I can't trust you. Don't you."

I listed them off on my fingers. "I've been acting weird since I saw Araphel, I killed somebody without your express say-so, and the shards have… done something to me."

"You have been acting super weird, I didn't think I needed to tell you not to murder people, and… I don't know what the deal is with the shards, but you're… different. I wouldn't have had to tell the Maulkin I know that murder is not okay. When I first met you it was fun all the time, and now… there's something else going on. You're angry. Not pissy about little stuff like me, but real proper hate-rage. I thought it was Seren. I thought that after you'd smacked her around and made her a good little slave wench, she'd started feeding you her bull about you being superior to everyone else, but then I realized you still treated the Dvergar the same. Just tell me, what is going on?" She didn't sound angry at me anymore, she just sounded hurt.

I turned to face her with a sigh. Her eyes were burrowing into me, and the truth was on the tip of my tongue. But if I said it, everything would fall apart even worse than it already had. "Would you even believe anything I told you?"

She gave me the saddest smile I'd ever seen. "Maybe."

I gave her the next best thing to the secret I had to keep. I gave her the truth I never wanted anyone to hear. "I'm scared."

The sad smile turned into something like a smirk. "What? Big tough guy like you?"

"The plan for today—using my death god powers to jump into the afterlife." I let my shoulders slump. "I don't know if it is going to work. I'm kind of worried it might just kill us."

I'd hoped that being emotionally vulnerable and stuff would have helped Mercy to chill out, but as it turned out, she was stuck on raging bitch mode. "You sounded pretty damn sure when you were trying to talk us all into it earlier!"

My temper flared up, but it wasn't the cold murderous rage that Mercy was so scared about, it was my own annoyance. "Yeah, because nobody wants to hear the pilot saying that he doesn't know how to fly the plane!"

"So what?" She slugged me in the shoulder. "You thought you'd just try it and see?!"

"We don't have a whole lot of other options do we?!" I shoved her back, and she stumbled over the bundle of arrows I'd made her. "The shard was sent to the underworld because Eternals couldn't get it there. It is in the one place we aren't meant to be able to go."

She came back for me in a bounding jump, and I caught her around the waist with both hands as she tried to slap me. "What happens if you die, with all the other shards attached to you?"

I was yelling by this point. We were both yelling. The poor sleeping Dvergar must have been getting sick of all this yelling by now. "I guess we lose them too!"

She slammed her hands down into my inner arms, splaying them enough for her to drop to the ground. She didn't dive in for a sucker punch. Instead, she got nose to nose with me and screamed. "This plan sucks!"

"I know! That's why you don't make the stupidest guy come up with the plan!"

Her face crumpled into something somewhere between a laugh and a sob, and the noise that came out of her was more snort than either. She staggered back from me and flopped down to sit in the bare dirt. Without prompting, I slumped down too.

After all the yelling, her next words came out like a whisper, "I wish I could believe that you're still you."

I met her sad stare and felt it in my gut. "Me too."

We sat there for a long time, not saying anything but not fighting either. It was… well, it wasn't nice, but it was better.

Asher descended the tower before dawn and found us there, waiting for him. "It occurred to me that we might be best to set off without informing the others of our departure. Particularly if there may be some trial and error involved in the process of… dying."

"Probably a good call." I cast a glance out over the burgeoning little Dvergar town that we'd help to build. It was looking pretty good for having only sprung up a little over a month ago. Now that the mining had started, wooden buildings were being swapped out for hefty blocks of stone, and eventually, all the carvings and artistry that had marked Khag Mhor as an ancient Dvergar stronghold would find their way onto them too.

"I shall go first, if you do not mind." Asher surprised us all with that. "Maulkin shall have to go last by necessity, and Mercy, I do not wish to witness your death, while I am certain that you have dreamt of watching my demise many times over since our first arrival upon this plane of existence."

Mercy chuckled at that, then nodded her acceptance. I turned to Asher. "Have you spent all your experience and glory?"

"I am fully prepared, thank you."

Knowing that I couldn't take it with me unless it was strapped onto my soul, I had only the Lucis in hand. So when Asher slipped down onto his knees and bent his head down until his chin touched his chest, it was that lethal needle that I held up. "Make it swift, if you please. I do not know how long my composure will—"

I plunged the Lucis down into the back of his neck. All of my strength was focused down into that needle point, and it slipped between his scales and bit into his spine so easily I was startled. I was so shocked that it took me a moment to remember that I had to focus not only on Psychopomp, but also on where I wanted him to go. I furiously concentrated on Gorgafel's name. Wherever he was, I wanted us to go. Gorgafel.

Asher's body wisped away like it had never been there, his robes toppling to the ground, empty.

Mercy and I turned expectant eyes towards his shrine, but after an arduously long moment, it was clear that he wasn't coming back. "Okay. So I guess that worked."

Mercy tilted her head to one side as she prodded at Asher's remains. "Or you just killed your best friend for no good reason."

"Yep." I nodded. "Definitely one of those two options."

She looked from me to the Lucis and back. "I am not happy right now."

"Can't imagine many people are happy to die."

"You wouldn't know it from how they act." She snorted, then scrunched her eyes shut. "Just do it already. Do it. Do it."

I closed the distance with her and pulled back the sword for a lethal strike. I wavered. I really didn't want to do this. "Do it, you pussy."

Okay, maybe I wanted to do it a little. I swung for her neck.

She ducked. The blade humming past the top of her head without touching her.

I couldn't hold back a little yelp of dismay. "Mercy!"

"Sorry. Sorry. Force of habit." She dropped down onto her knees like Asher had. "Try again."

This time I was taking no chances. I stepped around her, grabbed hold of her shoulder so she couldn't move, then stabbed it in without a moment's warning. Blood blossomed up from the wound, throbbing out of her as she toppled forward into the dirt. My sword was slick with it, the blood of both my best friends running down it in rivulets to pool around the hilt and the shard nestled there.

She'd barely touched the ground before she vanished, leaving a heap of gear behind for me to loot. I guess Death was already on stand-by after I'd dropped Asher. Which left me with… me.

Hitting other people with swords was easy by comparison. I'd had plenty of practice at it. All of my training, however, had been pretty devoted to making sure I never hit myself with them. Not to mention the whole fear of accidentally permanently destroying myself slowing my roll ever so slightly. I couldn't hesitate. Not now after shunting both of them off the mortal coil without a second thought. I had to do it. I just never gave much consideration to how.

Swinging the Lucis at neck height wasn't going to smack me with enough force to get through much more than the top layer of skin. Angling the thing so I fell down on top of it was just going to end up with a slow bleeding hole in the middle of my stomach. I really did not think this through properly ahead of time, and now the other two were maybe already in hell or heaven or wherever they were headed, and I was flapping my sword around like I'd been startled by a wasp trying to work out how to actually kill myself.

In the end, I went for falling on my sword, extreme edition. With a quick burst of Artifice, I summoned up a lump of rock to grasp the bottom of the Lucis. Angled it a little, measured a step and a half away from it and then, when I was sure I had everything lined up, I just flopped down backward for my final rest while thinking as hard as I could about going to wherever Asher and Mercy were.

There was one moment of sharp pain at the back of my neck and then darkness. Which I took to mean, I'd done it. I'd died. Go me.

When the lights came back up, Death was already there waiting for me. *"Again? So soon?"*

"Hey big D. How's it going?"

The empty sockets turned to me, but he did not deign to answer.

Eventually, when it was pretty obvious that this staring contest was not going to go well for either of us, he gestured vaguely towards the shrines. *"Return to your flesh."*

I shifted uncomfortably above my corpse, very deliberately not turning my attention to it. "Uh. No. Actually. I'm going somewhere else this time."

Throughout all of history stretching back to the dawn of the universe, I can't imagine there were a whole lot of times that Death was surprised. It wasn't like my man had a face to look surprised with, but the way that he rocked back spoke volumes. *"You are Eternal. Return to your flesh."*

"I'm a psychopomp, and I want to go to the afterlife. Asher, Mercy, and me. We're all going. To the afterlife where you dropped off Gorgafel and his shard." Probably needed to up the politeness levels a bit. If there was one person in all of creation I genuinely didn't want to piss off, it was bone-face here. "Uh. Please."

Death didn't immediately smite me into a thousand little motes of soul-stuff, so I guess he wasn't too mad about it, but at the same time, I didn't get the impression that he was pleased to be taking orders from some lowly pleb like me. *"As you wish."*

The gentle wave that had annihilated my body last time was a jerk of the hand this time around, and while my journey over Amaranth to be reunited with my new body had been smooth sailing, this time it felt a lot like I was being put through a blender.

Without a body and nerves I couldn't feel pain, but that didn't mean I couldn't feel anything. As I was ripped to pieces and dragged down into Death's waiting arms, the sensations came distantly, like when the dentist shot you full of Novocain and really started digging around in there. I knew what was happening in the abstract as my whole being was shredded, crushed, mangled, twisted, violated, and then crammed through a pinhole of swirling blinding darkness. That was bracing.

I squirted out the other side of that tiny black hole into a river, slipping into the torrent like an otter thanks to my soul having been traumatized too badly to take any real shape. I didn't know up from down, left from right, or myself from all of the other souls that were flowing along with me. There was no water in this river, just the bound-less tide of the dead pouring on towards their eternal resting place. Some of them darted around, while others scraped and dragged along the bottom.

When we collided, my Spirit Touch flooded me, and I was over-whelmed as the full sum of their life experiences struck me like a bludgeon. Have you ever been hit in the face with a whole lifetime of memories? It feels kind of like a sledgehammer. A sledgehammer mostly made out of boredom and drudgery, with odd little spikes of joy that really dig into you.

I was surrounded on all sides by the dead, and they battered against me, wriggling and twisting their way along the river as if I was their favorite thing in the world. Over and over they hit me until I didn't even remember my own name. One moment I was a Dvergar cobbler putting shoes together on some rocky world with nothing but bare stars burning above me, the next I was a Human back on Earth, riding a bike through crowded city streets. Thousands of them must have passed clean through me before I finally felt something solid closing around me, hauling me out of the cascade of lifetimes and into something soft and quiet.

Each morning at dawn I rose, stood out in the rising sun before my chamber, and breathed in deeply as the heat washed away the chill of sleep from my scales. In the library I organized the scrolls into their separate cubby holes, returning research materials to the stacks down beneath the stone floor. From the moment that I had hatched, this was the purpose that I had known would be mine, and unlike some of my brethren, I had never bucked against fate. Why should I when there was such peace to be found here among the papers. The world beyond these walls was chaos, and I was grateful every day that I was shielded from it. This was the purpose that I was made for, and I relished each moment of my solitude, when I could fulfil that purpose without interruption.

Asher dropped me onto the shore, and the wriggling mangled worm of my soul, left at last to its own devices, unfolded again into a proper shape. I remembered who I was in a rush and then flopped back until my horns touched the stone. "Oh, that was fun."

Mercy was down on her haunches, panting for air just a few feet away, almost invisible through the mist that whorled around us. "Barrels of laughs."

Asher seemed to be the only one who wasn't shaken by the whole experience of dying. "It seemed that you were having some trouble working your way to the bank. I hope that you do not mind that I intervened."

"Thanks for the intervening. Much appreciated. That was rough."

"What, you can't handle a little swim through some wiggly dead people?" Mercy scoffed, even while I could see that she was shaking.

Trying to put what had happened in the river into words was a struggle. "Spirit Touch. It made them all… they were in my… it was… yeah, let's just never do this again."

"I concur." Asher nodded, and I saw the air around him blur, his solemn face in two places at once before the after-images caught up to him. He wasn't solid, not any more than the things in the river had been. We had no bodies here. We were in our familiar shapes, but they weren't flesh.

Off in the mists, something howled.

"Oh come on, we're dead, and we still have to fight monsters?"

"No rest for the wicked." Mercy rose to her feet, empty handed but still ready to tussle with whatever was out there making those ungodly noises. I noticed the Lucis still in my hand with a start. Guess the whole soul-bond thing meant that you could take it with you when you died. The other shards had been in pockets and things back on Amaranth, but here they were just stuck to me. Embedded in my side like lizard scales. The transparent skin that I'd given myself here was turning black around them, veins of darkness seeping off into my spectral form. Probably better if I didn't think about that too much.

Turning my attention inward, I probed at my Bestiary to see if it had any intel on what kind of monsters were roaming around the land of the dead, but it had nothing. Guess that my supernatural knowledge of all things spooky and scary only stretched as far as Amaranth. Now we were elsewhere, it was useless. Great. How many more of my hard-won skills and divinities were going to do nothing for me here?

The Pillars of Divinity were still glowing nicely, except for the pillar of Ascension, which was shrouded in the same mist that pervaded the world outside. No body meant no buffing that body, I suppose. My void pillars seemed to be a lot more obvious now than before I'd bound the Lucis, so if there had been any doubt about the reason they'd appeared, it was pretty much gone now. One of them, opposite Ascension, was also shrouded, so I guess it was a good thing I hadn't dumped any Glory into Corruption. Primal was, improbably, still working fine. So I guess making life here in the realm of the dead was still possible, even if the metaphysics of it confused me a bit. At least Artifice was still working as intended, and we already knew that Aether worked fine after bath time, too well.

The howling was getting closer. Asher should still be able to use magic, and I had my sword, but Mercy was currently dual-wielding a hope and a prayer. She needed a weapon, fast. I reached out with Artifice, searching for anything that I could use, and my senses were almost immediately overwhelmed.

Spirit Touch worked whether I had a physical body to touch things with or I was just stretching my awareness out, and everything here was somebody who'd once been alive. The ground beneath our feet were the calcified and settled souls of the long-forgotten dead. The mist and fog were all the living things that had never been seen or known at all, the vague recollections of them too nebulous to take form. There were hints of lives in there, but they drifted away when I reached to touch them. They wanted to be forgotten.

Still, I could feel all these things in my sphere of influence, which meant that somehow, they weren't beyond the limits of my Artifice. I reached out tentatively at first, but once I realized just what I could do, it was no work at all to haul the mists together and weave them into a cohesive shape. With a little grunt, a bow made of mist dropped down to land by Mercy's feet. The arrows were actually trickier. When I wound the souls down into smaller things, they were more inclined to split apart and flee like they needed the comforting press of more of the dead around them. Still, in the end, I worked out how to spiral them around until they were trapped in a never-ending tumble around themselves and stretched them on out into arrows.

She picked it all up with a grin that she didn't even try to hide. "Did you just make a bow out of clouds."

"Uh, no. I made it out of ghosts."

She dropped it again. "I'm not using it."

Probably should have expected that really. I held up my hands. "They're cool with it. Well, the ones that still know what is going on around them aren't, but the rest of them, it is just… they don't care what shape they are. It doesn't hurt them."

Asher didn't even bother to look around at us as all this played out. His attention was locked firmly off in the mists, tracing the shadows that flitted there just out of sight. "I believe that the thinning of the mists may also serve to our advantage if we face predators for which this is familiar territory."

"Right. One cleared-out bubble coming up." This time the spooky scary mist ghosts knew what was coming, so as I stretched my power out towards them, the smart ones fled ahead of me. I let them go because there was still a ton of them drifting around aimlessly as fog. I considered making armor with all the collected material, but the prospect of having them crawling all over me all the time made me a little bit squeamish. Instead, I compressed them tighter and tighter until they were solid as the rock beneath us, and I wrapped them around the Lucis to make it a bit more substantial.

When I slipped back together, I was holding a great big sword, and I couldn't have been happier about it, Mercy had begrudgingly collected her ghost-bow and was trying out the string, and Asher had been experimenting a little, pulling up magic the way that he usually did. Everything seemed like it was going to be just fine. Until Chernghast came bounding out of the mist, baying for blood.

CHAPTER 16

Now you might be thinking to yourself 'But, Maulkin, I thought that the gods couldn't directly interact with anything on Amaranth. I thought that was part of the rules of their game'. Well yeah, but we weren't in Amaranth any more, were we? We had wandered outside the field of play, and that meant that outside interference was all above board.

The giant wolf's fur was jet-black, his eyes burned with moonlight, and he moved like nothing on earth. Not like a living thing, but like a flowing shadow.

If I'd hoped that he hadn't noticed that his patronage had slipped off my soul, then I soon lost that hope. He only had eyes for me, not Mercy or Asher, who should have been his natural enemy as lackeys of the Solar Courts, but me. I was having some nasty flashbacks to my last day on Earth when a big black wolf came along and chewed me to death. Didn't fancy doing that again.

Chernghast leapt, and I brought my ghost-sword around to meet him in mid-air.

It was only when I felt the impact of blade on flesh that I realized that this particular murderous wolf thing was only about half the size of the demon god I'd left behind when I first set out for Amaranth. If anything, it was only a Chernghast puppy—bigger than me, but not the ridiculously gigantic thing I'd faced when I was just picking out my new body.

Mercy wasn't having flashbacks or religious crises, all she saw was the big bad wolf. She unleashed an arrow into him that bit at the same moment as my sword, unleashing a thunderclap that rocked us all back. She'd obviously been practicing with that wind-powered arrow thing that she could do so that it was more useful than just one big boom a fight.

Asher was casting, all too slowly, as the death-wolf clawed back to its feet with a noticeable limp. My lip began to quiver. "Aww, the poor puppy."

"Maulkin!" Mercy practically screamed with exasperation. "It is trying to eat you!"

"It's a good boy is what it is." I turned back to the looming shadow of death. "Who's a good boy?"

When the wolf lunged, I was ready. I might not have wanted to kill a dog, but I wasn't letting this thing rip the face off my soul either. The same spinning parry that had turned aside Orphia's glaive smacked it in the jowls and knocked the lunge off course. The huge hairy body still carried on with all the momentum of the leap, but the chompy parts missed.

I threw my shoulder into the boney ribs of the thing and launched it back, just in time for Mercy's next shot to lance through its tail and pin it to the rock below. The next time I tried to spring forward, it abruptly stopped with a whimper. It spun on the spot, chasing its tail to find the source of the hold up, and Mercy looked at me with continuing disgust as I smiled down at the big goofy critter. "Will you hit the damn monster?!"

"Oh, right. Yeah. Sorry."

I stepped up with my sword braced high, ready to come down on the wolf the moment it showed the first sign of aggression. It was still whimpering, teeth locked around its own tail and trying to drag it's butt free of the grip of Mercy's arrow. "Can we just... leave it?"

"It is a giant murderous demon wolf, what do you think is going to happen once it gets free? You think it is going to invite us over for cocktails? It is going to eat us!"

"Maybe it will realize that we did it a favor and let it live, and then years from now at a dramatic moment a big wolf will jump out and save us."

Asher unleashed his spell, a solid column of lightning leaping out from between his hands to explode through the wolf in a shower of sparks that burst out to the very tips of each strand of hair before it dispersed into the mists, strobing off in every direction.

The monster really jumped out of it then. All the wispy black shadows I'd taken for fur snapped in tight against the wolf's skin into a black and hardened shell, and the moonlit eyes seemed to multiply along the length of its newly streamlined head. It no longer looked like a good boy. It looked like a very bad doggy indeed.

I leapt for it, sword sweeping down at that armored skull with all the force I could muster without any actual muscles to use. When it's head turned up and it howled again, the sound to come out was not wolf, it was somewhere between a shrieking violin and a murder victim's last gurgled cry. My blow cut it off short.

The shiny black beetle-hide may have been tough as nails, but when you get hit with a giant sword made out of the souls of the dead you feel it, no matter how thick your plating.

Jaws that had been stretched unnaturally wide to unleash that awful sound were met by the sharp edge of my sword, and while I didn't have the power to break through the armor, I did have the strength to rip whatever that gruesome grey gristle it had underneath it. The jaw spread wide and wider under the blow, then with a wet, crackling sound, the lower jaw broke clean off.

Oh gross.

Where before the wolf-beetle thing had been straining to get free and chomp us, now it was running in a very different direction. It leapt back, tripping over its own pinned tail and tumbling to a heap before it managed to get paws back on the ground and launch into an extremely short sprint before it reached the end of its tail-tether.

Mercy's next concussive arrow bounced off the newly hardened shell and detonated in the air, knocking me back a step and sending all the mist that had started creeping back in around us away in a big puff too.

Asher was already well into his next spell, with flames coiling around between his clawed hands like he had a glowing version of one of those worm-on-a-string toys. When that was ready, I had no doubt it would bake the bug-wolf in its shell, but I really didn't want to smell that.

Where Mercy's last arrow had failed, the shell was blistered and cracked. I brought my sword around and swung for that spot.

The wolf bucked at the last moment, and my hit went wide of the weak spot, but it seemed like the damage was more widespread than any of us could have realized. When I struck against the back leg, the shell shattered between there and the spot Mercy clipped.

A howl started up again, and I leapt back when I recognized that the sound wasn't coming from the wolf's broken mouth, it was coming from the gaping black hole where its leg innards should have been. Black smoke flooded out, spiraling around the wolf like an octopus squirting out ink to mask its escape but doing nothing to muffle the awful mournful wail at its point of origin.

That must have been what Asher was using to aim because when the burst of fire washed out, it was centered right on what was left, burning away all the black fog and showing the sorry state that the beast had been left in. It had withered and crumpled inwards, all that shiny black shell marred by cracks as it collapsed. When the flames washed over it, the howling stopped, but I couldn't say if that was because the pain got so bad it couldn't scream anymore or if Asher had just put it out of its misery. Regardless, there wasn't much left of it beyond an oily stain on the rocks by the time that the torrent of flame had cleared.

Legendary Foe Defeated!
Celerity increased to 23
Airstrike: Rank 4/10
90 Experience Gained
200 Glory Gained

It was nice to get a bit of experience and glory back in me after losing it all after my first death on Amaranth. It wasn't like I strictly needed it, but it just felt a bit better to have it sloshing around inside me like chicken soup for the soul, except made out of giant bug wolves. Giant bug wolf soup for the soul didn't have the same ring to it. Regardless, it was going to be a long climb to get enough glory to reach the next tier starting over with nothing, so I was glad I was back on the horse. Figuratively. I didn't actually have a horse, which was kind of a shame because it looked like we had a fair bit of distance to cover between here and anywhere.

The other two were looking at me expectantly. I looked right back at them until Mercy rolled her eyes. "Okay, which way?"

That stopped me poking at the wolf-stain. "How would I know?"

Asher's tail lashed behind him. "Do you mean that you have brought us to an entirely new plane of existence with no means of navigating it?"

"I kind of hoped that we'd just land right next to Gorgy and get stuff over and done with fast." I rubbed the back of my neck as I realized just how dumb that was.

Mercy had folded over trying to suppress her laughter, but apparently, Asher wasn't quite ready to laugh it off. "It didn't occur to you that any plane large enough to contain the dead souls of every creature that has ever lived across all creation may be somewhat on the expansive side?"

I couldn't even find it in myself to get mad, really. It was just so nice being back together, adventuring again. "Ok. Everyone that found out where a shard is and worked out a way to transport us all to a different plane of existence to get it put their hand up."

Mercy immediately stuck her hand up. I mean, no hesitation whatsoever. Then we both stared at each other until gradually she lowered it to her side, smirk never budging.

Asher rubbed at the point where his snout met his forehead like he was trying to fend off a headache. "I swear that I must have committed some great wrong in my past lives to have been incarnated here as your babysitter."

The fog had swirled back in all around us, and while I could slip out and push it back, it seemed like a lot of effort for very little payoff. The odd snippets of ghost-memories that brushed over me were barely a distraction now that I knew what they were. I kept my ears pricked for any more Chernghast-like howls, but nothing was forthcoming.

I turned my attention back to Asher and Mercy, and they were both staring at me again. "What? You don't have any bright ideas? I'm the sexy one; you're the smart ones."

Mercy looked like she'd choked on the word sexy, but other than that, I got no real response. I sighed. "Up until now, we've always landed pretty near to the next shard, right? So it's probably somewhere around here. I mean it is going to stand out since it is the only solid object in the whole of the afterlife, except for the chunks I've got."

Asher's attention was drawn to my embedded metal chunks. "The shards that you carry. Do they differ from one another?"

He was doing that thing where he asked me simple questions to lead me to the right answer. Shame I had no idea what he was looking for. "I mean, they're different shapes, and one is stuck in a sword but—"

He held up a semi-transparent hand to stop me. "To your spiritual sense."

Again, I felt like I was missing something. "Oh no, they all read the same to Spirit Touch."

"Then might I suggest that they are all parts of a great whole, rather than individual items." He said it nice and slowly as if any of this was meant to mean something to me.

"You can suggest that. You can suggest a lot of stuff."

He was looking at me with that special stare he reserved for when I was saying something extra specially stupid. Like, toddler-level dumb. "What?"

"My apologies. I understand that the fundamentals of magic are not taught in the world from which you came, but I had thought that certain things were self-evident." He held up his hands once more, shaking one in the air, then shaking the other a moment later. "If each of the fragments behave as one when exposed to your spiritual senses, then all other fragments will resonate in the same manner."

My brain was still running on empty. "Uh…"

Mercy snorted. "Maybe you need to use smaller words."

My mouth flew to offer a vicious rebuttal, but then I giggled at the butt in rebuttal and spoiled it.

There was a momentary pause as Mercy looked confused, then I explained. "Re*butt*al."

And she gave a little smirk of acknowledgment.

Asher pressed on as if neither of us had spoken, which was honestly probably his best bet. "When you lay your hands upon the pieces, each one should call out to the greater whole. The more elements of the whole that you have in your possession, the easier it should become to sense the resonance."

"Ah. Right. Yeah. When I touch them, I don't get directions so much as I get the ghost of the Voidgod screaming 'doom, doom, doom!' at me."

Mercy's wry amusement had faded away all too quickly back to the stern frown I'd been faced with ever since that silly little decapitated head incident. She wasn't happy about the Voidgod speaking to me. Well, that was something we had in common. It was not the highlight of my day either.

"If Araphel seeks to prevent the assembly of the blade, then it seems entirely likely that his intrusions are an attempt to prevent you from sensing the resonance that would draw us to them. I would suggest that you simply ignore any"—Asher seemed to struggle for the right word for a moment before settling–"hallucinations that appear and focus instead upon the goal."

Mercy wasn't happy about this. She would back me up, I was sure of it.

"This seems like a really bad idea," I said. "I'd really like to not see Araphel any more than I need to so I can kick his ass. Can we maybe try something else? Keep this as a backup plan?"

She shrugged, and any hope I had of support vanished.

Asher seemed genuinely annoyed with me for the first time that I could really remember. "Certainly, let us set aside our only guidance and wander aimlessly around a barren, shrouded afterlife devoid of all landmarks in the vague hope that we eventually happen upon the one dead person that we are hoping to meet within the multitudes. It shall only take us several centuries, and I'm sure that Araphel will be kind enough to wait patiently for our return."

"Damn, Asher," Mercy cackled. "Tell us how you really feel."

He paid her no mind. "Maulkin. Use the shards."

They seemed to leap into my hands the moment I thought about them like they were eager to be held. I didn't like that. Within my ghostly body things moved like they did in my Sphere of Influence, which was handy but also a bit disconcerting. I ended up with a bundle of shards in one hand, the blade of the Lucis in the other, and my Aether flaring to life whether I liked it or not.

I tried to concentrate on whatever connected the different bits, but I was not very good at the whole Aether thing. It was all new to me. It was like trying to learn how to dance after spending your whole life with flippers. All the bits were there, but I was doing it so wrong. I was dancing like nobody was watching—which mostly involved flailing around wildly. Sometimes I'd feel a little tug or vibration as I poured my Aether senses all over the bits, but the moment I tried to latch onto it, that sensation vanished. This was magic stuff, and there was a very good reason that I left all the magic stuff to Asher.

Araphel did not show up immediately, and for one glorious moment, I thought that I'd escaped his reach. Maybe I was too far away from wherever his soul was lingering? Maybe his spirit was stuck back on Amaranth. Maybe he was… Oh no, there he was.

Araphel rose like a shadow behind Asher, clawed arms splayed and barbed tail coiling around my friend like it was evil god lap-dance time. *"Such a frail physical presence, but a mind blazing like wildfire. I can see why you adore him so. Do not fear, my dear Harbinger. I will not kill him when I return. His destruction would be scant punishment compared to what I have in store."* Those long spidery claws closed around Asher's head, and all that I could do was watch. *"All of that magic, churning around inside him, so easily twisted out of shape. So that the flame and storm leap not from his hands as he commands but turn back on themselves into that prodigious mind. I will hollow him out. I will leave him a simpering, drooling, nothing. And every day as you look into his dead eyes you will know that he is never coming back, and that it was all your fault."*

Squeezing my eyes shut, I went on trying to feel the other shard, wherever it was, searching for that little tingle when my senses brushed against whatever invisible force connected all the shards. It was out there, I knew it was out there, and I had everything I needed to find it, if I could just concentrate.

The Voidgod whispered into my ear, *"All that you have to do is nothing. You are so good at doing nothing. You spent a lifetime without distinction or achievement. All you need to do is stop. Stop pushing yourself, stop hurting yourself, stop striving to be more than the nothing that you know in your heart that you truly are.*"

Man, I was getting real tired of this asshole. Even if he hadn't been an evil god hell-bent on destroying all life in the universe, I'm pretty sure I would have taken a swing at him just for being this much of a dick. "I hate you so much."

Then he grabbed my face in his icy claws, and I lost my grip on whatever tenuous tickle of a direction I had. My eyes snapped open, and I let out a little squeal before I realized that it was Asher holding onto my face, staring into my face so intensely I thought he was going for a smooch. "Pay no attention to what you hear and see. It is not real. The Voidgod deceives by his very nature."

"Yeah, okay." Memories of his life were flooding into me through his fingertips. The crushing pressure of shell all around him until he could gather the strength to break out. The dread when all the eggs around him had already hatched, and there was nobody waiting to greet him. Nobody to imprint on or offer sustenance even as his newborn body screamed for both. "Uh. Don't grab me, please."

He snatched his hands back, and the Voidgod was right there where he had been, featureless black face inches from mine. "*Pathetic. You are all so small. So worthless. How could you hope to defeat me? Give up now. Submit to my will. You do not need to die. You do not need to suffer. Amaranth is not even your world.*"

I closed my eyes against him. Araphel wasn't here. This was all just a distraction to keep me from finding the shards. He was running scared, and he was throwing every trick in the book at me to keep me from finding the weapon that had already killed him once.

Concentration was not my strong suit, but I could do spite. Bearing down on the shards, I poured more and more Aether into them until in an instant I realized where I'd been going wrong. When I tried to focus on the connection between the pieces, I lost focus on the pieces themselves. When I focused on them, the connections sprung back into view. It was like a magic eye picture, and the moment that I lost my focus, the full image popped into view. The resonance between the shards was like an echo of the whole sword, repeated over and over between them.

"This one I shall kill. Slowly and agonizingly. Flayed perhaps. All that soft skin. No. Perhaps I shall make you kill her when your will is broken. I think that would be best. She already thinks that you are a traitor and a monster. Would it not be a joy to prove her right? To make her watch as the one she had always suspected would be her end tore her bones from her flesh. Imagine her horror when I make you use the gift that I bestowed on you to blot out her light forever." Without looking, I knew that Araphel was hovering around Mercy now. But I wasn't going to look. Not now when I could feel the echoes of the shards stretching out towards a distant horizon. Not when I could feel the distant shard chiming in answer.

I raised up the hand wrapped around the Lucis, and I pointed to where I could feel the next shard singing. Then I let every one of the shards drop from my grasp.

The darkness that I hadn't even realized was surrounding us flooded away, leaving fluffy white clouds of ghosts in its place, and I nearly toppled with the effort. I forced my eyes open. My hand was still up. My finger was still pointing. I'd done it.

When I shook. It was like the outline of my body blurred, shifting endlessly between the many positions that it would be in and never quite settling solid. "Let's not do that again for a while."

"Aww." Mercy gave me a big pout. "Was your best buddy Araphel getting too friendly? Did he try to slip you the tongue?"

"Okay, first off, Araphel doesn't have a tongue. Or a mouth or… much of anything face-wise. Secondly, he is not my buddy, pal. He's a dick, and I really do not like spending that much time listening to him yammering on about how he's going to torture us all to death unless we admit we're worthless and give up. And thirdly…"

Even through the swirling mists and the shudders still running through me and blurring the outline of my spectral form, I'm pretty sure Mercy could work out which finger I was showing her.

She rolled her eyes, but I could still see the old Mercy showing through the gaps in her mask of hate. Even if she thought I might be a servant of evil and all that junk, she still liked me. There was no getting around it. She managed to grumble out, "Real mature."

Asher had already started off in the direction that I'd been point-ing, and we had to jog to catch up before he faded into the mists and we lost him in the Land of the Dead forever. Could have been an awkward one to explain when we got back.

I hadn't spotted it before through all the thick dead people clouds, but the big river of souls that had dragged us all along was only one of a great many of them trickling their way through the land of the dead. Most of them weren't nearly as vast as the one we'd gotten caught up in, barely more than little dribbles of souls that carved shallow courses through the rock beneath us. We'd been stepping over them this whole time without even noticing. There were wider ones up ahead, where Asher was striding forward with all the intensity and awareness of his surroundings that it would take me a bottle of tequila to accomplish. In my old body. This one wouldn't even get drunk any more. Damn poison resistance.

Mercy caught him by the tail just before he trod right in a big rock-pool of congealed dead folk. He jerked it away from her in dis-may, but once his fixation was broken, all she had to do was point down to make him understand. After that, we followed very carefully in her footsteps. Making sure not to slip and trample on someone's little slice of heaven.

Once we'd been trudging for a bit, and I was sure Mercy's attention was on the road ahead instead of dunking on me, I turned back to Asher and asked him, "How come you never mentioned the whole bits calling to bits thing before?"

After his near tumble into that first pool, he had proceeded through the land of the dead with his nose turned down and his eyes locked on the stone beneath us. That didn't change when he answered back, "You may recall that until this moment we were well equipped with both direction and purpose. Not to mention that a grasp of resonance is so fundamental a part of an arcane education that I assumed you had already made attempts and failed."

"Maybe don't assume I know anything in the future."

His tail lashed, but it wasn't the angry one. It was too fluid and floppy. I was getting good at reading Inyoka body language; he was amused. "I had hoped to avoid the appearance of condescension, but I shall endeavor to abide by that rule moving forward."

Mercy paused to call back. "Don't worry, Asher, I've been treating him like a moron since we first arrived, and I haven't been wrong yet."

I'd walked into that one, but it still stung. I opened and shut my mouth a few times before finally mumbling out, "Your mother hasn't been wrong yet."

She pretended not to hear that one—probably because it was non-sense—and we turned our attention back to the road ahead. The world of the dead was not a small place. As Asher had so politely pointed out earlier, anywhere that was going to serve as the afterlife for all the different worlds of the universe had to be pretty substantial, but even so, it felt like a long time of just walking forwards with nothing much to see. After the first death-wolf attack, I'd kind of hoped that we'd be fighting all the way to the shard, but it turned out that this place was as quiet as death. No pun intended.

We had to jump a few broader rivers as we went, and sometimes the stone beneath our feet was a bit lumpier and bumpier than before, but overall, nothing much changed. "I've got to tell you, if I lived a very boring life according to some religious book, and then when I died I ended up here, I'd be really pissed about it."

Mercy snorted, but Asher looked… angry. We'd never really had a chat about whether the Inyoka where he came from believed in crystal dragon Jesus or whatever, but apparently, he had some sort of deal going on. "This is not the only world where the dead find their rest. Only the one where Gorgafel lies. We cannot assume that this is the afterlife that we were all predestined for. This is not the paradise that was promised."

This was not a subject I really wanted to go stomping over. "Hey, I'm not impressed either. I'm pretty sure I was promised seventy-two virgins."

From up ahead, Mercy snarked, "Couldn't you have just gone to an anime convention?"

"Hey, first off, Japanese animation is an artform that is respected around the world. And secondly, no. I was banned after slapping a security guard with a body pillow."

Mercy actually had to stop walking to get herself under control again. There were spectral tears running down her ghostly face as she wheezed for breath she didn't need. "Every time I make a joke about how pathetic you are, the truth turns out to be even funnier."

I growled. "He had it coming!"

Asher was looking increasingly bewildered as the conversation went on. "Did he say something bad about the cartoon girl you wanted to kiss?"

I crossed my arms. "He took a picture up my friend's skirt."

That shut her up promptly, but it also sucked all the laughter out of the foggy air too. Eventually, she mumbled, "That's messed up," but I could almost feel the edge of suspicion in her voice again. Like she was wondering if it had really happened or if I was trying to win brownie points with her. Because I'm totally smart enough to be a manipulative asshole.

We marched on and on through the land of the dead, never quite able to relax after the first wolf attack but never encountering anything interesting enough to actually hold our attention. So we were stuck here in this halfway state. In limbo.

There was what felt like another hour's trudging and hopping rivers before Asher sighed. "It feels as though we have already traversed a great distance, yet there is no indication that our goal is any closer."

"I mean, this whole place kind of looks the same?" I stepped over an outcropping that looked just like every other outcropping and nearly dunked my foot in a rivulet of souls before I overextended and hopped clear. "We could be going around in circles and never know it."

Mercy snapped at us. "I've been leading us straight."

I was ready to snap right back, but Asher, bless him, cut her off. "How can you tell?"

She opened and shut her mouth a couple of times. "I've been walking in a straight line."

"She has." I felt obliged to defend her, even though she had been less than pleasant the last few days. "If she'd turned then her whole ass wouldn't have been wiggling in front of my face the whole way. There would have been partial cheek coverage on one side."

An arrow glanced off my left horn. "Stop helping, or I'm telling Seren that you spend all day staring at my ass."

"Don't go getting an ego now. I stare at Asher's tail swishing about too, and he doesn't swish nearly as much as you."

The next arrow hit my other horn. Even here I could feel the impact vibrating down into my head. Good times.

Asher's tail was swishing from side to side when I looked his way, but I couldn't be sure if it was amused swishing or irritated swishing. I really needed a guide book to this sort of thing. Men are from Mars,

Women are from Venus, Lizardmen are from Jupiter. He spoke as calmly as ever, "Would you care to make another navigational check, to ensure that we are still headed in the correct direction?"

I shifted uncomfortably. "I really don't want to."

"You are such a man," Mercy scoffed. "Never stopping to ask for directions."

"Never stopping to ask directions from the evil god of evil that gloats about murdering and torturing us all every time I stop to ask directions."

She conceded that point with a shrug, but Asher didn't want to let it go so easily. "It would set my mind at ease if you were to double-check that we remain on the correct course."

Once again I reached for the shards and found them flowing through my ghostly form to my hands. Out of curiosity, I stretched out into my Sphere of Influence and found that I could fling the shards about anywhere within it. I could even swing the soul-coated Lucis back and forth just as easily as I could with my bare hands, all in real time instead of the slowed down treacle reality that Artifice usually took me to.

New Skill Discovered! [Active Artifice]

Whatever that was, I wanted it. I just needed another two hundred and ten experience to grab it. That was just four more death wolves. Tops. Bring on the death wolves.

None of them miraculously appeared to save me from having to take a hold of the shards in my hands and listen to them sing. This time I'd barely taken a grip on them before my Spirit Touch started them resonating with each other and the other piece. It was still distant but getting closer. I lifted my hand to point and then jerked it back in terror at the sight of Araphel, just standing there, doing nothing but existing and watching me. "So do you go invisible when I let go of these shards or do you stop existing? Because if you've just been following me around staring all this time…"

The smooth black face of absolute darkness came closer and closer as I spoke until my voice died in my throat. *"Believe whichever version makes you the most unhappy."*

It was so petty even I had to laugh. "Gods, you are a charmer. No wonder everyone wants you gone."

Before he could answer back, I let the shards fall from my hands, and he blinked away.

Asher and Mercy were both looking at me with horror on their faces, but I just pointed. "That way."

It should have been enough to get Mercy off my case at least, but even though my wobbly pointing was a vindication of her amazing ability to walk in a straight line, apparently me laughing in the face of the Voidgod was more pressing business. "Are you trying to make friends with the Voidgod?"

"Uh no? I was laughing at what a dick he is." I was trying not to frown because this felt like it was turning into more and more of an argument. "You know, like I do with you all the time."

She was scowling like I'd just caught her eyebrow piercing with a fishing hook. "Yeah, because we're friends."

"We're friends again?" She did not seem impressed with the absolute delight that had come bubbling up onto my face from somewhere deep down in my soul where I was apparently some kind of Labrador. I tried to put my face back to stern and failed utterly. "You think I only mock people relentlessly when they're my friends?"

Asher cocked his head to one side. "I believe that you would attempt to extend your friendship to an inanimate object were you in its presence for too long."

"Hey!" I couldn't help but laugh, even though he was totally wrong.

Mercy shrugged. "You did adopt Seren."

"Don't say I adopted someone I'm sleeping with, that is creepy and weird!"

"And all of those Dvergar." She added with a wicked little grin.

"They came along because their city got destroyed!"

Asher chimed in, "And the two of us despite our natural state being that of enemies."

"I… I like you guys." It seemed a little bit flat compared to how I actually felt about them. But since I was trying to convince them that I didn't get overly attached to everyone I met, professing my undying love and friendship probably wasn't the way to go. "And I really do not like Araphel. I don't think there is anybody I like less than Araphel."

Mercy's brows drew down. "What about the Elf Queen?"

"Or our dear associate Orphia?" Asher added. Mercy held up a finger for each one.

With a start she seemed to remember. "Or that dude you called fantasy-land Mussolini?"

I held up my hands, laughing despite everything. "You know what, even with all those options, I still like him less. I'm going to go ahead and say he's the worst."

The two of them looked at each other, feigning shock. Mercy stage-whispered, "Harsh words from Maulkin."

"I mean it!" I was almost shouting now, and I could see the two of them trying not to laugh. "He's a real dick. Even outside of the whole destroying the world stuff, he's a real… dick."

Asher bobbed his head knowingly. "I am certain that when the histories of this tumultuous time in Amaranth are recorded, the fact of the Voidgod being 'a real dick' shall be inscribed into a stone tablet so that it is never forgotten."

Mercy cackled. "Maybe a real dick monument."

I stared down at my feet and tried as hard as I could not to picture a giant dildo statue. Through the transparent surface of my feet I could see the whorls of calcified souls below us, and so I tried to concentrate on that instead. "Can we just get going, please?"

"Aww don't get shy now." Mercy looked like she was liable to rupture something if she didn't stop holding in her laughter.

Asher took pity on me at least. "Did it seem to be closer?"

"It was definitely... I want to say louder? I think we're getting closer. And Mercy was even taking us the right way."

"Told you so." She had clearly been dying to say that all along. Smugness radiated from every surface of her body. I was surprised it wasn't melting the soul-stone beneath her feet.

We set off again, not a moment too soon for my liking, and I found myself wondering if the sun was ever going to go down here—if there even was a sun beyond the mists or if it was just the mists themselves that were glowing with that unearthly pallid light as far as the eye could see. Although I suppose that technically it wasn't as far as the eye could see. We didn't really have eyes here, just the memories of eyes. The ghosts of eyes? Did they actually make any difference to what we could perceive, or were they entirely decorative? The fact that I could cobble things together out of souls using Artifice was kind of scary too. I didn't like what that meant. Could I use Artifice to mess around with the shapes of souls back on Amaranth too? Could I mold a soul like clay and make it into something that I could use. Something I could touch with Psychometry?

Thankfully, a wolf howled up ahead and drew me out of my introspection before I started asking the kind of questions that you were only meant to voice after consuming copious amounts of liquor. The questions that you kind of mumbled while staring up at the stars at three in the morning when the party was meant to be long over but you're still hanging on to consciousness by a thread. The same kind of questions where the right answer was usually someone else, who was just as messed up as you by that point, looking over at you like you were a genius and saying: "Whoa."

Anyway, there was a wolf, so I didn't have to worry about it.

Snapping back to reality, I noticed that the terrain around us had finally started to change. There were more sticky up bits, to begin with. Then some of them started to look less like rocky outcroppings and more like plants. Saplings, maybe. I probably wouldn't have jumped to that conclusion straight away, but the farther on we strode, the more tree-shaped the twisted soul sprouts seemed to be. The mist looked pretty much the same everywhere we went, so the only thing that we really had to look at was the ground or Mercy's butt. And since all the comedy potential had already been sucked out of talking about her butt, I was watching her feet to see where I should be trampling next.

The trickles of souls were pooling here amidst the saplings. Shimmering pools of spiritual energy that shifted and shimmered like there was an oil slick on top of the water. The howling seemed to be coming from deeper in. The wolf wasn't coming to us, we were lining up to be its dinner. We had already been moving way too slow for my liking, and now that we were heading into what increasingly looked like a swamp, and expecting an ambush at any moment, that dawdling pace had turned into a crawl. "Can we go a little bit faster? I'd like to get back before the heat death of the universe."

Both Asher and Mercy snapped around to shush me, but that just made me want to yell louder. "Oh come on, it is a big puppy!"

Asher looked genuinely furious. "Do you know what will happen to us if we die in the land of the dead?"

I had kind of wondered about that. "No?"

"Nor do I. And nor do I intend to find out," Asher replied. Mercy's head snapped back around. The trees actually looked vaguely like trees this far in—dark and twisted like they'd been dead a long time, but still tall enough and dense enough to block our line of sight. Still, Asher snarled on, "In the very best case scenario, we would be returned to Amaranth and have to begin this pilgrimage anew."

Mercy snapped. "Guys, shut up."

There was nothing moving up ahead of us—or at least nothing moving that we could see through the fog and the trees. Presumably there was something moving somewhere in that direction, or Mercy wouldn't have been freaking out at us, but whatever it was, I couldn't see it.

Turns out, I shouldn't have been worried about what was up ahead of us. I should have been worried about what was coming at us from both sides. I wasn't sure at what point exactly my dumb ass had forgotten that wolves hunt in packs. Maybe I was just so used to seeing them on their own after that one dick of a wolf that killed me, and then Chernghast, and then Diet Chernghast that we'd bumped into when we first arrived here.

One giant wolf leapt at me from the left, and another leapt at Asher from the right, jaws wide open and drool trailing behind them. Chances of making contact with either one of us? Zero.

The Lucis leapt to my hand as I turned, and the downward sweep of it met the power of the critter's leap head-on, battering it to the ground. The one that was going for Asher got a whole different surprise as I threw up a wall between them, and it crashed into it snout-first.

The air here was thick with soul-mist that I could turn into a solid object with only a moment's concentration. This might have been their home turf, but I had all the advantages.

There was a double yelp and both beasts fell back for another try. My one had upgraded its original mouth into a gnarly new one with a four way split and the tongue dangling out the middle. The one circling around the wall had launched itself as a wolf, but now it had begun the long, sad evolutionary journey to being a pug.

Neither one looked too eager to come at us again. Good for them. They were learning.

Asher started to cast, so I threw up another wall, this one under his feet, launching him up out of reach of any snapping teeth until I had the chance to knock them out. Turning my attention back to old cross-mouth, I hefted the Lucis for another swing, only for the whole damn wolf to get blown away before I had the opportunity.

Mercy had gotten a lot better with those wind arrows of hers, and every one of them hit like a freight train now. "Hey! That one was mine!"

"You can get the next one!" she called back to me as she leapt, kicking off the side of the podium Asher was on to gain height before rolling to her feet on the first wall, already taking aim.

Damn kill-stealing archers. "What next one?!"

That was when I saw them. Wolves hunt in packs. Not duos. Packs. "Oh. That next one."

Two more leapt past the one I'd shut down with the first swing, and they were not making things easy on me. My sword might have been big enough to catch the two of them in one hit if they'd politely jump at the same height, but one was after my ankles and the other my face.

There wasn't really time to make a decision about which one I'd rather live without, but even without muscles, I still had that muscle memory from the month of Seren training. She fought with two swords, coming in high and low whenever it looked like I was getting complacent. I was leaping the ankle-biter and meeting the overly affectionate kisser with the flat of my sword before I knew what was happening.

The impact hammered me down, and I ended up straddling the back end of one giant wolf while the other skidded across the flat of my sword, right past my tasty face. I was the meat in a death wolf sandwich.

Usually being in the middle of a giant pile of puppies was exactly my idea of a good time, but these were not good boys. They were bad dogs. Bad. No biscuit.

The one beneath me squirmed and bucked, trying to remove the weight on its back. The one on top snarled and snapped, trying to get past the smooth expanse of sword and into the yummy Maulkin filling. It wasn't happening.

I tried to surge my Potency and toss the pup in the air, but I had no body. Couldn't buff up muscles that weren't there. Instead, I just had to hold on as they continued their struggle and buck—like a bull rider if a bull was also riding him.

It wasn't easy to feel things without nerves, so I heard the crunch before I understood what it meant when yet another of these big fluffy murder machines latched onto one of my feet and started pulling. The pain came because I wasn't lucky enough to skip out on it entirely, but it came from a distance, like I was nicely numbed up for the dog-tooth surgery being performed on my ankle.

With a jerk, I was hauled out from between my bread-wolves and hit the ground like the sad slice of salami I was about to become. At least it freed up my arms. I swept the Lucis at the wolf on my ankle, and the blade bit through one eye and burst out the other. The crunching loosened off, and with one more kick of the foot that wasn't dangling dead and useless, I got the dead death-wolf off me.

The double-decker wolf I'd just escaped lunged down at me in unison. Mercy's arrow caught the top one in the snout, forcing it to rear back, but the one on the bottom, in the driver's seat, chomped down onto my arm. More accurately, I fed it my arm. I'd rather lose that than my neck.

Teeth closed through my ethereal form, and seeing them sinking in made it more real somehow. I felt it more, knowing what was happening. Escaping steam of life drifted out of the monster's jaws to join the rest of the fog. Most of it was being gulped down, inflating the wolf until it was somehow even bulkier, but enough escaped that I could see my life drifting away.

When I reached out to it with Artifice, that drifting puff didn't feel any different than the rest of me. Just distant. With a flex of effort, I hauled it back into me, ripping soul-fog right back out of the wolf as it tried to gulp down more.

"Bad dog!" I roared as I launched myself up with another podium of stone before the rest of the swarming wolves could latch on and start chowing down. I didn't get far. The one latched onto my arm was not willing to let go. Well, that was fine. I wasn't done with him either.

I rolled off the podium before it got any real height when the weight of the wolf pulled me down, using that weight to fuel my next swing. The Lucis hit it square in the center of mass, and the wolf broke.

Fur that could have turned to armor never had the chance. Flesh woven from the same soul-stuff as everything else here fell apart at the touch of the blade. I didn't cut all the way through the wolf, but its back was broken, and its grip went loose.

"Play dead." That came out as more of a grunt than a joke, but I'd live with it. So long as I went on living.

Mercy, gods bless her, was raining pointy death down on the wolf-pack like the avenging angel that I knew she was. Wolves were leaping up to snap at her heels, but she didn't even spare them a glance. Not when she was aiming. That rain of arrows gave me the space I needed to get back on my feet.

The ancient and glorious weapon known in modern times as the Lucis worked great as a crutch until I'd hauled enough soul-smog around my ankle to form a solid brace and keep myself upright.

Not a minute two soon either. The top dog had tumbled free of its ride sometime during the scramble, and now it came bounding right for me, going for the face again. I know I've got a kissable face, but this was ridiculous.

"Sit!" The Lucis spun in a full three hundred and sixty degree flip, from pointing to the ground to the sky and then back again.

Twisting to the side in a panic had saved the wolf from a killing blow, but it was opened down the length of its ribs, and inky black fog came pouring out, obscuring my view of just how badly I'd hurt it.

Not that I had a lot of time to play vet right now anyway. Not with even more of the damn wolves coming on. How many wolves were there? I couldn't count them all in the frenzy of motion. This time I roared, "I said sit!"

There was no difference from the stone below and the mist above. I could use them all the same. So this time I didn't haul a wall of condensed soul-stuff up from the ground, I slammed one down. It felt like when I'd hit Leo with the rock walls back at the Bastion. Where it hit their flesh, it stopped dead, but the goal had never been to crush them to death.

Passing seamlessly around them, the stone pinned the wolves in the front ranks to the ground. They'd sit, whether they liked it or not.

I couldn't see through the wall and the wolves to the next lot, and Mercy was already lining up shots on the trapped wolves now that they were sitting ducks. I needed them out of the way. "Roll over!"

When I shunted the wall along, most of them just slid without any tumbling, but a few of them were good dogs. They flopped and rolled over as the solid stone around them trundled along out of my way.

Waiting around to be attacked was a fool's game, and I was no… Well, I was pretty dumb, but I was not dumb enough to wait until I was turned into doggy kibble. I charged in as the wall slipped aside, sword swinging before they could pounce.

I dashed across their line, blade singing as it went, gathering more and more mass around it as I pulsed my Artifice between each step, flickering back and forth from my body to my Sphere, gathering up more and more mist into metal until the Lucis was so heavy even I couldn't lift it, and my swing ended with a clunk and a furrow of stone dug up. Then the howling started.

A half-dozen wolves were dead from that single cut, and even as

I let the fog wisp away from my sword again and made it usable, I realized I wouldn't need to. Whatever will had driven these wolves at us had been broken. They were not equipped to deal with prey that could actually fight back, and it showed. The front rank lay dead, and the rest milled about, tripping over each other in their haste to leave, helped along by another shower of arrows from Mercy.

There was no howling behind me, but there was a big "woof." Although on reflection, the sound was less puppy noise, more petrol-bomb.

Glancing back at the hounds that should have been at my heels, all I could see was black smoke.

Little licks of flame danced on what was left of the winter-bald trees, but of the wolves there was not even a bone left to be chewed on. He might take a while to wind up, but once he got going, Asher was downright scary.

I called up to Mercy, "All clear?"

Legendary Foes Defeated!
Celerity increased to 24
Airstrike: Rank 5/10
240 Experience Gained
1400 Glory Gained

Apparently, the universe thought we were done, so I wasn't going to argue with it. The last glimpse I had of the wolves out in the woods were their rapidly fading shadows. Then as swiftly as they'd appeared, they were gone, and we were safe. I blinked for a second to pick up the Active Artifice skill, then turned my attention to the other two.

When I reached out to my Artifice to bring down the walls and podiums it was already there and waiting. I didn't need to jump out of my body or drift around in a cloud of consciousness while my body lay useless. Everything that I had wanted to do, I could do while still striding closer. Oh this was going to be really handy. The only downside was that now I had full control over my limbs, I couldn't help but wave them around a bit as I told the soul-stuff I was working where to go. Like a conductor. Or an idiot.

Mercy laughed as I waved her wall down into the ground beneath us once more and even more when I had to clench a fist before I felt like I had a proper grip on the podium to haul Asher back down. "Oh my god, have you been doing that the whole time?"

Faun skin didn't show a blush very well, but my spirit-body was practically glowing with my embarrassment. "Only in my head."

She bounded over and pinched my cheeks. "You are *adorable*."

I was laughing right along with her until I saw her remember. She remembered that we weren't meant to be friends. We weren't meant to be having fun. I was her enemy. For some reason I still didn't fully grasp, she didn't trust me anymore. She jerked her hands back, and I tried not to let her see just how much that hurt me.

CHAPTER 17

On the subject of hurt, I reached for my Primal Pillar and shoved some life back into my body with Restoration. It spread out like a green glow through my spectral form until it closed in on my busted up ankle and arm and flared brighter. The hasty patch I'd made fused into my leg hole seamlessly, and just like that I had a bunch of somebody else's ghosts as part of my leg. I was one hundred percent sure that wasn't hygienic. Still, they didn't seem to be screaming all their memories into my head, so maybe Restoration had sterilized them or something. My arm dragged in a little wisp of fog to patch itself up too. It was kind of weird being somewhere that all of my different Pillars interacted so directly with the same stuff. It was like we were in a simpler version of the world where everything ran on the same system.

Asher looked around at our handiwork and nodded, satisfied. "I believe that all attempts at stealth can now be entirely abandoned. If there is anyone in the land of the dead who did not hear that, then they most certainly will not hear our footsteps."

Mercy shrugged, walking along the line, plucking ghost arrows out of the wolves I'd pinned in place. Some of them jerked and jumped as she pulled the arrows out of their heads, but most of them just quietly evaporated away into nothingness, adding their bulk to the fog.

At least that explained what happened if you died in the land of the dead. I'd come pretty close to being a puff of cloud myself back there. I'd dragged most of myself back in to form a solid lump, but who knew what I'd actually lost.

My gods, I couldn't speak Spanish anymore. No wait, I'd never learned to speak Spanish.

Maybe I had just lost some of my encyclopedic knowledge of funny memes from the internet. That would be a real heartbreaker. Those burger loving cats that couldn't type well were probably about 90% of my personality. Without them, who would I even be?

Regardless of what bits of myself were floating off, we moved on at a much better pace after wolf attack two: electric boogaloo. The ground was liquid as much as solid after a few minutes of striding on, and once we were clear of the explosions that Asher had belched out, the trees came back on thick and fierce. Mercy fell back into line with the rest of us, and I took up the vanguard position. I started off hacking my way through the trees as we bunny-hopped our way deeper, but before long I gave up on even that level of subtlety and reforged everything I was carrying into a shield with a raised ridge down the middle, creating a bulldozer blade that I held out in front of me with both hands as I charged on.

Active Artifice was really getting a workout as I went, hauling solid soul-stone up in teeny tiny podiums the size of lily pads in the many stagnant pools of souls beneath us. They'd make stepping stones for the other two, but for me, they were mostly just a workout as I determined just how well I could use Artifice while I was moving. It took a lot more concentration than I would have liked. If I was doing anything more complex than just running with my arms up then I probably would have screwed it up a million times over. My brain was struggling with being in two places at the same time. It struggled with being in one place at the same time normally, so this extra dimension of thinking was… well, it wasn't painful, but it was pretty close. I was straining myself. Maybe I needed a brain upgrade. Oh! I unlocked one of those back when I was fighting Koschei. I was assuming that whatever had let him shoot a billion different thought-ghosts at me would definitely help me focus up enough to plop rocks under my feet as I ran. At the same time though, I was kind of reluctant to do any magical brain surgery on myself to become smarter. It could totally change who I was as a person if I wasn't a giant dumbass. Did I really want to find out who I could have been if I'd scraped together more than three brain cells to deal with every situation?

Mercy cried out a warning from behind me just before I rammed into something rock solid and was flung off my feet. I didn't do a full flip up and over my shield, but I did headbutt it pretty solidly. That was a clang that I was going to be hearing echoing in my skull for quite some time. I shouldn't have worried about gaining new brains changing me too much. Apparently, I was just going to mash them up anyway.

I staggered back, melting the shield away so that I could see what I'd rammed into and regretting it immediately. It was a foot. More of a hoof really. A hoof-foot combo that looked an awful lot like mine—if I was the size of a building. I craned my neck to look up, following calf to knee to thigh to massive dangling loincloth and the expanse of muscled torso beyond. This Faun was so big that I couldn't even get my brain to accept that he was a person. He seemed more like a bit of the landscape. The fog swirling all around his immobile form did nothing to change that impression. Neither did the dangling growths of soul-moss and vines hanging from his huge, hooked horns and draped around his shoulders like a cape. Even as that huge heap turned its head towards me, I was still half-sure that this was just some big-ass statue.

Then he swung for me.

He was ten times the size of me, swinging an axe so big that I was pretty sure the rough blade could have passed for a tectonic plate, and even knowing and seeing all of that, I still tried to block it. The Lucis had reformed into a great-sword almost by habit, and I swung it up to meet Gorgafel's blow.

Probably a mistake, though I didn't realize that until I was flying.

Asher and Mercy flitted by beneath my feet, both yelling something that the wind snatched away. I lost sight of them, and the giant monster looming over them, as I soared off into the dense mist. The dead claws of the trees caught me the moment I started to fall, hooking into me and ripping through me as they splintered and crumbled beneath my weight.

That distant sense of pain was back, and I saw some of myself misting off to join the fog, but it was a fair trade because every scratch and blow slowed me down until I could tumble back from the side of one particularly sturdy tree to land on my feet.

Distance had kind of lost all meaning by this point, but I charged right back towards the massive Faun as fast as my ghostly legs could carry me.

Even puffing and sprinting as fast as I could, I heard the howling pick up at my heels. I had no time for small-fry, not while Asher and Mercy were standing toe to toe with a titan. I staggered as I split my attention to throw up a wall behind me, but it seemed to do the job. I never even saw the wolves pursuing me, I just heard the chorus of squeals as they hit solid rock.

Hopefully, they wouldn't follow me all the way back to the real fight, but if they did, at least Asher would be able to Kentucky fry them with ease. The fog shuddered out towards me as I ran, and a sound like thunder rolled out. Something so huge and powerful was happening up ahead that it would have terrified me in my old life, but here and now, I knew that it was my friends. They were the ones rocking this place to the foundations. The giant Faun might have made a clap of thunder with every step, but Mercy and Asher were the lightning that made the horizon flash.

There was no real way to tell time here in the land of the dead, but now that things were finally happening, I felt like I was late to the party. I was running all out, tossing up stone steps beneath my feet as I ran, no time to look down and see when there was a pool and when there wasn't. As the shadow of Gorgafel loomed out of the mist up ahead, I pushed more and more rock up with each bounding step until I was jumping up to meet them as they rose, a stairway of jutting pedestals heading up and up until when I finally broke through the fog, I was level with the giant's face.

The last pillar of earth shot up at an angle, and I coiled every muscle in my spectral body, folding up on myself and then unfurling at the last moment to launch at Gorgafel's big, ugly face.

He had those same sharpened teeth that I'd been uncomfortably into on Mhirka, and his horns were huge and wide like a water buffalo's. To my eyes, he looked just like any other Faun, except for the missing eye and the fact he was capital B big. That eyepatch was what caught my attention as I soared, blade raised to meet him. It wasn't leather, and it wasn't held onto his ghostly body with a ghostly strap, it was a hunk of metal, embedded in the midst of the scar tissue. A rusty hunk of metal that sang to my Spirit Touch. All the shards I carried thrummed at the closeness of their other part, and I was going to go right ahead and blame that thrumming for distracting me. That was definitely why he was able to slap me out of the sky like an annoying fly.

Mercy stepped on my back as she ran by. Not even pausing to snipe at me. "Nice comeback."

I started pushing myself up, only to have to fling myself flat again when Gorgafel's axe scythed by again at waist height. I spat a mouthful of soul-water out when I finally raised my head again, doing my damnedest not to absorb any memories through Spirit Touch tongue. "So sympathetic."

Mercy had enough time to spare as she leapt gracefully over the same axe-swing that floored me to yell, "Get off your lazy ass!"

Despite her snark, I was trying. It was just a little bit on the painful side, after me being tossed around like a rag doll. Dull and distant pain was still pain, and when you stacked up enough of it, it started to feel just like the real pain I'd have felt if my physical body was slammed through a forest and slapped into the dirt. By the time I was up on my knees, Mercy's flip over the axe swing had ended with her standing beside me, readying another one of those windy-arrows she was so proud of. "Why's he's so big?"

She unleashed that shot straight up to meet Gorgafel's next blow. The axe blade was so high up in the fog that I didn't even see it coming before Mercy's shot intercepted and blew everything away. Before, it was an overhead swing that probably wouldn't have just split me in two but created a canyon underneath where I'd been standing that was big enough to kickstart local tourism. Now, the titan rocked back on his heels. The face that the fleeing fog unveiled did not look happy with us. I had to force my mouth back into motion. "I mean, I saw some big dudes, but this is ridiculous."

Asher dropped from the sky like a bird doing an excellent brick impression. He was getting better at zipping around with his gravity snares, but he still couldn't land worth a damn. I had to catch him if we didn't want him to wipe out. "I would hypothesize that the ancestor worship that you described among the Faun may have translated into a legendary physique here? Or perhaps he has simply been consuming the souls of others to increase in power and girth. That would certainly seem to be a natural extension of the Void corruption that looks to be affecting him."

There certainly were an awful lot of familiar black veins running through Gorgafel's spectral body now that I looked. There was a thick root of darkness heading down from that ruined eye-socket, branching out like a nervous system to stretch throughout his whole ghostly body. No matter how big he got, that cancer grew with him.

Whatever momentary break Mercy's arrow had won us was over now. All of the wild swings and careless chops appeared to be done too. Now Gorgafel was looking down at us with something I'd like to describe as cunning in his eyes, although it was probably more like a slight dialing down of the berserk fury. The next time he came at us, his attacks were precise.

It's weird to describe an axe bigger than your whole body being swung at you as precise, but every movement he made now was tighter, more focused on his goal. That goal being us dying.

I brought up my sword to meet his next swipe and deflect it away from Asher. Mercy was already springing to the side, but that lizard man moved like he was in molasses compared to us buff warrior types. This time I couldn't afford to be knocked back, so I gathered more and more mass around my sword until it was as big as it could get without tipping me over.

Anyone who tried to swing something that heavy would have no luck, but conveniently enough, it was already swinging by the time it put on all the weight. For that one parry, it was big enough to bounce Gorgafel's swing. Then it was useless.

If he'd still been flapping his axe around like crazy, it might have bought us some time to work out a plan, but the moment that I turned the first blow away he spun. That colossal mountain of a body spun, using recoil from the first deflected hit to fuel the next.

Dude really knew his stuff. I could have picked up some pointers if he wasn't actively trying to carve me in half. At least it was aimed at me, not Asher. Sure, he might lose his tail if I dodged, but that would grow back, right?

I threw up a wall between me and impending death, but it wasn't going to be enough. The stone shattered under the axe blow and it came on as if the stone hadn't even been there. There was barely a moment to think, but I'm proud to say that I still managed to flick another wall up. Shooting poor Asher back into the sky with a yelp.

Thinking back through my old life, I don't think I got hit a lot.

I mean, I definitely got hit a lot less often than I deserved given the words that came tumbling out my mouth. There were a few good solid slaps from women in bars, and a few punches on the playground when I was small, but none of it could have prepared me for Amaranth and the constant beating I'd been taking since I arrived. And nothing that I'd suffered on Amaranth was like this.

His axe had a thick line of that oily black void energy along its edge, and it bit right through my ghostly body like it wasn't there. My legs went left, and I went right. That pain that had been holding off, giving me the silent treatment, came rushing back to meet me like it had forgiven me for all my wrongs. Thanks, pain. Thanks for joining the party. So glad you're here.

[6/1270 Health]

Smoke billowed out from me as I landed on the ground in two bits. Again. I was really making a habit of this whole getting chopped up thing. My life bloomed out of me in a great cloud, and for a moment, I was just going to let it. Then I remembered why we were here.

Pulling myself back together with Artifice was not easy—maybe one of the hardest things I'd ever done with my new godly powers. The pillar trembled inside me as I hauled my ghostly bits back together, and then Primal sprang to life, taking over. I still had to concentrate on pulling all the spilled Maulkin juice back together, but Restoration rushed through me, sealing the gap, filling in what was missing.

I gasped in a big old mouthful of air, pushed myself back up onto my elbows, and then I saw the axe coming straight down on me again. Gorgafel didn't leave jobs unfinished. Guess that was why he was such a big hero back home.

Good thing I had my own heroes to come save me.

Asher's spell had been slow to cast, and we'd interrupted it more than once with all the jostling around, but when he finally unleashed it, it was worth the wait. A roaring ball of flame and lightning leapt out from wherever he'd landed, heading straight for Gorgafel's big, dumb face. It was going to roast him and toast him and knock any idea of chopping me up right out of his head.

Or at least it was meant to. Instead, Gorgafel moved much faster than anything that gigantic had any right to, following through on his swing and diving forward so Asher's patented murder-ball soared right over.

Mercy caught it.

She'd been leaping from one of my podiums to the next, bouncing off treetops when she had to, gaining height every step of the way. One last wild leap put her into the path of the ball-lightning-inferno and another wind-arrow sent the whole thing flying back on a new course.

Right up Gorgafel's ass.

If you've never heard a pig getting its testicles electrocuted while simultaneously being dunked in napalm, then it would be pretty hard to describe the noise that came out of Gorgafel's mouth when the arrow struck home. And with him looming over me, I got to see the expression on his face too. That was a thing of beauty.

Needless to say, he fumbled his swing, just narrowly avoiding lopping off my arm as I flung myself to the side. And there, just waiting for me, was my sword. Oh sword, I missed you.

Of course, it was way too big to lift in its current configuration, but a quick puff of Artifice brought it back down to ridiculous-sized, instead of super-ridiculous-sized. All the rest of the spooky ghost matter fell away in clumps, and I turned to face the enraged giant who'd already killed me once today. I could not have been happier.

Even as I charged, I was bellowing, "Nice one, Mercy!"

Maybe she heard me, maybe she didn't. I couldn't see her, and there was no way I was letting Gorgafel turn around and spot her either. Asher was still somewhere off in the mists, and I couldn't see him glowing up anything new and nasty just yet, so for the moment, I had the big guy all to myself.

The smooth flow of attacks had stuttered after Gorgafel's butt got violated, but he was back on balance and ready by the time that I got close enough to launch myself at him again. No way I was swinging for his ankles when I had a chance for something better. One long up-spurt of stone launched me at his chest. Even through the pain and the rage, I could see the contempt on his face. The same attack again? Didn't I ever learn.

His axe hilt swept up to meet my strike, and I let it. Abandoning the Lucis to go spinning off into the mist as I soared on by.

You would think that a Faun would realize that my sword wasn't the only weapon I was toting. My horns hammered into his chest.

The pained roar this time wasn't nearly as impressive as when he got toasted buns, but I was close enough to feel it reverberating up from his guts.

Now I was inside his guard, it was time to have fun. He abandoned his grip on the axe and reached down to grab me with a hand that was about the same as a normal human being, to pluck me off like the annoying little thorn in his side that I was.

That was when I called the Lucis back to my hand. Not just the little one that I'd been left with due to silly little things like "not being able to pick it up" but the whole damn thing. Every bit of it that I'd shaken off was still a part of the whole. It was connected, the same way that the shards were, and even though most of it was well outside my sphere of influence up here, it still leapt to attention when I called.

Lumps weren't of any use to me though. I needed swords. Lots and lots of swords. The Lucis hit my hand, and I plunged it into Gorgafel's chest. The echoes of the Lucis that I'd pulled together with Artifice struck a moment later, and the stuck pig noises just kept on coming.

Although Gorgafel looked less like pork and more like a porcupine.

Despite all that, it wasn't enough to break that martial discipline. His hand still came up, and I was still slapped right off him like a bug. Again.

Asher unleashed a bolt of lightning as I fell, and it passed close enough to make every hair on my body stand on end. On its own, maybe it wouldn't have been enough to stop the giant looming over us, but there was an answering crackle of electricity already inside him, leaping up to meet the bolt as it struck. I was never going to understand how magic worked, how all of the complicated scribbles in his books translated into bitching awesome explosions, but this little bit of it made sense to me now. The resonance part, anyway. He threw fire or lightning at something the first time so that there was fire and lightning for the next spell to latch onto. Maybe I wasn't a complete dumbass, after all.

Black burns spread everywhere that I could see, the veins of darkness blossoming out as the pure destructive power of the lightning tore through. It was the kind of blow that could have felled a mountain, and I could barely believe that even this ancient terror could still be standing after it struck.

Despite all that, Gorgafel kicked me as I fell.

[449/1270 Health]

It hurt. Big surprise.

I was sent tumbling end over end, and I would have hit the trees again if it wasn't for Mercy. She was still leaping about, trying to keep high while she peppered Gorgafel with arrows. Chipping him down, bit by bit. I just happened to be her next stepping stone.

She looked so dainty when she was springing and flipping about that I really didn't expect that second kick to hurt as much as Gorgafel's. Stupid really. She had much better reasons to kick me.

It knocked me down instead of out, though, so I suppose I should have thanked her. Maybe later. When I didn't have a face full of soul pond. Again.

Another push up, another mouthful of dead people trying to tell me their life story, and another panicked moment of looking around for my sword before I remembered I could summon it to my hand as easily as thinking. Gorgafel loomed over me like a mountain, surrounded by his very own ring of cloud cover, smog pouring out of his massive form, and the life draining out of him through all the holes that I put in him.

Time to add some more.

I drew the Lucis back, and through Artifice, I could feel every bit of it still stuck in Gorgafel's ghostly flesh straining to join me. Well, who was I to say no?

Keeping track of every bit when I hauled them out was way above my pay-grade brain-wise, but they felt like one thing, so they moved like one thing too, all parts flying out to me as one. Just a big old avalanche of spiky sword bits. I really didn't think this through.

Luckily sprinting for my life from the flying spray of razor-sharp blades also kept me ahead of Gorgafel's sweeping attack. Maybe he didn't see the other two as a threat despite them being the ones to ignite his rear. Maybe he thought I was challenging him to be top Faun. Either way, I had his undivided attention, and I wasn't giving it up any time soon.

He chased me around in an arc, stomping through the trees and the forest of blades I'd just planted like they weren't even there. His axe trailed along behind him, ready to sweep me off my feet the moment that he closed the distance. And, of course, he was gaining on me. I had these little stubby legs to run with, and he could have done the splits and bridged continents. There was no getting away from him. So why try?

I spun on my heel and thrust the Lucis out behind me with all my strength, directly away from him, into the empty air. I was getting the hang of this whole Active Artifice thing. The rest of the swords leapt at me again, but this time there was a huge hunk of man-monster in the way.

For someone as big as Gorgafel, each little stab must have felt like a needle, but as it turns out, if you hit anyone with enough needles at the same time, they'll feel it. He bowed over with the impact of my hundred tiny blows, and his sweeping attack swept on by me.

There was no point hauling any harder on the echoes of the Lucis in Gorgy's back. There was no budging them from this side. Instead, I had to go back to basics. I charged him.

He saw me coming and reversed his grip on that massive axe, waiting to see which angle I was coming at him from before he moved to block, or more likely, to chop me in half again.

Asher's casting glow was over in the tree-line to my right, underneath where Mercy had launched herself from to give me a helping hand or… uh… foot, earlier. I knew that he could see me running in, and I knew that he'd have my back. I bellowed as I ran, "Can I get a lift?"

He couldn't reply, not in the middle of weaving his magic, but that didn't mean he didn't hear me. Gods, I hoped he heard me.

Gorgafel was in motion, the axe falling towards the place I would be arriving by his feet. I didn't have time to launch myself up with Artifice steps, and I didn't have the strength of the pillar of Ascension to launch me over the strike on my own. All I had was hope.

I leapt, and Asher's Gravity Snare blossomed above me, a tiny black hole that jerked me up towards it harder than the ground tried to pull me down. The axe head swung cleanly beneath my feet, wobbling as even Gorgafel's might was tested by the teeny tiny black hole Asher had opened up for me. I soared up to that black dot until it blinked out, then I soared right on by to hit Gorgafel full force in the loincloth area with my regular-sized great-sword.

You might be a hero of legend, you might be a ghost, you might be empowered by the awful might of the Voidgod bleeding out from a fragment of the weapon that was used to slay him, but when someone wallops you in the nuts with a giant sword, you feel it.

Gorgafel roared in agony, in a much higher octave than his last snarls, and I fell through a black cloud of his escaping lifeforce to tumble to my feet again behind him. No pond water in my mouth. I was calling that a win.

When I yanked the Lucis back this time, I was ready for all the echoes to come flying at me. I caught them with my Artifice as they came, holding them at bay and marveling as they started to orbit me unbidden. Everything was so much easier here, when everything Artifice was working on had the same resonance. If I'd tried something like this back on Amaranth, I'm pretty sure I would have caught one blade and died a pincushion, but here, everything answered my call.

For the first time, I actually felt a little bit like the god I was meant to be becoming. Gorgafel was turning, rage vibrating through every inch of his titanic form, and I was not afraid. I was not cowed. For the first time, I really felt like we were on even footing.

Rage made him clumsy, hefting his axe and hammering it down on me like he was splitting wood. If any part of him was still thinking, then he meant for me to leap to one side. I stood my ground, sweeping up the Lucis and the hundred ghostly blades around me to meet it.

I turned his blow aside.

Mercy hit him in the eye with another wind arrow, and when the storm unleashed, it looked like it took half his head off in the sudden explosion of fog. It might have killed him, but I was already moving, leaping onto the haft of the titanic axe and running up the length of it to where it was tucked under his arm. I sprung up from there into the whirling cloud of dispersing soul-stuff, flying blind until my hand touched ghostly flesh, and I took a grip.

Furry and sticky, it only took a moment for me to realize I was up to my elbow in his nostril. Oh well, at least it gave me something to hold onto. I shed mass from the Lucis until it was only a broadsword, and then I plunged it in.

In and out, in and out, stabbing his stupid face over and over. A blinding bright bar of flame burst through him somewhere down below, but even seeing it go in one side and out the other, I still wasn't convinced he was actually done for.

The echoes of the Lucis sung when I reached out to them, and they gathered around the original, I a wash of Artifice, making a sword so impossibly huge I wondered how I'd ever thought I could swing it. Good thing I didn't need to. All I had to do was hold on and let gravity do its work.

Gorgafel broke as the sword came down. One horn heading to my left, one to my right. The nostril I was hanging from went limp, and I started to fall, but I hung onto the handle of my sword as it parted his spectral flesh, and I rode it all the way back down to the ground floor.

Taking one staggering step back from it, I got ready to run, but it was over. The dead hero of the Faun fell in half, and the roars of pain and fury became nothing more than echoes in the mist.

New Skill Discovered: Twin Strike
Legendary Foe Defeated!
Potency increased to 48
Celerity increased to 25
Piety increased to 9
Twin Strike: Rank 1/10
Airstrike: Rank 6/10
Aether Resistance: Rank 5/10

390 Experience Gained
4300 Glory Gained

Asher and Mercy came staggering out of the fog to meet me over by the steaming heap of Faun that had something worth looting. Both of them looked exhausted, and considering we had no bodies to actually get tired here, it was kind of funny that I felt just the same. That had been a long fight. I definitely preferred the ones that were over quick. Preferably so quick I didn't get murdered in half. "Guess we win?"

Asher tripped over his own tail and stumbled into me. "It would appear that is the case."

It took more effort than I'd like to admit to pry the shard from the clinging flesh that surrounded it. Even though he was double-extra-strength dead, the shard didn't want to be parted from this spirit.

Quest: *Return of the Voidgod*
  Acquire Rusted Blade Shards: 4/6 Complete
  400 Glory Gained
  Tier of Glory Ascended!

That was a relief. I'd been starting to worry that I'd have to give up on all the glory we'd gathered here when I suicided myself back to Amaranth. "You both get a Tier from all that sweet Glory?"

"Yup." Mercy eyed the shard warily. Like it might bite her. "Might spend it on candy. I've earned a little treat."

I tossed it to her. Instincts overrode her common sense, and her hand lashed out to catch the rusty, juicy, hunk of metal. "I've got a better idea. Spend it on Aether. Grab Soulbond."

She looked down at the shard in absolute disgust and went on trying to deny what I was obviously saying to her. "So you can make me a bow that I can't lose in case we go dimension hopping again?"

"So you can take this shard back to Amaranth." I spelled it out to her.

She tossed the shard back at me, and it bounced off my chest. "I'm good. Thanks."

"You think the shards are doing something to me, corrupting me." I took a deep breath. "Well, maybe you're right. I am different than I used to be. Every shard I attach to myself is just making it worse."

"Oh so now you admit it." She came at me like a tiny little storm of rage, all pointing fingers and snarls. "And you want to infect me too?"

Asher stepped up. I wasn't expecting him to do that. "I do not believe that our friend wishes to do you harm, rather I believe that he wishes to earn back your trust."

She rolled her eyes. "Hey, Mercy, shove your face in this nest of scorpions to prove how not poisonous they are."

"Venomous," Asher corrected her.

"Really?" She threw her bow at his head. He didn't have our reflexes, and it hit him on the snout, and he made a little whimper. "Really? Now is the time to have that argument?"

Despite all that, I didn't take my eyes off her. I was giving her the full in the cage with the tiger treatment right now. "If you take one, I won't get any worse. I didn't even start to get really weird until the second one."

She sneered. "Pretty sure you tried to murder Seren with just one shard attached."

"Pretty sure you were in the pro-Seren-murder camp at that point!" I snapped back.

"Pretty sure I still am."

Asher piped up again before this could turn into a brawl. "The salient point remains that each time another shard is bound to Maulkin's soul, there is a notable… darkening both of his aura and his attitudes. If that could be abated by simply sharing the burden, then I'm all for it."

Mercy pointed to the lump of metal lying on the ground in between us. "Great, you attach a bit of rusty metal to your soul then."

"To shoulder that burden would mean that we would have you turning upon the both of us each time that there was a momentary disagreement? I think not." He turned to Mercy with a downward slope to his shoulders like he was trying to make himself smaller and less threatening. "You know your own mind; you would trust in your own judgment. Just as we would place our trust in you."

He had too good a point for even Mercy to just shout him down. She was flustered. "You… I…"

I'd been thinking about all this for a good long time. "It gave me a bad temper. I think. I can't really remember getting angry the way I do now before I bound the first shard. But that was about it."

"You want me even angrier?" She glowered at the shard now, not me. Probably an improvement.

I shrugged, even if she couldn't see it. "I think that Mercy with a bad attitude is going to be pretty much the same one we all know and love."

She showed me the fingers that she used to draw back her bow. "I hate you."

I blew her a kiss back.

She glanced up long enough for me to see her fighting a smirk. "Alright. If it keeps you from getting more evil, I guess I can take it."

I let out a little breath of relief. "You'll feel what I felt. You'll know that it didn't make me evil or whatever."

"I already said I'd do it. You don't have to make a big deal."

We all settled down for a moment, turning our attentions inward.

I already knew what I wanted before I even tried to spend my Glory. Ascension may have been dull and grey here in the land of the dead, but I could still pour my power into it. The moment that I felt the next Tier of Ascension settle into my being, I flicked over to the list of new Divinities I'd unlocked and grabbed Ascendant Cognition. Maybe it would make me a different person, but maybe I needed to be a different person if I was going to make it through all this and win.

I certainly didn't feel any smarter after I'd picked it, but then again, I don't actually know what being smart feels like, so how would I know? Maybe if I sat down with some math problems I'd get through them quicker. Or… at all.

Either way, the important thing was that, hypothetically, I'd be able to control more than one thing at a time with my brain. That was pretty exciting stuff. Since up until now I'd been able to control one thing: me—and even that was only about 50% of the time. Who controlled me when my brain wasn't in charge? Don't ask me.

Opening my eyes, I wasn't amazed by the sudden change. Everything looked the same as it had before I'd blinked. Asher was still lost in thought, probably buying up a whole new catalogue of spells that he'd only use once. Meanwhile, Mercy had done her upgrade and was now down on her haunches beside the shard. If I didn't have Aether, then what she did next probably wouldn't have looked like much of anything, but with my godly eyeballs, I could see the coils of soul-stuff stretching out from the core of her body to entangle the shard.

A dark, horned shadow loomed around the shard, what was left of Gorgafel's essence still clinging to it for all that he was worth, and for a moment, I wondered if she'd even be able to bind it with him still clinging on. She struggled and strained; her first steps into the world of Aether were a lot like a baby deer's first steps into the world, all wobbly knees and shaking. Once again my body was off and moving without any input from the thinking parts, yanking the central blade of the Lucis back out of the roiling mass of soul-stuff that had been a giant Faun and cutting through that shadow, severing the connection that he had to the shard.

With him gone, it leapt right into her waiting hands, and her soul and the shard seemed to sing to each other, wrapping around one another in a constant dance, not a struggle for supremacy, but a waltz between two lovers, entangled and entwined so deeply that they could never be parted.

If Asher had watched, he would have seen a hunk of metal hop into her hands. I saw her and the shard being remade into a new whole. She met my eyes when it was over, and the anger she'd been radiating since the Bastion just seemed to have vanished. She was like the old Mercy again.

My voice was so soft when I spoke, I wasn't sure that she even heard me. "Okay?"

"Haven't turned evil yet." She shrugged. "Maybe later."

Asher's soul flared a little brighter in our Aether sense, then his eyes opened. "Are we prepared to return to Amaranth?"

I opened my eyes after pumping myself up to the next tier of glory and then hefted my sword. "Who's going first?"

CHAPTER 18

The return trip was just as weird as the outbound flight. There was less turbulence once we'd taken off, but trying to kill everyone in such a way that didn't result in the cloud of their being dispersing throughout the whole plane was trickier. I had to send them one at a time while still holding their cloud bodies in place until the reaper reaped them so that they didn't arrive missing their whole personality—although with Mercy that probably would have been a drastic improvement.

I sent the other two off without much argument from Big D, but when I turned my sword on myself, I was definitely getting a vibe from him. "Sorry for demanding all these trips back and forth. I promise it won't happen again."

The weight of his words hit me like a solid rock slab. *See that it does not.*

Then it was off through the funnel tunnel back to the wonderful world of Amaranth, traversing the void between realities without delay … or an inflight movie. Not that I'd bought headphones for it anyway, but I could have made up my own dialogue; that was a good way to kill a few hours and make anyone sitting nearby rabidly hate you.

Landing in my body felt weird after the freedom of just having my spirit to haul around. The added weight of the armor I'd strung up to be spawned into didn't help with that sensation. Still, it was kind of nice having muscles to flex again. And there was something undeniably pleasant about going for a breath of air and some air actually going into your lungs, even if it did kind of taste like burning. Wait, what was burning?

Things at Talon's Keep were not exactly as we had left them. I wished that they were. I sincerely wished that they were, but instead there were some Dvergar lying around on the ground that I was pretty sure weren't just taking a nap. The side of the white-stone tower had a big black scorch mark across it, and the wooden barrier marking the outside of the village had been reduced to ash in a few big patches. Normally, that wouldn't have been a problem. Normally, the most dangerous thing left in the jungle was the various deathtraps that Seren was using to train me to be less likely to be murdered by deathtraps. Today was not a normal day.

Inyoka were storming through, throwing spears at any Dvergar that had been too slow to get inside and hacking down any of them that were fool enough to actually stand up to them. These were not the feral creatures we'd found out among the trees when we first arrived, they were the same shape as Asher, lithe and wicked-looking in their lacquered armor. That armor was stained a deep green to help them blend with the forest, but out here in the open, it just made the pallid scales that covered the rest of their bodies shine even brighter.

It must have been near midday judging by the sun shining down. All of this had happened in just a little over a day. We really couldn't turn our backs on this place for a second.

A shadow passed between me and the sun while I was peering up and made me shut my damn mouth. Big serpentine body. Wings. Fire shooting out the front. I was seeing my first real life dragon.

No matter what else happened today, win or lose, I got to fight a dragon.

Mercy scrambled up beside me after snatching up her bow, and Asher stalked forward from his shrine with magic already pooling in his hands. I had the Lucis in hand and the iron heap close enough to make it a great-sword again.

The whole place was swarming with armored Inyoka, but we could take them. One at a time, or all together, we could take them. "Split up. Drive them back. Get the Dvergar under cover."

Asher's head bobbed. "Agreed."

"And I want to kill the dragon."

Mercy took off laughing, but she didn't argue, which I think meant that I got dibs. I was just trying to work out how to get up there when I heard a scream from off in the woods. Seren. Where was Seren?

I'd have to cross the whole damn village to get to the source of that scream, but if there was one thing I was good at, it was chopping my way in one direction. The Inyoka hadn't even noticed us yet. Not really. We were just new warm bodies for them to prey on, so they didn't give us the respect, or terror, that we really deserved.

The first one that came bounding up to me with his axe held high looked genuinely shocked when I snapped it out of his hands and then snapped his hands off at the elbows with my return stroke. I kicked him out of my path and moved on.

Everything seemed so much easier to follow now. There was no doubt or confusion about where my sword was or my legs were or anything else. All the things that Seren had been trying to drill into me so that they'd be my natural response, I could keep track of it all now. The swivel of my wrists as I turned the Lucis to strike the face off the Inyoka creeping up behind me, and the positioning of my feet, knees slightly bent, to drive forward with force into the slash that split the next one in two. Ascendant Cognition was meant to help me pull off Artifice tricks on the fly. I had no idea that it would change everything.

I didn't even need to reach for Artifice once as I made my way across town. It was like I knew exactly where everything was and what I needed to do to get through it. Keeping track of everything was Cognition, no doubt, but the rest, that was Seren. She'd kept on going for a whole month when it was abundantly clear that I was too damn stupid to keep up with all the complex switches and stances and grips she was showing me, and now it was finally paying off.

Another blood-curdling scream went up from the jungle. If they'd hurt a single hair on her head, I was going to kill every dragon on Amaranth, on principle.

There was an ambush waiting for me as I rounded the old white stone outbuildings that Talon had once used as bunks for his students. Behind the wall, my Lifesense warned me of a couple of Dvergar in hiding, but it seemed like the majority had retreated elsewhere—probably into the mine, knowing Dvergar. I should have guessed that the enemy would be massing here, out of sight of the tower. That was probably where they thought we were camped out.

There were twelve Inyoka crouched here, listening for my approach—ten in armor, and two in tight fitting robes. Fair guess they were going to be throwing magic around. I didn't have an answer to magic, so I needed them stopped first.

A wall burst up from beneath my feet and launched me over their front ranks, and they all reacted much faster than I would have liked. Spears jutted up into my path, and I had to slap them aside with the flat of the Lucis. That left me no time to swing for the wizards. Good thing I could just land on them and do almost as much damage. With the power of my gigantic grey ass, I crushed one as he started to cast. I probably didn't kill him, but a face full of buns was enough to put a halt to whatever electric death he was planning on shooting my way.

The other one went on casting as if his buddy hadn't just been Mario-stomped, and the rest of them moved with all the precision of a well-oiled machine, spears abandoned and axes drawn as they closed in around me. Perfect.

In this close, the only thing they could do was hack down at me if they didn't want to risk chopping up each other, which meant a quick spin of the Lucis overhead knocked every attack aside. The wizard was still doing something or other, but I could split my attention enough to deal with the leaping lizards coming at me and keep track of how far along his spell was. I'd been watching Asher casting since we first landed, and it wasn't hard to work out when the bubble was going to pop.

With their first attacks rebuffed, my ten choppy friends started to circle like I was in the center of an Inyoka whirlpool, every one of them waiting for me to make a move so they could exploit the opening.

Well, I wasn't going to keep them waiting. I swung the Lucis in a wild arc that made the whole bunched mass of Inyoka in front of me leap back and the ones behind me lunge forward to attack. With a stomp of my foot, I hauled a wall up behind me. Not big enough to stop them dead, but more than enough to trip them up as they darted in.

Turning my back on a whole posse of angry Inyoka probably wasn't the best idea, but I did it all the same. I spun on the heel of my stomped foot to slash through the tumbling row of Inyoka. Gouging through their armor and their flesh in one long bloody line, stretching from body to body.

The ones behind me rushed back in, and I had to launch myself over the waist-high wall of screeching wounded to avoid being chopped up.

They followed, trampling all over their buddies to get at me, driving me farther away from the caster, who was just about to unleash that big ball of fire from between his hands. No, thank you.

With a jerk of my hand, I brought the stone wall down on him, not in a collapse but in a wave. Where it hit his flesh, it stopped dead, but that didn't stop me hauling stone around him until he was encased.

The same stone exploded out a moment later when his spell went off, peppering me and the rest of the Inyoka with shrapnel. I caught a glimpse of something burnt and sticky in the hollow where the mage had been, but he wasn't going to be pulling any rabbits out of hats again any time soon.

The Inyoka closest to him stopped when they got backs full of rock-hunks, but the ones to my right just kept on coming—explosion or not, they wanted blood.

I turned one away with a parry, but the next one dove into the gap that it left in my defenses and hammered an axe into my guts. It bounced off, driving the rear of the axe back into his face, Surged Vitality and armor combining into something impenetrable. The next one didn't make the same mistake, but his attack scraped off my thigh without leaving a mark all the same, then all three of them were off balance, and I had the Lucis singing in my hands, sweeping back through the lot of them.

Blood and bone and bits flew, and I was laughing. They might have been faster than me, better trained and smarter too, but I'd been fighting Seren for a month. They were small fry.

Lightning struck me, and I staggered. The poor wizard I'd assed to the floor was back up and casting again, but there was no way that I was letting him take advantage of the static roiling over me now. He had another spell already casting, but it wasn't going to be finished. I swung the Lucis at him from twenty feet away, and it shattered mid-swing, hunks of ragged iron leaping out in a wave that flew with all the force of my swing to rip through the flimsy cloth and scales that were his only protection. He went down screaming, and the spell died.

A quick glance confirmed that none of these Inyoka were getting up to cause trouble, so I called back the mass of my sword, then I took off running again. In the haze of fighting, I had no idea how much time I'd lost, but it had been too long since the last scream in the jungle.

The trees flew by me in a green blur, and I stretched every sense I had to their limits, searching for Seren, searching for any sign of the struggle I knew she would have put up.

I burst out of the tree-line and into our training grounds, and there were bodies everywhere. A half-dozen dead Inyoka were scattered across the packed dirt, slit with careful, precise cuts that avoided their armor and left them in puddles of their own blood.

Up on the raised podium platforms of cut off trees where I'd spent weeks tripping and stumbling and falling, Seren danced.

Blood was streaked through her golden hair, but if she was hurt, then there was no sign of it in the way she fought. Some foolish Inyoka were up on top of the course, leaping from stump to stump, trying to get around the shining wall of death that her blades were spinning. Down here on the ground floor, some more Inyoka were clustered around the base of the stump where she was balancing on one foot, hacking at it with their axes as if she was going to be caught off guard.

I'll be honest with you, I was feeling a little bit stupid after charging in to rescue her, only to realize that she is at least ten times more competent than me and probably could have wiped the floor with all these lizards without breaking a sweat. Still, I was here now. I might as well help out. "Honey, I'm home!"

The Inyoka down on the ground turned to charge me immediately, but Seren didn't even spare me a glance. One blade leaped out to parry a thrusting spear, and the other lanced through the exposed throat of an Inyoka that had wobbled too close when he leapt over to her. "Took thy time."

It almost felt lazy pulling the same trick again, but Seren hadn't seen it the last time. So it probably didn't count. A stomp of the foot to bring up a short wall and trip all the Inyoka, a wild slash to keep them from getting up again, and then I surged Potency to step off that wall and launch myself up to land beside her, casual as I could play it. "Sorry, babe, I didn't realize there was a party going on or I would have come home sooner."

She leapt right at me, and I caught her around the waist, spinning to toss her onto the next podium along as her one finally collapsed. There was an Inyoka on the raised pole next to the one she landed on, and he didn't like his chances against her. He tried to jump away, only to meet a fresh made jut of stone coming up from the earth. The tip hit him in the throat, and he went down, tumbling end over end, gasping and croaking.

Some of the blood in her hair was definitely hers—I could see it oozing from a wound in her scalp that I had to lean over to her to heal with what a passer-by might have interpreted as a head-pat. "So, how have you been?"

She leapt away from my touch as soon as Restoration had gone to work, spinning as she fell to the forest floor, blades swirling around her to knock aside a thrown spear and to part the back of one fleeing Inyoka's neck. "The wyrm attacked while I was training. I have been detained here since then. I cannot speak to the safety of thy underlings."

I guess we didn't need the high ground any more now that there were two of us. I jumped down to land on the dude I'd throat jabbed with a rock, and he squelched. "The Dvergar? Well, some of them bit the big one, but most of them seem to have holed up somewhere, I'm guessing the mine? Maybe the tower?"

She raised an eyebrow at me. "Perhaps a plan in case of attack should be prepared?"

"Yeah, kind of dropped the ball there." I shrugged. "Didn't expect anyone to know about this place."

She took off without even checking to see if I'd fall into step beside her. I did, of course. I'd been following her lead for much too long to let her shake me off now. "We should reinforce the village with all haste. There are few wyrmspawn left in these woods."

I overtook her, still gaining speed, forcing her to pick up the pace. "Sounds like a plan."

"Nay, a plan would have been to withdraw to the choke point of the tower entrance and then perform a fighting retreat up the stairs so that the populous would have every benefit of its defensive structures. This is not a plan. This is an action. Responsive to crisis, and all too late." Turns out making her run faster did not mean she'd be too breathless to bitch me out.

I smiled back over my shoulder at her and almost hit a low hanging branch. "Missed you too."

There was no softening of her razor-sharp features. No twinkle in her eye. It was kind of hard to tell when she was genuinely mad at me, and when she was just being Seren a lot of the time. "Ah, yes. Thy dazzling wit. I am certain it will be of great comfort to those of your peons that have been slain this day."

My falsetto voice carried off into the woods as we rounded the corner in the path, and the burning village appeared ahead of us. "Oh, Maulkin, I missed you too. I can't wait until all the murdering is over so we can make out."

"The killing never ends. Thy know this as well as I. For so long as you hold power, others will seek it." She was real fun at parties.

The worst of the Inyoka had been driven off by Mercy and Asher's combined efforts. There was a solid wall of fire along one side of town, replacing the missing barricades, and Mercy was perched up on top of one of the wooden houses that had been thrown up, launching arrow after arrow through those flames, wrapped up in little pockets of wind so that they'd carry the fire on with them.

For his part, over by the base of the tower, Asher seemed to be holding his own against the few casters that the enemy had brought to bear. Every time I saw one spell springing to life, his magic already seemed to be lashing out to break it apart. Water met fire, and lightning met waves of earth. The whole catalogue of magic that he'd memorized was being flung out to keep any resonances being built up. On his own, he was keeping every single one of them at a stalemate.

Which was where Seren and I came in. She darted off among the burning buildings, already zeroing in on the casters' locations, and I honestly had no fear for her up against some poor squishy wizards. She could move faster than they could cast. Unless she really screwed up, they wouldn't have a chance.

Rounding a corner, I tripped over a pair of dead Inyoka and almost ran straight into Gunhild and her crossbow. She was propped up against the wall, face shredded by an Inyoka's claws and shoulder pinned by a spear that had managed its way through her heavy armor and stony skin. She didn't shoot me, which was nice, but she didn't shoot me because she was almost unconscious. I didn't even know if she'd seen me. I pumped Restoration into her face, then yanked out the spear. She toppled forward like a brick, ripped face mashing into the ground. She'd live, but she'd be mad about it.

Two of her boys lay dead farther along, each of them fully armored, ready for battle, and more than willing to lay down their lives to keep their Matriarch safe. There were not many fighters left among the Dvergar, and up until today, I would have said that they didn't need them anymore. Now I wished that there were a hundred more. I wish I could stop being wrong all the time. If only because Seren was eventually going to run out of verbose old timey ways to say: "I told you so."

There were more dead Inyoka about than dead Dvergar, so I was choosing to call that a win, but the fight was far from over. Even if Mercy and Asher had driven them out of the village proper, there were still a whole load of Inyoka out there, just waiting for the chance to come and murder us all. As if to remind me just how outnumbered we were, the dragon took a swoop over the town.

It was as pale as all the Inyoka, but where they were white—like the kind of things that lived in deep, wet caves—the wyrm herself was shimmering and opalescent. Her elegant neck shimmered with the heat passing up it, and then the flames leapt forth from her gaping maw to destroy everything beneath her as she soared. Unfortunately, I was one of the things beneath her.

Dropping to my knees and throwing up a dome of stone overhead meant that the flames didn't hit me, but it didn't take long for me to realize my mistake. I had basically just built an oven with me in it, and the air was growing hotter by the second. My hair started to crispen and burn with a smell like popcorn, and every breath hurt. Where my hand was touching the metal of the Lucis' guard, it seared me. Where my knees touched the cracked earth, they burned. I had to push up and out with all of my strength to crack the eggshell of scorching stone I'd encased myself in, and only then did I realize the destruction that the dragon had wrought.

The tower and the old outbuildings were stone. Everything else in town was wood. Where the shadow of the dragon had passed over, the thriving little village that had been here the last time I looked was just gone, ash and cinders left in its place. The only solace I could take was that the people who lived and worked in these buildings were already gone.

As she passed over the jungle, the wyrm turned. She tilted her wings, so that the tip of one almost touched the green foliage, and made a graceful arc around to come in for another pass. Another swathe of our home burnt away to nothing. To hell with that. The Dvergar had been working too hard for too long to make a home for themselves after I wrecked the last one. They weren't starting over from nothing again.

I'd been making my way to the tower at a steady pace so far, checking each corner before I rounded it. Now I ran, and smoke filled my nose. All the hopes and dreams of the Dvergar were burning away to nothing. If there were any Inyoka still in the village then they were idiots. That wyrm didn't give a damn who she burned.

Asher was looking almost relaxed by the time I got to him. Every one of the enemy casters seemed to have stopped at some point between me leaving Seren and me arriving here. Mysteriously. Almost as if an enraged Alvaren Paladin had gotten to them.

The wyrm wasn't coming right at us, but she was passing close to the tower on this run. "We need to bring her down."

"My snare?" I could almost see the numbers buzzing behind his eyes. "I doubt it will have power enough to fell her."

I shrugged that off. "I'll meet her halfway. Let's go."

With every bounding step of my charge, I got higher. Building a staircase to heaven with uprooted rock, each step just big enough for one foot to touch before I launched myself to the next. What had been a clumsy panic before came naturally to me now, the whole world bending to my Artifice until I was too high up to reach the stone beneath the soil anymore. I was halfway up the height of the tower, still falling short of the oncoming dragon's flight, but then that perfect little black dot appeared between us. That colorless nothing that dragged everything and everyone closer. The vast white dragon above me strained against the sudden pull, and I surged up into it. Sword ready and a roar of triumph escaping my lips.

She lashed out with her claws at the last moment, trying to bat me down, but there was an edge on my sword and all my strength behind it. I snipped through her blackened claws and buried my blade in her sternum.

Maybe if she hadn't slowed me down with those claws, I would have made it through the scales and the bone to something soft and vital underneath. As it was, my blade wedged into the thick battering ram ridge of solid bone where her ribcage fused beneath her elegant neck, and I dangled there.

I could see her scaled throat working above me, feeling the heat radiating up along it as she swept down to scorch our town off the map, so I punched her in the hottest part I could reach.

With a run up or some better leverage, maybe I could have done some real damage, interrupting the flow of fire up her neck, but dangling here uselessly, all I did was interrupt the lethal breath, making her cough out a plume of black smoke. "Knock that off!"

She tried to claw at me then, to shake me off with a sudden drop, but none of it worked. I had my hands tight around the Lucis' handle, and I was stuck right into her someplace that her mighty limbs just couldn't reach. No wonder the Wyrms needed Inyoka servants, they couldn't even scratch themselves without assistance. I had become everything that I hated. I was that itchy spot in the middle of my back that I couldn't reach, except for a dragon.

Of course, wyrms are thinking creatures, not dumbasses like me, and this one had worked out what to do much quicker than it took me to deal with an itchy back. A solid minute or two would pass before I found a doorframe to rub up against, but this clever lizard was diving for the rooftops already.

I could see it all now, the wood splintering under her weight, the wood slipping harmlessly across her scales, and me turning into a red smear down her front. Not today, thank you very much. I strained out with Artifice, pulling the building apart before we reached it, tearing shingles and rafters open like waiting jaws and then slamming the mouth of the house shut on the dragon.

The wyrm took no notice, smashing through as though the whole thing was made of paper, but I wasn't done yet. We were low enough for me to reach beneath the earth now, and I grabbed onto the stone with every scrap of will and hauled it up.

Spikes of stone burst from the ground, through the ruin of the house, and almost through me. Where they hit the wyrm they stopped dead, unable to press through, but the goal wasn't to kill her, it was to stop her. Every jab of stone was more friction, fighting back against her dive. Every little brittle ping of stone snapping off was music to my ears because soon she was moving so slowly I had time to react instead of just clinging on for dear life.

We were so low now I could have jumped clear without even

having to do the goofy three-point superhero landing or risking my kneecaps, and that meant that I could reach even more of the stone beneath us.

My first thought was a wall, but I was pretty sure she'd jerk up at the last second, and I'd be the one to get a face full of masonry, so I reached for those funky little spikes again, not aiming to jab her but to pen her in.

She saw them coming this time around, and I was too busy concentrating on what I was doing to realize what she was doing. The flames burst out from her mouth, ripping through the stone as it formed, blackening what was thick enough to withstand the blast and melting away what wasn't.

This close to her throat, the Lucis sucked up all the heat until it was burning through the leather grip, my gloves, and into my hand. I could let go and fall, abandoning my sword, or I could hold on and hurt. I grit my teeth together and flung the next house open before we hit it.

There were still Dvergar inside that one. If I hadn't popped it open at the last moment, then the whole thing would have come down on them. Instead, they just had a close encounter with me screaming by, dangling off a dragon, and throwing up lumps of rock to catch the flames the wyrm was still spitting out in every direction.

We whipped through to the next building so fast I couldn't believe it, and all attempts to trap the wyrm were now abandoned in favor of just holding on with my rapidly blackening crisp of a hand. Lifesense warned me of one living body in the next building, up on the roof. "Maulkin!"

That was a girl's voice. Either Mercy or Seren—I didn't have time to look. I just stretched out my spare hand and caught them as they leapt. There was a flash of metal as Seren soared past me and into the dragon's wing, slashing through the fine pale skin there with the sword I'd made her.

At once, we lurched to the side, all attempts at flight falling apart as the wyrm's wing tore. On reflection, that fragile bit of skin probably should have been what I went for. Oh well.

I did my best to throw up walls to keep the village intact as we spun to the earth, but by this point, I didn't even know up from down. We hit the ground hard enough to rip me and the Lucis clear of the bone where we'd been wedged, and I heard Seren's yelp of dismay as she was thrown free too.

We both rolled back to our feet and faced off with the ton of angry fire-lizard that we'd just dropped on the doorstep of the tower. I could already tell this was going to be epic.

I had one moment before it all kicked off to glance over at Seren's bloody face, and I knew before I even did that she was going to have the same grin plastered on her face as me. Oh yeah, we were a match made in heaven.

The wyrm snapped for me, blackened obsidian teeth shining, each one of them as big as my head. I swept up the Lucis to parry, and the blade scraped over teeth and gums. The bite was knocked up, but like a snake, the head was whipped back before I could counter. Seren had closed the distance, going for the same injured wing that had brought the wyrm to ground, and with her feet on the floor, she had both hands free for a sword.

A flap buffeted her back before she could do more damage, but that just made her circle farther back until the dragon's own bulk was blocking her from sight. My job was obvious: keep the dragon's attention pointed this way. I could do that.

Rearing up, the wyrm tried to rake me with both sets of front claws, trying to drive me back if she couldn't rip me up, but only one set still had their points, so I danced in past that one, surged Vitality, and took the hit. Blunted claws raked down my armor, the force of the blow enough to stagger anyone, but not enough to knock me back.

Not when I was surging Potency for a cut thrust through the gaping wound I'd already put in her chest.

The bone gave way beneath the blow this time, an explosion of blood and flame leaping out to greet me as I slid it home. One hand was already charred to bones, but now dragon-fire tore up my arms and hit me square in the chest. Surged Vitality or not, I felt that. Eyebrows? Gone. Face? A fair bit of that was gone too. The force of the escaping flame launched me back to tumble end over end.

The wyrm was not impressed. She reared up, letting out a strangled scream somewhere between an eagle's cry and a monitor lizard with its tail in a blender. That blender may very well have been Seren. I had no idea what she was doing around the back end of the wyrm. All I knew for sure was that I was not going to be suffering through any more dragon fire.

Even as I darted back, giving the wyrm some distance as she furiously flailed the ground beneath her with the whipping of her neck, I could see her trying to breathe flame at me. It was sputtering out that hole I'd made in her chest each time. Blackened blood exploded out with each coughing attempt at fire, sizzling where it landed.

There was a smoker's cough joke in here somewhere. I could feel it.

Electricity danced over the wyrm's scales, and it took me a second to realize that Asher was still here, fighting alongside us from the relative safety of the tower's entrance. The wyrm spun to face him, but that just opened up her neck to me.

With one leap, using up those last moments of my surged Potency, I was there, swinging with all my strength. The dragon's scales were tough, but they weren't nearly enough. The Lucis bit deep into the wyrm's neck, and the furious warbling screams cut off abruptly.

In the sudden silence, I could hear Seren's shouts, but they were the same bellows of exaltation she let out every time she thought she'd landed a killing blow. With a wet thump, I saw the wyrm's tail flopping off to land useless and dead against the side of the smelters.

Whatever pride the wyrm had been clinging to was gone now. She beat her wings in a pathetic frantic frenzy, desperate to get up, to get away. The wind she was throwing out was enough to send me skidding from my spot at the chopping block, so there was only time for one more chop. I didn't bring my sword down on her neck again. Instead, I swung it down into the joint of back and wing.

Without surged Potency, I didn't make nearly as much of a dent as I'd have wanted. Blood was flowing, but the wing still moved as if I'd done nothing at all. She lunged forward, spreading her wings as wide as they'd go, and I was knocked off my feet, into the air, end over end. Next thing I knew, I was landing on my head.

Seren was on the Wyrm's back when I got the right way up, swords shimmering into sight and then vanishing, again and again, as she butchered her way along its scaled spine. She didn't have the strength to drive a blow clean through that armored hide, but I'd seen her fighting golems made of solid stone in just the same way, carving weakness into things without a weakness and then punching through. Given enough time, I was pretty sure she could kill anything with the same precise cuts she used to kick my ass all around the jungle.

Normally I'd be happy to leave her to it, but despite the injured wing, and the blood pouring out of every end, the wyrm was still taking flight, beating frantically to gain height. "Jump!"

Seren didn't need told twice. We had that trust. She just sprinted the remaining length of the wyrm and jumped.

The wyrm snapped for her, bloodied and blackened jaws stretching wide to swallow her lithe form whole. Without even thinking about it, I parried.

The length of the Lucis shattered into fragments, the original weapon the only thing that was left in my hand. The rest of the metal leapt out, still sword-shaped but fragmented. It wouldn't cut a damn thing like that, but the force of the blow was still there, thumping into the wyrm's throat, turning the bite aside.

I caught Seren with my other arm, still kind of stunned that worked.

With hate burning in her eyes, the wyrm beat her way up into the air and out of reach.

Even before I'd set her back on her feet, I could feel Seren gearing up to yell at me about letting another enemy live. She obviously hadn't seen what I'd seen before I shouted out to her.

Asher's spell went off with a roar, and a column of lightning struck down from the clear sky and all the way through the wyrm as she tried to gain height. This wasn't a pretty little zap to stop her hearts, it was a violent torrent of primeval power exploding though every part of her. Her whole midsection exploded, and wings, limbs, and head soared in every different direction. Seren pirouetted behind me so that the worst of the splash zone fun smacked me in the face instead of her.

If it wasn't dead after that, I was pretty sure it never would be.

I gave Asher a salute as he flopped down onto his knees, and then I took off running once more. Mercy was still up ahead on the rooftops, raining a steady stream of arrows down on any Inyoka fool enough to step forward out of the trees. Sometimes a spear would sizzle away to ash before it reached her. Most of the time they never even got that far.

At my heels the whole way, Seren reached out to grab my blackened hand. I managed a juicy squeeze before we were launched up into the air on my rising podiums again. It was harder to concentrate on hauling stone up for the two of us. I knew exactly where my feet were going to be next, but I had to keep glancing down to Seren's to make sure I didn't miss.

Obviously growing frustrated with the dawdling pace, Seren leapt from her podiums and onto my back, kicking off my lower back as she passed, then balancing on my shoulders like she was standing on solid ground. She was light enough that I only almost fell to my death before I got my balance.

We were higher than Mercy's rooftop now and running out of stone fast, so for the last length between there and the fire wall I shot up only spikes of stone barely big enough for the balls of my feet to keep us level before I leapt over and down into the Inyoka. They did not look happy to see us.

Without the wyrm overhead to direct them, it felt like these Inyoka had lost all semblance of strategy. After I Mario-stomped the first one into paste and chopped the one beside it in half, the rest broke and ran. I may have slightly broken my legs with that landing, but Restoration put that, my fried face, and my crispened hand back together in a soothing wash of green energy.

Seren was off and pouncing before I could even move again, and I just let her scamper off and have her fun. What was I going to do? Stop her mass murdering the people that had just tried to do the same to us? Sometimes bad guys needed killing, and she was more than happy to do it. Why not let her have her fun?

The wall of fire died down behind me as I turned, looking for some Inyoka of my own to slaughter. Mercy came bounding up, sprang high enough to slap me in the back of the head, then sprinted off into the woods to go lizard hunting herself.

Organized, the Inyoka had been a threat, but now they'd be easy pickings. There was nothing in the woods that even resembled a predator, and everyone was too far gone for me to catch up, so I just left the girls to it. My fight was done.

I turned back to the village in flames and let out a sigh. Then I thought it again, louder; my fight was done. This time the universe agreed.

Skill Discovered: Fire Resistance

Skill Discovered: Ascendant Potency

Victory!

Potency increased to 50

Celerity increased to 26

Vitality increased to 20

Twin Strike: Rank 3/10

Airstrike: Rank 7/10

Fire Resistance: Rank 1/10

670 Experience Gained

The rest of the day was a lot less fun. While Seren and Mercy stalked the remaining Inyoka on the island, it fell to me and Asher to try and put the village back together, put out the fires, retrieve the Dvergar from the mines, and then, worst of all, admit to Gunhild that I could have built them stone houses this whole time but I just didn't want to. That last revelation earned me a pretty solid kick in the shins. Dvergar don't wear steel-toe-capped boots. The whole boot is steel. They clang when they stomp.

So while Asher was put to work dousing fires and burying the dead, I was cornered by every civil planner and architect from a whole society obsessed with civil planning and architecture to receive my marching orders. There was no denying that I'd screwed up, leaving the Dvergar and Seren to fend for themselves while we went off questing after promising we'd take care of them, so instead of bitching and moaning the whole way through, I decided to take my lumps and only bitch and moan about half as much as I wanted to.

By the time that Mercy had come stalking back into town, completely out of arrows, I had been reduced to a blubbering pile of misery, throwing myself at her feet and begging, "Mercy! Save me. They're making me do work."

She kicked me. "You sat on your ass while they built a whole town without helping when you could do all this just by thinking about it?"

"Mercy!" I sobbed. "It's hard."

She kicked me again. "Harder than actually building it? With your hands? Would you rather do that?"

"You're so mean."

She sneered. "Get back to work."

The wooden buildings that hadn't been leveled in the clash with the wyrm were well on their way to being torn down now. The planks snapped and sheared into workable firewood, doors, and shutters by the devoted craftsmen who were now completely delighted to realize that I could adjust the new buildings I'd made from solid stone to fit their fixtures instead of them having to do it the other way around.

As it turned out, I was every stonemason's dream, and even though the earth beneath us had already subsided several times as I hauled more and more stone up, the Dvergar were too excited to give a damn. I could see my whole future in Amaranth stretching out before me. An eternity of being hauled around from one Dvergar settlement to the next, building them things. I was in hell. I'd done bad things, and now I was in hell, working a steady job until the world ended.

At least I could rely on the Voidgod to show up and end the world before too long. There was some end in sight.

Gunhild was back on her feet, looking surprisingly fine for somebody who'd been nearly dead less than an hour ago. She took a lot of interest in the work I was doing for all her little minions, carefully prodding me in the hip and pointing out where something wasn't completely straight or completely perfect. I've heard of micro-managers before, but having to remake the same doorframe seven times when there was still half a village to haul up had me at my wit's end.

Night had fallen by Seren's return. I didn't even bother to beg her for help—she'd probably just start giving the Dvergar pointers on how to exploit me harder. The stone walls that I'd brought up to replace the old barricades wouldn't be thick enough for her. Neither would the shelters I'd built to protect the mine entrance and the giant crossbow things that they made me build in case of dragon attacks.

The only ones who didn't seem happy with all of this were the miners themselves. They felt like all of this was cheating. Like I was robbing them of their purpose—not to mention the number of promising shafts I'd collapsed by pulling stone up.

By the time it was all done and they finally left me alone, the whole village sat in a depressed basin from all of the collapses, every bit of rock that I could reach hauled up from beneath the soil and painstakingly shaped into all the myriad shapes that the Dvergar demanded. I'd never be able to do the engraving that they loved so much, but that was fine. I'd given them stone to work, and from what I'd managed to understand from all the whispers, it would be a way for them to feel like this place belonged to them, not me, if they got to put their mark on it.

There were songs being sung around the fire that night as I still trudged about, reinforcing a wall here, raising a roof there. The dead were being remembered. All their great deeds, and all the stupid stuff that made everyone crack up. Mercy was out there in the middle of them. Asher perched perilously on the very edge of a bench, ready to leap up if things grew too raucous. The only one I couldn't see was Seren.

I'd kind of hoped she might be up in the tower, waiting for me in the bedroom we'd claimed, but I only had to go halfway up the tower before my Lifesense informed me that I was alone in here. Except for the damn butterflies.

Eventually, I found her perched up on one of the new roofs, staring down at the gathered Dvergar with contempt. I didn't like that look on her face. When she was happy, she was beautiful, but when she was bitter, all the elegant angles of her face turned jagged and cruel. It seemed to be the same for all Alvaren—a big reason they never let their emotions show. Got to stay gorgeous.

The walls may have been built to the dvergar's specifications, but I'd added in a few details of my own—like the handholds just where I could jump up and catch them. I scrambled up beside Seren, but she didn't bother to look my way. Her eyes were narrow and cruel. "Why do they celebrate defeat?"

I opened and shut my mouth a few times. "We won?"

She waved my words away without breaking her death-stare. "I do not speak of thee, I speak of the slain. Each one of them faltered and failed. Why do they sing in their praise?"

"Because even if that was true, which… uh… pretty sure it isn't"—sometimes I forgot just how much growing up with the Alvaren had messed Seren up—"they still cared about them. They were friends, family. Why wouldn't you want to remember them?"

She shrugged a shoulder. "Grieving is weakness."

"Wow, uh no. Feeling stuff doesn't make you weak. Do you think I could have done half the stuff I did today if I didn't care about all these people?" I hoped she couldn't see me blushing this far from the campfire. "About you?"

Abruptly, she leaned into me. It was enough of a shock that I didn't know what to do for a moment, before I realized I was meant to put an arm around her. Normal boyfriend stuff. Right? She sighed. "You would have fought to the best of your abilities, regardless of your attachments."

"I'd like to think I would have, but I don't know." She could probably feel my words vibrating through my sooty breastplate more than she could hear them. "Do you think having something to fight for made a difference?"

She twisted to look up at me, allowing just a hint of confusion to show on her face. It was amazing what she considered being vulnerable looked like. Any admission of anything resembling weakness, any hint that you didn't know everything and anything, and the Alvaren read it as opening them up to danger. "I fight because it is my duty to fight. Just as you do."

"Hah, I wish that was true too. Most of the time I fight because I don't want something big and scary to eat me. Or my friends. Sometimes just because I'm mad. I don't think duty really crosses my mind."

She pushed away from me a little farther, lacing her fingers through mine to keep herself steady, but not willing to look at me. "So you would not have come to my aid if you did not have a… personal attachment?"

Thank the gods she was looking away because the blush was getting worse and worse. We were talking about our feelings. Oh no. "Well… even if we weren't uh… what we are… we'd still be friends. So yeah, I'd have come helped?"

She met the dull glow of my eyes, and I was startled once more by just how pretty she was. I mean movie-star breathtaking. So damned beautiful that I sometimes forgot to listen to the words that were actually coming out of that pouty little mouth. "I am sworn to you, so I will serve you however thou would have me. It is not a matter of whatever affection I hold for you, it is simply the natural order of things. The powerful lead, the rest follow."

"That's not… I… I don't want you to do things because it is your duty. I want you to do them because you want to… I…" This was the conversation I'd been trying to avoid for more than a month now. The relationship killer.

She didn't even seem to realize it was an issue. "To serve you is my pleasure."

"Okay, that's uh… that's kind of the problem." Why did talking about this stuff have to be so difficult? "I don't know if you actually want to be with me or if you're just… obliged?"

She finally turned to look up at my face. "How would it differ?"

And just like that, I was feeling like the biggest pile of trash on the whole of Amaranth, and that was including Orphia. That big trash heap. Seren must have seen it on my face because she tried to make it better. By philosophizing. Oh gods.

"Would I take more pleasure in my acts if I were to choose each in turn, remaking every moment of my life into a debate instead of simply taking joy in my service?"

I wasn't getting dragged into another roaming discussion about how weird the Alvaren mindset was. I needed a real answer. "Seren, are you in my bed because you feel like it's your job?"

"Thy have the most comfortable bed in the settlement. I would wish to sleep upon it, even were we not carnally entangled." She had a little blue flush to her cheeks, even now with just the two of us here talking about it.

Time to give up on subtlety and just bite the bullet. "Would you be having sex with me, if you didn't think I was your boss?"

"Nay. I think not." That was a real punch to the gut, but she said it with wry amusement. "Were you… less than you are, I doubt thy could have inflamed me so. Thy power, thy strength, it draws me to you."

Alvaren ranked and filed everyone and everything. They understood everything in hierarchies, with their position in the rankings determining how they dealt with everyone above and below them. It kind of made sense that they'd be attracted to people they thought were superior. Even if the word superior kind of made me queasy in this context. Like I was good breeding stock or something.

"Wouldst thou have hungered for me if it were not for my comeliness?" She caught me off guard with that one. Both with the point and with the bat of her eyelashes. Where did she learn that? I didn't teach her that. Was Mercy training her up to devastate me using only facial expressions?

My mouth worked uselessly as I tried to put an answer together, like I was chewing cud. "I'd like to think so? I mean, even if you weren't pretty, you're still pretty awesome."

"Yet it was a part of the attraction." She squeezed my arm. "Just as thy might draws me to you."

"Yeah but…" With her this close to me, looking all pretty and flushed, my train of thought was up on one set of wheels, wobbling dangerously close to completely derailing.

She leaned in even closer, but instead of softness and flirtation, there was steel in her words. "I must ask thee, do you take me for some doe-eyed milkmaid, set to lift her skirts to any man of mention and quivering with dread of him?"

"Well… no." The idea of Seren being scared of anyone was kind of laughable.

"Then have faith that I know my own mind." She placed a gentle kiss on my cheek. "Have care for me enough to trust in my choices."

I squeezed her even closer. "Even when you could definitely do better?"

"Let me by thy judge."

Maybe all of our problems weren't actually sorted out after that. Maybe I was still just fooling myself. Remember all that stuff I said about how throughout the eons of human history, men have done a lot of really dumb things to get laid? Ignoring problems is definitely one of those dumb things.

In other news, can you call it make-up sex when you didn't technically have a fight? Just a kind of arduous conversation? Regardless, it was a good thing that all the Dvergar that hung around the tower on a normal night were down in the village partying.

Despite whatever may or may not have happened in that bedroom, we were still both back on our feet at dawn, looking well-rested and heading down to greet the gathered council of Dvergar and Eternals that had filled the town hall that the little darlings made me build for them yesterday.

Gunhild was the first to speak—as usual. "Nice of you to be crawling out your pit to join us. Even if the rest of us have been here an hour."

I chose to be the bigger man and ignore that. It was easy to be the bigger man when you were literally three times the size of somebody.

"How's everybody holding up?"

The few Dvergar that had been designated as Elders by their peers looked too uncomfortable to pipe up, but Mercy certainly wasn't. "People are pissed at us. We left. They died."

Asher looked up at me from his stone pew with a sigh. "They are rightly unhappy. We provided them scarce defense against invasion."

"Look, I'm sorry, but we really didn't think anybody else knew about this place." I appealed to the Dvergar Elders. "I mean Tsangaanax did, obviously, but that was like… a thousand years ago? It seems kind of nuts that he'd be sending over his little soldiers now."

Gunhild had settled back into her seat, but she still had that angry energy about her. "But he bloody did, didn't he."

"No," Asher said so softly that the blazing row Gunhild was gearing up for died before it could even start. "I cannot say with any certainty that these were his servants. In all accounts of Tsangaanax, he was described as a great black wyrm, 'dark as the tempest's heart.' I would suggest that these pale scaled Inyoka are the servants of another master, seeking us out for some other purpose."

Mercy rolled her eyes. "You don't think the different Wyrms talk to each other?"

"It is not in the nature of Wyrms to be cooperative. Rather they seek dominance in all things. They are territorial, viewing most other races as tools that they might use to gain traction against others of their own kind. Nor is it in the nature of the Wyrm to take prisoners and slaves when Inyoka are so easy to breed. Had Tsangaanax conquered another brood, he would simply have exterminated them, not run the risk of betrayal by deploying them against us." Damn it was handy having an Inyoka on our team.

Still, that didn't actually answer any questions. Just raised more of them. "So some completely unrelated dragon also wants to kick our asses for no reason?"

Asher shrugged. "Perhaps."

"I can think of plenty of reasons," Mercy piped up.

I cut them all off before it could turn into a bitch-fest. "Will the new fortifications help?"

Gunhild was forced to give me a begrudging nod. "Aye, we'll be holding off anything shy of an army with them."

I clapped my hands. "Cool. So we can get on with our job now?"

Apparently not. Gunhild rose to her feet and tried to square off with me. "Sixteen dead and buried. More hurt. Three trapped in the mine, still getting dug out today."

I threw up my hands. "I should have built the walls before. I should have made this place a fortress. I thought we were hidden here. I thought we were safe. It is all my fault. Is that what you want to hear?"

"I be wanting to hear my dead boys' voices again. Can you be giving me that?!"

I hadn't realized just how angry I was until she said that. It took the wind out of my sails. Then I realized I was basically screaming at an old lady who'd lost her friends or possibly her kids. I still wasn't 100% on what her relationship to the younger dvergar who followed her around like lapdogs was. I really hoped they weren't her harem.

Mercy put a hand on Gunhild's shoulder, but the Matriarch shrugged it off. "You all be high and mighty, saving the world from some doom you've imagined. Well, those boys did nothing wrong, and now they're in the dirt."

Asher was giving me a very level look. He wasn't saying "I told you so," but I could tell he was thinking it. Right from the start, he'd objected to me involving myself in people's lives, trying to help them when I could. Not because he didn't want to help people, but because he was certain that saving the universe was too important for us to get sidetracked. I'd kind of hated him for saying that back when we were first starting out, and now, looking down at Gunhild, flushed and fighting back her tears, I hated him all over again. This didn't stop being important just because there were bigger things going on. People didn't stop mattering just because they didn't have powers or gods to kill.

I scooped her up in my arms. I didn't mean to—I knew she was not a big fan of being picked up—but what else was I meant to do, lie down? She struggled in my arms for a moment, like I was trying to hold her still instead of just hold her, but then she heard my voice rumble down and went limp. "I'm so sorry."

Her fists beat helplessly against my blackened breastplate. "Sorry won't be fixing nothing."

"It's all I've got." She could feel me crying along with her now. She had to feel it, even if she couldn't see the tears or hear the sobs. Seren was looking away from me like I was taking a crap on the floor, but Mercy had suspiciously watery eyes. Asher looked disinterested as though this was all irrelevant to his interests.

When we finally parted, both of us were sheepish enough that the conversation was put to bed. She thought the fortifications would be enough to keep them safe in the future, and I couldn't do any more for the Dvergar, short of sitting here on the off chance of dragons. I was sorry that Gunhild had lost people, it ached in my gut when I thought about it, but I couldn't spend my whole eternity babysitting. I just couldn't.

Seren didn't have any compunctions about trampling all over that moment. "Regardless of which seeks thee, there is but a single way to put an end to their encroachment. Ever has it been so that the only language the wyrms understand is that of brutality."

"Loathe as I am to concur with this rather grim assessment of my people's psyche, she is correct. Only a show of force will prevent further attempts." Asher slumped back on his seat.

"So, even if we were giving up on the Rusted Blade, the best way to keep the Dvergar safe is heading to dragon town?"

Mercy stared at me. "Dragon town."

"Yeah, where the wyrms live."

She glanced to Asher and stage-whispered, "Does he think that there is actually a town where all the wyrms live together?"

"No," I grumbled, even as I saw Seren fighting to keep the smirk off her face. "Shut up."

"There be roosts beyond the mapped Khags of old." Gunhild piped up. "Mountains and steppes the wyrms call home. My lads will be pulling the papers for you. That's where you'll be finding the scaly scum."

Asher looked put out, but we all said nothing. Any other day, I probably would have piped up about not all lizard men being bad guys, but things were still a bit tender with Gunhild, and I didn't fancy missing out on those maps.

Mercy coughed. "That would be great."

When Gunhild stormed off to get the paperwork, I turned to the rest of them with a huff of relief. "So, we definitely know how to kill dragons now. I'd say it's time to go get our boy Tsangaanax. Right?"

"Might be missing a few steps in the middle there, dumbass." Mercy rolled her eyes.

"What am I missing? Kill a wyrm, take his shards, make a sword, kill a Voidgod." I ticked them off on my fingers. "Naked party for the rest of eternity."

"The part where we find the wyrm first?" She paused for a moment, then added. "Also, I'm not committing to the naked party plan."

"Come on, it isn't like Asher has any fun jiggly bits to look at."

She even tried appealing to Seren. "You cannot be okay with this?"

"If thy succeed in slaying the Voidgod, I shall forgive a great deal." Seren might have been joking, she might have been entirely serious, but regardless, she wasn't going to show any hint of dissent or weakness in our relationship, even if it meant agreeing to a future of eternal nudity.

"As for finding Tsangaanax, well, we've got even more shards now than we did before." I held out my hands. "We can just do the echo thing."

Gunhild bustled back into the room with her arms full of rolled up papers. The Elders had mostly scarpered back to their own various tasks, and there was a nice broad table up at the front of the room, almost an altar. This whole place had a vaguely churchy vibe that I hadn't really noticed while I was building it. They hadn't asked for it to be a church, they'd asked for arched ceilings and rows of seats, and I guess my own childhood memories had stepped in for the details. The fact that a pair of artisans were all excited about making stained-glass windows for the place had really just amplified the churchiness.

With all the maps spread out and Gunhild tapping here and there around the edges at the places marked with Wyrm-sign, Asher looked down at it all and sighed. "The vague direction of our quarry shall matter little in comparison to the vast distances that must be traversed. Even the closest of the draconic territories is many months of hard travel from Witchglass Overlook."

His clawed finger was tapping on the spot on the map where fresher ink had been added in Gunhild's handwriting. I had no real interest in that though. For the first time I could see the name of the whole region where we'd first arrived, freed the Alvaren city, and inadvertently destroyed the Dvergar one. The Dverbal Hinterlands. That rang a bell. "Hold on… why do I know that name? That was… Leofric said that the waygates went to the Dverbal Hinterlands"—I was searching frantically about the map for the words I needed, then with a start I saw them—"and on to the Serpent's Gate!"

That was some real old ink, almost faded away to brown to match the paper around it. It was one of the many patches Gunhild had suggested as potential wyrm territory, but beyond it, the map was basically empty. "What's over here?"

Gunhild just shrugged. "Never been."

I looked at the others with a grin. "If there's a waygate over there, and the shard is over there, we could get there today. Wrap it up by dinner time."

With a flex of concentration, the Lucis and the other shards all drifted around me. The only one missing was Mercy's, which she reluctantly laid down on top of the map. They slipped together easily now, balanced on the flat of the Lucis.

Just a touch, just to check. That was all it would take. I stripped off my glove, took a steadying breath, then grabbed on.

"You pitiful wretch!" Araphel snarled an inch from my face. *"What do you think I shall do to these runts you shed tears for if you do not submit. Do you think your walls will stop me? Do you think anything can stop me?"*

Squeezing my eyes shut, I felt for the familiar pulse of recognition. The echo of the whole Rusted Blade that every part of it contained.

"What do you think I shall do with your treacherous sow when I lay my hands upon her? Do you hope her death will be swift? Do you think that she will turn on you if I offer her life? She will. I have no doubt. She will bury a blade in your back as soon as the opportunity arises. I'm amazed she hasn't turned you in for a pat on the head from her little queen already."

The echo was off to my side when it bounced back. So far away, that there was no way that I would have felt it if Tsangaanax hadn't been dumb enough to hoard both his shards right next to each other. The two pieces sang back and forth, calling out to the rest. We were so close now. So close I could taste it.

"Abandon this course and I shall reward you. Not only shall you survive, I shall make you the king of all Amaranth. This place means nothing to me. It is merely the cocoon I must shuck before I ascend to the heavens. You can have this world, just leave me in peace."

My hand was up and pointing to the distant echo now, the last parts of the blade that we didn't already have crying out to be united with the rest. I could feel, rather than hear the presence of the others around me. The warmth of their bodies in the chill air.

"Open your eyes and look upon me. Witness my glory—" I let the shards drop to the tabletop and cut Araphel off mid-rant.

The others were bent over the map. Gunhild and Seren were the only ones who hadn't seen this trick before, so while the Dvergar did her best to completely ignore me, Seren was the only one staring at me with concern. I managed to give her a shaky smile. "He's running scared."

The mask of neutrality slipped over her face before I'd even finished speaking. Whatever was going on in her head, she didn't want to share. I couldn't really fault her for that. If I'd just watched her communing with the big bad god of super-evil, I'd probably have some concerns too.

Everyone else had sprung into action, swiveling the map and pulling out a compass to match my vague pointing to an actual direction. Mercy was grinning down at the maps. "The Serpent's Gate. Bang on."

Asher was less certain. "It is certainly in that vicinity, but given the distances involved, we may still find ourselves many leagues away from the specific target that we are seeking."

"The Serpent's Gate?" Until now, Seren had been silent in our planning—doing the whole seen but not heard thing she seemed to believe was required of her. "Beyond it lies not the domain of the wyrm, but the site of the Revelation."

That put a damper on all our excitement. Even Gunhild, professed doubter of all things to do with the Voidgod's existence, turned sullen and silent. Mercy was the only one who still had the wherewithal to answer. "What?"

"T'was the last line we meant to hold. A valley mouth between the ancient underkingdoms of the Dvergar and the outskirts of the Alvaren Empire where escaped slaves had built their own savage domains. A choke point where the Voidgod could not bring his legions to bear."

I'd seen the Bastion, hundreds if not thousands of miles farther in. They definitely had not stopped the Voidgod at the edge of the map. "Guess that didn't work out?"

Seren's slender fingers stroked over the little scribble on the map's edge as if she could remember just by touching it. "All our powers were arrayed against him, all allies gathered. His abominations and monsters broke upon our lines like spray on the cliffs. It was the turning point of the war when we set our feet and declared an end. An end to his voracious appetite for conquest. An end to the destruction and slaughter. It was a battle the likes of which none had ever seen, all of Amaranth bending against the tide of fate and holding off the end by courage alone."

Her mask did not break, but a single tear escaped and ran down her cheek. "Then he came, striding untroubled from amidst their ranks. Living darkness given lethal form. The Voidgod. Shields shattered at the sight of him, swords snapped in their sheaths, and the very earth beneath our feet gave out and cast us to our knees. Our courage… it faltered. Araphel was a god. What were all our arts and majesty in the face of the divine?"

There was a tremor in her voice, and I almost wanted to stop her, to hold her, but letting all this out had to be good for her. Better than holding it in forever anyway. "It was a slaughter. With our lines broken, the Voidspawn swept through, killing for neither gain nor fodder but sport. Neither Dvergar nor Faun saw the field that day, already turned from warriors to slaves. This was the Voidgod alone. His flesh and his blood, unleashed."

She leaned back into my arms when I came up behind her, showing ever more weakness to the people around her. I didn't know why she was doing this. If she was trying to show humanity to the others. If she was trying to convince them that she was vulnerable, so that she would have the advantage when they came for her. Not that they would, but if you grew up believing everyone was trying to climb the ladder using you as a stepping stone, of course you'd assume everyone was out to get you. "The wyrms came to feed upon the battlefield when the storm had passed. It was there that Briar by Moonlight made her compact with the Twilight Betrayer as he sought to feast upon Alvaren flesh. He who you hunt. Even the enemies of Light came to realize that they would be consumed by the Void."

She choked off before she could say any more, but it was enough to make it clear we were heading into enemy territory on a whole different level from what we'd been expecting. Up until now, none of the Voidgod's old critters had shown up to cause us trouble, but if Tsangaanax had set up on Araphel's home turf, then we were almost guaranteed to cross paths. Beyond the Serpent's Gate, there was no telling what we'd be up against.

Mercy pressed on without a word of sympathy. "There's a waystone there. It's the direction we need to go. What we find on the other side doesn't matter. It's still where we need to go."

"In this we are in agreement. But if we truly expect to face the remnant of the Voidgod's armies, perhaps we should plan accordingly."

"Turn up the ass-kicking to eleven?" I grinned. "I'm ready."

CHAPTER 20

There was a possibility that we had over-prepared. Everyone was geared out in the finest armor that I could make for them, every weapon was upgraded as far as I could take it, and my own body was wrapped in so much metal that I clanked with every step. I was not planning on getting caught out without materials to work with again, even if it meant I looked like a tank on legs.

The Voidgod had screwed up the area around the Bastion by accident. If we were heading into some battleground where he'd been using his destructo-powers on purpose, then I didn't plan on getting caught out again. On top of all that, Asher and a small army of Dvergar helpers had strapped a backpack onto me that probably would have broken the spine of most beasts of burden. I was pretty sure he had half the library, a metric ton of miscellaneous magical junk he'd stolen from the tower, and maybe one of the giant crossbows I'd made for the walls crammed in there. If there had been a kitchen sink, it would have been in the bag.

Only Gunhild came down to the beach to see us off, since a solid half of the other Dvergar were still furious at us for leaving so soon after the wyrm attack. I'd tried explaining the timeline of stuff to them, that the sooner we left, the more likely it was we could cut off any further attacks before the flights of dragons took off. Since they'd only just managed to dig some of their buddies out of the collapsed mines, they weren't really buying that line. Not that their opinions really mattered. We had to go. I'd rather have left with everyone happy, but if we had to leave them sulking, that was what we'd do.

As we sweated through the jungle, I dissolved a few of the outer layers of my armor into a second great-sword to match the Lucis, on the basis that at least having two swords on my back wouldn't make me walk like I'd been riding a horse too long, the way that the real thick armor plates had. Sure, a strong breeze might tip me over backward, but at least nobody would accuse me of waddling.

Before Asher could cast his spell, Seren took a hold of my hand. She really did not want to be left behind again, and since dying wasn't the only way to make this trip, there was no reason to ask her to. If anything, the other two had been enthusiastic about bringing her along after the battle with the Inyoka. Mercy might not always like Seren all that much, but at least she could recognize her value.

The first jump took us to Witchglass Overlook. This was the closest thing we were going to have to familiar territory on this trip, and we wanted to make sure that we had somewhere to retreat to if we hopped to the Serpent's Gate and discovered it was completely overrun with monsters.

Before we'd even begun to move from the courtyard where the spell had dumped us, Seren halted us with a raised hand, stalking forward on her own in a half-crouch. I glanced to the other two with a little bit of amusement over her never-ending paranoia, but they looked just as stressed out as her. "Really?"

Asher had his hands up and waving around like he was doing interpretive dance, feeling around for the magic. "This was the point where we shed the pursuit of Briar by Moonlight and her Paladins. It does not seem unreasonable to assume that some entrapment may have been left behind in case of our return."

"If it was me, I'd have trapped the place." Mercy shrugged when I appealed to her.

Seren had crept back and forth across the whole courtyard by then, eyes narrowed, pointy ears twitching at the echo of her own footsteps. The dead Alvaren that we'd left behind were gone. So either some hungry monsters had passed through, or Briar's minions had come to clean up. Since there wasn't a load of chewed up elf-bits spread on the floor, I was leaning more towards the second option.

Even beyond the courtyard, it seemed that their fears were un-bounded. The magic inside the school had kept things pretty much as we left it, so we didn't go messing around with that. The never-ending feasting hall still stretched out forever, and the plates were still full of their evil poisoned food that made you turn into a glow in the dark skeleton. Maybe I wasn't remembering that bit right, but I still wasn't going to take a bite of that chicken, regardless of how good it looked. In a stunning twist, Asher did not want to go down and check out the library, having already cleared it out pretty effectively the last time we came through. Maybe he just remembered the mess we'd made.

Even the outbuildings looked clean and tidy where before they'd been filled up with sand and leaves. Like they'd been swept out and prepared for use. Maybe we weren't the only ones planning on using this place as a base of operations.

The whole situation felt weird. We'd left this place in a hurry last time around, and coming back to the scene of the crime felt like we were asking for trouble. Not to mention that this was the first place that I'd almost murdered Seren. Still felt a bit weird about that too. Pretty sure that beating a girl up and dragging her back to your cave by the hair was frowned upon these days. Sure, we'd talked things out now, but just remembering the things I'd done to her made my skin crawl.

So I just stood around, stagnating in my misery and bad memories for a while. It felt like forever as the three of them combed the place looking for anything that might have been a trap or an alarm or… well, anything really.

Eventually, Seren let out a little call from the hillside overlooking the school, and I clank-jogged up to find out what she was excited about. As it turned out, it was an arrow. "Uh."

She had a blue flush to her cheeks, and her eyes were bright and wide. "My absence was noted. My queen, she left this here so that I might reach out for aid."

"That… seems like a stretch? It's just an arrow." I peered down at the object she was cradling in her hands. At a glance, it really was just an arrow. Definitely Alvaren in make, with a beautiful crystalline head and soft gryphon feathers as flights. The engravings along the length of it definitely marked it as something fancy, but given how fancy the Alvaren made absolutely everything, I was quite ready to just believe that they'd forgotten to pick it up.

"Maulkin, this is… this is an incredible honor." For the second time that day, there were tears prickling at the corners of her eyes. "To be personally acknowledged by the empress. To be offered a means to return despite my failure. This was more than I ever could have hoped for."

"So…" I tried to move onto a less contentious subject than how I thought her beloved queen was a psychopath. "Magic arrow?"

She smiled at me, and that was the first time I realized just how emotional this little twig had actually made her. Her smiles were not easy to come by. "I forget thy lack even the most basic sense for the arcane."

"So, how does it work? You use it, and you can talk to her, or you use it, and it calls her to you? How does it…" Anxiety was churning in my guts, and I caught myself glancing around the horizon without meaning to, in case the Alvaren flying city was already zooming toward us.

"Dost thou still fear her? There is no need for such dread. Thy art a true and brave warrior—Amaranth's best hope against the forces of darkness. Whatever quarrel you had with my queen will surely be ended once she learns of the Voidgod's return." It was almost endearing how Seren could be 100% cynical about everything else in the world but completely blind to just how bad her own people were.

"That uh… doesn't seem likely. She didn't take kindly to the whole headbutting thing."

Seren flinched when I mentioned that, but even so, she pressed on with her little fantasy of a happy reunion. "We were all disoriented in the wake of the curse. Now that time has passed and tempers have cooled, I have no doubt that peace can be made. If she cares enough for me to leave this beacon so that I might be saved from the land of the savage, then surely she shall take my word into account. If you are mine, she will not harm you." She reached out, and I took her hand, extremely not used to being treated like I was her boyfriend rather than a piece of furniture she hadn't quite gotten bored of sitting on yet. "And thou art mine. As sure as the sun rises."

I had to keep looking around because if I looked at her and started feeling things I was going to end up blubbering. Subject change. Rapid subject change. "Do you have to use it now?"

Her brows drew down when I finally dared to look back at her face. "What is your meaning? With the Alvaren Empire at thy back, we can take the battle to the foul wyrm Tsangaanax. Your quest might be ended in mere days!"

"Seren. I know you love your queen. I know you're loyal to her, but—"

She cut me off with a finger on my lips. "There is no but. I may have sworn myself to your service, but thou art no king or conqueror. What love I bear for you can never replace my loyalty to the empress."

"Love?" I mumbled into her finger.

Her smile was wicked. "Didst my tongue slip?"

I was getting off topic again. She was putting me off topic with all this romantic stuff. "Just… listen. I know that eventually we're going to have to deal with Briar, and I know that we'll need to put what happened behind us and team up to take down the Voidgod, but I just think… later might be better?" I had been freewheeling up until now, but an idea popped into my head before I crammed my foot in my mouth again. "I mean, right now the only proof we've got that Araphel is coming back is our word, some prophecies we've never even read, and the fact we've managed to grab so many shards. If we were to hold off until Araphel stuck his head up…"

Her smile began to fade. "Then thy would be too late to muster the forces of Light against him."

Yet again, I had to drag us back to the question. "Do you need to use it here and now?"

"Nay." She shook her head, hair swaying golden in the sunlight. "All I need do is hold it aloft to the heavens and speak the name of my liege. The beacon it lights can be seen from anywhere on Amaranth."

"Then maybe we can hold off until we've gotten a little bit farther. I uh… I'm sure Briar would want to help us out, but maybe going ahead to scout first might be a better idea, you know? Maybe we find out where Tsangaanax is camped out, grab his shards sneaky style?"

She raised an eyebrow, obviously amused by this latest attempt. "You do not wish to test thy mettle against the wyrm?"

"I mean, obviously I do. But if there's a way to grab the shards quietly, maybe that would be better? Right?" Desperation was starting to build up again. Where were the other two? They'd have been able to talk her out of this. Mercy would have sarcasm-ed her into submission by now. "Plus, I'm sure there would be no uh… no opportunity for Briar to get the wrong idea about me if I had the whole Rusted Blade first."

"You wish to bargain from a place of power. I can respect that. Yet you must know, I serve her still. The moment that I feel we are straying from the path…"

I spread my arms wide and smiled. "Seren. It is me. Have you ever known me to get distracted?"

She broke down laughing, loud and bright and sparkling. The slip only lasted a moment, but it was enough to bring the other two running from where they'd been working away, hunting for any sign of Alvaren infestation. Mercy reached us first, in a wild sprint. "What happened? Did he punch himself in the balls again?"

"Hey!" My head snapped around to Seren who now looked terribly interested in the lapping waves out by the waystone. "That was private."

Her face was back to a barren mask of absent emotion by the time she replied, "That was hilarious."

I opened and shut my mouth. It had been pretty damn funny. Even if it did mean I had to resort to frantically using Restoration on my own crotch in the middle of the night.

Asher mounted the hill with a gasp, "Is all well? I heard a strange sound."

Mercy shrugged. "Maulkin hit himself in the nuts again."

"Ah, that would explain it."

I carefully put both hands over my face so that I didn't start screaming. Even so, I was sounding a little bit strangled when I muttered, "I hate you all."

Seren presented the arrow as a distraction that I greatly appreciated, and Asher ooh-ed and aah-ed at the magic that had been layered onto it as if it was something we could all appreciate. "Truly a magnificent piece of craftsmanship."

Mercy scoffed. "Yeah, it's a real fancy poking stick."

Both Seren and Asher started waxing lyrical about the amazing and wonderful enchantments on the damn thing, again, so I took a walk. We'd only been out of the Hinterlands for a month, and already so much had changed. The brown scrub was starting to take on a purple hue, and the distant forests had gone from looking like bloody smears on the horizon to a bubblegum pink as blossoms opened up. We hadn't really talked much about the seasons changing here in Amaranth, but I guess that either spring had sprung or winter was on its way. I couldn't feel much difference in the temperature, but I had skin as thick as a rhino's at this point, so I'd probably only notice winter had arrived when I walked directly into the side of a glacier.

Now that I knew it was there, it was easy enough to spot a waystone relay shimmering against the distant hills, still standing tall enough that I didn't need to worry that it had been toppled in any of the recent seismic activity that may have been entirely my fault. Even if one of the towers had broken down, we were still saving a solid day's worth of travel for each one that was still up. If we got lucky, we'd make it to the edge of the map today. If we didn't, we'd still only be making a fraction of the journey we would have had to do overland.

The less of this journey that we had to make out in the open the happier I'd be. Last time we were here the Alvaren floating city-fortress had been hanging in the sky, and the fact I couldn't currently see it didn't make me feel any safer, especially given that the damn thing could teleport around.

Normally, I could put that hunted feeling out of my mind and get on with things, but between the location and that arrow-beacon, I felt like we were going to get jumped by Briar by Moonlight at any moment. I'm not saying she was scarier than all the giant monsters and dragons and stuff that we'd fought up until now, but at least none of them held a grudge—probably because they're all dead? I really should have made more of a concerted effort to murder her when we had the opportunity.

Mercy whistled me back over before much longer, and we headed back to the Overlook to take the next small-step slash giant-leap of our journey. They'd talked Seren out of using the beacon arrow thing using the same logic I'd already attempted to deploy. It worked better when you sounded like you knew what you were talking about, apparently.

The persistent feeling of dread took a backseat as I looked around at us all, geared up and ready to adventure properly again. It had been way too long. Was that pride I felt bubbling up inside me? Horny and hungry were my go-to emotions on a regular day, so all these more complicated ones kind of threw me.

Asher bobbed his head as he spoke. "We shall travel the waystone relays to their natural end or to the Serpent's Gate, whichever is closer. From there we shall disembark, scout out the immediate area, and then return here to plan our next moves. Are we all in agreement?"

Mercy groaned. "Yes, mom."

His tail lashed in irritation, but he started casting, and I reached out and took Seren's hand, anticipation building as the magic gathered around us once more. Here we go, here we go. The magic glowed all around us, the waystone behind us crackled with power, and the one on the distant hillside shone brighter and brighter. I gave Seren a squeeze and one last grin, then the spell went off, and we were whipped off our feet and into the blinding light.

Last time the trip went by so fast I didn't even have time to notice every part of my body being ripped apart by magic and reassembled. This time it lasted just long enough for me to have some awareness of all the waystones that we were zipping through, humming around us as we flew across the continent. If I had a mouth, I would have been screaming "Weeeeee!" the whole way, but as it was, I didn't get the opportunity.

Has something ever gone wrong, but you didn't realize until after the fact? Like you drove home and then discovered you had a flat tire for the last mile, or the coleslaw on your sandwich had turned sour but you didn't smell it until it was in your mouth. That was the sensation when we came flying out of the waystone at the Serpent's Gate. That big oops.

Maybe it was the whole army that was deployed around us, maybe it was the fact that we came out sideways as the relay was pulled down to smash apart by a squad of burly dudes with ropes, or maybe it was Orphia's shit-eating grin.

Oops.

CHAPTER 21

We might have been in a little bit of trouble. Our exit had just been smashed to pieces, we'd all landed face down in the open plain ahead of the mountain pass, and there were more people around us than I was capable of counting. Tired, angry looking people. Then to top it off, there was Orphia standing right ahead of us in full battle regalia, something like a dress made out of plates of armor, her glaive shining with gathered electricity, the banner of Leofric strapped to her back. It was a golden lion, predictably enough.

I pushed up onto my knees, and the spears all around us were leveled. "Fancy meeting you here."

Orphia called out to her army instead of replying. "Just as was foretold. Our efforts have been rewarded. The traitors are here."

I felt Leofric before I could turn around and see him standing behind the acid-etched base of the waystone-relay, hands still glowing green. "All has come to pass as I predicted. They sought to join with the Wyrm."

Now I'm not going to say that the idea of Leo coming after us for stealing his ancient relic magic sword and the symbol of his authority hadn't crossed my mind. I just assumed it would take him a lot longer to get his ass in gear and haul a whole army across country. Even with the ugly naked horse things, they must have left the Bastion at more or less the same moment that I did to get all the way over here in this time.

From the haggard look of the soldiers, it had not been an easy march. They hadn't looked terribly well fed and comfortable back at the Bastion, but the journey over here looked like it had left them at breaking point. I wondered how many of them were true believers in Leo's messiah schtick and how many were just scared of what would happen to them if they got left behind. I suppose it didn't really matter all that much, but I still felt obliged to offer them a way out. "Hey, soldier guys. We don't actually want to kill you."

Seren interrupted. "I want to kill them all."

I kept on going as if she hadn't just said that, "So if you walk away right now, we aren't going to come after you. We aren't going to blame you for hitching your wagon to the wrong horse. We aren't going to look for revenge. And there isn't going to be enough left of Leo for him to come after you either."

Orphia bellowed, "the first man to shirk his duty shall fall by my blade."

Mercy had an arrow drawn by the time she righted herself, and it was lined up straight for Orphia's open mouth. "Not before I put this through you."

None of the grandstanding and shouting had done much of anything to the soldiers. They were still staring at us with the same determined glares as had been on their faces when we first arrived—except for the ones that were getting a good look at Seren.

Whispers spread out in a ripple, and the word "Alvaren" seemed to be on everyone's lips. Even Leo looked taken aback when he spotted her.

I could smell doubt in the air. "Yeah, that's right. Did we not mention that we'd brought the Alvaren back? And we've got them on speed dial."

The last bit obviously made no sense to them, but the Alvaren being back, that made all the difference in the world. Confusion abounded. Murmurs and dissent in the ranks. Leofric hopped up onto the ruins of the relay with a flourish and a bow. "Herald of the Alvaren, I offer you greetings. If you will stand aside while I retrieve what these blackguards have stolen from me, then it would be my pleasure to welcome you back to Amaranth."

Seren kept him talking as the rest of us found our feet. "It is thee who must stand aside, Leofric. These Eternals are on a quest of great import to the Alvaren Empire. Those who do not offer them succor shall incur the wrath of Briar by Moonlight."

Leo flinched at the mention of the queen of all bitches, but he didn't stand down, and he didn't order his people to stand down. I could almost hear the whirring between his ears as he tried to work this new information into his plans. "Whatever it is that your vassals provide, there can be no doubt that I can offer it threefold." His moustache twitched in what might have been a smile. "Had I known that they were in your service from the beginning, they would have been greeted as your envoys and offered all aid, but that opportunity has passed. Now justice must be served.

He drew a sword from the scabbard by his hip that used to hold the Lucis. It wasn't magical, and it wasn't reverberating in my consciousness the way that the old sword had, but it was certainly a very long and sharp piece of metal that was going to hurt when he jammed it in me.

The next step that he took forward, all of us flinched into battle-readiness. Even Seren. He was still making excuses as his muscles coiled beneath his shining golden armor—as if saying the right words would make what he was about to do acceptable. How many times a day did he have to lie to himself just to get by? "I am certain that you would not want thieves in your employ."

Predictable as the sunrise, I was the one he launched himself at. I was the one who'd stolen his sword, and I was the one who'd made a fool of him. He didn't even look at anyone else.

I shredded the straps of my bag as I shed the excess metal from my armor into hunks all around me. He was expecting to fight the same Maulkin he'd pushed around back on the Bastion. Things had changed. I brought the Lucis around to catch his blow, and he pushed down against my parry, expecting me to crumble. Instead, I matched his strength. My newly acquired Ascendant Potency meant that I wasn't going to be getting thrown around by anything short of an actual god anymore.

Everyone else had exploded into motion around us. Asher had dropped to the ground, digging in my abandoned backpack, and Mercy had thrown up a wall of fire to hold back the right flank of soldiers and was peppering the left with arrows so fast that I couldn't even see her hands moving. Just the thrum of her bowstring. That just left the other third of the army and Orphia for Seren to deal with.

One hundred men and an enraged Eternal? That seemed doable.

Confusion was written all over Leo's face as he pressed in closer, forcing me back one step, then the next. My heel touched against Asher, and I knew I couldn't give any more ground.

Leaning forward the last inch and Surging Vitality so I didn't need immediate dental attention, I bit onto the blade of his sword. The confusion turned to disgust as he strained to twist the sword so it bit into something more vital. The dead stone beneath our feet began to crack under the pressure he was exerting.

It was enough though, enough of a hold for me to take one hand off the Lucis, and draw my other sword. He saw it happen. Saw my hand reach out. Saw the great-sword on my back leap from where it was strapped to land in my waiting palm. He didn't wait for what came next.

Leo abandoned his attack, leapt back, and I had to open my mouth or risk giving everybody a real wide smile. I tossed my offhand blade to the ground and spun the Lucis back into a high guard with a grin. "I liked the original recipe sword better."

"Then I shall feed that too you next."

Mercy was amazing. She was always amazing. But there is only so much that you can do when you are one person trying to fight back against dozens. The firewall helped, but at the end of the day, it was just a wall. They could go around it. And now they were, pouring in from either side, charging at Seren, at Mercy's turned back, and at Asher where he was still down on his knees struggling. There were so many of them. Hundreds of them. Leo's whole army stretched out all around us until they were all we could see, all brought along for some petty vengeance on me.

Seren let out a yell, and it dragged my attention away from where it needed to be. She had Orphia's electrified glaive pinned between her swords, and that bark of victory had been the sound of her plunging it into the first soldier taking a swipe at her back, discharging all the gathered lightning out through him and into the ranks behind him. We were running out of time. I needed options.

As I'd feared, the ground beneath us felt like nothing to my Artifice. Whatever had been unleashed by the Voidgod here had robbed the place of all the vital energy I needed to move the stone. Good thing I'd brought all that metal with me.

I swept the Lucis in an arc, and the hunks of metal that I'd scattered around the battlefield leapt up to match it. Resonating through my Artifice with the sword. Dozens of soldiers fell to that one cut, dozens more fell back in fear of the next one, and once more I could see the confusion and fear showing on Leo's face. He was ancient and powerful and stagnant. He was all that he'd ever be, and I was becoming more every day.

On the backswing, I sent my second great-sword flying at him from where I'd dumped it. It was a clumsy attack, and he batted the blow away with all the contempt that a feint deserved. Still, it gave me the time to close the distance though.

Rebounding from the other blade, he spun to catch the Lucis and turn my chop away. I reared back, far further than his parry should have made me, and the other sword jumped at his back.

With a practiced ease, he spun his blade behind his back to deflect it. Smug prick didn't even look. Well, that was fine. I didn't need him to look. I just needed to keep him busy.

Asher leapt back from my bag as soon as he'd wrestled the lockbox open and leapt to the side just a moment later. The butterflies from Talon's tower fluttered free.

Back at the tower, those little bugs had been the old Archmage's anti-air defense system. Out here in the open, they were chaos. With each flap of their wings, they threw up a cyclone. There was no limit to them now—no walls to pen them in, and no clever architecture to keep each gust of wind from tapping into the weather systems around it, so each spiral of wind grew larger and larger as they spun away from us. A million tiny storms all leaping to life as the dozen butterflies fluttered to gain height.

I might not be a smart guy, but I was glad I had one on my team.

When one passed through Mercy's wall of fire, the wall snuffed out, and the tornado became a firestorm, scorching a line through Leo's army. Everywhere else, the soldiers didn't get to burn. Instead, they got picked up and thrown—into the air, and into each other. Everywhere you looked, they went flying by.

Whatever Leo had been expecting, it wasn't that. He gawked up as one of the wagons that he'd rode in on lifted up from behind the shattered waystone-relay, ugly naked horses still dangling, and scream-ing, from the front as it spun.

Couldn't ask for a better distraction, really. I hammered the Lucis back down at him. He managed to get his blade up in time, but he'd been expecting the same sort of whacks I'd been dealing out to him so far, not Surged Potency. His own blade was slammed back into his face, only stopping short when the ends hit his giant gold lion pauldrons.

The roar he let out was less lion and more cat-whose-tail-got-trod on. I hauled the Lucis back, and like it was attached by a string, the other sword leapt up to hit Leo in the back with the same force. Once more his armor stopped the worst of it, but the impact knocked him stumbling forward to meet my next attack. Off balance, bleeding, surrounded. I had him.

I brought my reforged Lucis down like a butcher with a cleaver. Planning to split him in two the same way I had Gorgafel.

A body hit me. A soldier. In that first moment of confusion, I assumed she'd been thrown by one of the butterflies, but then another hit and another. Not one of them trying to hurt me, just clinging on. Trying to stop me. Trying to hold me back from killing Leo.

"Come on!" I roared as more and more of them heaped on. Dozens of them. A mass of bodies that only my surging Potency let me overpower. I took one dragging step forward and brought the Lucis down, only for Leo to flick aside my clumsy attack with a sneer. "No more than you deserve."

With all the time in the world to act, he lined up his thrust and plunged his sword clean through the head of that first soldier girl and into my chest. She died for him without a whimper.

I did plenty of whimpering. That sword hurt as much as I'd thought it would. And I'd only been planning on some flesh wounds, not a collapsed lung.

He pulled back, drawing the red tip of his sword out through the dead girl with a horrid sucking sound, and then he readied his next attack. The rest of the idiots didn't even try to get clear. They just held on. They were all nuts.

I hauled up with all my strength against them and even though the Lucis in my hands moved so slowly that I'd have had better luck intercepting the killing blow with hopes and prayers, the mirror sword didn't. It crashed into Leo's back and sent his swing wide, carving another of his soldiers off me but leaving me untouched.

Before my eyes, I could see the open wound across his face closing up, and it reminded me that I could do the same. Flaring my Regeneration to fix up the hole he'd put through me. I strained once more, hoping that the loss of another body would make up for my Surged Potency running dry, but I was still stuck.

Leo had one foot on my flying sword and his eyes locked on me by the time I gave up the struggle. His own sword was sheathed, but there was a green glow between his palms that I really did not like to see. Getting doused in acid once was more than enough for one lifetime, thank you very much.

I twisted to see if rescue was coming from anywhere else. It really wasn't. Mercy and Asher were back to back in the midst of a tightening circle of soldiers. She was keeping them at bay with her wind-arrows, but there was no opportunity for them to break out. Asher's casting had been interrupted with a crossbow bolt to the shoulder somewhere in all the chaos, and he still hadn't gotten it going again. Seren was the only one who seemed to be having a good time. There was a circle of corpses around her, and though Orphia kept dashing in and taking swipes at her, they were useless in the face of my girl's ludicrous skills.

The false Alvaren had rage ingrained on her features, but her movements were slow and stunted compared to the real thing. The fancy armor that she'd been strapped into was just making her even more awkward. I kind of wished that I could have just kicked back and watched the show. Instead, I had to deal with acid-bath-time.

Stretching out with Artifice to my very limits, I grabbed every piece of metal and hauled them in. At the same moment as Leo pushed his hands forward to douse me in burning chemical agony, my iron-maiden snapped shut around him. It wasn't pretty, and it wouldn't last. It was just a big thick slab of metal wrapped around him.

He did not make a happy noise when all that acid splashed back in his face. I was upgrading it from "stepped-on cat" to "cat-that-fell-into-a-bath." Less surprise, more anguish.

And, of course, his loyal followers all leapt to his rescue, dropping off me to run over to the acid vat now surrounding their boss and trying to pry it open with their bare hands. The geniuses.

I had maybe a few seconds before Leo realized that he could stop squirting out more acid and just bust out of there, but they'd have to be enough to turn the tide of battle. I charged back over to Mercy and Asher, slapping a heal on the lizardman and catching a crossbow bolt headed for Mercy in my shoulder. The soldiers around Seren were understandably scared to get too close to her, but despite how casually she was handling everything, I could see the strain in her face. There were too many enemies, too many angles of attack, too many ways that everything could go wrong, so the usual beautiful dance of blades was stilted and halting as she had to keep spinning away from Orphia's clumsy attacks and handle whichever soldier was getting too brave. I could help with that.

I plowed into the ranks of soldiers that had gathered around her back, leading with my shoulder and following with my blade. It wasn't that I wanted to avoid killing them—they'd been given their opportunity to back down, back off, and survive—it was just that I was short on time and using everything I had handy.

Orphia herself got a blast of mind-strike to keep her off balance. The image of me yelling at her for being a loser would hopefully haunt her dreams for many years to come.

The soldiers folded under my charge, proving themselves to be made of the same stern stuff as their cannon-fodder buddies back at the Bastion. The Lucis shrank down to its original size, and a shield formed up on my other arm. I'd had to dump almost all my metal to keep Leo contained, so I was down to the bare minimum. A whack from my shield sent most soldiers flying, and the ones that fell by my feet, instead of soaring, got the unique experience of being skewered with a legendary relic. Lucky them.

Seren had been ignoring them for the most part, too focused on Orphia to give them much attention. Now that they had an enemy actively trying to kill them, the soldiers were quick to switch focus. She had her shot at Orphia. Now I just had to fight this whole damned army before Leo got loose.

I led them back with me towards Mercy and Asher. Maybe it wasn't fair, but instinct always told me that being closer to them increased my odds of survival. Mercy was still holding up well, her barrage of arrows keeping all but the most suicidal of the soldiers cowering behind their shields. They were trying to outlast her quiver, and normally that would have worked perfectly, but I was here.

Splitting my attention between the body holding a shield up to catch another crossbow bolt and the mind spreading out through my Sphere of Influence to snatch up every broken scrap lying around—the bolts that had missed, the arrows that had snapped off, and the scrapings of steel thrown off their armor when Mercy's arrows grazed by. Everything leapt up, twisted together into arrows, and slipped into the leather case on her back, ready for action.

Between shots, Mercy managed to snap, "Finally decide to join in?"

All I could do was laugh. Even with the storms tearing through them, there were still a hundred soldiers to any one of us. Even with all the damage that we'd done, the endless tide of living, breathing people who were willing to die for Leo's megalomania kept coming on.

I cut them down.

More and more soldiers rushed in towards me, heedless of the inevitable. They were trained, they were confident, and they had no chance at all in the face of my strength. Their blows rained down on my shield, and my sword lashed through their defenses as if they weren't there. It didn't matter how well you parried or blocked a blow when it had the force of a runaway train behind it. Their swords shattered.

Their shields splintered. They bled.

With the pressure of holding back the charge from every direction gone, Mercy's wind-arrows came slower, one or two bursting on the most aggressive soldiers on her side to drive them back, but most of her shots slipped through to knock out the crossbowmen in the rear ranks. Asher was back on his feet between us, and while I didn't think there was anything he could do that would deal more damage than the bugs he'd already set loose, he had something big and angry looking coiling between his hands.

We were about to turn this whole battle around when Leo leapt back into the fight.

His acid bath had eaten through most of his golden armor, and the shiny golden hair and beard were long gone. Underneath where it had been, I was annoyed to discover he had a chin with one of those little butt dimples in the middle. Continuing the bad news, his sword and skin seemed to have made it through unscathed.

He brought that shiny length of metal down on me hard, and I had to twist around to catch it with the Lucis while still pushing back the closest soldiers. The poor stone beneath my feet shattered with the impact. It had already been ravaged by the Voidgod and a good few millennia of wear and tear. By the time we were done here, it was probably going to be called the Serpent's Gate gravel pit.

I was off balance, surrounded, and trying to protect myself and Asher, and the demi-god still dripping acid from the cracks in his armor was not a happy bunny. "How dare you?"

Mercy flung up a fresh wall of fire between us and Seren's battle. Then she cracked up, "What, is this your first time meeting Maulkin?"

His irritation with her was just enough of a distraction for me to twist out from under the crushing weight of his blow. If I'd hoped he'd fall forward, I was sadly mistaken. Even enraged and dribbling, he had the kind of discipline in his movements that it would take me centuries to master. He spun into another attack, and I had to haul my shield overhead to knock it away, opening my side up to the massed soldiers and their spears. They didn't need a special invitation. Three of them hammered into me, and more probably would have followed if the soldiers could have squeezed past each other.

My armor did what it could, but that wasn't much. The three pointed tips nipped between my ribs and started wiggling around in me with every movement and breath. That was uniquely unpleasant. But worse, the pain, the damage, and the sticks poking out my side slowed me.

Leo's next blow lopped off one of my horns and bit into my shoulder before I had a chance. There was a manic grin on his face as acid suddenly exploded out from the sword's blade in a sticky green wave. "Ow. Ow. Ow."

Ever get lemon juice in a paper cut? Imagine that, except the paper cut is a foot long and the lemon juice is deadly acid.

Mercy blasted Leo square in the chest with another wind-arrow, but he just tanked right through it and laughed, twisting his sword to smear a little more acid in me as he withdrew. I remembered this feeling, the acid gradually eating out through my body until I fell to pieces, and I didn't want to do it again. Not again.

I took a wild swipe at him with the Lucis, but he didn't even bother to do more than lean back out of the way. That was fine. It wasn't about him. The shield on my arm shattered as Artifice made it resonate with the blade. The broken fragments of it soaring out in the same arc as my cut. Leaping past the spears still embedded in me and slicing into the soldiers behind them. That sudden burst of shrapnel gave me space to breathe, and I used it to rip the spears out.

Leo was back in my face again. The wind was still swirling out from Mercy's arrow in his chest, buffeting me as he abandoned his sword and grappled with me for the Lucis. Normally, I'd have put money on myself in any wrestling match, big money, but today I was sporting a gaping wound in the shoulder above my sword arm, and acid was seeping down into the joint, burning away my strength one snapping tendon at a time.

He wanted the Lucis? He could have it. I threw it off into the crowd of soldiers as far as my wrecked arm could manage, which admittedly was not far. It vanished into their ranks, and Leo took off after it like a dog chasing a stick.

Asher flung his arms up at almost the same moment, and fire exploded from between his hands. The shattered earth beneath his feet blackened, Mercy's bowstring snapped, and heat and pain washed over me as the roaring fireball spread out from him, through us, and on into a massive dome covering the battlefield. The sky burned above us, and the earth burned below. Every single soldier was licked with flame. Then as fast as it had come, it was gone. A blackened crisp of a butterfly fell past me, then the roar of the wind picked up again as the surviving bugs fled from the heat and light with all haste.

Every tornado carried fire in it now, and every soldier fell screaming and roaring, trying to be free of the flames that clung to them. I knew that they were not burning, not really. That explosive display had just been Asher priming the field for his real attacks. The flames would hold onto each and every one of us, so that his next spell had somewhere to take root.

With a desperate pulse of Artifice, I managed to haul my backup sword away from the bubbling wreckage that had been my iron maiden and into my hand. It wasn't much compared to legendary swords of legend, but it had an edge. I tried to heft it, readying myself for Leofric to come tearing back with the Lucis and a bad attitude, but something went wrong. I mean really wrong. Even by my usual standards of things going wrong.

When I tried to lift the sword, my arm fell off.

For a moment I just stood there staring at it in stunned silence. Asher gawked at it too, though his hands and mouth were already moving into the next spell. Between holding off a whole army solo, Mercy took a moment to bark. "Everything is going to be all right."

Even in my state of shock, I couldn't let that crappy joke pass by without commentary. "That *was* my right arm."

She fired an arrow past my severed horn to catch one bold soldier in the eye before he could close in on me. "At least you have one left!"

I fell to my knees as the acid ate down into my chest, fumbling with my off-hand to try and pluck the sword out of my own rapidly cooling hand. Turns out I had a really solid grip on it. There was a hysterical edge in my voice as I rumbled out, "I… I've been disarmed!"

Leo came flying back at me over the ranks of his own screaming soldiers, the Lucis upraised and ready to plunge right through me. I grabbed onto my own severed arm and I swung. The sword dangling from my locked fist met the Lucis with a clatter, and while it had no real power behind it, just the force of the impact was enough to save me. At least from that stab.

The Lucis hammered into the stone where my shoulder would have been if I still had one. But Leo came down on me like a ton of bricks, knees hammering into my guts. I retched. Good thing we hadn't stopped for breakfast, really.

He roared in exaltation, raising the Lucis for a killing blow. "Taste my vengeance!"

Desperate times called for desperate measures, so I shot a Mind-Strike into his face. He'd fought old Koschei for centuries, so he'd have been braced for any of the old tricks, which was why I filled his brain with an image of me, naked, flexing and wiggling in front of the bedroom mirror in Talon's tower.

The sudden change in his expression made the inevitable murder that was about to follow completely worth it. First surprise, then confusion, then horror, then confusion, then disgust, and then bewilderment. He actually stopped before he struck to ask, "Why?"

I grinned up at him. "Just wanted your last memory to be something nice."

Seren came flying through the wall of fire, coiled into a ball around herself. She had a sword in one hand, Orphia's crackling glaive in the other, and absolutely no intention of stopping.

The glaive blade clipped off the side of Leo's head as she spun back to her feet, discharging lightning through the both of us. Ow.

She didn't even pause between strikes, discarding the glaive as he snatched for it and pressed in closer before reaching for the second sword on her belt, parrying the Lucis, and then swiping at him with the same motion as her draw.

Leo had rolled to his feet as she came on, and I have to admit that looking up at her as she stepped on me, I was in love.

Her golden hair was so pale that it was almost white, singed black at the tips by the walls of fire she'd walked through to be back by my side. There was a sheen of sweat on her face from the heat and the effort, but best of all was her smile. That same crooked little smirk that I only saw when I was pushing her to the limit in our training. This was what she lived for.

Leo was fast, but she was faster. Leo was clever, but she'd not only learned every trick in the book, she was also there when they were first being written down. Both of them moved faster than my eyes could follow, blades shimmering in the bonfire that surrounded us all.

On my best day, I could beat Seren with a trick she hadn't seen before. Some divine power that she hadn't had a second to think about and concoct a counter for. And poor Leo, he was trying to take her on with skill alone. I'd almost pity him if he wasn't such a colossal dick.

Maybe it was just the massive blood loss talking, but I was pretty sure she had him running scared. I was so caught up in the drama that I didn't even realize what Asher was doing until he brought his flaming hands and my severed arm together with the gaping wound where my right side used to be.

Cauterize had to be my least favorite spell in Asher's whole arsenal. Yes, it could heal me back from the point of near death or dismemberment. Yes, it was more effective when I just so happened to be lit up with fire already, like I currently was. Yes, it was probably going to get me back up on my feet and into the fight, but it really, really hurt. I mean, top ten most painful things I've ever experienced kind of pain. I've been murdered in some pretty cruel and inventive ways, and none of them came close to the flames shooting out from Asher's fingertips to scorch their way through every nerve in my body.

I might have blacked out there for a second because the next thing I knew, there were soldiers all over the place, dragging me away by the feet as Mercy screamed something incoherent but almost inevitably rude after me. I blinked up at the soldiers hauling me along and realized that somehow, despite my arm having been removed and reattached to my body, I was still holding onto my sword. Sword, meet soldiers. Soldiers, meet sword. You're about to become intimately acquainted.

The right leg crew definitely got it worse than the lefties. I cut one of them in half and lopped through most of the neck of the girl behind them. That gave the left leg team time to think through their life choices, let me go, and run like hell. I managed to hamstring one of them as I was hauling myself to my feet, but their buddies hauled them along before I could do any real damage.

Back on my feet, I could see just how much of a mess we'd made of the place. The earth was blackened and cracked, and tornados swirled around us in every direction, blocking sight of almost anything beyond the battlefield. The soldiers outside of that circling storm might have been dead, alive, or indifferent—there was no way to tell. Inside the storms, fires blazed on every flammable object and on more than a few patches of decidedly non-flammable rock. The rock itself had been smashed up by the forces unleashed by me and Leo's scrapping. If this place hadn't already been a bombsite, safe to say there would not be a booming tourist trade in the coming months.

Mercy was firing into the crowd just beyond my reach, driving them back and giving me enough time to backpedal towards Team Us, and Asher was casting something huge and complicated that would probably solve all our problems if he ever finished it. Seren and Leo were still dancing about, but he looked like he had his confidence back, and he was using his superior strength to screw up her perfect form, battering blows aside far harder than was required and grinding the Lucis against her blades to push them back into her, just the way I'd done to his stupid face.

I'd forgotten about Orphia. I suppose we'd all forgotten about Orphia. Leo included.

She came charging at me out of the enemy ranks with a borrowed battle-axe in her hands and blood pouring down her chin. Seren had slit her cheeks open from ear to ear. I'd always said she should smile more, but this was ridiculous.

I managed to dodge the first wild swing, but she didn't come alone. All the other soldiers that had been wavering and scared at the sight of the big scary Eternals felt like they had a shot at us now. I kept the first wave of the snarling horde back with a swipe of my sword, but their buddies were already pressing in behind them, driving them forward whether they'd be getting carved up or not.

Orphia came around, aiming her axe for the back of my head and very nearly hitting it this time. "Swing and a miss."

This time there was no pretense in my swipe at the coming soldiers. Some of the soldiers had their shields ready, some didn't. With the strength in my arms it didn't much matter. They all broke.

Orphia didn't give a damn about them any more than Leofric had.

She was completely consumed by bloodlust. Or maybe just regular lust. I didn't know what she was into. Either way, she just went on throwing herself bodily at me while waving her axe around. The next overhead cut required a parry to stop it from splitting my pretty head in half, and that gave the damn soldiers time to close in and start poking at me with spears again. Their jabs were half-hearted, but those spears were still pointy. They skidded off my armor but bit through the holes that acid, swords, and spears had already put into it and then right on into the juicy bits.

[739/1670 Health]

I was getting really tired of pointy things in my juicy bits.

Mercy was backing towards us now, carrying Asher along with her and abandoning all attempts at holding off her side of the encroaching army. Seren was heading back our way too. Leofric seemed to have finally worked out that he couldn't beat her in a sword fight, but he was holding his own in an acid spraying and worm summoning fight.

Whole patches of the battlefield were flooded with that same acrid smelling goop that he'd used to melt me before, but while he'd been pretty direct when he was spritzing me all over with chemical agony, he wasn't getting the chance against Seren. Her sword was darting in at his hand every time he tried to shoot something her way. He'd given up on actually hitting her. Instead, he was taking away the ground beneath her feet. Every patch he covered in acid was somewhere else she needed to avoid with her fancy footwork. It hadn't been enough to make her slip up yet, but it did stop her advancing on him. Meanwhile, he waded through the caustic soup barefoot without it leaving a mark.

As for the worms, I didn't know when he'd had the opportunity to summon the pair of bloody red khorkhoi, but they sure seemed excited to be here, darting in to bite at Seren every time she turned her attention away for a moment, and always working with their master to keep her pressed to the limit of her speed.

Instead of the Alvaren over there, I should have been paying attention to the Eternal in front of me. Orphia brought her axe in at an odd angle as I struggled to pull free of my trendy new liver-piercing, slipping under my parry to batter across what was left of my horns. Something by the root of the one that was still intact cracked under the impact, and since they were growing out of my skull, that was kind of concerning. I didn't instantly forget how to speak or anything, so I decided to worry about it later.

She thrust the spiked top of the axe forward to spear into my chest, somewhere in the bare region that all the acid earlier had opened up. It hurt, but compared to an acid bath, I barely even noticed the prick. More importantly, it gave me the time to grab onto the haft of her axe. Even when it was obvious there was no way she could win, Orphia wouldn't back down. She was reliable that way. I picked her up by the axe and bowled her right into the soldiers coming up to spear me some more.

The front ranks fell into the next and all the way back until four whole rows of Amaranth's bravest idiots were down like dominos. I called the shards of metal that I'd cast out into them earlier back to my blade, and they tore up through armor and flesh like they were hungry to spill blood. Every little lump of iron glistened with gore as they soared to me, then lashed back out again as I swung. Another arc of soldiers fell to the shrapnel.

Over and over I tore the metal back and lashed it out again. Over and over it ripped through the soldiers as they came on, but they just wouldn't stop. I was slaughtering them. Why wouldn't they stop? I saw Orphia churned up in the midst of them. One of my swipes had torn through her leg, and there was blue-tinted blood gushing out of her, but still she kept stumbling on towards me. All of them were.

Relentlessly coming on despite everything.

That was when I realized we couldn't win. Not like this. I'd dealt with bad odds before, I lived for bad odds, but this was beyond that. They were going to bury us in bodies and drown us in blood. Leo didn't care how many people he lost. He didn't care that these were real living human beings that were dying to serve his whims.

Mercy was by my back, a hand stretched out to rest on my elbow, stopping me in my tracks. "We need a new plan."

"Definitely need a new plan." I heaved in a breath, then unleashed one last swipe past Mercy, shattering the sword in my hand and sending those shards flying out into the charge coming in from the other side. It stopped them, but it still wasn't enough. There were just too many bodies.

Mercy told me what I already knew. "Leo and bitch-face, we could turn into chowder. The army, we could turn into chowder. All of them together"—she ducked a crossbow bolt—"it's too much."

The only direction that wasn't full of enemies was covered in acid. Unless we learned how to fly, we weren't getting out that way. There was nothing my Artifice could move or touch except for the metal I'd brought along, and there was no way we were getting across the newly made acid lake on a silver surfboard.

Asher unleashed his spell, not at the gathered soldiers but at Leofric. He was a smart guy. He knew that cutting the head off a snake was the quickest way to stop it wriggling. We all should have been focused on Leo from the start. Why was I so dumb? Why didn't I think of that.

Unlike the fireballs and lightning bolts I'd seen him tossing around before, this latest spell came out like a thin beam of dazzling red light. The heat pouring off it was enough to make me flinch back. When it passed by Seren, she leapt aside with her hair curling and crispened black. Maybe Restoration could fix that, and she wouldn't have to kick

Asher's ass or get a bob cut.

Leo must have sensed it coming because both of his worms leapt up, crisscrossing directly in the spell's path. Both of them exploded into waves of slime, and the red bar of searing heat punched right through.

Bald, breathing hard, and battered from his clash with Seren, I thought that Asher had finally got him, but the wily old bastard had both hands up between him and the death-ray. At a glance I thought he was trying to push it back with that acid spray of his, but no, it was grosser. Slime exploded out from between his hands, slopping down all around him, but then as he bore down on it, more and more hunks of worm sprayed out around the sides. Whole coils of khorkhoi tumbled out around the beam as I watched, wriggling and writhing without any mind to control them. Creatures without any thought or purpose beyond suffering.

Asher's beam blinked out as suddenly as it appeared. He slumped, exhausted, and Leo was still untouched. Untouched and smug.

Seren was back by my side before I even knew it, panting for breath. Leo's army were lapping in around us in a wide circle, shy of coming closer now that there was someone of a higher paygrade to handle us but still cutting us off from any escape. "We must break through if we mean to escape. Focus our efforts in a single point, so that we may punch through their lines."

Leo forced out a laugh. "Yes cowards and thieves, flee before me. Show me your backs so that I might cut you down."

The Lucis shimmered in his hand, and the green glow in the other one meant that he was pulling some more Primal energy out to do something terrible with it. When he jerked it up suddenly, all four of us flinched, and I hauled my metal back into a shield between us. I shouldn't have bothered. That green light swept out in a wave over his minions, and the screams of the wounded became cheers of victory.

Orphia put her full weight down on her once-injured leg and gave a satisfied nod as the wound closed up. She bounded in ahead of her soldiers now that she could walk again, a borrowed spear replacing her axe.

Mercy fired off shot after shot at her, but with her Celerity surged, Orphia ducked past them all as if they were hanging still in the air. Asher let out a ragged breath that sounded like a sob behind me. I twisted my shield back into a sword. If we were dying here, I was going to make them pay for it.

With a lurch in my stomach, I realized that dying wasn't something all four of us could walk off. Mercy, Asher and I would pop right back up again and start over if we dropped dead, but Seren wouldn't. If they got her, then she was gone. "We have to get Seren out. The rest of us will lose a bit of gear, but Seren…"

The whole enemy army crowded in around us, but I only had eyes for my people.

Mercy nodded, and Asher bobbed his head in what was probably assent. I turned to Seren to make sure that she wasn't going to demand the opportunity to make a suicidal heroic last stand—even that would totally be in character for her. She was standing with her back to me, the Alvaren arrow held high. "Briar by Moonlight. Your servant calls for aid!"

CHAPTER 22

Oh no. Oh no. I reached out for the arrow, but it was already too late. "Oh no, no, no, no, no, no."

The magic bound within that little twig had been unleashed. An invisible wave of power swept over us, and a single needle thin beam of light shot up into the sky. It was a nothing of a spell. An arcane answering machine beep. But with Briar's power behind it, it turned every head and rocked us where we stood. Mercy caught my eye and panic sank in. "We've got to go. Now."

She snatched the arrow out of Seren's hand and fired it off as far away from us as she could muster. If it was some sort of homing beacon, we needed to get it as far away from us as possible. Seren turned with a hint of confusion painted on her usual mask of indifference. "All will be well, my friends."

It really, really, wouldn't. The only good thing that I could think of to say about Leo was that even though he was... who he was, at least he didn't have the power to back it up. Briar was a whole different level of trouble.

There was one long blissful moment when all the soldiers were looking to each other panicked, when Orphia's charge faltered, and when Leo looked like he was ready to turn and run. Then that moment stretched on too long, and they decided that maybe the Alvaren Empire wasn't going to appear out of thin air. They started in for us again. Crossbow bolts twanged loose from their rear ranks, soaring through the air towards us and then stopping dead. Everything stopped moving.

Deathly silence swept over the battlefield. Even the fires and the winds were frozen in place. It was like time had stopped. Maybe time had stopped. Maybe the only reason I could see everything held in place was whatever little spark of divinity made me an Eternal. It didn't make much difference either way. We were all frozen in place as the Alvaren arrived.

Their city appeared first, hanging in the sky directly above us as though it had always been there. It was soundless and seamless like the world had just been rewritten to make it so it had always been there. Still, we stood still, frozen in our ridiculous poses and facial expressions as the shadow covered us all. Light, then dark. Moving, then still. All in an instant. My eyes could still move, which was maybe a blessing, or maybe a curse because it meant that I could see my doom coming, drifting down from on high with what I would have once said was a blank expression, but which weeks of Seren had taught me was something like a condescending smirk.

The first and last time I'd met the boss of the Alvaren Empire it had been a few seconds after yanking the Rusted Blade shard out of their Keystone font of magical power thing and turning them all back from goblins. Even in rags, she had looked regal. Now she was in actual clothes the effect was stunning.

I'm not going to pretend to know anything about fashion—my current look was not hobo-chic, I just had most of my armor melted off by acid—but I figure that most people dress for where they're planning on being. You wouldn't wear high heels to go hiking through the woods, and you wouldn't wear a pair of Hawaiian shorts to go to a fancy restaurant. Briar by Moonlight was dressed to fly.

Ribbons of intricate white lace trailed down from her black skirts to drift around her, buoyed by the same winds that slowed her descent down to among us peasants on the ground. If she walked like a normal person instead of floating around like a snow-globe ornament, then those lacy whatevers would have been dragged through the mud all day every day. The skirts that looked longer than her legs would have been a problem too. Even the dangling drapery of her sleeves would have gotten underfoot and tripped somebody up if she'd been strolling around. Since she was flying, it all made an impact. Her clothes screamed: this is the person to look at, the center of attention, the bee's knees, the highlight of your low life. Look how much prettier than you she is, how much more powerful and graceful. Look at how much *more* she is than you. How dare you even look at her?

Basically, if she had literally any personality other than superpowered mega-bitch, she could have spat in my mouth, and I would have liked it. Unfortunately, she was her.

The Alvaren are the center of their own universe, and nobody who isn't Alvaren matters. We're less than them. Sometimes that is unpleasant, like if you're trying to have a conversation with one or date them, but right now, I couldn't help but feel a little bit relieved that Briar kept me paralyzed and useless so there was no way I could blurt out something stupid that could get us all killed.

"Serendipitous Winds, ever faithful. Long have I awaited thy call."

Translation: bitch, what took you so long.

"Your Majesty, I cannot thank thee enough for this audience." Seren's face broke my heart. Even after everything we'd told her, she was still looking at the floating Alvaren empress like she was Santa Claus come to grant all her wishes.

Briar drifted closer, cupping my girlfriend's face in her hand. "Nonsense, my child. You are mine. All who are mine are worthy of their mistresses aid. That thou have brought my enemies to their knees before me only sweetens this joyful reunion."

Seren's voice was tiny when she tried to reply. "Beg pardon, Your Majesty, but there is much that I have not yet had time to tell you. These Eternals—"

"The vile sycophants of Araphel responsible for our corruption." Briar stared at me as she corrected Seren. Guess she hadn't forgotten about the whole headbutting thing. "They were the ones who doomed our people to millennia of base savagery. There is no punishment cruel enough to make up for the curse that they inflicted upon us."

Where was a daytime TV host when you needed him to come running out and announce that the polygraph had determined that was a lie? Briar was the one who'd jammed the rusted blade bit in their big magic pyramid and turned them all into goblins. She'd admitted as much when she was trying to grab it back from me and shove it into place. I had no idea why she wanted her people to be goblins—I had no idea about most things, if I'm being honest—but the fact she was trying to shift the blame onto us suggested that the rest of the Alvaren weren't going to be happy with her for doing it. No wonder she wanted us dead.

"I cannot speak to the gold clad tyrant, who by my reckoning has been in this place since the Revelation, but I can attest that the rest are newborn to this world." Still, poor Seren went on talking as if there was any hope of changing Briar's mind. Like this was all just a misunderstanding. She had never believed a word I said against her queen, even now, seeing Briar lying to her face she couldn't believe it. I strained against the invisible restraints that held me in place, but it did nothing. It was like the whole world had crystallized into something solid. Even with all my strength, there was nothing to push back against.

Once more Briar's elegant pale fingers brushed along my lover's cheek, trailing over the places I had touched and kissed. Ready to snatch her life away. Seren didn't even know she was in danger. I should have fought her more. I should have made her understand. I'd just wanted for things to be good between us. I'd just wanted us to be happy together instead of arguing. "They have deceived you, my sweet. You need not worry about them any longer. You shall never need lay eyes upon any of these servant of the void again."

Seren leaned away from her touch, blue flushing over her cheeks at the attention. "You do not understand. They are on a vital quest, Your Majesty. They are gathering the only weapon that can strike the Voidgod down upon his return."

The silence went from absolute to deafening. The pressure holding us all in place doubled until I could feel the air being crushed from my lungs, and the flesh being squeezed to my bones. Briar went from soft spoken to shouting in an instant. "I do not understand? I do not understand?!"

Seren dropped to her knees, gasping. "I misspoke, Your Majesty."

Briar toppled forward with her, still hanging in the air in a nimbus of finery. She caught Seren by the chin and dragged her eyes back up to meet hers. "No, no, humble paladin, please share your boundless wisdom with the empress of the Alvaren. Please tell me how you came to know what I do not, to have reasoned with more clarity than she who can name every star with a glance and track their passage through centuries. Tell me once more that I do not understand what you do."

There was a frantic edge to Seren's voice, but still, she kept trying to argue, kept on trying to prove that we were the good guys. She didn't understand that Briar already knew. She didn't understand that was why Briar wanted us dead. "I have traveled amongst them, Your Majesty. I have seen their purpose. I know them."

Briar's eyes closed, and she took a deep breath through her nose. I almost had hope for a moment. Hope that she might hear reason. That she might be calming herself and thinking rationally, and this might all actually have just been a big mistake. When her eyes opened again, I knew that I was dead wrong.

"Is a paladin so easily swayed from her purpose? How little it took before you embraced doubt. I can smell the beast-man's rutting upon you from here. Should all Alvaren abandon their virtue and lay down with beasts of burden?" She flung out a hand towards me, and

I was jerked forward, hauled off my feet to hang suspended in the air beside her. "If I were to mount this animal, would I understand then what you understand now?"

There was panic on Seren's face. She obviously hadn't thought anyone would find out about her dirty little secret just yet. Maybe she was hoping they'd get to see some of my heroics and be so overwhelmed by how awesome I am that they might overlook the fact that I was Faun-shaped. "Your Majesty..."

"Be silent." We all rocked back at the impact of her words. Not just me hovering in the air, or Seren cowering before her, but the whole damned battlefield. Even the fires snuffed out. "I have heard their lies, and I have found them wanting. To learn that you have believed every word of their deceptions when your queen tells you that they are to be ignored... it is an insufferable betrayal."

Seren had tears in her eyes, but she still couldn't let it go. Even now, she had to argue. "Your Majesty..."

Briar snarled. "I said, be silent."

This time the power behind her words didn't rock over the battle-field. They were focused in on one single point. Seren broke.

Her head was flung back, but then it kept on going. Twisting back off her shoulders until it was hanging by skin. Her back arched back, then curled all the way over until the crackling of bones felt like it was the only thing I'd ever hear again. Her arms broke, twisting back at the elbows, and her legs gave out even as they were mangled and twisted too. By the time she hit the ground, she was dead. Dead, and ruined. All of her beauty and grace and vibrancy blotted out with a vicious cword. Folded up into a mockery of a body.

I couldn't even scream. That monster had killed Seren for noth-ing, and I couldn't even scream. I couldn't move. I surged my Potency, I strained with everything I had, but nothing worked. I lashed out with Artifice, grabbing anything and everything I could take a hold of, but none of them would budge in this frozen world. Every power that the gods had given me, I strained against this paralysis. I raged, and I tried to turn away as the girl I loved slopped out across the dry stone, and through it all, I made not a single sound.

Briar turned to face me, as emotionless as if she had just swatted a fly. "Now what shall I do to remind you of your place?"

I tapped my Void Pillar. Slaughter. The antithesis of Primal. The opposite of creating life.

All of the time I'd been hiding it, I hadn't even dared to look at the Divinity I'd bought or tested it out. I knew that Deathtouch was bad news. I knew it was a sign that the Void had some hold over me. It had been a stupid decision, but I couldn't regret it now. Not when it passed untouched through whatever spell Briar was using to pin us in place. Not when the total darkness of the Void tore out from my body in a wave of destruction, sweeping over Leofric's gathered soldiers and blinking them out like birthday cake candles.

There was no gruesome display, no blood exploding or bones breaking. One moment they were alive, the next they were not, toppling to the ground like puppets with cut strings. Everywhere the darkness touched, death followed.

Briar saw the wave coming, and whether she understood what it was or not, she darted up into the sky with all the speed she could muster. She could not escape me. She would not escape me.

Her spell on us was broken. My Potency was still surged. I kicked off from the stone into the sky after her, and the Sphere of Slaughter followed me up and swallowed her down.

Her beautiful clothes were untouched, but her pristine immortal flesh began to pucker and wrinkle. Too powerful to die like any decent person would, instead she withered. She let out an ungodly wail as her beauty faded, then that wicked old bitch gravity caught me by the heel and dragged me back down to earth.

Mercy and Asher had been untouched by Slaughter, Orphia and Leo too. They were true immortals, not just long-lived.

"You killed her!" My voice. I didn't recognize it. Nothing seemed real. Seren was dead. How could she be dead?

Briar opened her mouth to dismiss Seren as nobody important, to insult the woman I loved who'd believed in Briar's decency and died for it. I didn't let her speak. She didn't deserve to speak. Nothing she had to say could save her. My sword shattered into pieces as I swung, every shrapnel fragment lancing out at the haggard Alvaren Queen.

Despite the cataracts I'd put in her eyes, she still saw well enough to dodge aside, throwing up shields and spells that it would have taken Asher a month to learn like they were afterthoughts. In the midst of it, I heard her croaking voice. All the silk burnt away from it by the touch of death. "Voidgod."

Even now she was spinning lies. I kicked off the ground again, but she had already soared too high, and without stone to call with Artifice, I had no way of reaching her. I swiped the wetness from my cheeks and roared, "Get down here so I can gut you!"

She called down, not to me, but to everyone else. "Legends will have told of me, the queen who faced the Adversary. I have felt the touch of darkness, and I have gazed upon the void. Hear me, and know I speak from dread familiarity. Araphel is no more." She pointed down at me with a shaking finger. "A new Voidgod rises."

Then she was gone. Her and her floating city both blinked away so abruptly I didn't even get the chance to throw anything at her. Which was probably for the best, given that the only things available to throw were Mercy and Asher.

Silence returned. The tornados had long since blown clear, and the fires had all been smothered. Even the scattered stragglers of the army that fled from us made no sound as the meaning of Briar's words sank in. I sank down beside Seren and tried to straighten her out, slipping her head out from under her torso where it was wedged, and smoothing her arms out at her sides. Even her fingers had been broken, and I flinched as I tried to hold her hand at the alien feel of the dislodged parts. The tears were flowing freely now I had no Briar to focus on.

It still didn't seem real. Like this was some sort of trick. Like this was just some broken doll, and the real Seren would be waiting for me back at home. This wasn't the real Seren. All of Seren's beauty was in her grace. She was always in motion. Even when she was standing still, she was poised. Even in her sleep, when I lay there looking across at her lit only by the light of my eyes, she was in motion. Every breath perfect. She had never been this still. Never.

What was I meant to do now? We were meant to have forever.

The spear took me in the side. All of Orphia's weight was behind it, so she bowled me right over, vaulting through the air using my flesh as the fulcrum to land by her beloved master's side. The sucking wound in my side hurt me as I scrambled back to my knees, but I couldn't bring myself to care about it. Not really. Not now.

With a shudder of effort, I stopped the flow of Deathtouch, and the sphere of darkness around us shimmered away. The few soldiers beyond its limit were already running for their lives. As it turns out, having some all-powerful Alvaren queen wet herself and flee while screaming "Voidgod" had been enough to scare them off.

Let them run. They didn't matter. The only one who mattered was getting cold on the ground beside me.

"Aww." Orphia's face contorted into a hideous pout. "Did your little whore die."

I didn't even have the energy to be angry. "Shut up."

Leo had regrown his hair and his beard while my attention was away from him, but it had lost the slicked-back look of when we first met him. It burst out around him like a wild mane now. A better match for his half-dressed, acid-dribbling state. "So the Voidgod is born again. As I warned you all from the start, this treacherous beast is the only thing we needed to fear. Asher, my brother, Mercy, my sister, you have been deceived. But this accomplished liar took us all in; feel no shame, only righteous fury."

That charisma or presence or whatever you wanted to call it was back in full force, washing over us all. It was only now that I realized he wasn't the most handsome man on the planet, he was using some sort of power on us. So persuasive that it even had me nodding along. Yep, I'm a liar and a monster. He nailed it.

Asher was not taken in for a moment. Trying to rile him up was like trying to squeeze blood from a stone. Emotions didn't come into his decision making, even when the subject was something near and dear to his heart, like me.

Mercy was looking at me like I was the monster he said. Since we'd beaten Talon, she knew I was keeping secrets, and every time I let one slip, she demanded that it was the last one, that I told them everything. The fact that I had one of the Voidgod's powers probably didn't help with her theory that I was being corrupted and turned into one of his servants or whatever.

"All this time," she whispered. "All this time, I thought you were a good guy. A bit of a dick, but a good guy underneath that. And all this time, you've been…"

"Nothing has changed, Mercy. Our friend simply withheld the details of the corruption you had already ascribed him to prevent this very upset." Asher had it all worked out. I didn't need to fight her. I didn't need to argue. I couldn't. Not now, with Seren dead before me.

"He's a monster." She spat the word with venom.

"Did you see what he did to those people? Just being near him is enough to…" She choked on her own disgust. "We've spent all this time worrying about a Voidgod coming back, chasing after prophecies and shards, and… what if it was him? What if he's the Voidgod that's coming?"

Asher didn't even flinch. "I have faith that he is not."

"Why?" She sounded almost as broken hearted as me.

Whatever Asher was about to say to make it all better was cut off with a kick. Orphia had cleared the distance in a single vault. Her heavy boot slammed into Asher's gut, and he folded around her. She looked absolutely delighted when she hissed to Mercy. "The wyrm-spawn has chosen the path of evil."

Mercy didn't move, she didn't speak, it was like Briar's spell still held her. Inside, maybe she was wrestling with all the things she'd seen. All the things we'd done. It didn't matter. She did nothing.

Leo was standing with his arms crossed too, waiting to see what came next, no doubt. Watching his apprentice to see how well she'd learned the art of being a complete asshole.

Orphia looked down at me huddled over the corpse of my girl-friend and gave me a razor-sharp smile. "Come meet your death."

There was no pause before she spun her spear around to whip across my shoulders. "Get up."

If she'd had her glaive still, it would have cut into me. As it was, all it did was knock me down. My hands splayed in Seren's blood.

"Get up." Another crack of wood across my back.

"Face me, you coward!"

She didn't swing for me this time. Instead, she thrust her spear down into Seren. The tip scored across my palm as I caught it. At the far end of the spear, I could see Orphia's smile widen. The perfect picture of every bully to ever find a weakness to exploit. "I'm amazed that anyone was desperate enough to spread their legs for something like you."

She jerked the spear back out of my hand, spraying blood across the bare stone.

[689/1670 Health]

The spear spun as she circled me, twisting hand over hand as she waited for her opportunity to strike. "Did you have to torture her before she gave in? Did you have to force her? You seem like the type."

She jabbed at me, and through the numbness, I felt the pain as the spear pricked my shoulder. "Or maybe it was pity. Maybe you were so pathetic, she had to do it just to get you to stop whining and pawing at her."

The pain helped. It helped me to focus. To come back to myself, to this body. It dragged my attention away from Seren and that hopeless lost feeling. Still, Orphia rambled on. "There must have been something truly wrong with her to want your filthy hands anywhere near her. She must have been a real twisted pervert. Someone that wanted to lie down with animals."

Rage found me then. Not the prickling of annoyance or the burning of anger, cold dead rage that froze everything inside me. She was taunting me, insulting Seren's memory because she wanted to goad me into a fight. She wanted lost in anger and easy to manipulate. She had never seen my rage.

I held out my hand and called out to my sword.

"Oh gods, I just realized. It is all about your obsession with me, isn't it?" She feigned a retch. "She was the pauper's version of me. Did you pretend she was me in the dark of the night? Did you call out my name. How grotesque. How pathetic. Did she know that she was nothing but a—"

The Lucis leapt from Leofric's scabbard and into my waiting hand. The iron scattered around the battlefield forged it into my great-sword. My Lucis. I cut off her vile words with a slash.

She managed to duck underneath it and away unscathed, but at least it shut her up.

Asher was just fumbling his way back to his feet as I passed him by. His eyes were still bulging out of his head a bit, but at least he could stand. She hadn't done any permanent damage.

Orphia opened her mouth to spit out some new horrible lie, and I fired off a mind-strike into her face. She didn't get to see me naked, she didn't get any of the polite jibing I'd sent her way before, I showed her what I was going to do to her corpse when I was done with her.

The blue flush faded from her face as she paled, leaving behind a twisted mask of disgust and horror. I spun my sword overhand and then advanced.

For the first time in her new life, Orphia made a smart choice. She ran.

She was faster than me, there was no denying that, but I didn't tire. She could run as fast as she wanted, and I'd always be there right behind her.

Every blade on the battlefield sang as I ran by, every piece of metal resonating with the Lucis through my Artifice. All blades were one blade. All metal was one metal. I picked them up behind me as I went. A whirling mass of weapons and scraps followed me like a wave. She twisted to launch a bolt of lightning back at me from the tip of her spear, and I ran right through it. The electricity splashed into my chest, set every muscle twitching and burning. It couldn't stop me. Nothing could stop me now.

She still tried to distract me. To make me lose that focus. "Did your whore know you were a monster? Did she know you were the Voidgod reborn? Did she know that you were always going to end up killing her anyway?"

I cut at her, and the wave of iron leapt past me. She had to leap to the side to avoid the sheet of blades flung at her back, and she had to stay down to avoid the torrent of shrapnel that followed. I caught up to her when she was still lying face down in the dirt. A quick kick rolled her over, and a quick stamp shattered her spear. Staring up at me with her chest heaving, there was a moment where I almost believed her lies. I saw Seren lying beneath me.

I saw the hatred in Orphia's eyes, and I knew that they were nothing alike. Sharing a shape meant nothing. I raised the Lucis to put an end to her, once and for all.

That was when I realized that Orphia was smiling. Not at me, never at me, but past me. I spun to defend myself, but Leo wasn't there.

Leofric was fighting Asher, and Mercy wasn't helping. She was just standing there on the sidelines as they threw acid and lightning back and forth, watching it happen like she couldn't decide whose side she was on.

CHAPTER 23

"No." The cold rage in my stomach withered and died as fear for Asher throttled it. I couldn't lose anyone else today. I couldn't let him get hurt. Not for the sake of petty revenge. I turned and ran.

The battlefield that had passed in a blur when my eyes were locked on a target now seemed to be a thousand miles long. I reached out to the weapons of the fallen and stripped iron from their armor, but all of the best pickings had already been wasted on Orphia, and I struggled to gather more than enough to forge a second sword. It didn't matter. It would do. It would have to.

Asher rarely fought alone. He always had me or Seren at his side, protecting him while he cast his spells. I knew that he could move at a decent pace because we never had to slow down for him during our cross-country hikes, but I'd never seen him ducking and dodging around acid-blasts before. The serpentine quality of his appearance really jumped out when he was leaping and lunging like a striking cobra. Even so, I could see his robes being eaten away by acid in more than a few patches. Making matters worse, he didn't seem to see the horde of Khorkhoi coming up from behind him. The ground here was too solid for them to burrow, but by staying low to the ground and slithering they were surprisingly stealthy despite the bright red of their segmented bodies.

I didn't know what Asher was casting, but it seemed ridiculously fast compared to his usual spells, and ridiculously slow compared to the rate that Leofric could pour out his attacks. Little thunderclaps popped, and flashes of white-blue lightning leapt out towards the other Eternal. Never coming close to making contact, but providing Leo with some dodging to do so he couldn't focus exclusively on drowning Asher in acid.

I was running wild now, wishing I'd picked up Celerity Surge or at least put some effort into improving my speed. The three figures on the horizon flew towards me as fast as I could make them but even so I knew it wasn't going to be enough. Leo's worms reared up behind Asher to strike, and Leo raised both his hands to unleash the glowing ball of green energy he held between them. Mercy stood there, just watching it happen like it wasn't her best friend in this whole world dying.

In desperation, I swept the flat of my blade at the worms, but I had no focus. The mass of metal chasing along beside me didn't leap out in a clean cut to strike them down, the gathered metal thumped into me instead, blasting me off my feet, sending me tumbling through the air.

Riding the wave of shrapnel. I hit Asher full-on. I wrapped my arms around him as he tried to squirm free, and I bore him down to the ground. Leo's lethal blast passed overhead.

The Khorkhoi lunged for me. Each one of them was bigger than it had any right to be—twice the size of the ones I'd found out in the desert. Like Leo was printing them off magnified. Their lamprey teeth skidded off what was left of my armor, but when they found a gap, they plunged right in, hooking into my flesh, burrowing inside me as deep as they could go.

Teeth scraped over ribs that spear strikes had already cracked. My bare shoulder was gouged open, and the largest of the Khorkhoi coiled itself around me as it's throat worked, sucking blood and fresh shredded meat up its tubular body.

I reached for the Primal Pillar and found my Restoration was still dull and grey. I should have saved it. Even when I touched Asher before the constricting Khorkhoi dragged me up and off him, it didn't light up. I'd wasted it on some stupid crossbow wound. "I do not suppose that you have any other powers gifted from the Void that might turn this situation around?"

"Nope." I strained against the Khorkhoi, trying to pull its jaws out from where they were scraping into my collarbone. "Just that one really stupid impulse purchase."

Leo's next acid blast came, and all I could do to save Asher was throw myself off balance and into its path. The green spray washed over the Khorkhoi without leaving a mark, then started eating my flesh away. Now felt like a good time to start screaming and never stop. Being dissolved is not fun, kids. Don't try this at home.

I'd kind of hoped the acid might stop the worms, but apparently, they were made of the same goop. Leo's primordial ooze. Where the conqueror worms weren't already gorging themselves on my flesh, the acid did its work, burning away skin and flesh and bone and leaving puckered sores everywhere it had splashed. I was making some truly animal noises as I fought to straighten up and fight using muscles that had been dissolved away. It felt like using Artifice on what was left of my armor to puppeteer myself around was the only way I could even stay standing.

Leofric closed in on us now, more worms curling out from his hands, swelling as they fell to the dust and then springing forward, only half-grown, to catch Asher's frantic lightning crackles and die. The Eternal himself didn't flinch or slow. He knew now that he had us at his mercy.

"Mercy." It slipped out in a desperate wet gasp as the shoulder worm broke through and burst my lung. "Mercy!"

One moment, Leo was strolling in with as smug a look on his face as I'd ever seen, the next he took an arrow to the knee.

A barrage of them came, piercing through the worms that feasted on me, plucking them off and casting them aside. As more tried to lunge in at Asher, she hit them too. Everything that she should have been doing from the start, she finally did.

She was beside us a moment later, kicking worms away, hooking her fingers into what was left of the ones hanging onto me, and hauling them off. I nearly fell without the crushing support of the Khorkhoi, but that same hand was there to catch me, to hold me up.

Leo was keeping his distance, and Orphia was closing the distance from where I'd left her. We had a moment. "Why?"

The tears in my eyes were all from pain, not from emotion. Honest.

Mercy met my gaze for just a moment, then she forced herself to look away. "You're... you."

I coughed up blood. A lot of blood. That was probably bad news. "Always... have been."

She slapped me on the back of the head, and I nearly toppled right over. "Shut up, you ass."

"Yes, boss," I spluttered.

"I thought that you were changing. I thought that you were..." She looked at me again, and this time her gaze didn't falter. She didn't even blink. "I thought the bad stuff was taking over. When you went off after the bitch, I thought... This is it. This is who he is now. A killer. A monster."

Orphia had come to a halt, and Leofric was pacing around us. Asher had returned to his feet casting a glance between us before he set himself to gathering power for his next spell.

I wheezed, trying to get a word out. "Always..."

"Shut up." She shoved and caught me again. "You threw yourself in front of the acid, the worms. You didn't care if you died, you just... you care about us. Voidgod voodoo or not. You would never do anything that would hurt us. Never."

"I wouldn't..." I struggled in a breath. "I couldn't."

"Right back at the start, someone shot an arrow at Asher, and you caught it. It went right through your hand." She chuckled. "I thought, my god he's dumb. A complete and utter idiot. How did he even tie his shoes by himself?"

"Circle back… to good stuff." I tried to shove her back, but I was about as strong as a wet noodle at this point.

"But even though I knew you were a total moron, I could see you were a good guy. Right then and there. I knew."

Restoration flared back to life, and the same green energy that Leo had been using to blast us and spurt out worms flooded through my body, stitching me back together, closing up the worst of my wounds, even crunching my horn back out of the stump and into its place. I hadn't expected to get that back. My lungs popped back to full capacity too, and all my words came pouring out, "I should have told you everything. I know I should have told you, but I was scared. You didn't trust me, and if I suddenly announced I'd picked up murder powers from binding too many shards … I thought you'd… I didn't want you to… I didn't want things to change. I wanted us all to be friends and go on adventures and… I just… I just want a quiet life, you know?"

Mercy raised an eyebrow. "How's that working out for you?"

I took one good deep breath and then I sighed out: "I'm sorry."

"Me too." Mercy shifted uncomfortably. "But if you ever make me admit that in front of another person, I will shoot you in the face."

Orphia had circled around behind me, yet another weapon borrowed from yet another corpse in her hand, but Mercy had eyes locked on her. I kept my focus on Leo. He had let the neon green of Primal power fade from his hands, but there was no question he was just waiting for his moment to strike.

I clapped a hand on Mercy's shoulder and willed a new load of arrows into her quiver. Asher gave us a nod. That was when Leo's voice echoed out once more. "So you have chosen the path of wickedness and sin too. Do you have no shame? Did you think that the Solar Court blessed you with their gifts that you might use them against your kin?"

"We're family, Leo." I said it, but Asher's head bobbed along with my words. "Not you."

"Orphia!" Leo roared out, all the divine charisma draining away as he barked orders. "Together!"

A plume of dust and gravel was kicked up as he charged. Behind me, I could hear Orphia's battle-cry. Even with their army dead and scattered, they were coming for us. Even with just the two of them, given Leo's overwhelming age and power, they could still win against us, battered and broken as we were.

So you cannot believe just how hard I started laughing when I realized that Leo's charge had curved. The first few steps had been right towards us, but then once Orphia was barreling at us and too late to change course, he spun on his heel and headed for the mountain pass as fast as his little legs would carry him.

It might have been a ruse—he might have been planning to rain acid down on us from a distance—but it wasn't. I'd seen his face. He was scared. Just the same as Briar had been. He knew that I could permanently kill Eternals, and now that he didn't have overwhelming odds on his side, he didn't want to play anymore. It didn't matter that if he'd had the balls he could have taken us all on. It didn't matter that I still had his ancient-relic symbol-of-station sword. It didn't matter that if he turned and ran, Orphia was certain to die. He didn't give a shit about any of that. All Leo cared about was Leo.

I spun to face Orphia as she charged, and I saw the exact moment that she realized he'd abandoned her. I'd seen her killed before, and I'd seen her hurt before, but nothing would ever be as satisfying as that moment when I saw her betrayed. When the realization sank in that she meant nothing to this man she'd devoted herself to, body and soul.

For the first time since Seren died, I felt something like a smile creeping onto my face. There was no joy in this, no pleasure, not really, but there was a grim satisfaction in watching her lose everything, the same way that I'd lost everything. Maybe I *was* a monster. I could live with that.

There was no strain when I leapt forward and parried the blow she had aimed at Mercy. There was no effort in twisting and turning away each desperate swing of her borrowed sword. Seren was with me in those moments—I could still feel her cool touch on my wrist, adjusting my grip, my stance, making everything she touched just a little bit closer to perfection.

I didn't need the strength of my godly body. I didn't need any magic or powers. I knew how to fight.

As we spun around each other, I could see that Mercy and Asher had turned their attention to Leofric. Even as he sprinted away, he was unleashing worm after worm to cover his escape. The Khorkhoi leapt up to meet Mercy's arrows as they soared across the distance. Each one dying making a perfect catch. A never-ending trail of corpses just so that he could run away. How many of them had he left through the millennia he'd walked this world? How many good people had died for his egomania?

Orphia didn't have a chance when it came down to it. I'd had the best teacher in the world, and she'd had Leo. I'd had someone with infinite patience while she had a man who'd break her jaw for talking out of turn.

She had her back to Mercy and Asher now, frantically parrying away my attacks as they came but never able to launch a counter. She didn't have the time. Every movement of my sword was another link in the chain, and while I grew more and more confident and skilled with every motion, she was only becoming exhausted. Her parries became clumsier, her movements more sluggish. She tripped and stumbled about the battlefield, falling over the corpses of her army where I had laid them down.

There was no challenge here, no risk, just a petulant child who thought that she was better than everyone else. How would Seren have dealt with her?

My next lunge knocked Orphia's feeble attempt at a parry aside, smashed through the lacquered pauldron on her shoulder, and slit along the side of her neck.

She dropped her sword and grabbed for her throat, frantic and scrabbling at the sudden fountain of red. Every step that she stumbled back, I matched, until she fell back and switched to crab walking away. That was when I let my foot come down on her ankle, and the farce of a chase stopped.

Even to the last moment, she was defiant. She spat blood at me and hissed, "You're nothing. This is nothing. I'll be back. I'll come back and then…"

She was so pathetic that I almost stayed my hand. Almost. "No. You won't."

I brought the Lucis down into her chest.

[196 Damage]

You never know that Death is at your side until he decides to make himself known. He comes and goes so fast that I can't imagine most people would spot him even if they were looking the right way. But for me, time ground to a halt as the black robed figure hung there. *"What is this one's destination?"*

Until now, all I'd had to do was will them not to come back. To wish for their deaths to be permanent. But I suppose that now I knew there were other worlds that they might get dumped on, I had to get more technical. The trouble was, no matter where I sent Orphia, she was going to be a problem. Back on Earth, she'd probably try to hunt down everyone I ever cared about and torture them. In the land of the dead, she'd probably swell up into a monster like Gorgafel. "Is there somewhere I can send her where she is just gone, forever?"

"*The Void.*" Death didn't sound disgusted or disdainful, he'd seen it all before.

"Then take her to the Void." I remembered my manners at the last moment. "Please."

He seemed to pause for a moment when I said please, then swooped back into motion. "*As you wish, psychopomp.*"

Time snapped back into action as blood exploded up from Orphia to cover me. Lying there, split open and oozing gore, it was the best she'd ever looked. There was no point in staring down into her face and watching as life left her body, I already knew she was dead. Big D didn't show up for near misses.

I hauled my sword back out as I passed her by. Bigger fish to fry.

In the gap between the mountains, the Serpent's Gate, Leofric fled with all the speed he could muster. A trail of dead worms lay behind him, and the open expanse of the Voidgod's home turf lay ahead. A whole open world for him to lose himself in, find cover, find allies, come back at us again when we least expected it. No.

He was as responsible for Seren's death as anyone. If he hadn't ambushed us and driven her to desperation. If it wasn't for him, she'd still be alive. He didn't get to walk away unscathed.

Mercy lined up her shot, and Asher tossed the roiling ball of lightning and fire that he'd spent all this time preparing into her path. With a gust that cleared all the grit and dust of the shattered stone away, the tempest arrow soared forth. Fire, wind, and lightning coiled around that arrow's flight, soaring all the way across the open plain in a beautiful arc.

At the very limit of my vision, I could see Leofric throwing up worms to intercept it. Huge monstrous things. Tangles of blood red flesh that did nothing to slow the storm that was coming down on him.

The arrow struck home, and the spell detonated.

Normally, I don't get to see Asher's handiwork as I'm too close to the epicenter of the explosion to really appreciate all the pretty blossoming flames, the shots of lightning leaping out in fractals, the colors, and the roar. When it cleared, Leofric was lying still on the ground. Then a moment later, there was nothing left to see at all but the shattered and melted remains of his golden armor.

Legendary Foes Defeated!
Potency increased to 54
Piety increased to 10
Twin Strike: Rank 7/10
Resonant Dominion: Rank 1/10
860 Experience Gained
8000 Glory Gained
Tier of Glory Ascended!

That was the last of them. The other soldiers were dead or scattering, and the leftover worm parts were done twitching. The battle was over. I let the Lucis fall from my hands as I tried to get a breath and found myself choking on it. The cold hate, the fury, it had held everything down until now. It had crushed everything with vengeance, but now it was spent, and I was done. Hollow.

CHAPTER 24

Mercy crossed the distance to me, already yelling, "Don't think you're off the hook, you lying piece of…"

Asher caught her by the sleeve, and she spun to face him snarling, "Did you know about this? Did you know what he'd done?! What he'd become?"

There was never a readable expression on Asher's face, but he shook his head slowly at Mercy.

I was already away from them, back to the place I needed to go, kneeling beside all that was left of Seren. I returned to my task, uncurling each broken finger and smoothing them out, unwrapping her spine until she lay in the shape of something human again. Every time my hands touched her, I hoped that Primal would flare to life. That I was somehow mistaken. That the vital spark that was her was still here. It didn't. I wasn't. She was cold to the touch.

"You can spin any lies you want about him not knowing that binding the shards would connect him to the Voidgod. None of us expected that, but this is different. He chose it. He chose to put Glory in it and make himself into a monster." Mercy was still ranting, and I could hear her, even if my brain wasn't letting me respond right now.

Asher was trailing along after her. "Mercy, we will discuss this in great detail, and we shall seek his reasoning in what was clearly a serious lapse in judgment. But not now…"

"What is so important that…" She trailed off when she saw me. When she saw Seren. "Oh."

Asher led her away and left Seren and me alone.

My body shook, but the tears didn't seem to come. Maybe the

rage had frozen them all solid. My hands were quaking as I smoothed out her hair, and when I brought her swords up to rest on top of her chest, curling her fingers around the hilts. I'd made her those swords, and she'd sworn herself to me.

She'd never even had time to realize that she was way too good for me. She never had the chance to break up with me and tell me I was a worthless loser in some old timey language I wouldn't properly understand. Everything that we were going to do together, it was all done. There would be no more.

It took a little tug of Artifice to bring every sword on the battle-field to me. Then another little push to shape them into a jagged tomb around where Seren lay. I didn't know what the Alvaren do with their dead. We'd never talked about it. Funeral arrangements had seemed so distant a worry, what with us both being immortal and all. Except, apparently, we weren't. Not both of us.

Sometime between me kneeling down here and me building the sword shrine to Seren, the sun had slipped down into the mountain peaks, and Asher had come to stand by me. "I never observed any time that she faltered in her courage."

"It wasn't… she wasn't brave. She was too stubborn to let anyone see her scared."

He still pressed on like he could give a whole sermon to me on Seren. As if I didn't know everything he knew and so much more about who she was. "We are Eternal, and she was not. Yet she flung herself into danger as readily as those of us who could walk away from it unscathed, regardless of the outcome."

I smiled, but it didn't reach further than my mouth. "Yeah, she was crazy."

Mercy was lingering behind Asher like she didn't want me to know she was there. Like she was embarrassed just to be seen with me right now. "You know we weren't besties, or whatever, but… yeah. She was pretty decent, for an Alvaren. She was… good people."

"She was a psycho, and you hated her, and that's okay because I… I didn't." The tears started to gather in my eyes at last, and the last words came out in a croak. "I liked her."

Mercy scoffed. "Well, yeah, that's why I wasn't the one shtupping her."

Asher made a little strangled sound "Mercy."

I almost managed a laugh, but it caught in my throat. We stayed just a little bit longer as the sun sank the rest of the way down, and the alien stars came out above our heads.

"Are we done here? We've still got a dragon to slay and a world to save."

Asher sounded truly appalled. "Mercy!"

"I'm done." I said it before I thought it. Pushing myself up off the ground. "I'm… I'm done."

Mercy kicked me in the back of the knee, sending me stumbling towards the jagged edifice I'd hauled up for Seren. "So now can we talk about why you decided to make yourself into a Diet Voidgod?"

Why I'd thought she'd give me a minute to breathe before she started in on me about this was beyond me. I held up my hands. "I'm an idiot, and being able to kill enemies with one touch sounded cool. I didn't know it would work across my Sphere of Influence. Pretty sure it wasn't meant to. Like… I don't think I'm meant to have both sets of powers? I don't think they're meant to mix."

Her brows were drawn down, and she didn't look all that impressed with my answer when she kicked me again. "Why did you do it?"

I stumbled back, but the violence was actually helping. My heart felt like it was beating again. The brief thumps of her boot on my skin drew me back into my body. "I'm an idiot. Did we not cover this?"

"No." She swung for my face again, and this time I dodged. "You're not an idiot."

That stopped me dead, so her next slap hit me square in the face. "Mercy, are you feeling alright?"

She was so angry that she actually stopped hitting me. "Shut up. You're not this stupid. You're not so stupid that you'd make yourself into… him, just so that things are a little bit easier. I don't believe it. So tell me the truth, right now. Or we're done."

Both her and Asher were just standing there, staring at me, waiting for me to announce I was the devil in disguise or something. The silence dragged on and on until I felt like I was going to crawl out of my skin, and then finally, I admitted what I hadn't even wanted to think before. "We're going to lose."

They both looked stunned. I was the hype guy, the one who always insisted we were going to win, even when there were giant monsters chewing on my guts. That we were the best. That we were awesome. We were, we are, that wasn't the point. "We're still babies compared to the Eternals that went up against the Voidgod before, and he wiped the floor with them. Compared to Briar? She can make the whole world freeze just by thinking it, and the Voidgod kicked her ass. Unless someone does something different, he is going to beat us."

Mercy covered her face with her hands and screamed. Good thing we were all alone in the middle of nowhere. "So what, you thought you'd beat him at his own game? He's a god! It's in the name!"

"I can kill Eternals because I'm a Void Eternal." Felt weird saying that out loud. "I can… I can send their souls away so that they never come back, and I thought that if I could make that stronger—if I could make myself stronger—then when the time came and I had the Rusted Blade back together again, I could… I could do it. I could kill him. For good this time."

Asher cocked his head to the side, probably still dead on one side from Mercy's bellowing. "If that was the case, then why did you fail to inform us of all this from the start?"

It was even harder to force this out than the admission that we were going to lose. It took all my courage to finally put it into words. "Because I was scared. You already thought I was kind of shady because the Lunar gods picked me, then you started acting all suspicious, and… I didn't want to lose you guys. I can't… I can't do this on my own."

Mercy squatted down, hands still covering her face, and groaned. "I take it back. You are a complete and utter idiot."

"That's what I've been saying."

"A dunce," Asher added.

"Right!"

He advanced on me, pointing a finger, and despite the fact that he was smaller than most of my meals nowadays, I found myself backing away. "An imbecile."

"Okay…" I grumbled.

"A half-wit moron, with intellect comparable to that of a crustacean."

I opened and closed my mouth a few times, wondering where he was going with this. "Um."

"An ignorant, vacuous cretin."

"Ow?"

His clawed finger jabbed into me, and the suddenness of it shut me up. This was Asher who never lost his temper, never raised his voice, and never even bothered when Mercy and I were doing our best to tag-team annoy the crap out of him.

He was shouting now. "If you had approached us with the choice that you faced, do you not think that we would have taken your fears into account? That we would have not weighed all of the information available to us? Did you not believe that we had sense enough to see the correct course?"

In hindsight, yes, maybe I should not have been so stupid. "But… what if you thought…"

"Fear cannot govern you, and no choice that we undertake is made in a vacuum." He jabbed me, again and again. "Whatever any one of us has decided, it has changed the course for all. You were a fool to do this without us."

"I…" There wasn't really any way to deny that. "Yeah?"

"And you were twice a fool to keep it hidden from us. To hobble your own power when you could have turned the tide of our battles, again and again. It is this that I struggle to forgive, Maulkin. Not your impetuous choice, nor your deceptions, but the simple fact that our quest has been imperiled by your refusal to take responsibility for your choices."

My mouth was hanging open, and I had to force it into motion to mumble out. "I'm sorry."

He looked me in the eyes, and he hissed, "If you had not been such a coward, your lover would have lived."

"Asher!" Mercy bounced up and took him by the shoulder, but the damage was already done.

I could see it all playing out in my head. Everything would have been different. Still, Asher raged on, "Would you have me deceive him in turn to repay this buffoonery? If he had slain Leofric's minions from the beginning, then there would have been no escalation of the conflict, and his retainer would not have sought to summon allies. If he had just…"

Mercy clamped her hands around Asher's snout and whispered, "Shut up."

"He's right." That hurt almost as much as losing Seren. Knowing that I could have saved her if I'd just—

"That doesn't mean he should say it." Mercy cut me off. "You're going to have to carry that for the rest of… well, forever."

I sank down to the ground once more. "It wasn't like I didn't know it was my fault."

That put an end to the arguing, at least for a little while. The other two set about the business of getting us ready to get back on the road again, scraping together what supplies they could and handing me anything that needed repairing or replacing to fabricate them a new one. The special glass cages that we'd borrowed from Talon's Keep to transport the butterflies were smashed to pieces, their inhabitants long gone by now, causing havoc somewhere out there in the world. The butterflies that hadn't been crispy fried anyway. We just left them where they lay when I put the backpack back together.

Most of the iron I'd carried in with me was gone. Melted away to nothing by Leofric's acid. Most of the metal from the fallen soldiers had been cobbled into the shrine to Seren. I scraped together enough to put my armor back into some sort of decent shape, then strained a little more off the dead men, pulling out hobnails and shattered links of mail to form a second great-sword to match the Lucis. The other two crept up on me again when it looked like I was done.

Mercy had her arms crossed. Great. Stern talking time. "Maulkin. You need to trust us. If we haven't run away from you yet, we aren't going to. Okay? So this is your chance. Are you keeping any more secrets?"

I racked my brains. "I sometimes look at your butts when you're walking in front of me."

"Something we didn't already know?" She was trying not to laugh. That was probably a good sign. That probably meant that we were going to get past this. That things might be okay again. At least between the three of us.

"I'm sorry." To my eternal shame, my voice broke a little bit as I said it, and then suddenly, Mercy was there with her arms wrapped around me, and a moment later, hesitantly, Asher tangled his scaly limbs about us both too.

We were only there for a second before one of us had to ruin the moment. Asher mumbled into my back, "I do not approve of the butt staring."

"Oh, like I haven't caught you staring at mine," I mumbled back into Mercy's hair, drawing a wet sounding laugh out of her.

He couldn't help himself; he had to snap back, "Solely because your posterior fills such a large proportion of my line of sight."

"So then why do I keep seeing you staring at Mercy's?"

He let out a little exasperated huff and pulled away, leaving me and Mercy still clasped together. It sounded like she was trying really hard not to laugh out loud, vibrating against my chest instead. "I look to Mercy because she is scouting ahead of us, and I am attempting to ascertain which direction she is headed so that my spells do not intersect with her and cause undue injury."

"And you're just checking which way she's going every time she's bending over?"

He sounded genuinely aghast, and I could feel Mercy's tears of laughter soaking through my armor now. "Maulkin! I do not know what you are attempting to imply."

I lifted my own tear-striped face up to wiggle my eyebrows. "Oh, you know what I'm implying."

He huffed and stormed away from us both, heading towards the Serpent's Gate. Then before he was out of earshot, some terrible magnetism seemed to draw him back around to very carefully declare, "The idea that I could take a carnal interest in someone occupying a human form is obscene."

She'd shoved me away by this point, doubling over with laughter and conveniently presenting the subject of our discussion to Asher. I pointed to it. "But if that was an Inyoka booty, you'd be down to clown?"

Asher looked genuinely perplexed. "The inclusion of harlequins within your mating rituals only serves to further prove the incompatibility."

Mercy gave me one last look before setting off after him—one without any mirth or forced kindness. It was pity, and I hated it. "You'll be okay."

I took one last stare at Seren's shrine and shook my head with a rueful smile. I might be able to pretend I was still alive, and I might be able to keep on fighting, but "okay" felt like an even more distant fantasy than killing a Voidgod right now.

Until today, I had never understood why so many of the Eternals had gone mad in the end. Not just the ones that had just given up and slinked off into obscurity or let themselves stay buried when they died, but the few who still remained active and fighting who had all completely forgotten the first thing about being a decent person, treating other people like they were people, not things to be used. For the first time, I got it.

If every death hurt this much, if every day that ticked by took another person you cared for, no wonder they ended up not caring. I could barely stand to be alive right now knowing that I'd never see Seren again, but if you added that up a dozen times, how long would it take before feeling nothing was better?

Anything had to be better than this.

I trudged after the other two as the night rolled on, passing through the Serpent's Gate without even noticing and heading out from that dull grey passage into the lush foothills that lay beyond it. I'd set out thinking we were going to be face to face with some dead wasteland like we'd encountered by the Bastion, but it looked like there was no sign of the Voidgod's occupation left. Bushes and trees blossomed, even growing out of the cliff-faces at odd angles, and the colors were so powerful that even by moonlight it looked so vibrant as to be almost fake like the bright berries and fruits were Christmas tree decorations that someone had forgotten to pack away.

Dawn was a long time coming, but the deep shadows of the night were a fine fit for my mood. I'd make it a few steps sometimes without remembering, then I'd turn my head, and Seren wouldn't be there, and I'd feel a tiny tug of panic in my gut that we'd forgotten her. We'd left her behind. I'd catch myself stopping and turning before I could convince myself that she was gone.

And she was gone. That settled over me like a shroud after the first few twitchy glances back, and all the pretty scenery in the world couldn't punch through it. I trudged onwards, following in Mercy's footsteps because what else was there to do? I'd come this far, I'd been through everything I'd been through, and I'd made the biggest mistakes I'd ever be able to make. The only way to go was forward because these people were dumb enough to trust me again, and I'd rather die myself than let them think for a moment that they couldn't.

At sunrise, the other two stopped to get their bearings, and I slumped down onto the road by their feet. I say road, but there wasn't even a dirt track out here. The area around the Serpent's Gate had been cleared thanks to Araphel's deathly powers, but this far in, everything was overgrown, thick with scrub and ferns. The purple grass we'd seen in the hinterlands had grown here into something massive and abundant, stretching up past my knees and humming as the breeze ran over its blades.

Mercy's hand came down to stroke over the grass almost involuntarily as it tickled by her, twisting the leaves between her fingers. Asher was quite firmly a city boy, and he treated every touch of the grass like he was bumping into somebody. You could almost hear him struggling not to apologize to the shrubs when he tripped over them.

I didn't feel anything towards these plants one way or another, but a quick flex of Artifice skinned some down to their roots and used the fibers to make new flights for Mercy's arrows. I wasn't up to the task of weaving anyone a jungle-style outfit from the grass, but those same fibers made neat little patches for where Asher's robes had been eaten away. As long as I kept myself busy doing things, I didn't have to think. As long as I didn't have to think, I didn't have to remember.

In pursuit of busywork, I turned my attention inwards. I had a new Tier of Glory to advance, pushing me a little bit closer to godhood, and I had enough experience to buy some new skills or divinities too. As we traipsed on, I read through all the different skills and powers that were already available to me that I'd just completely forgotten about.

The obvious Pillar to upgrade was Aether since if all went well, we'd soon be coming into possession of another pair of shards, but the prospect of a battle with some ancient dragon between now and then gave me a little bit of pause. We needed to win first. And besides, once we had all the shards and stuck them together, wouldn't that make the whole sword just count as one thing? Maybe I didn't need to bind any more bits to my soul.

It felt like a slap in the face when I looked at all the Aether Divinities and realized how badly I'd screwed up. Right there at the lowest rung of the ladder of abilities that I could purchase was Soul Stone. When Seren died, I could have caught her. I could have trapped her soul in a gemstone or something and carried her around with me and found some way to grow a new body for her once I had gone a lot further into the Primal upgrades. I mean, okay maybe that last bit wasn't true, if somebody like Leo had gone centuries and only mastered worms, putting together a fully functional girlfriend would probably have taken an idiot like me a long, long time, but I still could have kept her. I could have trapped her soul and carried her around with me for all eternity and... yeah, she probably wouldn't have liked that.

The few times we had brushed up against Alvaren theology in conversation she had been pretty hyped about their afterlife. I wasn't sure if what had happened to her counted as dying in battle strictly speaking, but I figured it to be close enough. It was still a battle, even if you didn't know the other side were your enemy. If I'd taken that away from her, trapped her in a shiny rock, just so that I could keep forgetting I was carrying her around like a Tamagotchi, she would not have been impressed.

When all of this was over, when we had the shards, and the world was saved, then I could start thinking about getting Seren back. I knew the way to the land of the dead, and even if Big D wasn't exactly my best friend, we were on speaking terms. Someday, I'd work it out, pull her out, and give her a rocking body again. Death was not the end. I knew this.

That helped me pull myself together a little bit.

"Hey, guys, what should I level up?"

It was the first thing I'd said in about twelve hours, so the other two were understandably surprised. If you've never surprised an Inyoka before, their tails go rigid for just a moment like they've had an electric cattle-prod jammed right up under there.

Mercy let out a little splutter, struggling to sound mad at me. "Oh now you want our opinions."

I managed a smile. Everything was going to be okay. Even if I had to tear down the heavens and burn the whole world to get Seren back, it was going to be okay. "Well, yeah, I figure if I'm going to unlock the new Betray All My Friends and Ruin Everything Forever power, I should run it by you first."

She snorted in a very unladylike way. "Maybe skip that one."

"Well, I'm wide open to suggestions." I spread out my arms as I strolled along to catch up to them. "If you want to know what the Void Pillars can do, just imagine the uh… evil version of all your ones."

Mercy flinched when I said that, but Asher notably didn't. He just tilted his head to the side as if he was weighing something up. "Evil seems to be a less than helpful descriptor."

"Okay, let's say… destructive instead?" That was probably more accurate too. "Like, whatever you can make with the shiny light ones, the void one can unmake."

"Your display with the soldiers was the antithesis of…" Asher paused for input.

"That was the opposite of Primal. Slaughter." I was still not feeling super comfortable talking about my Voidy powers, even now that everything was out in the open and I wasn't being quite as much of an idiot as before. So needless to say, I was babbling a bit. "Maybe you could call it unhealing?"

"Given that our task is the removal of life from a specific powerful individual, perhaps it would be best to focus your investments there." Asher seemed more amused with my gibbering than annoyed, so I was calling that a win—although it might have just been that I had already used up his full year's allocation of annoyance already today.

Mercy piped up, "Or you could get better at healing. That thing goldilocks did where he healed everyone with a wave could definitely come in handy."

I blinked shut, searching for anything resembling the mass-heal that he'd used. Mercy was right, being able to get a whole army back on its feet like that had been amazing, even if the one doing it had been a giant poop wrapped in shiny gold tinfoil. "That one… I think that's a fair distance up the Pillar. I can't even see it yet."

Asher's pupils narrowed to slits as he considered me. "Perhaps you could tell us what is available to you if your Primal antithesis is advanced?"

I closed my eyes to do just that when Mercy coughed, aggressively loud, in my ear. "Or he could stop putting glory into evil void powers?"

Asher shrugged it off. "As I said, I do not believe there to be any particular morality tied to any one of the gifts of godhood, only in the manner in which they are used."

"I could always just stick with Artifice and get better at building stuff," I said hopefully. Making stuff did not make me uncomfortable.

Making stuff was fun, and being able to lob things around with my Artifice was making it even more fun. I hadn't dug too far into the mechanics of my new Resonant Dominion skill, but it seemed like the natural extension of Twin Strike, tapping into more and more things of the same type, just like when I'd called to all the swords on the battlefield.

Asher dismissed it with a wave. "As tempting as it is to have marginally improved equipment, I suspect that something more potent may be required if we mean to put an end to an ancient wyrm and a god in the coming days."

Okay, Slaughter powers. "I've already got Deathtouch, then the other starter Divinities are: Slaughter Infusion and Extinction."

Mercy was grinding her teeth as she walked. Did Eternal life come with dental? I'd need to check next time I spoke to my union guy. "Oh yeah, none of that sounds evil as hell."

I pretended not to hear her. "Infusion just lets me put uh… murder power into my sword when I'm whacking things…"

She rolled her eyes. "Isn't that just swords anyway…"

"And Extinction…" I read through the description a few times because the first time it sounded insane, and then every follow up read-through made it sound even worse. "Yikes. That is about hurting everyone related to the person you're killing. Hitting people so hard that even their grandma feels it. Wiping out bloodlines. Looks like I could clear out whole species at the higher levels. That… doesn't sound good."

While Mercy's jaw was hanging open in abject horror, Asher just nodded along. "I can think of tactical advantages, certainly. The ability to target a weaker family member to do injury to a stronger one? Or to remove a swarm of related enemies in a single blow. Consider our encounters with some of the more monstrous denizens of Amaranth, surely there are certain species that the world would be better without?"

I considered it for a moment. "Mosquitos?"

"Abominations?" Asher countered.

"This is real supervillain stuff." Mercy had that look on her face, that one she always got when she was right, and she knew that I knew she was right, and the whole argument was over. "Wiping out whole families. That is messed up."

That had been what I was thinking, but I didn't want to make any snap decisions since all my snap decisions seemed to end in me alienating everyone and getting my girlfriend murdered. "I'm with Mercy on that one."

It was Asher's turn to look perplexed. "Did I not just observe you massacring an entire battlefield of people?"

"Yeah, but they were trying to kill me, so it was… fair?" I trailed off towards the end there. It was fair, right? I'd given them more than ample opportunities to go away and not get murdered. They were the ones who'd insisted on having a fight, even though we were patently Eternals, and their boss was patently a dick-hole.

Mercy clapped her hands to get us back on topic. "We can do moral philosophy lessons later. Let's just… what will you unlock if you pump up the Slaughter?"

A blink provided the less than savory answers. "Drain and Blight."

Have you ever heard someone chortle? It is not a good sound to be on the receiving end of. Give me a good guffaw any day. Mercy chortled at the name of my new options. "More good news!"

"Drain lets me steal health to heal myself," I read out, "and Blight lets me permanently damage someone's stats."

Asher's head tilted back the other way. We really needed to get him a stabilizer for that thing. "Stats?"

"Their Potency or whatever."

He nudged me along, verbally. "Both of those seem supremely helpful for a frontline combatant."

Mercy looked reluctant to agree with him—presumably because she spent every waking moment arguing with everyone—but eventually she gave a terse nod. "Weird as it is to vote yes on you making yourself a vampire, if you could start healing yourself more that would be handy. You do keep catching swords with your face."

I held my hands up to frame my face. "Steel facials are how I stay this pretty."

"That explains a lot." She snorted. "I'd say bump up your Slaughter, grab them both."

I blinked to do just that, then paused, squeezing one eye open to peer at her. "And you aren't going to go nuts at me for picking the evil powers."

"No. I understand what you're doing now." She rolled her eyes. "Dumbass."

"Love you too." I blew her a kiss, then got to work.

CHAPTER 25

Maulkin – Chagnar Faun of the Lunar and Void Court –
12th Tier of Glory
Statistics:

HP: 1670/1670

Devotion: 440/440

Attributes:

Potency: 54

Celerity: 26

Vitality: 20

Piety: 10

Divinities:

Aether – Rank 4: Soul Bond

Aether – Rank 4: Spirit Strike

Aether - Passive: Psychometry

Ascension – Rank 4: Ascendant Brutality

Ascension – Rank 4: Ascendant Cognition

Ascension- Rank 4: Ascendant Potency

Ascension – Rank 4: Potency Surge

Artifice – Rank 2: Active Artifice

Artifice – Rank 2: Inferior Architecture

Artifice – Rank 2: Inferior Weapons

Artifice – Rank 2: Inferior Armor

Artifice – Rank 2: Inferior Shrine Construction

Artifice – Passive: Sphere of Influence

Primal – Rank 1: Restoration

Primal – Passive: Lifesense

Slaughter – Rank 2: Deathtouch

Slaughter – Rank 2: Drain

Slaughter – Rank 2: Blight

Slaughter – Passive: Deathsense

Skills:

Combat: Rank 10/10

Sword: Rank 10/10

Mace: Rank 1/10

Polearm: Rank 2/10

Phalanx: Rank 8/10

Brawling: Rank 10/10

Brutality: Rank 10/10

Twin Strike: 10/10

Resonant Dominion: 2/10

Acrobatics: Rank 7/10

Climbing: Rank 1/10

Poison Resistance: Rank 10/10

Aether Resistance: Rank 5/10

Fire Resistance: Rank 1/10

Airstrike: Rank 7/10

Bestiary: Rank 3/10

Dungeoneering: Rank 2/10

Ancient History: Rank 1/10

Traits:

Relentless: *The Faun are the greatest hunters on Amaranth, known for pursuing prey for days or even weeks at a time before closing in to strike.*

Effect: *Faun are immune to fatigue, their Attributes do not degrade over time without rest.*

Psychopomp: *You are a conveyor of souls, a guide or guardian akin to the reaper, who may push their incorporeal victims beyond the limits of the world and on into the next.*

Effect: If you so choose, you may guide those who have been slaughtered to the afterlife of your choosing, sundering whatever connections they have to their mortal shell.

With that all done and dusted, I took a look around me with fresh eyes. Not literally. My eyeballs were the same, I was just feeling less sorry for myself. The terrain had been continually changing through our night-time march, and while the initial valley of the Serpent's Gates was far behind us, more of the same pale sandstone jutted up everywhere I looked. Not very high though. There were raised plateaus dotted all over the place, breaking my line of sight to the horizon but never quite managing to achieve hill status. The same luminous fruits grew on every tree, and those trees seemed to spring up everywhere, out of the side of the plateau cliffs as often as on top of them or down here.

There was some treacherous part of me that really wanted to eat some of the glowing fruit, but I was 100% sure that I'd get yelled at for it. There was no way that they weren't poisonous or radioactive or something. So I just stared at them longingly as we passed them by.

More and more of the plateaus soon covered the prairie until we found ourselves having to wedge our way through the bushes growing in the gaps between them. Mercy fell back, and I took point, turning the ancient and hallowed relic of the Lucis into a handy pruning tool.

Asher actually fell into step beside me, peering at the plants as I carved my way through, taking interest in the neon sap trickling out from every hole I hacked in the tangled wood. "Curious."

That was all he said. I kept on waiting for some follow up, but no. That was his full opinion expressed. Yet still, he lingered at my elbow, making me pull every other cut to avoid slapping him with the back end of the sword. He was studying something—I was sure of that from his faintly dazed expression—but I couldn't have told you what he was looking at.

"What?"

He didn't seem to hear me, so I stopped with the chopping and turned to face him. "What is it?"

He crouched down at the side of one particularly robust shrub with berries so orange that nobody would believe they didn't contain artificial colors. "The planting. It is… familiar."

"Mercy, help! He's being a vegetable detective."

She didn't bother to turn her head from her ongoing attempts to stare the undergrowth into the form of something she could shoot. "Good for him."

"The positioning of these heavily rooted shrubs in the gullies where water would pool feels like a deliberate choice to maintain the structure of the area. The plantings on the plateaus appear erratic to the casual glance, but on examination, I see many pairings of a substantial fruit tree with a rather more lackluster appearing plant. As though attempts are being made to balance the nutrients within the soil. For all the appearance of chaos, I believe that we walk cultivated land."

Mercy's ears finally pricked up. "And what, you learned about chaos-farming in the library?"

He didn't rise to the bait. "It is the manner in which my people traditionally managed our land. Though I had no firsthand experience, even the flowerbeds of the imperial palace were operated under the same principles, balanced plantings of flowers and vegetation in proximity to maintain the vitality of the earth."

"So we could be strolling through Inyoka farmland right now?"

Asher shrugged his shoulders as he drew himself up. "Indeed."

I hefted the Lucis and felt a little bit bad for chopping down some poor farmer's hard work. "Should we be getting ready to fight?"

"It seems likely that there will be conflict should we encounter Inyoka, however"—he glanced around nervously, making Mercy reach for an arrow—"I would say that when an area has been planted with such devotion to appearing natural, it is likely that whichever Inyoka are present in the locale may be seeking to avoid confrontation. It is quite possible that we shall not encounter them at all. In keeping with that desire for stealth, it is likely that these plantations are in fact quite distant from wherever the planters reside, so we shall not come upon them by happenstance either, unless they have the grave misfortune of having positioned themselves directly between us and our goal."

Mercy deflated a little. "Could you skip to the bit where nobody is about to ambush us a bit quicker next time. All that blabbing to get nowhere."

"It was essential that you understood the situation fully."

She grumbled past us and vaulted the next bush to start scouting ahead again. "Probably no ambush. There, three words."

Asher took a step back so I could get chopping again. "It would be quite impossible to gauge the probability of either outcome at this stage. Perhaps we shall encounter the planters, perhaps we shall not. Perhaps this was all established long ago and the Inyoka who once dwelled nearby have moved on, and this is merely a leftover testament to their talents."

Mercy bellowed from deeper into the gully, "Then just say you don't know!"

"But, Mercy, that does not account for even a fraction of the truth. My knowledge of many things is one of the reasons that I am an asset to this group, and providing you with—"

I held up my hand to stop him. "Quiet."

Immediately he fell silent, and we all tensed. I didn't know what I was hearing, but my other senses sang. Lifesense or Deathsense or something was humming away at the periphery of my awareness. Not down here on the ground with the rest of us, but up there in the big blue open sky. "Hide."

Mercy was already pretty well covered by the bushes she was digging through, and Asher was as light and pliable as he'd always been when I scooped him up in my arms and leapt us up into the trees of the nearest plateau. Not a moment too soon.

The flight of wyrms passed over barely a moment later. The same opalescent sheen that had marked the one that had assaulted Talon's Keep was reflecting sunlight down on me, not once, but dozens of times. Most of them weren't as big as the one we'd killed already, but what they lacked in bulk, they made up for in numbers. Could we have beaten them? I think so. Did we want to fight them if we didn't have to? I certainly did. I was feeling particularly in the mood to kill something. But Asher, he felt differently.

When we'd killed the wyrm back at Talon's Keep, it had hit him hard. He'd been weird and introverted, even for him, in the hours that followed. I suppose that if I grew up thinking a certain set of oversized flappy lizards were gods walking the earth, seeing one of them carved up by some random dude you hang out with might be upsetting.

He kept it all to himself, of course. He was Asher. He could have a full mental breakdown going on inside that scaly head of his and we'd never know a thing about it until it was too late, but after all this time with him, I knew something was up. He'd never argue with us about going after Tsangaanax, not when it was so obvious that the old wyrm was hoarding the last two shards we needed, but that didn't mean that the whole prospect wasn't upsetting to him.

If we could have shaken claws with the big black wyrm and walked away with his shards on loan then I'd have been happy to go with that plan, but between the Inyoka attack on Talon's Keep and the swooping monstrosities in the sky now, it didn't look like he had any intention of letting things resolve peacefully.

Still, if there was a way to keep Asher's brain bubbling to a bare minimum, then I wanted to keep it tamped down. So we hid in the trees until the wyrms turned a gentle loop and soared back the way that they came. Which was, coincidentally, the direction we were headed. Interesting.

"White wyrms once more. It makes no sense!" Asher grumbled as we clambered down the cliffside to land beside Mercy in a little pond she'd found. There were tiny little fish that nibbled at my legs as I strode through it, each of them as shimmering blue as the sky in the sunlight. Little cuties.

Mercy was fiddling with her bow as if I hadn't made it perfectly for her. "You want to explain that one to us again?"

Asher furiously wrung out the bottoms of his robes where they'd dipped into the water. "Inyoka and lesser wyrms are bred from the stock of whichever wyrm rules the roost. If and when rulership changes, the previous wyrm's servitors are allowed to take their rest with their master, and a fresh batch are born. Tsangaanax is a black, and there is no logical way that these albino deviations could come from him. And there is no possibility that he would allow any ally to know of our mission, lest they attempted to wrest his prizes from us. Or indeed from him."

"So back in your library," I approached the subject as carefully as possible, "you were the baby of your dragon?"

He waved his claw. "Distantly related, but I would not have been accepted in the hierarchy if I did not bear her colors. If the patterning of my scales differed too greatly from my liege, I would not have been allowed to come to maturity."

"Well, that is really messed up." Mercy was not so bothered about approaching the subject carefully. She was quite happy to trample right over Asher's feelings if it meant getting him to the point quicker. She's such a charmer. "Are you sure it is the same here in Amaranth?"

"All that I have read since my arrival indicates that it is." His head bobbed along, eyes narrowing as he fiddled with his robe's seam, and one of the tiny fish was ejected back into the pool. "That these norms are a constant across all draconic cultures, regardless of the world."

"So what does it mean?" Mercy grumbled. "Some white dragon has killed Tsangaanax and taken his shards? Some random white dragon is out here, camped out on his doorstep? We know the shards are here."

"I have begun to formulate a theory with regards to their location as a matter of fact." Asher was off on a tangent, but I might as well let him. It wasn't like we had anything to do all day other than chat. "While the maps provided by our Dvergar benefactor offered up the most current information on the lay of the land, they were limited to the areas in which they traded. As they did no trade with the Inyoka, this region was not mapped."

"Thank you, Captain Obvious." Mercy was already pacing again, ready to move on.

Asher's tail lashed, flicking us with water. "My point, if I might be allowed to reach it, is that the most current maps were not the only ones available to us. I perused the atlases of Talon's Keep before our departure to the Bastion, so that the lay of the land might be familiar to me prior to any potential mishaps with the waystone network."

Mercy was at her limit. "Asher, I swear to the gods, if you don't spit it out I'm going to shove an arrow so far up your—"

He held up his hands. "Voidcrown Spire."

"What's that then?" I asked.

"There is a mountain beyond these plateaus, a place where there once lay bountiful fields and a kingdom at peace. It was there that the Voidgod rose from the underworld, and with his rising, so rose the very earth. A volcano, spilling forth not flame but darkness."

Mercy grimaced. "So it is the zit that Araphel popped out of."

"While those are not the terms I would have used, there is some accuracy to the comparison," Asher conceded.

"And you think whoever's got the shards is camped out there now?"

Asher's head bobbed along with my words. "It would be one of the few places in Amaranth that servants of light would fear to tread. Where even the boldest and most mighty would rightly fear their powers being blunted."

"Okay. That makes sense. Same logic Koschei was using when he hid out on the death-spot." I stretched out and got ready to start hacking through some more shrubberies.

"Slow your roll, ride-on-mower." Mercy caught me by the elbow before I could start weed-whacking again. "What are we walking into if it isn't the big black wyrm of doom?"

I shrugged. "Does it matter?"

"Does it matter?" She slugged me in the shoulder. My armor went clang, and she shook the pain away from her hand while pretending it didn't hurt. "Of course, it matters. There could be anything in that Voidzit! Araphel might already be chilling there for all we know. Do you really want to just walk in without any idea?"

"What's the alternative? We've got to go where the shards are. It doesn't matter who is trying to stop us. It doesn't matter what is in the way. The shards are how we make the weapon that can kill him." I started cutting through the bushes, looking for any little rabbit trail that I could bludgeon into a proper path forward.

Mercy had the good sense to stay clear of my swings. "I thought you were getting your super murder boy powers so you could kill him?"

Asher was hanging back too, but I suspect that was less about common sense and more that he was still trying to get the pond-weed out of the straps on his boots. "Multiple viable solutions to the impossible problem of killing something immortal sound better than relying on something entirely untested."

"I mean, the sword works." I shrugged mid-swing, making an

ugly mess of some poor berry bush. "We know it works because it worked before."

Mercy was quick to snap back. "If he's coming back, doesn't that mean it didn't work before?"

I paused to pull up a less impressive looking plant that was almost inevitably going to trip Asher. "It took him this long to pull himself back together after he got whacked last time. Maybe this time it will finish him off. Or maybe the combo of the magic sword meant to kill him and my murdery powers will do it. There was a prophecy about the sword killing him again too, right?"

Asher agreed with me in the least helpful way possible. "I cannot say that I have come upon it yet, but that was certainly the message that our benefactor bestowed upon us when we arrived."

"Benefactor?" Mercy scoffed. "The guy who dropped us in a dungeon?"

With one last wild swing, I broke through the brush, and there was open grassland again. "Can we not have this argument again? It never goes anywhere."

There was sullen silence as we trudged on across the open space, eyes darting from the plateaus overlooking us to the sky and all around. Just waiting for doom to come. Arrows soaring. Dragons roaring. Doom, doom, doom, everywhere I looked. Any minute now. Mercy mumbled behind me, "Your face never goes anywhere."

I elbowed a tree aside as we passed into another gully. "Your mother never goes anywhere."

Mercy gave me a little curtsey as she passed me by. "Your mother's face never goes anywhere."

Asher came along behind her, and I gave him a lift up onto the plateau above, calling after Mercy, "Your mother's face's mother never goes anywhere."

With a sigh, Asher found his footing on the clifftop and plodded on. "Were it not for the gift of tongues that the gods bestowed upon us, I would swear that the two of you speak a language entirely unknown to sentient people."

From down in the scrub, Mercy chirped back, "Your face speaks a language entirely unknown to sentient people…"

And so went the rest of our day. Plodding on. Fighting nothing more fearsome than overgrown rabbit food and the ever present specter of boredom. Mercy and Asher had about a dozen minor arguments that I happily blundered through without any knowledge of who was in the right, and in the end, the result was always just the two of them sulking for half an hour, then pivoting to some whole new argument about nothing.

The sun passed overhead and began to sink once more.

I groaned back to Asher when we were faced with yet another high plateau directly in our way. "Any idea when we're actually going to see the gloom volcano?"

He didn't meet my eye. "The accounts were very ancient."

"So, no?" Mercy asked, gleeful to get one over on him.

"I am afraid that the scale of the illustrations escaped me."

"Wait, so you could understand the words but not the pictures?" She was grinning so wide you'd think she'd won a prize. "You're like… the opposite of Maulkin."

I threw a berry at her, and she caught it in her mouth. Her damned Celerity was through the roof.

She chewed it thoughtfully as we walked. "Kind of spicy?"

I reached out to the nearest bush for a taster of my own, but instead of squishy fruit, my fingers brushed over something solid and scaly. Uh-oh.

The Inyoka leapt back out of the shrub with a yelp of terror. She must have been about half the size of Asher, and her scales were greens and brown in a pattern like a snake's. I reached after her as she sprinted away, but she was way too quick for me, throwing herself forward to scurry on all fours and vanish into the plants.

I gawked after her. "Did anyone else see that or am I hallucinating Inyoka?"

"Our mystery farmers." Asher hissed. "One of the casteless judging by her look. Perhaps we have worried overmuch. It seems that this place is populated not by organized defenders but by disorganized savages."

Mercy laughed. "Damn, Asher, tell us how you really feel."

"There have always been Inyoka born outside the natural order of hatcheries and broods. Matings that were not approved of. Acts of passion." He said the last word like it was something dirty.

I tried to conceal a smile. He'd never seemed all that prudish before, but maybe it was because what Seren and I had been up to didn't register with him as hanky-panky. No eggs involved. "Pretty sure none of us would be here if it wasn't for a little passion."

"This is not our way." Apparently, this was no laughing matter. He strode off through the trees with his shoulders hunched. "Inyoka are nothing if not prolific when left to our own devices, but there is a great danger of mutation in our bloodlines. Our pairings are carefully selected and regulated to ensure that the offspring remain true to their purpose."

Mercy got it though. Right away. "Because if you come out the wrong color, they kill the baby."

He was moving faster than I'd ever seen him, pushing through the woods with all haste, doing his best to keep his eyes forward as if catching a glimpse of one of the little brown Inyoka would pollute him. "Purity of patterning is a good measure of mutation. It is necessary to keep us from degenerating into the wild beasts we faced when we first approached Talon's Keep. We are bred for sentience. If we stray too far, we cease to be capable of rational thought. We become beasts. That pygmy would have been exterminated the moment their mutation was detected—at least, in any sane world."

"Killing babies is the sane thing?" I couldn't quite swallow that one.

"To prevent further degeneration as the generations proceed. What if one of them coupled? You would end up with… it does not bear consideration."

He obviously thought it was one of those greater-good situations, but I couldn't picture it. "I'm still kind of hung up on the baby killing."

He waved his hands as if he could dispel our worries. "It is a very rare occurrence. Careful breeding prevents the need for it. Except in the wild places where Inyoka have no governance and such monstrous things become necessary."

Mercy met my eyes, and we shared a moment of concern before we took off after Asher. He didn't talk about his life before coming back here. None of us did really. It felt too distant. Like a dream you had years ago. Now I was hearing more about Asher's old life, it sounded more like a nightmare.

We caught up to him, and he seemed to realize that he'd been ploughing on ahead with nobody to protect him if any of those Inyoka he was crapping all over happened to jump out and stab him. I wanted to move on to another subject, but I just couldn't quite let this whole thing go yet. "I don't think I'd be happy if somebody told me who I could and couldn't… breed with."

"That is where we differ." Asher let out a sigh. "Duty always comes first for Inyoka."

Mercy's concerned gaze was visible from beyond him. Just a moment of eye-contact that spoke volumes. How much had our boy Asher lost when he died? "You… had kids?"

"I could not say the exact number, but I made my contributions as required." He shrugged off my hand as it touched his shoulder, and we had to press on to keep pace with him.

It seemed like Mercy was struggling to wrap her head around the

Inyoka way of doing things. "And if one of them had come out the wrong color, then you would have been fine with them—"

"If there had been an issue with the purity of my progeny, I would not have been invited to continue making further contributions!" Asher snapped.

That was the end of the conversation as far as he was concerned, and the rest of the day passed us by without much more of an argument. I sometimes caught sight of what might have been another Inyoka ducking down out of sight, and my Lifesense sometimes sang out their presence where they lay in hiding in hollows that they'd dug out beneath the denser shrubs up on the plateau.

Asher was convinced that the hodgepodge colors meant that these Inyoka were mindless, but everywhere I looked, I could see signs of their careful planning. Sure, it was hard to get about these plateaus for us, but a big part of that was making sure it all looked natural so that attention wouldn't be drawn. The fact that they had these little cubby holes to hide in, that said volumes. They weren't fighters, but they knew that the world was hostile and dangerous, so they'd done what they could to make the people sent out here to gather food as safe as they could be, hiding under shrubs on the raised areas, so that they were invisible to ground troops and wyrms soaring by overhead. It was well thought out. Probably a smarter solution than I could have come up with. I probably would have made some sort of spicy berry catapult.

By nightfall, the plateaus had grown so high that if we wanted to cross the top of them instead of digging through the dense tangles of vegetation between them, I had to Surge my Potency and carry us all up in a leap and clamber maneuver that I was not fond of performing with so much weight on my back. Two swords, a backpack, two stalwart companions. It was enough to throw anyone off balance.

We were almost to the end of one of the biggest and highest ones we'd hit so far when Mercy made a little "urk" noise, and I immediately froze. We all stood there still and silent for a long moment as I waited for the ambush that had been promised all day to show up or wyrms to come swooping down from the sky. I got neither. Mercy slowly raised a hand to point out through the tree-line.

Voidcrown Spire was a big lump of rock, and I know big lumps of rock. On the dimly lit horizon it loomed up like a nail driven through the world from the other side. With the description of it being a kind of volcano, I'd been expecting a flat top, but nope, it was spikey all the way up. Maybe the jagged bit angling off into the clouds was where stuff had come pouring out, but I was already starting to suspect that Asher had been getting metaphorical on our asses.

The only thing that brought me any comfort about the looming spike of doom was that it had patches of green. The same persistent trees that they had planted to grow out the sides of the plateaus were poking out all over the place, and there was a layer of moss creeping up one side of the place that spoke more of a historic landmark gone to seed than the dark lord's fortress.

Between here and there was a much shorter distance than what we'd already traversed, but it was also a much more dangerous one. The foliage which had kept us shrouded from sight throughout the day's travel wasn't entirely gone, and nor were the plateaus on which so much was growing, but they had not been planted, and what life there was between here and the spire was low hung. The purple grasses barely came to my knees, and the gullies between raised areas which had been so carefully protected from rainfall in the farmlands we'd passed were muddy and flooded out here, corroding the sandstone to turn the cliff-faces that should have separated each heap into gentle inclines. Easier to traverse slowly, with the mud sucking at your boots, but practically useless for crossing with any degree of stealth or speed. Unless you could fly, of course.

In the sky above Voidcrown Spire, wyrms circled. In the twilight, it was hard to be certain they were the same white ones we'd already avoided, but there was no denying that they were wyrms. Each time one came swooping in to land on the jagged rock-face, another seemed to launch itself out from somewhere else. I couldn't keep count of them all. It could have been thirteen or thirty. "Oh, that's bad news."

Asher seemed a lot less concerned than I'd expected him to if I was being honest. "At least we can be certain that a wyrm holds dominion over this place. A single wyrm might be bought for the right rewards, but a whole flight? Impossible."

Mercy slumped down with her back to a tree. Apparently, we were stopping. I slung my bag off as she sighed. "Well, at least we know some of what we're up against."

Asher was trying to do the impossible and take a count of the wyrms arrayed against us, but his eyes weren't any better than mine. "Judging by the wyrms taking to the skies to ride the evening zephyrs, I would wager that their support staff number in the thousands. Most will not be competent fighters, of course, but all of them would willingly die for their brood."

I flopped down on top of a berry bush with a moan. "Of course, they would."

Asher continued, unfazed by my grumbling. "And then, of course, we must account for whatever fortifications are in place. Both the current residents and Araphel's minions when he held court here are likely to have reinforced the natural structure to make it as impregnable as possible."

"None of this is a surprise." Mercy cut off his doomsaying before he could sap any more of our life away. "We knew we'd be fighting our way into a fortress. We knew it was going to be hard. None of this is news, you know?"

Asher folded up on himself and sank down into something like a yoga pose with his tail coiled around him. "I, for one, had hoped that we would have only the single great wyrm to confront rather than all of his children also."

I shrugged, upside down and stretched over the gradually collapsing bush. "And I'd hoped that they'd come out and offer us their shards on a nice plush cushion. This is what we've got, and we'll deal with it."

"What I wouldn't give for but a single one of the butterflies that we squandered in conflict with Leofric. Just think of how many of them might be driven off by inclement weather."

"I'd rather have Seren back."

That seemed to cut his bitching off dead, and even Mercy shuffled uncomfortably to look away from me. I realized how maudlin I'd sounded a moment after the words came out. "I just mean, she'd have loved this. You know? I could have made a big catapult and launched her up to murder wyrms. It would have been her favorite thing ever."

Asher's misery train had been derailed. "I am sorry that you have been parted from her."

"It's okay." I blew out the breath I felt like I'd been holding all day. "This is only temporary, you know?"

Both Asher and Mercy looked at each other with no small degree of concern. Eventually, Mercy forced herself to pipe up, even if she did end up flinching at how blunt her words came out. "Pretty sure dying is the most permanent thing that can happen."

"I mean, yeah, normally. But we've already been to the land of the dead and back this week. We come back from the dead every day. It isn't a big deal. When all the Voidgod stuff is over, I'll just hop into Alvaren Valhalla or whatever and see if she'd rather come back and hang out. Or maybe we could do the long distance thing? Or like… timeshare?"

Both of them were staring at me with undisguised confusion at this point. Asher hissed, "Do you mean to say that you intend to resurrect her?"

I couldn't help but laugh at the looks on their faces when I sat back up. "Oh come on. It isn't that crazy."

Asher turned to Mercy with genuine worry on his face. "Would such a thing even be possible?"

I shrugged. "Only one way to find out."

"And if you can't?" Mercy looked shrewd—the kind of look that usually resulted in me losing at cards.

"I'll find somebody who can." I squished my way down across the berry bush to sit beside the two of them. "I figure that after we've saved the universe, the gods might owe me a favor."

Asher seemed to be stuck with asking the awkward blunt question this time around. "And if Seren chooses her eternal rest rather than a return to your—"

"Banging." Mercy chortled at Asher's horror at having that word put in his mouth.

I was grinning despite myself. "Wouldn't be the worst breakup I've ever had. Given a choice between me and Alvaren heaven, I'd probably choose me. But that's just because I'm not a big fan of harp music."

Asher seemed quietly delighted to be in on the joke instead of the butt of it. "Woodwind instruments are definitely preferable."

Mercy shook her head at us both, trying to hide a smile. "Nerds."

CHAPTER 26

It was deep into the night when we made our charge. Until now we had been relying on stealth to close the distance, but now that was no longer possible, we had turned to speed. The land beneath our feet had not been wiped clean by the power of the Void, but it had been painstakingly cleared by Inyoka servants to give their masters the best protections that could be mustered. Against any normal invaders, that would have served perfectly to slow progress and allow swooping wyrms all the time in the world to crispy fry the poor fools trying to get in. However, we were not your normal household or garden variety invaders.

With every step, I pulled on the stone beneath the earth, and a road was built. Strip by strip, step by step, I hauled it up. At first it was halting, setting off landslides and rockfalls, but soon I found my rhythm, and the three of us got up to a steady run, each of them trusting in me to put the ground beneath their feet before we fell. No pressure.

In the dark, you might have thought that we'd have made it a good distance before we were spotted. Sentries might have been stationed, but come on, who really expects someone to show up building a road in the middle of the night? As for the wyrms up in the sky, they had to have something better to do with themselves than stare down at the ground all the time, right?

Wrong and wrong.

Before we were even close enough to see the base of the tower, the wyrms were swooping down at us, and fires were bursting to life all up the rocky face of the spire. At first, I couldn't make sense of the sudden lines of glowing red appearing on the otherwise dead stone, but then the fireballs started raining down towards us. Organized artillery fire. Great.

Our headlong charge towards the spire turned into a zig-zag. Great eruptions of flame burst up from the ground where the balls rained down, with some going wide, but most landing right in the place that we would have been running to next. The swooping wyrms laid down lines of flame, crisscrossing that same patch of charred land and then swerved around when it became clear that we weren't sticking to the "charge directly into the jaws of death" plan. They missed us. Even twisting their serpentine necks around and spritzing fire every which way, they missed.

Back when I lived on Earth, I didn't run into fire all that much. I mean, I cooked sometimes, and I'd been camping once or twice when I was a kid, with all the requisite burning of marshmallows, but actual proximity to big old fires? Never really happened. So I wasn't aware that the flames are not the only hot bit. Any dumbass kid who's seen a picture book knows fire is hot, yes, I'm aware that it isn't a revelation, but in my head, the flames were the hot thing, not the whole area around them. I could feel my skin crackle on one side as we sprinted past the fireball explosion. That eyebrow was a lost cause too.

The next load of fireballs lit up on the spire, and I could really have done without it. There was always the option of throwing up walls to block them, but that would slow us down even more than zig-zagging. And there was no guarantee some of them wouldn't get through anyway. So back and forth we went.

Screaming and shrieking, the wyrms came after us. Looping and dive bombing at us even as we zigged and zagged and dodged the fireballs with ease. Well, not with ease. They were getting closer with each volley. Maybe their aim was getting better, maybe we were getting into the right range for this kind of bombardment, or maybe it was getting easier to see us now that the whole plain between us and the Spire was on fire.

The wyrms were definitely getting closer on each swoop too. Four of them had come down, each varying in size from what had apparently been a little one that had come for us at Talon's Keep and at the other end of the scaly scale, a gargantuan jumbo jet of flesh that I mentally dubbed Jumbo Dumbo. And while Jumbo Dumbo was dumping out enough fire with each pass to make my eyeballs sting even at this distance, it was the little ones that were setting the path behind us alight, so close behind my backside that I had to remake my backpack on the run to stop it from falling apart.

Probably a good thing we'd used up all our butterflies. If I'd waited to let them out now, I'd have been flicking some very flat pieces of charcoal into the air.

All the moisture in the air had been burned away, so every pant of breath came in aching from all the heat. Still, Mercy managed to croak out, "Kentucky Fried Eternals."

My lips were cracking as I laughed. Then before our course reversed yet again, I managed to point up at the dragons and rumble back, "Side order of Hot Wings."

When Mercy tried to fire off a shot at a swooping wyrm as we made our next turn, her bowstring snapped. I had it repaired an instant later, but every time she tried to pull it taut, it twanged uselessly apart again. I turned to Asher, and he wasn't there. His arms were raised, and blue lights were swirling all around him as he prepared his spell, but I wish the dumbass had told me he was casting so I could have adjusted our plans accordingly.

I stamped my foot down, and a sudden upshoot of stone exploded out of the road, scraping up under Asher's feet to launch him to me. I caught him in my arms and marveled that he was still managing to cast his spell all the same.

Then it was time to run like hell again. Weirdly, it was almost easier to keep my balance while running and making road while I had Asher to carry—he was a nice counterweight to all the stuff on my back. The winds that whipped out from him as he intoned ancient rituals and waggled his hands around also served as air conditioning, so it was a win on all counts.

The next wave of fireballs hit, not in a cluster where we were expected to be next, but in a row. I missed fighting disorganized monsters, they were so much easier to handle. The wall of flame roared up between us and the spire, penning us in so that the next pass of the wyrms would have no trouble toasting us. We had to punch through, but given the height of the wall of flames and the fact that I was losing my eyelashes by just looking at it, I didn't have high hopes we could just run on in and make it out the other side with enough of us left to heal.

Mercy skidded to a halt and looked helplessly at her useless bow, then we barreled into her, and suddenly, I was carrying both of them as we charged headlong into spicy burning death. Reaching as far as my Sphere of Influence would go, I tried to haul up stone, to make a tunnel through the fire that we could make it through. It didn't work. The heat was so intense that the rock crackled apart before I could make it solid. It was las though the air was shaking it into gravel before it could set. Were they still applying physics to a fantasy world? That wasn't fair. We were two steps from hell when Mercy hauled the Lucis out from behind my back and poured a swirl of power into it. The same gift that made her arrows explode with wind when they struck infused the great-sword that she could barely handle, and when she lost her grip on it, I dropped her to catch it.

The swipe of the Lucis, empowered with Mercy's tempest, still wouldn't have been enough to clear the firestorm ahead, but the echo of the blade was twice that size and forged from the same power. It tore out from my haphazard cut, parting the sea of flame for us to leap on through.

Behind us, before the flames closed back in, I could hear a frantic thumping sound as the wyrms that had been descending on us had to flap like crazy to avoid crashing into the same wall of fire we'd bypassed. Sucks to be them.

"Nice…" I panted to Mercy as she scrambled up the stairs I was making to get us back above the level of the plateaus again.

"Someone has to do"—she gasped in some of the cool night air from up ahead—"the thinking around here."

Jumbo Dumbo didn't have enough time to stop before they hit the wall. In a shrieking and flapping explosion that would have made any fireworks company extremely excited, the massive dragon exploded through the firewall and crashed to the ground, tucking in their wings to avoid the worst of the damage as it rolled first across the open ground, then right into my staircase, shattering every rock I'd hauled up with its weight.

One down.

The casters on the distant spire had stopped, obviously assuming that their work was done now that they'd thrown up an impenetrable defense. Sure, one of them was probably peering down to see if there were any gaps where we could have snuck through, but every moment that they didn't know was a moment that we could run straight.

Riding up on the rising heat, the other three wyrms soared back into view behind us. Beautifully up-lit in roaring red. I liked them better in red. It felt more like a dragon to me than the vaguely sickly things that had been chasing us so far. These pasty critters felt like they'd earned the name wyrm because they looked like pale things that burrowed beneath the earth never seeing the sun.

The sight of the dragons must have been signal enough to the spire guards that something had gone wrong, and in patches, the whole place lit up again. "Oh, come on."

There was still almost a mile for us to cross. Either the fireballs or the divebombing wyrms would have been enough to stop us, but combined, they were going to turn the whole distance into an unworkable nightmare of scorched earth and searing air. Even now I was struggling to keep the road ahead rising steady, and that was without the next barrage of flames. Mercy coughed out soot when she tried to speak, but a moment later, she was snarking away as usual, "Maybe we needed a better plan than running really fast."

Up ahead there was a plateau, so I had a moment's respite, during which I could think as well as running. "I didn't hear… you suggest anything."

The wyrms took another dive at us, the two smaller ones flying to either side of the bigger one in the middle, the tips of their wings almost touching as they glided down. Three lines of blazing fire chased along after us, too wide for us to dodge to the side, too fast for us to stay ahead of.

I threw Asher to Mercy and then strained with all my Artifice to haul up stone. There just wasn't enough. The whole plateau started to slip and slide as the stone beneath it was ripped out, collapsing in slow motion just as fast as the wall I was raising went up. Still, I pushed on, throwing more and more stone up into as thick a fortification as anyone had ever seen despite the mere moments I had to do it. Then the dragon-fire struck.

Better stone might have made the difference. If we'd been standing on a nice vein of granite or something maybe the wall would have held. But we had sandstone. The impact of the dragons' breath hit it and rocked it, and then the heat went to work.

Glowing cracks flowed out across my sandstone barrier, and molten rock started to eke through a blink later. Then before I even had a moment to come up with some new way to reinforce the wall, it was down, exploding apart into chunks as the air pockets I'd clumsily trapped in the sandstone blossomed out to join the flames.

Asher flung his hands forward. The same spell that he'd been casting this whole time finally went off, and it was a doozy. Lightning and fire had been his go-to elements so far, but knowing we were heading into the territory of giant fire-breathing lizards, it looked like he'd branched out. A wave of freezing air washed over us all as he unleashed an ice-storm right into the wyrms' faces.

Fighting fire with fire might not work, but fighting fire with ice magic is apparently pretty effective. Where the ice and flame met, there was a brief splash of water and then a concussion of steam knocked us all stumbling away. We were just little creatures compared to the wyrms, and they had two giant sails sticking out from the sides of their body. The gust of wind that knocked us down sent them flying.

Jumbo Dumbo was barely back on their feet when the cavalcade of wyrms came tumbling end over end into them. They should have just stayed down and saved themselves the pain.

What was left of Asher's ice storm dispersed into a wash of snow around us, and when he turned to meet my gaze through the swirling white, I could already see resignation in his expression. "Just say it."

I couldn't help myself. I really couldn't. "You're a lizard wizard in a blizzard!"

With a four-car pile-up of wyrms behind us, we turned to run again, just in time to come face to face with the fireball bonanza coming from the spire. Maybe we could take another holiday after this was done. I think we'd earned it.

Up until now, I think we'd been doing pretty well. We had drawn a bit more attention than we really wanted, but otherwise, we were making solid progress. This was the moment where that stopped being true. The moment that we started losing.

One minute Mercy was running, and the next she was gone. Not even a silhouette left behind. Completely consumed as the explosion where the fireball touched down. The concussion from that blast knocked me off my feet to crash into Asher, and it was only luck that had us flying down into the shallow muddy gully beside the plateau rather than into the path of another fireball.

We hit like a meteor, plunging down through the mud until we hit dry earth and stopped. The softness of the earth here had saved us, but then that same mud closed in over us, and suddenly, we were drowning. It poured into my mouth as I tried to cry out. Ever get mud up your nose? Not a good time. Smells like mud.

I lashed about, trying to get a grip on anything solid that would let me push my way back to the surface, and inadvertently, I shoved poor Asher even deeper into the goop. It took me a solid thirty seconds before I remembered I had Artifice and could just lift the floor up beneath us. A slab of mud came up with us, like a big nasty slice of lasagna, but it was easy enough to break free and breathe again once I had solid stone beneath me.

Asher definitely looked worse for wear when I hauled him out, puking out black soil like he'd been doing his best to eat his way out of trouble, but that was nothing compared to the state of the land around us. The earth was blackened, the grass was burnt away, and the sandstone was crumbling like ash everywhere it could still be seen. I had to drag Asher behind me like a lazy puppy as I mounted the slope up to the plane where I assumed that Mercy had been a minute ago. The last few seconds had been pretty hazy what with all the explosions, but I was pretty sure we only got thrown a short distance. If not I had no idea how we were going to find her again, short of us all dying.

"You okay, buddy?" I managed to pull Asher alongside me.

He was still spitting out mud as he went, sputtering out, "Unpleasant."

Being the gentleman I am, I turned away from him before I started to bellow, "Mercy?"

Another round of bombardment started thumping down around

us. Not up on the plateau where we were standing, but all around us as though we were the only island in a sea of fire. The explosions rocked me on my feet, but the light of the fire was just what I needed to pick out the blackened remains of Mercy where she lay moaning.

I skidded to my knees beside her, Restoration already glowing on my palms. "Shouldn't have caught it with your face, should you?"

The moment that her lungs were in good enough shape to draw breath, she started saying a lot of words that I can't repeat in polite company—words that only got louder and ruder when Asher cast Cauterize on her. The air was full of the delicious smell of roasted pork, and I felt a little bit queasy when I realized that it was also the smell of delicious, roasted Mercy.

The fireballs that had been pounding down all around us died down, and the next round had not flickered to life on the distant spire. For some reason, they weren't killing us right this moment. That was nice. In the aftermath of all the booms, my ears were ringing, but even so I could hear the steady thump of wyrm-wings behind us. Guess it was their turn.

Jumbo Dumbo was in the lead, with the other three skirting out to flank us. They'd learned their lesson from the last round of explosions, and they were keeping close to the ground, beating their wings once or twice to leap from one raised area to the next but never taking flight fully. When they saw us turn to face them, their wings snapped in tight against their sides, showing just how long and weird wyrm bodies were when they weren't being stretched out like a sugar-glider's arms. Looked like a snake that somebody had stuck some extra bits onto.

The downside of their cunning solution to the problem of their wings was that now I could reach them to chop bits off. I reached out a hand for Seren, ready to launch her up onto the snaking neck of Jumbo Dumbo, and then I realized that I was reaching for thin air. I staggered forward, then shrugged it off. We'd be together again, and when we were, she was going to be pissed that she'd missed this.

They had to stay grounded, but I didn't. With a surge of Potency, I leapt for Jumbo Dumbo, just where I was planning to land Seren. They snapped their jaws around to catch me like somebody was tossing salami slices, but that was exactly what I thought they were going to do. The Lucis was already swinging around to bite through obsidian teeth and fire blackened gums.

Deep down in the wyrm's throat there was a spark of flame churning towards me, but before the heat could even wash out, the force of my blow spun Jumbo's aim wide. It bit off the rush of flame before too much could be squandered. I swung around on the end of my sword, the force of that same blow spinning me through the air until the Lucis snapped free of the wyrm's tough hide, and I was twisting down to land on their back.

The twin of my Lucis leapt to my spare hand, and I slammed both down into Jumbo Dumbo's back, one in each muscular cluster where the wings took root. Even if it wanted to fly again, I wasn't going to let it. The scales shimmered like mother of pearl in the firelight, but the blood that came forth in great surging gouts from the holes I'd made looked black.

Jumbo's serpent head whipped around to snap at me, twisting the back under my feet and setting me sliding around with only the embedded blades to keep me steady. The first snap missed because of its own momentum flinging me out of the line of attack, but the next zeroed in on me perfectly.

Holding tightly onto the handles of both swords, I flung myself up into an acrobatic flip, my steel boots catching Jumbo under the chin and snapping their mouth shut. In usual circumstances, that would have hurt. When Jumbo was in the middle of trying to breath fire, it caused a whole other set of problems. Fire heading out, with nowhere to go, washes back the way it came.

Smoke poured out of Jumbo's nostrils as they pulled back, head snapping frantically from side to side like they could shake the burning away. When they tried to open their mouth to scream, the flesh inside had melted together, and so it came apart sticky and dribbling out. Those shiny obsidian teeth tumbled to the ground like cereal box prizes into the bowl. Dragons always sounded really impressive back when they were fictional creatures back on Earth, but meeting them face to face, I had to admit I was a little bit let down. Apparently, they weren't even fireproof.

Jumbo had clearly decided that they'd suffered enough. Instead of trying to bite me or roast me again, they flung their mass sideways, trying to crush me underneath by weight alone. If I'd been dumb enough to keep holding onto the swords in their back, it probably would have worked.

The force of that barrel-roll launched me off towards one of the smaller wyrms, and I rebounded off the blackened earth between them with a roar of victory, soaring towards the critter's side with my empty hands held high.

Both the Lucis and my other great-sword came when I called, leaping into my hands as I brought them down in a brutal cut that split clean through the wyrm's folded wing and bit into the flesh beneath.

These wyrms had bullied us all the way across the plain, so there was no way I was letting them get away unscathed. With these swings, I'd ensured two of them would never take flight again.

There was a distant roar as Mercy's wind arrows lashed out into the face of the other little wyrm, each thunderclap sending it staggering farther away from my squishier friends. Apparently, the last bow-repair had stuck, although I suspected Asher's blizzard bringing the temperature down to merely hot instead of skin-melting had done most of the work in that regard.

The medium wyrm—it seems kind of stupid to describe something as being medium-sized when it was bigger than a bus and twice as likely to crush you, but… oh well—leapt over the lashing tail of Jumbo Dumbo with one quick beat of its wings before she came plunging back down towards me, claws outstretched. Say what you like about wyrms, but they were at least smart enough not to keep falling for the same trick over and over.

I brought both blades about, fusing them into one titanic greatsword to parry the dragon's strike. It wasn't nearly as big as the nonsense I'd been waving around in the land of the dead, but it would have been more than any human being could heft around. Even so, I must have looked like a mouse with a matchstick to the wyrm, which made it all the funnier when her claws raked across the flat of the blade, her legs folded under the weight of the impact, and she went tail over teakettle, a giant lever flipping over with me as the fulcrum. Ascendant Potency might have been my favorite thing in the whole universe.

With a roar and a smash, the wyrm landed, her soft underbelly exposed to the stars. I didn't need a signed invitation on fancy stationary to know where I was meant to be. I split my swords and leapt up to start digging around in her guts.

She was saved by the combined idiocy of her two buddies. The little one-winged dragon came smashing into her, trying to charge me but swerving because of the new lopsided limb set-up, overcompensating in the other direction and ramming right into this poor wyrm's hip.

Meanwhile, Jumbo Dumbo, not content with completely melting the inside of their own head, was now rearing up to try for a third time to set me on fire.

I shouldn't have worried about it, Mercy was on the job. Her storm-arrow shot out, wreathed in wind and lightning, and struck the big dumb animal in the side of the head. The concussion knocked it aside so that the latest huff of flame went wide, and the electrical discharge made their eyes roll up into their head. Unfortunately, the same boom of wind knocked me off course. Combine that with the wyrm I was trying to jump onto suddenly being spun like it was on a DJ's turntable, and I was about to make a really unfortunate landing.

My swords swept through the empty air, and my face swung directly into the medium-bus wyrm's face. Did I accidentally kiss a dragon today? Yes, I did. Was she going to call me in the morning? Probably not. Instead, her jaws snapped open, and she lunged up, trying to swallow me whole. Not my worst first date ever.

"It's not you, it's me." Even as I was throwing myself back, I knew it was too late. I had no leverage to get clear, and the momentum of her lunge upwards was forcing me down into the bite. Good thing I still had swords in my hands. With a twist of my wrist, I shattered both the Lucis and the spare and set the shards flying forward to pepper the wyrm's face. Most of the shrapnel couldn't get through her scales, but the impact was enough to keep her pushed away from me until gravity could drag me off her face again.

I tumbled off her neck before landing face-first in the churned-up mud that was all that was left of the plateau we'd started out on. More mud in my mouth. Delicious and nutritious.

Once I'd plucked myself back out with a nasty sucking sound, I realized that things were progressing without me. Medium-bus was rolling towards me, trying to get the right way up again, and One-wing had sprung back with a lopsided flap to try and line up for another charge. I couldn't see Jumbo thanks to the flopping bus gal, but I could sure hear them, roaring and churning up the ground with their claws. I had no idea what was up with the fourth wyrm, but I had no doubt I'd be hearing from it soon. I called the iron back to my swords and tensed for action.

The moment Bus found her footing, I took a dive under her belly, scrambling forward through the mud as fast as my elbows could carry me. Up until now I'd been going toe to toe with these gargantuan monsters, and I didn't need to. I was tiny compared to them, and it was time I started using that tininess to my advantage. Above me, Bus twisted and flexed, her head whipping about to search for me. In the confusion, I thought for a moment that I'd gotten away with it, but then I heard One-wing howling, "Beneath you!"

Dragon voices were weird—like their mouths were the wrong shape for language, but they were forcing them to make the sounds anyway.

Anyway, the second Bus knew where I was, she hopped up into the air and slammed her body down against me. That pallid soft underbelly fell at me like an avalanche, and I almost felt guilty to twist around and stick the Lucis straight up. She stabbed herself, not just once, but three times. The first stab, I think she didn't notice, just that she wasn't getting the squishing sensation that she'd expected. The second one she definitely felt because she let out a yelp of pain that echoed down on me from every direction. That one made her jump away involuntarily, then gravity helped me out for a change, bringing Bus back down for one last wound, and her blood flowed down over me in waves. Every time she pulled away, her scales snapped shut over the jagged punctures, but when she pushed down, it was like I was in a late 90s kids' TV gameshow and buckets of slime were being dumped on me.

The Lucis was holding her far enough off the ground that I had room to breathe and move. I brought my spare sword up, scraping the tip up the length of the tentpole blade and wedging it into the same wound. Breaking through a wyrm's scales was hard work, but prying them apart was child's play. More blood, scalding hot to the touch, came pouring down on me. The more that she struggled to pull away, the more the blades jostled about inside her. I had no idea what to do next, but as it turned out, someone else was making the decision for me.

Bus tipped onto her side, and clinging to my swords, I was carried along for the ride. I'd assumed that Mercy or Asher hit her with something big and explosive, but as it turns out the only big explosive thing hitting her was Jumbo Dumbo, who was so intent on getting at me that they had no qualms about body-slamming one of their own buddies out of the way to do it.

I had to abandon my swords to leap clear of the incoming blast of fire, and if I'd felt bad about letting Bus stab herself, I really felt bad about using her as a shield against Dumbo's incinerating breath. The white of her underbelly blackened, and scales showered down around me like hail. She was wailing, a wretched sound that made my teeth vibrate.

The downside of jumping clear of one wyrm was that I was now face to face with Lopsided, and he had all his claws, teeth, tail, mass and flaming breath to bring to bear on me while I'd left my weapons behind to get toasted. Not great.

He came surging at me with his jaws wide open, and with no sword to parry that bite with, I was pretty much guaranteed a bad time. I tried to dive to the side, but fast as a striking cobra, his head whipped around, and he caught me by the leg, crunching through my armor like he was biting into a chocolate bar without taking off the wrapper.

I'd had enough practice by now to surge my Vitality before the crunch, but it still hurt like hell. "Ow!"

Worse yet, he didn't seem content to just chomp me and go. Instead, he kept that vice-like grasp on my leg as he whipped his neck back and forth, flinging me about and shaking me up. "Ow! Ow! Ow!"

I couldn't tell up from down or left from right by the time he got tired of waggling me about and finally threw me up into the air so he could swallow me.

With my brain all scrambled, I couldn't even sense my swords, let alone pull them to me in time. I guess I was about to start my next grand adventure—through a wyrm's digestive tract. I was going to constipate this lizard so badly. He was going to walk funny for months.

Mercy's arrow took me in the shoulder, and the tiny cyclone coiled around it exploded, launching me off course. Lopsided snapped after me, but he had no luck. The blast had launched me clear. I hit the ground rolling, and by the time I'd tumbled back to my feet, the arrow in my arm had snapped off. "Ow!"

The second it took Lopsided to close the distance was all I needed to get my swords back. They ripped out of poor Bus, who just wasn't even trying to get up again, and soared past the charging wyrm and into my waiting hands. The Lucis I caught, and the backup soared right by me and looped around as I made a vicious cut to meet his jaws head-on. He barely got his jaws open before I slammed the great-sword down on his face and shut him up again. The second sword shattered as I struck, the razor-thin fragments pummeling into the wound I'd opened across Lopsided's snout.

Maybe they weren't doing much damage, but apparently, they stung. Lopsided lurched back, trying to get his face out of my path. It was a good thing he did, because a moment later, flames tore through where his head had been just before.

Jumbo was not a happy camper. Maybe it was because the inside of their head got a bit melted, or maybe it was because they got smacked about a bit, I didn't know. All I knew was that despite it causing them obvious pain to vomit out more and more fire in my general direction, they were still going for it. They were standing atop what was now almost certainly the corpse of Bus, claws dug in for stability and fire pouring forth.

I stumbled back out of the first blast, then had to take off running as Jumbo's head snapped around to follow me. The furnace heat washed over me as I ran as fast as my little legs could carry me, but I knew it was never going to be enough.

Artifice came to my rescue again. As I tripped over a burnt-out hunk of grassroots and spilled face-first into the blackened soil, I hauled on the stone beneath me. It was probably the shoddiest wall I'd ever built—and I've left a trail of really crappy construction projects all across Amaranth—but it did the job. It stopped the flames from hitting me directly as Jumbo's head swung by.

Fun fact about wyrms: they can't actually see the thing they're breathing fire at. They can see to either side of it, or they can cross their eyes to see the fire, but their target is always going to be hidden. This gave me the moment I needed to jump back to my feet, leap the crumbling charcoal of my wall, and charge.

Jumbo saw me coming, but when your head is the size of an SUV, shaking it back in the opposite direction means overcoming some serious momentum. Their neck strained and cramped into odd angles as Jumbo tried to bring their head and the fire-fountain within to a halt.

Another dive, another close encounter with the cracked earth, another roll, and I came up underneath Jumbo's head. The Lucis whipped around and opened a line beneath the wyrm's jaw. It wasn't deep enough to bleed something that size out, but it was enough that the wild stream of fire already trying to escape had a new channel.

Heat was already radiating out from that overworked throat, but now the puckered edges of the slash I'd made blackened and flame burst free. On I ran underneath the bulk of the beast, so that neither eruption of flame could get me without scorching the wyrm to death too. Jumbo tried all the same, snaking their head under their own body, and scorching their already battered face with the flames escaping their neck-wound. Blinded and enraged, it didn't even cross Jumbo's mind that they were about to unleash all that flaming death into their own legs.

The flames washed over me, and it hurt like only a burn can—every part of my body facing in that direction crispened and blackened, flesh sloughed off, and muscles twisted into bitter little bands of ruined meat, all in the moment before I could stagger behind Jumbo's rear leg and gasp in a breath.

Restoration went to work putting me back together, and I frantically tried to pull the Lucis and the forgotten remains of my other sword together into a shield that might keep some part of me intact when the heat came again. I needn't have bothered. The fire burning out of Jumbo was choked out.

The elegant neck had been twisted into too awkward an angle to chase me beneath the wyrm's own bulk, and the flow had been pinched off.

My backpack, and all the clever little tricks that we'd stowed away inside, was gone, burnt away to nothing. The back half of my armor had been reduced to puddle of molten metal too. I had to strain Artifice to pull it back into shape over my raw, freshly regrown flesh. Couldn't have a heroic dragon battle with my ass hanging out.

One quick duck past the lashing tail and I finally caught sight of Mercy, Asher, and the wyrm they'd been scrapping with. It had seen better days. Maybe it wasn't dead yet, but I was willing to bet that it wished it was.

Where once beautiful pale scales shone across its length, there were now streaks of soot and blood almost as dark. At some point, it had been stupid enough to spread its wings, and now they hung limp and dislocated, dragging along the ground. That looked like the work of Mercy's concussive arrows to me. Just like the flames licking out from between the poor critters scales looked like Asher's work. Fire was everywhere around here, and the moment that Asher had realized that he could use it against the wyrms was probably the last moment of peace that the wyrms had known.

From the far side of Jumbo, where they were frantically trying to untangle their neck from beneath their collapsed body, there was an explosion. The roaring flames that had been backed up by the twisted off neck needed to escape, and if they had to do that by bursting out in every direction, apparently that was what they were going to do. The wyrm's head was still trapped under its body, but the two ends of the explosion-severed neck now flopped around, spraying fire to the sky.

I closed on Asher and Mercy's leftover wyrm with my sword raised to put it out of its misery, but Mercy had it covered. She was standing on the thing's head, aiming down with a storm gathered on her bowstring. With a thundercrack, she loosed. That final execution-style shot was all it took to put it down permanently.

I gave the two of them a smile, then turned back towards Lopsided. The last living wyrm. I could see it now beyond the heap of dead flesh, thrashing about as though it was still in agony. I guess the needles of metal jammed in the facial wound were even more irritating than I'd hoped.

As sore as they might have been, it still didn't explain why the wyrm was flapping frantically to take flight, even though one of her wings was completely out of commission. I couldn't understand what Lopsided was trying to do until the whole sky turned red.

The next volley of fireballs was coming down, and it was all coming straight for us.

Asher and Mercy looked from the sky to me with horror written on every line of their faces. All three of us were bruised and battered, and all three of us were in no way prepared for the doom that was falling down to burn us all to crisps. Just one of those fireballs had been enough to turn Mercy into beef jerky, I didn't want to see what a hundred of them could do. She was yelling, "Run!" at the same time as I was roaring, "Stay still!"

Asher glanced between the two of us and curled up neatly into the fetal position on the ground. Fair.

Now that Jumbo was dead, they were nothing more than a heap of materials, bone and scale that were built to withstand fire, even if the full temperature of the wyrm's lethal breath was more than they could cope with. I reached out with Artifice, grabbed all I could, and hauled it over us.

I had already been painted in wyrm blood. For the other two it was a new experience. Despite her instincts telling her to run, Mercy had listened to me. She'd dropped down on top of Asher like she was going to shield him with her own body. Cute, but hopefully, it wouldn't come to that. I flung myself on top of both of them, then piled wyrm above us all.

The fireballs hit while I was still stripping bone from meat, and it was all just a mass of corpse overhead. In an instant, the explosions blew my hasty shield to pieces, and the burning sky was revealed once more. The heat washed down over us before the fire, and I knew that I was out of ideas. Good thing smarter people were here with me.

Mercy had shoved me off as soon as I'd tried to shield her, and now she had her arms up creating fire of her own. It was the same solid wall of flame she'd deployed before time and time again, but this time the fire flowing through it wasn't coming from her—she was drawing it all in from above her. In less than a second, I could see her sweating and shaking, trying to control the barrier as more and more flame siphoned into it. Asher was casting beside and partially beneath her. The cooling winds of another ice spell were already forming between his hooked claws.

I was useless. There was nothing I could do to help. Nothing that would keep the inevitable from happening. I could already tell Mercy wasn't able to handle all the fire, and still more of it was hammering down into the barrier, licking through the line of her will and scorching us.

I reached for Artifice, but nothing was responding to me the way it should. The heat was too much. It made solid things waver, and anything I tried to move and shape crumbled before I could force it into any useful form. I didn't even dare to try hauling more wyrm-flesh to make another barricade because if I brushed Mercy's wall, I just knew that it would all come tumbling down.

Flames started to lick from Mercy's quaking fingertips, burning her. Still, she didn't falter. The fires spread, creeping down her hands to her wrists. Blackening her flesh and exposing her bones. Still, she would not stop. She strained with all that she was.

The Pillar of Creation within her governed the elemental powers that she flung around, and I knew that no matter how she'd reinforced it, there was no way that it wasn't cracking apart under this strain. Pushing my Artifice to use materials beyond my means had almost crippled me. I couldn't bear to think about what this was doing to her.

She was screaming now, not in pain but fury. Eyes narrowed. Voice cracking in the heat.

Time seemed to slow as her grasp on the wall above her started to slip. More and more fire spilled down in a rain around us, and the flames on her hands, the burning grass at her feet, and the fire bound up in the searing wall above us all sang to each other, roaring and crackling back and forth. All fires were one fire.

My throat burned as I gasped out, "Mercy, my sword! Put fire in my sword!"

Her attention wavered, and the wall of fire hanging above us shattered and rained down. As she fell to her knees, she caught her hand on the flat of the Lucis and pushed. Fire licked along the length of the blade, barely visible in the red hell we'd found ourselves. Fire. Just like the fire above us. Just like the fire all around us. All fire was one fire.

I looked up into the falling inferno, and I swung.

My sword swept uselessly through the air, trailing fire behind it. The echo of my sword was as wide as the sky itself. The fire that Mercy had been holding up became the edge, and the fires all around us whipped up to make its body. Everywhere that burned reached out to be a part of that echo.

The twin of my blade carved a bright red line across the sky and faded away.

CHAPTER 27

Probably worth mentioning that between the fight on the ground and the fireball bombardment, I had no idea that there were wyrms in the sky above us. So when two halves of a wyrm came tumbling down to land on either side of us, I was genuinely surprised. Three more wyrms that had been orbiting above us were luckier, only losing a tail or a wingtip. Two of them came spiraling down to crash atop the scorched remains of the four incinerated dragons around us, and another one frantically beat away, trailing blood all the way back towards the Spire.

I couldn't count all the wyrms above us, but where before they had been turning gentle circles waiting for their opportunity to pick us off, now they wove between each other, undulating and flapping for all that they were worth. My first assumption was that they were fighting to get to us first, but I was overestimating the courage of the wyrms. Having seen seven of their kin felled, they were no longer in a hurry to get to us. The swirl of wyrms blotting out the starlight were all competing to get above each other, to put the bodies of their brothers and sisters between us and themselves.

With them so high above us, we were wide open for bombardment, but it didn't come. Asher and Mercy had untangled themselves from each other's arms and were now pretending that there had been no cuddling going on. It was hard to say which of them looked more awkward. I asked, "What's going on? Have they run out of juice?"

Asher huffed ash off his snout, abandoning his spell to swirl away to nothing again, "Doubtful. More likely, following that last display, they believe that they are providing us with 'juice' of our own when they unleash their spells."

I hauled my aching body forward a step, scooping an arm under Mercy's shoulders to help her along as I waited for Restoration to ping back to life. "So the wyrms are scared off, and the fireballs have stopped. Are we in the clear?"

It was a sign of how exhausted she was that she willingly accepted my help without trying to beat me for touching her. Still, she was the one to snort, "Have we ever been that lucky?"

"Maybe we're due some good luck by now." I shouldn't have said that. I jinxed us.

Up in the swarm of wyrms above, there was a cacophonous roar, and as one, they turned and fled back towards the spire. At first, I thought that was another sign that everything was going our way, and as we lumbered forward, still dragging a road up to meet our stumbling steps, I could feel a little spark of hope. Maybe this didn't need to be a complete train-wreck like most of the times we went after a shard. It was just as I was having that dumbass thought that I realized the wyrms weren't going back to their roosts on the spire, they were landing in the open expanse of land between here and the spire, forming up into a battle line.

Even if they were too scared to fly and too scared to breath fire at us, that was still more reptilian tonnage than anyone could cope with. I tried to count them as we got closer, but my brain rejected what my eyes were telling it. There was no way there could be that many. "How many…"

Asher kept his eyes on his feet. "The answer is not going to make you happier."

Restoration came back to life, and I poured that soothing green energy through Mercy. In an instant, she went from dangling dead weight to struggling free of my arm around her. "That's a lot of lizard."

The way that Asher avoided looking at the wyrms made me

wonder how much of it was dread and how much was reverence. "We need not best them all. Defeating only a few should provide us with ample opportunity to pass through their defensive line and make it onto the rise. From there it should be a simple matter of finding an entrance too small for them to pursue and then proceed inside to face their… leader."

Mercy picked up the pace, forcing the rest of us, sore as we were, to keep up with her rejuvenated body. "That's still a lot of lizard."

The wyrms to the center of the line, directly between us and the spire, seemed to be the eldest. They were certainly the biggest, but maybe they didn't grow all their lives like goldfish do. Maybe the mass of massive wyrms in the middle were just the overeaters. The devoted fans of deep-fried dvergar. When we got close enough, maybe we'd see the cheesy nacho stains on their claws and settle the matter.

We were picking up steam again now that we didn't have to dodge diving dragons or swerve around fireballs. The other two were undeniably faster than me, but for every two of their steps, I only had to take one, thanks to my big Faun bod. The last mile between us and the spire seemed to be eaten up in no time at all.

Apparently, enough time had passed between murders that the world considered that last fight to be over.

Victory!
Celerity increased to 29
Vitality increased to 23
Piety increased to 13
Resonant Dominion: 5/10
Airstrike: Rank 10/10
Fire Resistance: Rank 4/10
2680 Experience Gained

Drawing closer, it became clear just how screwed we actually were. The wyrms were just the front line of Voidcrown Spire's defenses. A good distance behind them, great barricades had been constructed, woven out of living trees around uprooted rocks by the look of it. And behind those stood an army of Inyoka. The ones atop the barricades were in full lacquered armor, resting what looked like slings on sticks over their shoulders—hand-held catapults to rain rocks down on us. Charming. Around the base of each palisade there were a dozen ranks of spearmen, each and every one of them ready for war, all their pale scales glinting in the distant starlight. Whatever spellcasters they had were still sequestered up on the carved balconies that we could now see lining the outer face of the spire.

What had once been wild outcroppings, launched up and out by the explosive force of the Voidgod rising, had been smoothed and shaped by Inyoka artisans into platforms. Even the greenery that we'd seen clinging to the spire from a distance was resolved into tiered gardens around the periphery of those great open spaces. Even knowing they were there, it was practically impossible to make out the robed figures that had to be lurking up in those gardens.

Our crazy sprint slowed just a little as I sloped the road back down towards the ground level of the tower, now all the plateaus were behind us. "Okay. So not to crap on the plan, I'm sure 'smash through' will work fine on the wyrms, but what about the rest of them."

Asher had a frantic edge to his polite reply. "A moment to think, if you please."

"What… What can we even do?" Mercy mumbled, her sprint faltering at the sight of the whole army arrayed against us.

I strode on, spinning the Lucis in my hand. The other sword was still in fragments, embedded in the burnt-out skull of a dragon. I'd just have to do without. "We've fought armies before. This isn't any different."

Despite her obvious fear, Mercy was by my elbow. "We fought one army before, and we got whipped."

We got a bit whipped, but we turned it around. "I can Deathtouch any Inyoka that get close enough."

"They don't need to get close enough—they have staff-slings." She shook her head slowly from side to side, taking in all the massed bodies and wyrms arrayed against us. "They can beat us to death with rocks from way over there."

I shrugged that off too. "I can Artifice any rocks that get close enough."

She pointed up to the spire itself. "Then they've got wizards."

"I can…" I really didn't have a lot of solutions to those. The fire resonance thing had worked once when we were desperate, but I really didn't know how many more times I could pull it off. Or even how I pulled it off the first time. "Dodge the fireballs?"

"And the wyrms." Mercy couldn't stop staring at them. They had begun shuffling closer together in front of us as though the sheer mass of bodies would be enough to stop us. If we had a single braincell between us, it probably would be enough.

The handle of the Lucis was dry despite my sweating hands, the metal still warm enough to evaporate it all away. "I can fight them?"

"At the same time as doing all the rest?" The look she shot me was so dubious it had twisted her whole face, all of it contorted around that one raised eyebrow.

I couldn't help it. I laughed. "Man, we're screwed."

Asher piped up from behind us. "I cannot help but notice that despite this accurate assessment of the situation, you continue to move forward."

I glanced back at him. Every part of his body was rigid, his tail held straight, and his usual swaying completely arrested. "Don't suppose you've got a spell that is going to get us around all this?"

Asher didn't relax, and he didn't soften, but even so, his words brought a smile to my face. "I am devoted to the study of magic, not miracles."

Turning to give him a pep talk, I nearly fell right over when from the spire a roar ripped out: "Halt!"

Doing what the bad guys tell us to do is not generally the best strategy, but I think we were all so surprised that they were finally talking, that we actually did stop.

From the rear ranks of the wyrms, a behemoth of a lizard leap-frogged forward. It wasn't bigger than Jumbo-Dumbo, for which I was very grateful, but it did still manage to look like their buff big brother. Or maybe the bully that kicked sand in Jumbo's face on the beach and stole their girlfriend. It was a very burly wyrm, is what I'm trying to say.

Fire boiled out from its jaws, but not in the water-cannon way that the other wyrms had accomplished. More like it had been gargling with it and some had spilled out. While the other wyrms had all been opalescent, this one was completely devoid of color. Combined with its red rimmed eyes, I took it to be an albino. White even by the standards of the white dragons. "Which runt speaks for you?"

I glanced to star-struck looking Asher and sneering Mercy and stepped forward before they had the opportunity. The last thing we needed was Mercy's version of diplomacy.

"I'll talk to you." Both of my beloved companions let out a groan behind me. Nice little vote of confidence. Dicks. "Who am I talking to, and what are we talking about?"

The great white wyrm tucked in its wings and stalked out from their line to the halfway point between us, just like we were the leaders of two armies striding out to parley instead of one dude and his two buddies trying to break into their house. "You cower before Arataanax, prince among wyrms. Tell me why you have invaded our lands and slaughtered our kin."

I jerked a thumb over my shoulder towards the heap of scorched wyrm bones on the horizon. "Uh. They started it."

He stalked back and forth in front of me, tail swishing with each step, but his head always twisted around to keep both eyes locked on me. "They were defending themselves from invaders."

"Who said we were invaders?"

"You are here"—more flames spilled out between his teeth—"which makes you invaders."

"Couldn't we just be friends who're bad at calling ahead?" I tried to give him a smile. He did not appreciate my smile. He did not appreciate it at all.

His head snapped forward until he was only a foot from my face, and the heat of his breath made my eyelashes burn away with a sizzle. "You shall turn back now and make restitution for all the evil you have done. Then we might accept a single supplicant."

"Yeah, we really don't have time for that." I shrugged, refusing to step back an inch. "And besides, you set our Dvergar on fire. You don't get to take the moral high ground."

His head was the size of a horse, and he cocked it from side to side in confusion—like all of Asher's expressions done large. "What Dvergar? And what matter is it to Eternals if Dvergar were done injury? What is this nonsense you speak?"

I pointed a finger at his face, and he actually did pull back. "You sent a wyrm and a half-ton of Inyoka to Talon's Keep. You killed a load of our people and set the place on fire. You started this!"

You could almost hear the cogs turning in that massive brain of his, trying to parse the things I was saying into something that suited him. "You are servants of Talon?"

"No, we killed his ass and took his shard, and now we're here for the rest."

Wyrms of a certain age probably didn't run into things that they didn't understand very often. The fact that I was hitting him with all these facts he couldn't make sense of had him more off balance than the fact that three tiny humanoids had blasted their way through a half-dozen of his friends. He latched onto the one point in the whole conversation that he thought he could work with. "Such blatant lies. Eternals cannot die."

I shrugged, wishing I'd hauled along some severed heads to show off. That had worked pretty well last time I had to convince someone I could kill Eternals. "I've got a trail of bodies from here to the Bastion that say otherwise."

Arataanax stilled for a moment, and I genuinely wasn't sure what was going to happen next, whether he was going to pounce on me or fly away or start ranting and raving. As it turned out, it was none of the above. He narrowed his massive eyes and brought his head low enough to the ground that we were face to face. Then he hissed, "Who are you?"

Once again I did my best to flash him a winning smile. "I'm Maulkin, that's Mercy, and the Inyoka-looking guy trying not to bat his eyelashes at you is Asher."

He looked to each of us in turn as I made the introductions, and this time, it was Asher's turn to bury his face in his hands. "Who do you serve?"

"Uh… nobody. Or… the gods maybe?" Why did everyone always assume we were working for somebody else? I guess I just didn't look like a 'big ideas' kind of guy. "We're on a quest to collect the shards of the Rusted Blade? To kill the Voidgod when he comes back? You've probably heard of him at least."

Nictitating membranes flicked sideways over the wyrm's eyes, turning the blood-red stare milky for just a moment. He jumped to a new subject rather than dealing with the possibility that we were divine intervention. That was probably fair. If someone showed up on my doorstep saying they were on a mission from the gods, I would have slammed the door shut in their faces too. No matter how persuasive their pamphlets were. "Ayangarax could not have arrived at Talon's Keep more than three days hence. How could you have traveled such leagues, wingless, since then? Nothing you say makes sense."

"I get that a lot." I snorted. "Let's just say we have amazing godly powers that let us do all the stuff you don't understand and move on, yeah?"

He shuffled his massive body around until he was pointed right at me instead of coiled sideways, making himself a smaller target for when this all went sideways. Probably smart. "Regardless of whatever slight you feel our brood has committed, you have done far more harm than it could warrant."

"We aren't here for revenge." I let out a sigh. "We're here for the shards."

Once more the red eyes of the wyrm narrowed. "You mean to steal from our hoard?"

"I mean…" I opened and shut my mouth a couple of times, hoping something smart might pop out if I gave it enough time. "If you're willing to trade for them, I'd be happy to do that, but I'm guessing you guys aren't big on that sort of thing."

He growled, and damn, that was a good growl. It set my bones vibrating inside me. If I hadn't gone to the bathroom earlier on, then I definitely would have had to Artifice myself some new pants. When that rumbling roar resolved into words again, they were, "You shall trade your lives for another step forward."

"Ah, there it goes." I waved back to Asher and Mercy, who looked like they were getting ready to jump into the fight. The longer we were all chatting, the longer my healing powers had to cool down for the inevitable injuries we were about to suffer. More talking was good news. "Okay, so what is the chat really about if you just want to fight anyway?"

"A challenge," Arataanax growled with undisguised pleasure. "Your champion against ours. When I have defeated them, the remainder of you shall turn aside."

Okay, fighting one wyrm definitely sounded like a better idea than fighting all of the wyrms. If I could kill this one guy and that was the end of it, I'd be very happy. "And if I win?"

The prize I was hoping for was obviously a free pass into Voidcrown Spire, but I'd settle for just some of the enemy army going away and sticking their fingers in their ears until everything was over. It was pretty obvious to Arataanax that I was expecting an express pass too because he didn't even bother to offer up anything else. "My kin shall never abandon their duty to protect the roost. No matter the fate of one wyrm."

"So heads you win, tails I lose?" I rolled my shoulders and adjusted my grip on the Lucis. The fighting was going to start soon. I could feel it in my gut. Arataanax was too still after all his pacing and swaying, as tense as Asher had been just a minute ago when we were walking into the jaws of death. "Doesn't seem like a good deal."

Once more his eyes narrowed, but this time it wasn't anger, it was some savage delight. The prospect that I was going to back down. Wyrms were predators at heart. If you showed them weakness, they'd pounce. I didn't need my Bestiary skill to tell me that. I'd met enough bullies in my life. "You are too cowardly to face me?"

"Nah, I'll kick your ass. Just give me one second." I turned to shout back over my shoulder, "Hey, guys, he wants to do the duel thing. Stay out of it until I'm done beating his ass bloody, okay?"

Mercy put her face in her hands, but Asher nodded his assent. He understood that there was still a pay-off, even if this wyrm didn't actually offer me a prize for winning. First, we wouldn't have to deal with him when the actual battle kicked off, and second, all of his buddies would have just seen their biggest scariest fighter turned into mince before their eyes.

With that settled I turned back to smile at Arataanax. "So how do you want to do this?"

His head cocked to the side, but there was no doubt in his voice when he rumbled out, "To the death."

"Yeah, obviously to the death." I rolled my eyes. "But how do you want to make it fair? Do you want me to tie one hand behind my back or something?"

Who would have thought that would be the insult that broke the wyrm's patience?

He lunged forward, jaws spilling flame, and I surged my Potency to meet him head-on, catching him by the spear-blades of his blackened teeth and twisting him aside. He was insanely strong, not just throwing his weight around like the wyrms earlier, and I barely managed to get him turned away before a belch of blue-hot fire escaped, obviously meant to obliterate me but instead puffing harmlessly past me.

Asher and Mercy had to dive for cover, but even though they thought I was being a dumbass, they still did what I asked and left the fight to me. Bless them.

Normally that would have meant it was my turn, but before I could heft the Lucis to take a swing, Arataanax was already bludgeoning me with the side of his head, sending me rolling out of striking range.

The wyrm huffed another puff of blue fire after me that I had to dive around or risk being flame broiled. His words rumbled out with the heat: "Weak."

If he was trying to get me mad, he was barking up the wrong tree. I got bombarded with worse insults from Mercy just for existing in earshot of her. Still, it wouldn't hurt for him to think that I was some berserk idiot. I leapt for him, all the muscles in my legs bulging as

Surged Potency gave me the power to clear the distance between us in a single bound.

Arataanax followed my flight with his eyes, waiting until I was in mid-air and there was no way for me to change course to let out another burst of fire—just like I'd expected him to.

The metal of the Lucis exploded outwards into a blunt rectangular shield as broad as my body, superheating and becoming unworkable, but turning aside the brief burst of extreme heat without any of it touching me.

I smashed into his neck, my sword still only so much useless flattened metal, but the bulk of my body still made a decent enough club to whap him with.

The impact barely rocked the wyrm, but it got me inside of his reach, and that meant that the moment the Lucis cooled down enough to become a weapon again, he was dead meat. If only he'd just hang around for long enough for that to happen.

With a beat of his wings that knocked me skidding, Arataanax launched himself into the air. If he stayed up there, spitting fire down at me, this fight was probably done before it had even started. Regardless, my cunning plan to toss myself directly into him was thwarted before it had any chance to pay off.

At least I still had the shield-shaped Lucis ready for the inevitable wash of fire he unleashed down on me. This close to the Spire, the stone beneath us was hazy to my Artifice, some of it still intact, and some untouchable thanks to the Voidgod's power. Maybe I could have hauled up a shield of stone, maybe not, but I didn't fancy betting my life on it.

The flash of fire passed as fast as it had come, and I was just hauling the shield away to get a quick look at what Arataanax was doing next when he hit me. As it turns out, what he was doing next was dropping out of the sky like a ton of bricks to land directly on top of me.

There was no skill to the blow, no cunning or strength behind it, just the full weight of his front claws coming down on me like a pouncing cat—assuming that cats grew to the size of monster trucks. The Lucis-shield crumpled under his weight, the metal already softened by the heat, and stretched too thin so that it could cover me. My strength meant nothing if the metal I was pushing against collapsed.

I was borne down to the ground in a shriek of metal, the wind knocked out of me before I could make any witty comments. Pretty sure I had all my witty comments knocked out of me too, to be fair. Well, whether it worked or not, pulling up the rock with Artifice was the only thing I could come up with in that moment.

Just like it had back at the Bastion, the stone didn't come up smooth. The few patches I could touch leapt up in spikes while the rest lay useless and dormant. Where those spikes hit the underside of my shield, they stopped dead and started to crumble under the weight. Where they spurred up around it, they stopped dead the moment they touched wyrm-flesh. I couldn't drive them through a normal person, let alone scales like that. All I could do was haul up more and more of those spikes. Everything that I could pull up I did, until the earth beneath our feet felt dead and empty.

Even so, the raking claws of the wyrm above were ripping through that feeble protection, stripping clean through stone and iron. I guess I was screaming a bit, but I didn't really remember telling my mouth to make that noise. Maybe I could convince myself it was deliberate. I was trying to distract the giant murder-lizard. Yeah, that was it.

My surged Potency gave out, and holding up the Lucis-shield with my arms became pointless. Without my strength, the stone spikes I'd thrown up to support the barrier gave way, and the whole thing came crashing down towards me. The only good news was that the shredded shield was finally cool enough for Artifice to work again.

I cocooned myself as metal and stone swirled down around me in as solid a barrier as I could make. Arataanax's weight fell unhindered against it, and it began to collapse almost immediately. The original Lucis fell down to rest against my chest, so I was all set for being buried alive.

Arataanax bounced above me, flinging himself up in the air, then coming down, again and again. Bending the metal, shattering the stone, crushing it all down on top of me.

I took a grip on the handle of the tiny Lucis, and I thrust it up. The wyrm was off me for that moment, and both stone and iron shattered up with my thrust, all together, giving me a clear view of the spiky claws coming crashing down. It wasn't enough. The impact of them held off that crushing weight for a moment, but there wasn't enough power to break through the thick, armored scales.

Gasping between screams, I rolled to the side. The momentary delay gave me some distance, but then Arataanax was on me again, and his claw punched through my back, through my guts, and right out the other side to pin me to the dirt.

Pain is a funny thing. Sometimes you can stub your toe and feel like you're dying, and sometimes you can be covered in third degree burns and a dragon's claw can go right through you and it doesn't even feel that bad. Mostly I felt weight, then an awful sucking sensation as the claw started to withdraw as Arataanax bounced up again.

My body seemed to cling to the claw thrust through it, and I lifted up off the ground with the wyrm.

The Lucis dangled useless as a toothpick in my grasp as I was hauled up and then smashed down into the earth again like I was a ragdoll and the wyrm was an overenthusiastic puppy. The blow knocked me free, and pain and blood blossomed out from the new opening. I cried out, and the fragments of metal scattered all around me answered. The Lucis reformed, a great-sword once more, and I rolled and swung with more desperation than strength as the hooked and bloodied claws of my tormentor came down again.

It sheared through the claws. The full weight of the wyrm still struck me, and my bones made a noise not unlike somebody stamping on a bag of cereal, but the lethal, piercing claws were blunted. I lived through it.

Surging Vitality helped me to keep it together—and I mean physically keep my body together in one piece instead of just letting it splatter out into component parts—but it couldn't undo the damage. Only Restoration could do that.

That green light pulsed through my body, even as Arataanax bore his weight down on me, trying to turn me into Maulkin paste. I couldn't get a breath. I couldn't move. All I could do was wait.

Arataanax hadn't struck me as the patient type. Even though he could have just stayed put and won without moving another muscle, he decided to bounce again. I didn't try to get away. I was pretty sure that I was in no fit state to move anyway, and there would never be enough time. What there was time for, was using Artifice to twist the severed claws of the dragons into spears, their butts stuck in the churned soil, their points aimed right up at the descending hands. With a thrust of the Lucis, I drew the iron around its blade up into a jagged point too. If he wanted to keep smacking down on the same spot, I'd be stupid not to make it hurt.

His own claws were strong enough to make it through the scales, even if the point I'd put on the Lucis skittered off. What should have been a killing blow for me became an agonizing, cactus-slapping moment of stupidity for him.

The pain was enough to make him flap his wings to throw himself free of me again. Restoration had just finished melding my bones back together, even if the hole through my liver area was still oozing more blood than I even knew I had. I could move again. Which meant rolling to my feet, ignoring every ounce of sanity in my skull telling me to run away, and charging after the wyrm with a roar. "Get back here! I'm not done with you yet!"

Half of the dragon-claw spears were still standing, and the other half had broken off into him. When I thrust the Lucis forward as I charged, they leapt after me. Spear and sword were close enough for them to resonate, apparently. Even if they were made of different materials.

Without the wyrm's strength behind them, the spears couldn't make it through Arataanax's scaled hide, but the rattle of them against his armor seemed to rattle him. He beat his wings again and again. Gaining height, running from the fight. "Come back here, you big flappy coward!"

Oh that did the trick.

His wings snapped in against his sides, and he plummeted back towards me with fire already boiling up his throat. I didn't have the strength to leap up and meet him, but I did have the wherewithal to dart forward at the last moment before the fire was unleashed.

The tops of my horns burned off, and my hair caught fire. Everything above my eyebrows was screaming agony. It didn't matter, as I launched myself up to hit the underside of Arataanax's jaws with a swipe of the Lucis, slamming them shut on the flow of fire. He had more control than Jumbo Dumbo. He cut off the flames before he could irreparably damage himself, but now I was inside his reach, and I had a sword. I'd done a lot more with a lot less.

Rebounding off the sooty earth, I leapt not for the soft underside of his throat but for the closest leg, splintering my great-sword into two short ones, the Lucis in one hand and a hooked and barbed slab of iron in the other. They both served me well. I wasn't trying to hit hard enough to get through the scales, and I wasn't trying to rip him apart. I was climbing him. The hooks caught in the gaps between scales, the tip of the Lucis digging in to give me leverage to make the next leap up.

Arataanax spun around like a dog chasing his own tail, trying to catch me in the act of sneaking under him, so well protected by his dense scaly hide that he couldn't even feel me on it. I was up by his wings before he even knew it, and then I was between them, Artificing a spike onto the end of one boot that I kicked through the row of fins down the center of his back before splitting out to hold me in place. We were locked together now. Me on his back, him underfoot. The only way he was getting me off was if I was dead.

I smashed my swords back together into one and started hacking away. The wyrm's back got most of my loving attention, but I didn't neglect his wings either. He might not have noticed my climb up onto his back, but once I started chopping through scales to the meat beneath, he suddenly became aware of the monkey on his back.

The wyrm's great head twisted around and lashed at me like a striking snake, but now I was ready for him, and I'd taken his biggest advantage away. I met his bite head-on with a solid blow across the face. Again, his natural armor protected him from the worst of the damage, but he couldn't hurt me so long as I had my eyes on him and my sword in hand.

His tail lashed up behind me, but I knew without even looking that it couldn't reach. Simple mechanics. I was too far forward along the body. His head came around again, and I could see the exact moment that he realized he was screwed. The fire that would bake anyone fool enough to stand in one place while fighting a wyrm came boiling up his throat, flowing up from whatever weird apparatus they had down in their chests that let them do something as crazy as breathing fire. Then, as it reached the twist in his neck where he'd coiled it around to face me, the rush of heat stopped.

Again, he was smarter than the wyrms I'd fought before—he worked out that he was about to blow his own head off without needing me to tell him—and he whipped his head around to un-pinch the pipe of his throat and let the flames loose. He scorched over the top of his own wing, but it wasn't close enough to touch me.

He twisted around to come at me from the other side, and I laughed aloud as his fitful huffs of flame couldn't quite reach me again. He even tried craning his neck straight back and trying to burn me off him that way, but unfortunately, he had a spine, which meant that it was physically impossible. He let off a whole load of blue-hot flames straight up into the sky after that, in a scream of what I'm going to go ahead and call anguish.

Anguish because, while he was making all these little experiments, I was killing him. Blow by blow, his pallid scales were chipped away. Blow by blow, the flesh beneath started ripping out in great steaming hunks. By the time I was past flesh and into bone again, Arataanax had abandoned all attempts at snapping at me, breathing fire at me, or anything else.

His wings beat steadily as he lifted us off the ground, like he was waggling them at me, trying to distract me from my task. I won't deny that I was tempted to try and chop them off so his valiant last stand plan fell through, but I was so close to breaking through the wyrm's armored spine by then that I considered it a wasted effort.

Taking to the air, he hauled us up, high above the battlefield, spinning lopsided as he went, hoping fruitlessly that he might dislodge me. I could see all of the Inyoka arrayed against us and all of the wyrms craning their necks up to see me killing their prince. Even the Spire itself didn't look so massive from up here above the smoke. I could feel Arataanax's voice through my feet more than I could hear it over the whipping winds or the crunch of bone, steel, and gristle. "If I die. You die."

"Am I meant to be scared?" I laughed between swings. "I've already died three times this week. But you… you'll only die once."

CHAPTER 28

When he did die, it wasn't pretty or dramatic. One moment I was butchering away, and the next the wyrm's flesh went limp beneath me, and we began our long tumble from the sky.

Lifesense was a hell of a thing. I could feel Arataanax dying, inch by inch. I felt his three hearts stop beating, I felt the flow of blood stop, and I felt every part of him screaming out for nourishment, with nothing coming, and then my Deathsense took over, and I felt the growing darkness, spreading in from Arataanax extremities until it reached the point where the Lucis was still stuck. Last but not least, my Artifice began to sense the dead wyrm as a pile of raw materials.

I slung the Lucis into its place on my back, reached out my arms, and took hold. The bones of the wyrm were the kind of material that Artifice found the easiest to work, so it was the spindly bones in the wings that I seized control of, not tearing them free to use, but holding them steady. The plummet down to that scary crunchy landing became a spiral. Still more helicopter blades than helicopter cockpit, but at least we were slowing down.

Rigor Mortis wouldn't set in for a few minutes yet, so I had the time to make careful adjustments to the position of each bone in the wing until that deranged spinning became a smooth curve. Round and round we went, swooping lower and lower over the empty plain and the gathered army, back and forth, back and forth.

I had done the best I could with what I had, but I definitely did not stick the landing. Poor Arataanax hit the ground face-first, then that face, on the end of his flexy neck, got folded up under the body as it scraped its way along the sooty earth. Mercy and Asher had both come running to my aid, but when they saw that I was fine and I'd procured us a ride, their dread-struck expressions transformed into delight, and they scrambled up on top of the wyrm's back to join me. Free ride, all the way into the Voidcrown Spire, courtesy of Arataanax, whether he wanted to give it to us or not.

I grinned at the two of them, flipped off the army arrayed against us, and lifted my arms high.

The bones ripped clean out of Arataanax's wings.

Huh, that wasn't meant to happen. I flapped them back down again quick, hoping nobody had noticed, but Asher already had his face buried in his hands. "Okay, maybe I pulled a little too hard."

Mercy slugged me. "You think!?"

"I can fix this! I can…" I reached out with Artifice to try and repair the damage I'd done to the wings, but instead of repairing the torn skin and muscles, the whole membrane of the wing tore loose.

Asher groaned into his hands. "Gods preserve us."

"Look this isn't my fault. Most of the time when I Artifice stuff, I'm just throwing it around as hard as I can. I didn't know that I had to be delicate or whatever. Ah man come on, it is a wyrm. You'd think that they were built tougher than—"

Somewhere beneath us, whatever organ produced the fire that the wyrms spat quietly detonated, and blood and guts exploded out from beneath Arataanax's body in all directions. His head had still been under there somewhere, but I was pretty sure I could see a big dragon eyeball rolling around in circles under what was left of the left wing.

Mercy clambered down without any further prompting, and Asher followed a moment after, looking kind of sick. "I can still fix this!"

Mercy's laugh had a hysterical edge to it. "You really can't."

I was feeling a bit deflated after all that. I unhooked my boot from the carcass and hopped down to land beside them. "Well, maybe we can try again with another wyrm? There are plenty of them about."

"I am not certain that the wyrms will allow you free reign to desecrate the corpse of another of their kin." Asher pointed out.

"Eh, who cares what they think?" I joked.

Apparently, I should not have joked. Asher looked very serious when he said, "I am not certain that I would allow it."

Right, semi-religious devotion to the things that were trying to kill us. Slight conflict of interest there. Oh well.

The wyrms were bounding towards us now with their wings tucked in tight, looking very much like some extremely excited ferrets running towards a tasty hunk of bunny. Beyond them, the battle-lines of the Inyoka held steady. I closed my eyes against all of it. I'd harvested more experience than I knew what to do with in the last dragon fight, so I threw it as quickly as I could manage into every Slaughter divinity I could find. Slaughter Infusion and that real evil sounding Extinction were both mine now. I threw the remainder into Fire Resistance, on the basis that I was inevitably going to get huffed on by at least one of these wyrms, and that still left over a thousand experience to dump into three more ranks of Resonant Dominion. I still wasn't 100% clear on how it worked, but if it let me do things like grab all the fire being dumped on my head and throw it back in their faces, I knew I wanted more of it.

The more I amped it up, the more aware I became of everything in my Sphere of Influence. All the earth, all the fire still clinging to the wyrms remains, all the death, and the life, and the air and… It was almost overwhelming, this sudden awareness of how it all connected with the world beyond that sphere.

I opened my eyes to the charging enemy and rolled my shoulders. "Ready?"

Mercy drew back an arrow. "Let's kick some tail."

Asher's spell snapped up from between his hands and shot into the sky in a pillar of blue, punching through the smoke and up to the stars. It blossomed out from that point in fractal, jagged lines, spreading out across the sky, intersecting and shimmering. I had no idea what that was going to do, but it sure looked impressive.

The wyrms came on together, close enough to touch each other if they'd wanted. Like flocking birds, every motion was synchronized. I spun the Lucis in my hands ready to meet them, and then as an afterthought, I hauled the bones out of Arataanax to make myself a new host of blades. I stuck the new boney great-swords into the dirt behind us in a fence, and then it was time to party.

Mercy's storm arrows leapt out, thunderbolts striking at the wyrm's faces, blinding and stinging even if they couldn't make it through the scales. I poured Slaughter into the Lucis to make ready, and I felt the death all around me singing in harmony. The dead land beneath us, where the Voidgod once walked, and the dead wyrm scattered behind me. The shards and the Lucis sang the loudest. A tool made for killing, used to kill the greatest killer that ever lived. No wonder death spoke to it.

The wyrms were not making any mistakes or taking any chances. Before they even got close to us, they unleashed their fire. Six wyrms poured a line of fire out towards me, angling in from all sides. Asher and Mercy leapt to either side of the coming inferno, and I jumped it.

Potency Surge was back in action, and even if it wasn't, I was stronger now than I'd ever been. I soared over the fire of the blinded wyrms and came down blade-first into the back of the one nearest the middle. Deathtouch burst out through the wound, necrotizing tissue as it went. I felt the life go out of the wyrm before it even hit the ground, and then I was bounding off onto the next one.

Spread out through my whole Sphere of Influence, Deathtouch wouldn't even touch something as long-lived as a wyrm, but brought down to a single point, it did its evil job all too well. Just like Restoration, I wouldn't be able to use it twice in quick succession on any one enemy, but each new wyrm would taste it.

I poured Extinction into the next blow without thinking, and when I brought my sword down on the next wyrm's wing, the roar of pain that it let out echoed from all around me. I had no time to look and see what I'd done, I was already diving and rolling under the wounded wyrm to tumble out the other side.

It was only with the next wyrm in sight that I realized just how evil that power was. The same brutal slash marked the third wyrm's wing as the second. The exact same injury in the exact same place, echoing out through Extinction and their shared heritage.

Those shrieks of pain cut off the flow of fire. The heat that had been so fearsome just a moment before was gone now. The wyrms twisted, seeking out the source of their pain and finding nothing. All of them, that was, except the one who'd snapped her head around to see me standing there. She did not look happy.

I hacked at her leg and pulsed Deathtouch into the blade as it bit. If there was one thing I was learning about wyrms, it was that they were absolutely lethal, finely tuned murder machines that completely fell apart the moment you knocked any one part out of place. Like they were pulled too taut, and the moment anything got cut they completely unraveled.

Her leg came away before she could snap me up, and with it, her balance was gone. Necrosis rushed up from the severed wound, and I could already see festering pus squirting out from the wound before I dove beneath her to avoid the inevitable sideways collapse. She flopped, head whipping around at the last moment to protect her precious neck, but she was down, and I was standing in front of yet another pissed-off wyrm.

They might have been extremely loyal to their big daddy wyrm in the mountain, but they clearly didn't give a damn about each other. The next wyrm in line opened his jaws and belched flame right across me and my newly made tripod wyrm. Fire resistance did its work. The flames washed over me, hurting like hell but doing no damage that a good nine months in hospital wouldn't fix, but the poor wyrm behind me wasn't so lucky. Her body was engulfed in flames, scales blackening and flaking away.

Huffing and puffing out fire, the new wyrm couldn't see me charging through the flames, ducking under its chin or thrusting the Lucis up through its jaws and into its brain. Another Deathtouch, spreading out from so close to so vital an organ. There was no way this one was recovering.

The carefully coordinated line that had charged us was broken, and the wyrms milled about, under constant bombardment from Mercy, every one of them frantically searching for whatever enemy had struck them on their wing.

I broke free of the swirl of scales at a sprint and closed the distance with Mercy and Asher. "That worked!"

Mercy sighted past me to put the one wyrm with enough sense to come chasing after me in a very bad way. She didn't even bother to infuse her arrow with any elemental juju, she just shot the poor critter in the eye. "What the hell did you do?"

I turned to catch the half-blinded wyrm across the snout with the Lucis. Pulsing Deathtouch and melting its face off in a burst of slurry and gristly slop. "You know that super evil-sounding power that you didn't want me to take?"

"You…" Mercy took a steadying breath, then lined up her next shot. One of the wyrms had tried to take flight to get out of the mosh-pit we'd created, and she wasn't having that. The concussion of that thunder arrow flipped the whole wyrm upside down to crash onto its mates. "Of course you did!"

I thrust the Lucis at another likely looking wyrm, and one of my bone-blades shot out to skewer it through the chest. Fire came belching out of the hole. "Well, all these wyrms are related, right?"

"Looks that way." Mercy ducked a ball of fire spat in our direction, then snapped back up to fire a lightning arrow right down the throat of the wyrm who'd launched it at us.

A swing of my sword launched three more bone blades into the crowd. I didn't know if any of them killed anything, but they certainly made some very interesting noises. "So if I can kill one…"

She cut me off with an arrow passing so close to my face that I felt the wind tickling by my burns. "Just get on with it."

I dove forward, knocking her off her feet as a wyrm pounced by with claws outstretched. "Uh, I can't. It is on cooldown."

She shoved me off and shot an arrow right into the fleeing wyrm's… let's just say she did the opposite of what she did when she shot that other one in the mouth. Then she put a hand on my scorched face and shoved me out of the way. "Oh, come on!"

"It'll be back soon."

She kicked off my thigh to get some height and hammer another shot down into one wyrm that was feeling courageous enough to sneak around our flank. "We'll be wyrm-food soon!"

It was a funny thing, but I always assumed Asher was casting a spell whenever I wasn't looking at him. Sometimes, during our month at Talon's Keep, my head would snap around to see what he was doing, and he'd just be there sitting, reading. I'd jump when he joined in the conversation because I'd assumed his mouth was busy warbling magic words. Of course, now when I glanced his way, he really was casting, and whatever spell it was looked like it was going to be a big one. Both his hands were tracing out runes in the air, and he seemed to be singing three different songs, in four different languages. The fractal of blue light he'd spread across the sky was shining brighter in harmony with whatever he was working. Even the sunlight in his eyes seemed to be fracturing into little beams that were trying to join up with that pattern.

Of course, while he was doing all that wondrous magic, he wasn't paying attention to the giant wyrms coming to eat him. I snapped the Lucis around in a parry, and one of the remaining bone-blades leapt up to knock a snarling mouth off course. I reversed my grip and spun towards Asher, making that same twin to my blade loop around him and then slam right into the wyrm's nostril. Guess they didn't have any armor plating rammed up there, judging from the truly pitiful sounds the wyrm started making. Good to know.

I pulsed Deathtouch into my sword almost out of habit, and it echoed through the bone-blade. The wyrm's face collapsed in on itself as the rot set in. One moment it was whole and hearty, the next it was dying.

Asher couldn't even spare me the fearful look that I knew he wanted to give me. Not with his complex spell so close to completion. I stood guard over him for those last moments, fending off any wyrm that dared look his way as the chanting rose to a crescendo and then stopped so abruptly I almost felt dizzy.

The blue light leapt up, the fractals painted over the night sky ignited, and a blinding dome encased the battlefield for just a moment, then it all came raining down as icicles as long as lances plunged from the sky. I threw up my arms and hauled every scrap of bone, stone, and iron above us, and even through that, jagged spikes of ice still punched through.

Mercy slid under the turtle-shell on her back, face coated in a layer of frost. She was panting for air. It was too cold out there to breathe. Restoration was ready for her, and I turned it on myself afterwards to grow back my horns and face.

She managed to croak out, "Nice one, Asher."

"I am relieved that you offered us protection. I must admit that I was at somewhat of a loss as to how to—" Another icicle slammed through the roof of our makeshift cave, and Asher flung himself back to the ground with a whimper. Guess the storm wasn't quite over yet.

We gave it a few seconds more, then I pried the shield above us apart and dumped all the mounted spikes of ice off to the sides. The war was over. Everywhere I looked there was ice, but even where exploding wyrm corpses had melted it away, there was little more to look at. Deathsense told me more than my eyes could about the state of this place. Not a single wyrm had been left standing. There had been too many of them to count, and now they were gone. All of them. I turned to Asher with newfound respect. "Could you always do that?"

He looked pretty somber for the guy who had just won a whole war all by himself. "The libraries of Talon's Keep were bountiful, but it was only with our latest progression that I gained access to the Arcanum necessary to perform this particular spell."

Mercy clapped him on the back, and her approval was so alien to him that he flinched away, expecting another blow.

Victory!
Potency increased to 56
Piety increased to 14
Climbing: 3/10
Resonant Dominion: 9/10
740 Experience Gained

I turned to face the Spire and what was left of its defenders. Beyond our field of ice, the Inyoka still stood, stalwart and ready. I'm pretty sure if I just watched all the giant monsters on my side get wiped out by three tiny little people, I would not have been waiting there politely to meet the people as they came marching in.

I bought myself Celerity Surge with half the experience that fight had given me and dropped the rest into unlocking Twin Strike's close cousin, Twin Mantle. Projecting out armor or a shield was sure to come in handy if I ever found the time to practice it. And I wasn't leaving any experience to vanish when we inevitably got murdered by the rest of the army that was still waiting for us.

One last time, we set off towards the Spire. Exhaustion was setting in for the other two. Even if Asher hadn't been sprinting around like Mercy, killing wyrms was clearly taking some awful toll on his morale. As for Mercy, she'd been fighting off an army of monsters using nothing but a stick with some string attached and a bad attitude. Mercy's bad attitude could carry her through most things, but there was no denying that she was built for stealth and scouting more than for head-on slap fights.

I could hear Asher mumbling numbers as we came closer and closer to the enemy lines. If he was having a mathematical mental breakdown, at least he was being courteous enough to have it quietly. "We are in range of them now."

"To zap them?" I asked, hopefully.

Asher sighed. "For the launchings of their staff-slings to strike us."

Mercy looked across the expanse and made a little distressed noise. "I can't hit them from here."

I nudged her with my elbow. "I thought you could hit anything?"

"It isn't me, it's just… bows. Shooting that far… well, there are limits to the bend… I can't account for wind, I can't… It just doesn't work."

Asher's tail lashed as he stepped up beside us, inside firing range. "My thanks for your elaborate technical explanation."

"Go suck an egg." Mercy drew an arrow back all the same. Even if she missed, she'd probably hit somebody. There were enough of them.

I'd managed to retrieve the great-sword Lucis from the mangled mess of a shield I'd thrown together before, and a couple of workable bone-blades hovered behind my shoulders too. When the rocks started flying, I'd be ready to catch what I could and deflect what I couldn't.

If Asher and Mercy could deal with the fireballs, that just left us with all the foot-soldiers to work out.

We trudged forward into the shadow of the Spire, waiting for the fireballs and rocks and all the rest to come tumbling down on us, but they never came. Step by nervous step, we got closer and closer to the gaping cave at the base of the spire, and not one of the Inyoka fired down on us. That was… weird.

On and on we walked, and before our eyes, the illusion began to fall apart. Not a literal magical illusion, although that wouldn't have surprised me, but one of the old dirty tricks that people used to play when they needed to convince an enemy army that they had an actual enemy to fight. There were Inyoka manning the barricades, but most of the soldiers arrayed against us were stuffed dummies. Maybe ten dummies to every living Inyoka. Making matters even more confusing, most of the Inyoka that we did see weren't white. Once we were close enough, it became apparent that someone had just gone at them hard with a powder brush. The majority that we saw were in varied shades of brown and green, caked with white paint to cover up that fact. Some of them might have been genuine albinos, but you could count them on one hand.

Asher was the first one to get it together enough to shout out. "Who's in charge here?"

"Now that the wyrms have expired, I believe that duty falls upon me." That voice was all too familiar. It was the first voice that I'd heard on arrival in Amaranth, other than the gods bullying me out of my grave. The White Prophet stepped out from behind the palisades to greet us with a bow.

I had to slap Mercy's bow aside so that the shot went wide and hammered into the fencepost beside the Prophet's face instead of into his face. He didn't flinch. He never flinched. Why would he when he knew everything that was going to happen before it happened. "I must admit, I did not expect your arrival to be so… imminent. I had presumed that it would take you longer to gather power to yourself or that you would seek the other shards before confronting the Great Wyrm. If I had known you would be here so soon, I would have arranged for more flights to be away, to ease your passage."

"Nope, got all the shards already. Here to steal the last ones." I cut him off. "Why are you here?"

What I'd taken before as a blank expression in the face of everything had changed now that I'd spent so long with Asher. There was surprise written in every line of how the Prophet held himself. I was guessing it was only that surprise that made him so abruptly honest. "It is my pleasure to serve as Tsanganaax's castellan."

This time, when Mercy took a shot at him, I let her. He leaned out of the way, already knowing it was coming before she even drew an arrow. She was ranting as she reached for the next one. "I knew we couldn't trust him. I said, we can't trust him. But did anyone listen to Mercy? Oh no, she's just being crazy. She's just paranoid saying that the guy who dumped us in a dungeon full of monsters all trying to kill us was not our bestest friend."

Asher sounded heartbroken. "The prophecy was a fabrication?"

The Prophet bowed deeply to Asher, coincidentally avoiding Mercy's next arrow by inches. "It is with great regret that I must admit that while elements of it were entirely correct, such as the arrival of five Eternals upon the palm of the Hinterlands, certain parts were exaggerated to force you into action."

"So this whole time… what?" Long-unused machinery in my brain was swinging back into action, churning through everything that had been said and done, trying to find the reason. "You wanted us to gather up the rest of the shards for your master? He couldn't get the shards from Talon, or the Alvaren, or the Faun, or even Leofric by himself, so you used us?"

"With even greater regret, I must tell you that this is not the case." The White Prophet seemed to slump a little. "Perhaps it would be easier to show you."

He turned to sashay up to the cavernous entrance to the Spire, and our choices seemed to be limited to walking into what might have been a trap or staying out here with the fake army and the very real casters up on top of the Spire gardens. We didn't really need to take a vote to make that decision.

I was still trying to get my head around what we'd just heard. If the prophecy wasn't real, then why had we been collecting all the shards? Why had the universe dumped them in our path? Why was Araphel so intent on stopping us if it didn't mean anything? Had the Prophet accidentally told us some truth that even he didn't know?

Mercy had gotten her little "told you so" out of the way already, but it seemed that her curiosity wasn't going to be satisfied with a few words from the dude that sent us all off on this wild quest to start with. "So what's with the fake white-boy army out there?"

"Breeding for albinism, or simply paler shades, in wyrms is easy with their diversity, but there are too few albino Inyoka to produce a stable line. Too many of us have been destroyed for our mutation. I am forced to supplement our numbers with unaligned Inyoka."

Mercy snorted in derision. "So what, you go out, enslave them, paint them white, and pass them off as the home team?"

The Prophet didn't seem to take it personally. "They come to us. The rejected, the loathed, and the lost. We are a place that they can call home. A place where all may serve without the demands of perfection."

Asher let out a hiss. "It is… wrong."

The Prophet's step never faltered. "It is an imperfect solution to an impossible problem. The master must be served."

We passed by tunnel mouths carved into the solid stone with a smoothness that only Artifice, or its Void counterpart, could achieve.

We were walking into the warren that Araphel had carved for himself. His home. I'd hoped we'd get some glimpse in the way that he'd made this place that might give us insight into what the hell was going on in his head, but it was pointless. Everything was bare-bones and utilitarian. Nothing received more than the bare minimum of attention required to make it functional. At least all the walking gave me ample time to pulse Restoration through myself again. Burns closed and scarred over, and hair sprouted back out. I gave Mercy and Asher a heal too while we had the chance.

Mercy popped back into the conversation with what she clearly considered another 'gotcha' question. "So if you wanted us here, how come the wyrms—"

"An Inyoka, however well respected or regarded, cannot command a wyrm." He slowed a little in his relentless pace as if he was pondering his next words. "The masters are prideful. They would not have understood why you are here."

I piped up, "We also don't understand why we're here."

"You will, soon enough."

We were led off down one of the side tunnels, coiling deeper and deeper down into the earth. For some reason, I'd expected us to head up, what with the giant spike of stone shooting up into the sky, but down into the earth probably made more sense. That was where Araphel had come from after all—down in the dark places of the world where the Dvergar delved too deep.

It was weird. I'd expected this place to be more intimidating and evil-looking, but mostly it was just boring—like a Dvergar mine without any of the handcrafted charm. The boringness probably had something to do with the fact that my senses were all blunted by the Voidgod's touch. None of the stone around me felt like anything. All I could sense was static. It was like my leg had fallen asleep.

Mercy still wouldn't let up. "You know that if this is a trap, we're going to murder you first, right?"

"As is your right," the Prophet intoned softly. "But it is my hope that the truth will gain me your sympathies, and you might forgive my minor deceptions."

"I'm not big on forgiving." Mercy plucked her bowstring like a guitar. It thrummed.

Still, the Prophet could not be flustered. "If my life is the price that must be paid, then I pay it gladly."

We were so far down into the earth now that my ears popped. As deep as we'd ever been beneath the Dvergar city, but we'd gotten here so much faster. The tunnels that we crisscrossed and followed were so wide you couldn't see the sides in some places, and they were so tight I had to duck in others.

Finally, just when I thought Mercy was actually going to just shoot the Prophet out of pure boredom, we came to a halt by a tunnel opening, and he swept out his arm, whispering, "Behold, Tsangaanax."

CHAPTER 29

We beheld him. We beheld the heck out of him. Although it took a little while to completely grasp what we were looking at. He was white, which didn't fit in with what Asher had told us about big black dragons, and he was so big that it took my eyes some time to adjust to the idea that all of the thing that I was looking at was one thing.

The serpentine coils were rucked up on top of each other, so you couldn't really tell which end of the wyrm was which, and there was just so much of him that even if you could work out which bit was the head, he was liable to be doubled up on top of it with his butt or something anyway. There must have been wings in there somewhere, trapped under the body, limbs too, but I couldn't make them out. I could only see so far. For all I knew, this was just the midsection. The outer edges of the cave were beyond the limits of my vision. We'd seen wyrms before that I'd considered to be too big to be real, but this was insane. Tsangaanax wasn't a creature any more, he was a landmark, a country, a force of nature. And he was sick.

My Lifesense struggled to make sense of what my eyes were telling me was a living creature, but my Deathsense wasn't having the same problem. Focusing in on just that, I could feel the veins of dark energy shifting and drifting through the great wyrm's body. Outlining him. Burrowing through his flesh and his spirit, rooted to the two shards that were embedded in the place of scales.

I spoke as softly as the Prophet had. There was no way of knowing what might happen if we disturbed this creature's slumber. "He's poisoned."

The Prophet nodded with a little tremor, barely holding his composure. "The shards."

"All this time that he's had them, they've been eating away at him…"

The Prophet stepped back behind us, speaking as softly as he could. I couldn't turn to watch him. I couldn't take my eyes of the gentle shifting of the mass of flesh before us. Wind whistled through the tunnels, drawn and expelled by his breathing. "He believed that their power could be tapped, just as your Talon did. When the corruption took hold, he believed it to be a sign of progress. When the color and the fire were drained from him, he thought it was an even exchange for all he would gain."

"But he isn't divine." Mercy sounded almost respectful. That spooked me as much as anything else. "He couldn't use them."

The Prophet's voice broke, the pain cracking through. "They used him. Driving him to dark deeds. They hurt him. More and more with each passing day. The agony, the hunger for them, it has driven him to madness and beyond."

"You didn't trick us into coming here to bring more shards." Asher had been reverential of the wyrms we met before, but now he was awestruck. "Your desire is for us to remove his."

"Please," the Prophet whimpered. "I beg you."

Death had burrowed through the great wyrm where the flows of life should have been. Pumping through his veins. Coiling through his brain. The shards were the root cause, there was no arguing with that, but that didn't mean that pulling them out was going to make a difference. "They might be the only things still keeping him alive. You get that, right?"

His voice was so soft I almost didn't hear it when he answered, "Please."

I drew the Lucis and sighed. "We've come this far."

Asher shook his head at me hopelessly. Even Mercy looked overwhelmed by the task in front of us. "You two hold him down. I'll… I'll cut them out."

"Maulkin, this is madness." Asher had that same desperate edge as the Prophet's. "No spell I can weave will so much as crack Tsangaanax's scales. This is a task beyond us. Beyond any of us. The gods themselves would turn away."

"The gods did turn away. They left him here like this for… forever. They left the poison of Araphel to infect this whole world, when they could have put an end to it. We've got to do better. We've got to save Amaranth. We've got to save the universe."

Mercy caught my arm before I could step forward. "Dude, there is no way we can win this."

"Then we'll lose." I growled, louder than I meant to. "We'll lose, and we'll come back and lose, again and again, as many times as it takes until we wear Tsangaanax down and get the shards out of him. We can't leave him like this. And even if you could stomach leaving him suffering like this forever, Araphel is coming back, whether the Prophet or anyone else believes it or not. He is coming. I've seen him. We need a way to fight back."

For the first time since we'd met him, the Prophet looked surprised. "You have seen him?"

I tugged free of Mercy, and I jumped.

A cloud of dust puffed up from the great wyrm's scales when I landed on him. The white coloration that had resulted in his new albino army was decay. The outer layer of the natural armor he'd been born with was crumbling away to nothing as he was devoured from inside. Maybe he felt me landing on him, maybe he didn't, but either way, he didn't stir.

Back in the tunnel mouth, Mercy and Asher were frantically waving their arms and shaking their heads, neither one willing to risk shouting and awakening the beast below. That made things easier. I cupped a hand behind my ear like I couldn't hear them, then I shrugged and moved on.

I sincerely hoped that Asher had some big magical sedative ready to shove into Tsangaanax because the moment he started moving, I was going to be in some serious trouble down here. The two shards felt like they were a good distance down below in the coils of wyrm, wrapped protectively as close to his heart as he could keep them, which meant I was going to have to squeeze down through the gaps to get to them, and the moment the big white wyrm started moving, I was liable to get crushed by his tectonic shifting.

Fighting down my own nerves, I hiked over the breathing landscape, trying to tread lightly and not slip and slide as the length of wyrm I was following sloped down to either side. I'd get as close as I could up here before working out how to get down there. Since the wyrm had politely decided to stay asleep, I shoved the Lucis back into my baldric so I had my hands free for balancing.

At a glance, I could see Asher and Mercy having a frantic but stilted argument, both trying not to scream at the other, while the Prophet looked down on me with his strange pale eyes. I think that he would have been crying in gratitude if he had the tear ducts for it. All of his byzantine scheming had finally come to fruition. We were here, and we hadn't even told him to go and lay an egg when he switched up from Machiavellian manipulation to outright begging for help.

The stupid thing was, if he'd told us the truth up front, I would have volunteered to help anyway. All the lies and the tricks, they'd all been for nothing. If he'd just rocked up to me, fresh out of the ground and said, "Hey, there is a sick dragon, want to come help?" I would have been all over that.

I was above the shards now. It felt like they were embedded on two separate coils of the great body, but Tsangaanax had decided to twist himself around so that they were together, as deep into the heap of body as he could make them. His most treasured possessions, which I was about to pry off him and run away with. Oh yeah, this was going to go down well.

Taking one glance back and a deep breath, I slipped down into the gap. Almost immediately, the press of scales all around me stopped my descent. I had to wriggle around until I was head down, then pry the sides of the wyrm apart before I could make any progress. With every breath in, the scales crushed in around me, covering me in powdered wyrm, but with each exhalation, I was able to slip a little deeper into the crushing darkness. I could only see at all because I was an Eternal, and what I could see wasn't much. Scales made up the walls of this tunnel, and a patch of darkness in the middle was my only way forwards. My shards were humming in recognition of the ones below, all parts of the whole desperate to be together again. It was better than a compass, better than any of my other senses. I followed the song of the shards down and down.

The closer I got, the tighter the wyrms coils were wrapped, and the harder it was to push my way through. Even when Tsangaanax breathed out, these walls were so tight that I was only making it a few inches through before the next crushing came. Asher and Mercy must have been crapping themselves after watching me dive into the wyrm soup, but if they were coming in after me, I couldn't sense them.

There was a pocket of air up ahead—I knew because Lifesense and Deathsense showed me nothing, and because wind was gusting up out of it to hit me now that I was getting closer to it, squeezed up and out by the same motions that kept making my armor creak and crunch all about me. I dared to hope that it was a pocket of air that also contained at least one of the shards, but surrounded on all sides by the coiling veins of Death energy, I was finding it harder to see the forest for the trees.

I couldn't remember what being born felt like, but I had to assume it was something like being slowly crushed out from between a wyrm's coils head-first. My horns kept getting hooked on scales as I was squirting out, and if they hadn't been chalky and crumbling already, I likely would have stayed stuck there. I did not envy Faun mothers.

Wriggling and kicking, I managed to get my arms free, then used them to push the rest of me out. There wasn't too far to fall head-first. Which was lucky. Imagine if I'd made it all that way, then knocked myself out. The membrane of a wing was beneath my feet when I rose up to standing, and in the moment it took my eyes to adjust, I realized that no, the air in this air-pocket wasn't being gusted out by the undulation of the sleeping wyrm's body. Tsangaanax's head was here.

There was a thick white membrane stretched across an eyeball that was as big as me, and the majority of head and snout were buried under coils of body, but that was definitely his head, and his teeth were definitely the same size as me. I swallowed hard. Okay. Nothing to worry about. Just a gigantic terrifying wyrm that could kill me by turning his head slightly in his sleep. Stay cool, Maulkin, stay cool.

There were a lot of missing scales down here, where the rot had set in the worst. Even through the chalky powder of that shedding, I could smell the decay. I could even see hints of the darkness drifting about under the surface—dull grey patches shifting under the sickly white scales.

The shard was right beside Tsangaanax's eye, of course, wedged into place where a scale had gone missing before. It was tiny when you compared it to this massive creature—so overwhelmingly small it was impossible to imagine that it had done so much harm.

Getting close to the eye, the face, and especially the teeth seemed like a fundamentally stupid idea. So instead, I reached out with Artifice, fully intending on just yanking the shard out like you'd pull a rotten tooth and then running like hell. I yanked, but it didn't budge. The flesh around it had healed over the edges, and the roots of darkness burrowing off into the flesh were holding on tight. It was less like trying to pull a tooth and more like trying to pull a whole nervous system out through a scratch.

The membrane stretched over Tsangaanax eye shifted aside like a curtain being drawn back, and the black void of his gaze settled upon me. Oh crap.

Scrabbling for the Lucis, even though it would be like an ant waving a twig at me, I forced myself forward. Already the coils around me were shifting, and the colossal head was lifting from where it had rested. Dust rained down all about me, covering me and hiding me from the wyrm's pinning stare. I jammed the tip of the blade in beside the shard and tried to pry it free. Even with all my strength and an unbreakable lever, it still wouldn't budge.

The next exhalation from the great wyrm's jaws was hot and foul. Not the fire of a wyrm's breath but the stuffy rancid heat you found at the heart of a compost heap. The heat of decay. My Deathsense recognized it for what it was and strained against it. The same Deathtouch I'd been using to wipe out the wyrm's kin swept over me. If I'd been mortal, I would have been dead. Hell, even if I hadn't been mortal, I might have taken one hell of a hit and ended up looking as wrinkly as a shar-pei. Only the power of the Void protected me against it. Wasn't sure how to feel about that.

I'd expected Tsangaanax's voice to be a bass roar so loud it knocked me to the ground. Like my own voice, the voice of the Voidgod, the voice of Death himself. Instead, it was a mealy whisper. "Thief."

I held up my hands and kind of wished I didn't have a big sword in one of them. It made it sound less than convincing when I said, "I'm just trying to help."

"Thief." He wheezed a little louder, and puffs of his own disintegrating scales blew up to batter me.

"Whoa. Hey. No." I tried to back away, but there was nowhere to go. He was all around me. "If I can get the shard out, then maybe we can heal you…"

The whole of his face had been uncovered. It looked like he was untroubled by his own crushing weight. Probably should have expected that really. He tried to force out more of that Death-breath, but it washed over me without any effect.

He hissed, "Thief," again as if it was the gravest insult that he could think of. Maybe it was. The corruption had dug right into his brain. Maybe he didn't have much of the talking parts left.

"Dude, please just let me cut the shards out, then you'll maybe get back to normal. Or maybe die." I shouldn't have said that last bit. He did not like that last bit.

Tsangaanax surged forward, his massive jaws snapping at me, and all the tricks that had worked on his kids were not going to work here. Not with my back to a wall of wyrm and the sword in my hands about the size of a toothpick.

I did my best, of course I did my best. I surged my Potency, swept the Lucis around, and hammered it right into that charging wyrm's face, but being the strongest gnat in the world isn't going to help you when you're facing down the flyswat. The Lucis carved through his flaking scales, bit into the flesh beneath, and then I was steamrollered by the sheer weight of wyrm coming at me.

Despite being so massive they could have gone right through the whole height of me, every one of the teeth snapping shut on me was razor-sharp and serrated. The corruption that had wrecked every other part of his body had not provided any handy tooth-decay. Because of course not.

There was nowhere else for me to go, so I leapt forward into the wyrm's gaping mouth, and the jaws snapped shut behind me.

I don't know if you've ever been swallowed alive, but it is a lot wetter than you might imagine. I didn't have to worry about Tsangaanax breathing fire up at me since he'd screwed that up for himself, but there was still a hell of a lot of drool to go around. No tongue though, which I thought was a bit weird. All those teeth and no tongue. How did wyrms get stuff unstuck from between their teeth? Fire, right. Yeah. I'm an idiot. We've mentioned that before.

The floor beneath my feet was ridged with bone under the hard leather of blackened gums, same with the roof above. I still had my sword, and hypothetically I might be able to jab around enough to get spat out, but that was working on the hypothetical that I was going to get to stay put for any length of time.

Bone-ridge roof and floor became bone-ridge walls as the wyrm's head jerked up, and then shot through the coils of his own body to the surface. I tried to grab a tooth to keep myself from falling straight down his throat, but I only succeeded in cutting the tips off my fingers, then fell straight down his throat.

Let's just say the situation didn't get less juicy farther in. It also didn't suddenly start smelling like roses as I tumbled down the length of that serpentine neck to the parts of the wyrm that were rotting from the inside out.

I bounced off the sides a few times as Tsangaanax twisted and turned through the maze of his own flesh, and that helped slow me down, but that was all that helped slow me down. Luck more than anything else jammed the Lucis into one side of the big flexing sphincter at the bottom of the wyrm's throat, but I was dangling down into it, the meat pulsing in around me, slapping me around the midsection while I clung on for dear life. This was as far as I ever wanted to go through a digestive tract. Actually no, it was way farther than I'd ever wanted to go. I'm sure there were some folks on the internet who'd consider this a good time, but this just wasn't for me. Like feet. Don't get the appeal.

The sphincter had been closing and opening around me spasmodically so far, but now it opened out so wide that the point where my sword was embedded seemed to flop right over, and then I was dangling underneath it. Maybe the wyrm couldn't do fire any more, but the acrid reek rising from beneath my toes told me that he could do regular style digestion just fine. I did not want to be digested. I did not want to be dragon poop. This was not the future that I had envisioned for myself. I was not letting it happen.

When the throat contracted about me, trying to gulp me down deeper, I used that movement to power a swing, bringing my legs up to brace beside the Lucis where it was jammed and pulling it free.

End over end I tumbled down towards the wyrm's stomach, but I was not going to hit the bottom. The decay that had spread through the wyrm was everywhere in my Deathsense. Where it was nestled, none of my other senses could touch. But the corruption had wounded the great wyrm in ways that were unpredictable. Where the vines of death had coiled, they had strangled off life to whole sections of the wyrm's flesh—the parts that now rotted. There was dead meat and bone all about me, severed from the living body of Tsangaanax by the corruption, and if they were neither living nor dead, they were materials I could work.

With a strain of Artifice, I pulled a sheet of bone out from one of the wyrm's ribs. It was wafer thin, almost transparent between the ridges and nodules, but it was still strong enough to halt my fall.

Outside of the wyrm, I had no idea what was happening, and inside of the wyrm, it was too dark to read. I was being flung about, clinging to the edge of my bone-plate with my half-sliced fingers. I had to assume that the big fella was fighting Mercy and Asher by now and not just breakdancing on top of himself for the fun of it. It wasn't like they would have just run off and left me in here. Right?

The whole section I was in flipped upside down, and I started falling up off my bone-plate towards the frantically working sphincter again. I'd been sphinctered enough for one day, so I held onto the bone for dear life. A moment later we evened out, and I fell against the side of the throat as some awful rumble swept up from deeper in the beast. I felt it more than I saw it churning up towards me. It was that death-breath that he'd tried and failed to use on me. It didn't work on me, but that was because I was a Void Eternal. If it hit the others, what would happen? Would Mercy suddenly turn into a crabby old lady? At least she had the personality for it.

I couldn't let it happen. I reached out with Artifice and found basically nothing to work with. There were patches of dead tissue decaying around me in the neck, but nothing as substantial as the one hunk of necrotic bone I'd already hauled loose. I could flatten out the Lucis into a half-assed shield, but it wouldn't hold all of it back. I needed to put my whole ass into this.

Slaughter rippled out through my blade, and I could feel the answering echo of death within the wyrm about me, nowhere stronger than the wave of murderous black smoke pouring up from where once there was fire. There wasn't room to swing a cat in that neck, let alone a great-sword, so when the darkness washed up towards me, I pointed the blade straight at it, and I thrust with all my strength.

The death all around me leapt forward, and the death rushing towards me stopped dead. I couldn't throw the power around yet—I didn't have enough mastery of Resonant Dominion for that—but I could make it into a blade, and I thrust that blade down into the heart of the great beast. Well, in that general direction.

Tsangaanax might have been full of the shards' power, but he had no control over it. When I seized hold of that darkness and pushed, he had no way to resist. The veins of death woven through him were tugged free, ripping loose the rot and loosing blood from everywhere that had been stoppered. I was washed with it, scalded by the fresh blood plucked loose from ruined flesh. The whole throat was flooded with it. My platform was slick with it, and I was coated.

If the wyrm had tried to swallow me down again now, I would have been done for, but he didn't. Instead, he was trying to get me back up and out, like a bone stuck in his craw. The throat worked around me, and he swung his head back and forth, trying to knock me loose. I let him. I didn't want to be in here any more than he wanted me in here.

Back up the way I came, stumped fingers hooking into the torn parts of the wyrm's throat and blade carving in new foot-holds. There was a light at the end of the tunnel, framed top and bottom by the wyrm's terrifying teeth. I caught a glimpse of the cave tearing by as he twisted and turned, the flames that coated one side of his massive body were a red blur, and the lightning lashing down from some blind angle was a brief flash.

There was no way I was getting out past those teeth without getting shredded, so I did the only thing I could do. I rolled to my feet when Tsangaanax evened out to lunge at a blur that looked like Mercy, and I hacked into his gums. That skin was tough, and the bone beneath it was tougher still, but I had the advantage of this poor wyrm spending the last thousand years slowly decaying. What would once have been impenetrable was now spongy and porous.

Two teeth came loose from the bottom jaw, and by the time I swept my sword back around the other way, they were transformed into great-swords of their very own, swiping around on the same course. Back and forth I swung, and with every cut, and every piece of the wyrm I tore free, the bigger my arsenal grew. A dozen swords were spinning around me in an orbit by the time that I leapt free, each and every one of them sticky with gore. Tsangaanax's once fearsome grin was now peg-toothed and ridiculous.

I rolled to my feet outside the wyrm on what turned out to be the back of his great wing and was charging back in to send all twelve swords soaring into the bastard's face when The Prophet leapt out from a fold of skin and caught me by the arm. He'd found his courage again, it seemed. "You must not harm him."

Blood was coating the handle of the Lucis—mine and the wyrm's all mixed together. "Tell him not to harm us!"

When I tried to pull away, the flurry of the Prophet's arms twisted mine into a knot, and the Lucis was suddenly dangling limply from my hand as he strained to keep it locked in place. "It is not the master's fault; he is beyond reason with the pain…"

I wasn't much of a martial artist. If Seren had been given more time, maybe she could have taught me how to get out of lizard limb locks. All I had was strength. I strained against the hold he had on me, but still, he wouldn't let go. The tendons in my arm began to twang, and the bones ground together. My words came out strangled, "We can't help him if we're dead."

"We cannot help him if he is dead!" the Prophet snapped back.

"Then help us," I hissed. "Stop him."

He looked from me to the great wyrm he served, and he let go.

Asher's fireball took Tsangaanax in the face as he twisted after Mercy. Not enough to penetrate the scales, but enough to blind him and let her bound away unscathed. Her arrows peppered the great-wyrm's hide. Everywhere a scale had fallen away from rot there now seemed to be an arrow poking out. Blood trickled to turn the dust that had been his scales into a kind of chalky pink mud. It was every-where. Even the translucent membrane of the wing beneath my feet was smeared with it.

They were keeping the wyrm's attention, now I had to do what we came here to do. Even now the shards still sung to me. I could find them. I could take them. We could end this suffering.

A storm of swords followed me when I ran, looping around me in a spiral, lashing out when I twisted the Lucis to turn falling masonry aside, to bat the wyrm's writhing loops back into place—anything that I needed to do to keep me moving forward.

There was a shard on the far side of Tsangaanax's neck, but even as I came closer, the wyrm sighted me and twisted it away. Death-breath washed out towards me, and with no Slaughter in my blade, I had no way to work it. It passed me by without a scratch but behind me I heard a mournful wail. I didn't have time to look back, I didn't have time to see what the wyrm had done to his most loyal servant. The gore dribbling jaws of this titan were coming down at me once more.

I spun and I slashed, and the twelve bone blades I'd made from the wyrm's own teeth swept out to bat its lunge aside. They struck as one—twelve blows with all my strength behind them. The bones shattered to fragments, the scales on the wyrm's face cracked into powder, and his bite was knocked aside.

Tsangaanax's jaws snapped shut on his own body, jagged broken shards of tooth cracking through scales just as ruined. There was no time to watch him realize what he'd done to himself. No time to worry about the pain that could drive him to that madness. I leapt from one loop of the great wyrm to the next until the shard embedded beneath his jawbone was in sight.

All of the shards were one shard. The ones in my belt pouches, the one in the Lucis, and the ones in the wyrm. This time I didn't try to pull at it with Artifice or pry it with the strength of my body. I reached out through that resonation. The shards wanted to be together. They wanted to be one thing, not pieces. When I pulled back the Lucis, the shard in Tsangaanax's neck answered me. There was no struggle now. The veins of darkness that had hooked themselves into the wyrm's flesh came ready and willing along with the fragment itself, slithering back out through the warren of tunnels that they had made through the wyrm's body and soul and releasing their grip.

The shard flipped end over end through the air and into the palm of my maimed hand.

Quest: Return of the Voidgod
Acquire Rusted Blade Shards: 5/6 Complete
400 Glory Gained

I let out a shaky cry. "Got one!"

The wyrm shuddered and slumped helplessly beneath our feet, and fresh gouts of blood rushed out through the tiny hole in his neck as though I'd opened up a million wounds inside it, and this was where the pressure was forcing it out.

Mercy was too busy ducking and diving the wyrm's lashing tail to answer me, and I couldn't even see Asher. The second shard was singing even louder now. The one in my hand had been the Dvergar shard, and the other one had been in Tsangaanax possession longer—it had burrowed in deeper, closer to the last beating heart in his vast chest. I could feel it so much more clearly with all five pieces in my possession. Tsangaanax let out a long warbling wail: "Talon, I know it is you!"

I called back, "It's for your own good, buddy!"

I doubted that he could hear me, and even if he could, and it made it through to his Void-addled brain, I wasn't betting he'd believe it. I wouldn't have if someone started ripping bits out of me.

There was a whole lot of wyrm between me and the last part, and even though he seemed to be slowly dying, there was no way that Tsangaanax was going down without a fight. His whole body was in motion now, clawed legs shooting up out of the tangle of neck and tail, each limb three times the size of me and ending in claws that would definitely sting a little bit. He was reaching for me, kicking out with his feet at Mercy, and I'm pretty sure that even Asher was in the firing line for something.

Another burst of fire washed down over the wyrm from the tiny entrance to the cave, but in the chaos, the great beast had hauled up one wing like an umbrella to catch it. The membrane lit up from behind, blinding bright as Tsangaanax shielded both himself and me from Asher's strike. Throughout the skin, I could see the veins where the darkness had been, now filling in with pus and blood.

Weirdly, seeing that wing helped me more than anything else. From the wing I could find the back, and from the back I could find the chest. I set off running, even as the fire seared through the bubbling membrane and burst over us.

Fire Resistance kept the worst of it off me, and the Prophet definitely saw it coming, even if I couldn't see him. Tsangaanax though… he was like a powder keg. All the dust of his scales caught when the fire swept through, and it spread so fast it could only be called an explosion. The massive wing he'd brought around to shield himself snapped away from that burst with a crackle of breaking bone, and I was launched off my feet to smash into a raised ridge of fin that had lurched out of the morass as the wyrm writhed in agony. "Talon, why?"

I couldn't see Tsangaanax's head anywhere around, but that was probably for the best—he'd just use it to bite me if he saw me. Maybe he'd ducked into his own folds to keep his eyes and his wound away from the heat. I clawed my way forward, then got back upright somewhere between the end of one shifting coil of wyrm and the next. Everything was shifting so rapidly beneath me that the position of the last shard seemed to change every time I reached out for it. The ridge of fins I'd hit was probably the tail end of the body, and the broken wing was now subsiding down into the swirling scales, tentatively, like pulling it down slow would make it any less broken.

I chased that sinking sail of ruined skin, and I dove into the gap beneath it. Surrounded on all sides by scales once more, I squeezed through, crushed and battered as the serpent ground scales against scales. The last shard sung to me from up ahead, so close that I could taste it. So close that the rest of my shards were vibrating and dancing in their pouches and in my hand.

There was no need for stealth anymore, no need to pretend that this was anything but a violent invasion. I swung the Lucis back and forth, carving a bloody path through any flesh that would not part to mere shoving. I was almost to the shard again when, all of a sudden, I was tumbling end over end through open air. I hit stone, and it knocked what little breath I still had in me out. The bottom of the cave. Stone that had been the bed to the great wyrm for so long that I could still see the indentations of his scales in it.

The shard was here, nestled deep in the wyrm's flesh—so deep that if I were to shove my whole arm inside the wound, I didn't think that I could reach it. Good thing I didn't need to. The other shards were humming, desperate to be one again, resonating so much that the sound of it startled me. Humming aloud.

I got to my feet, set my stance, and was pulling the Lucis back when the great wyrm's head came hammering through the coils to lunge at me. I didn't have time to think. I didn't have time to do anything but move. Death poured out from the wyrm's mouth, and when I swung the Lucis with Slaughter rushing through it, I caught that wave and turned it back again.

This time there was no clumsiness, no awkward thrust in closed spaces. I made a clean swing of the sword, and the echo it made reflected that. The death that had permeated every part of the great wyrm leapt to answer.

The cut itself probably wouldn't have been lethal to something so unbelievable ancient and massive. His face was split apart on a diagonal, a quarter of his jaw dropping loose when the black arch passed through it, and I could see the white glint of bone up on his snout. One eye burst in a wave of gore, and scales all around rained down. If it had just been that cut, that would have been the end of it. But it wasn't just the cut.

The veins of death and destruction that were embedded throughout the wyrm's body leapt up to empower my strike, every part of them seeking to be a part of the murderous blow. It was those black veins tearing free that killed Tsangaanax.

Still staggered from the power I had unleashed, I felt the room spinning around me as I scrambled for the shard. All about me flesh was heaving, and I didn't know that the wyrm was dead yet. His head was still, his last eye staring blankly out at me with the same blank darkness it had always held, but that did not mean he was dead. Why would anyone have thought he was dead when every part of his body was coiling and twisting about me? When it undulated and pulsed as the long-restrained corruption was set loose throughout his flesh, it looked like the motion of an enraged beast. Just as it had moments before.

Surrounded by so much death, at the heart of the Voidgod's palace, it was a wonder Lifesense worked at all, and when my eyes were telling me clearly that the wyrm lived, I had no reason to doubt them.

I held up the Lucis before me, tapped into the resonation with the shard still embedded in Tsangaanax, and I pulled. There was a sound like a toilet being unblocked, and then the hunk of metal, still coated in a century's accumulated pus and poison, came soaring out to splat into my hand. Gross.

Quest: Return of the Voidgod
  Acquire Rusted Blade Shards: 6/6 Complete
  400 Glory Gained
Quest: Return of the Voidgod
  Reforge the Rusted Blade: 0/1 Complete

Just like that, our whole purpose on Amaranth was complete. I let out a little laugh that honestly sounded a bit hysterical even to me, then I remembered why I was here and what I'd promised. The slimy shard went into a pouch with the others, and I rushed to Tsangaanax's side, laying my hands on his wounds and pouring forth Primal power to heal him.

The green glow surrounded my hands and then went nowhere. I pressed it to the scales of the wyrm, over and over, as the beast writhed and quaked above me, but still, Restoration refused to work. The scales must have been in the way. I darted over to the gruesome, leaking wound in the wyrm's side and I shoved my hands right in. "Come on, heal."

Still, Restoration did nothing. With the shards gone, there should have been nothing left to interfere. My Deathsense couldn't detect those great black veins of destructive power running through the wyrm anymore—I'd removed them when I plucked the shards out—so why wasn't this working?

The coil behind me collapsed in on itself, and a plume of dust and noxious gases erupted. Through the gap I could see the cave above. I needed help. This wasn't working.

I scrambled and climbed as the impossible weight of the wyrm bore down on the remains, and the fragile encasement of scales proved too weak to hold shape without anything solid beneath. I leapt clear just as the unburned wing of the wyrm burst up from the far side of the cavern, rot already oozing through it. "Asher!"

Everywhere I looked, my Deathsense was screaming at me. The solidified power of the shards' influence was gone, but death itself felt like it was everywhere now, permeating the whole room as it spread throughout the great wyrm. "Asher! Use cauterize! Hurry! He's dying."

Asher stood up there in a tiny hole in the wall of this giant cham-ber, and he shook his head helplessly, watching one of his gods die before his eyes. Mercy came tumbling down beside me, rebounding off an exposed rib that was now glistening through a coil of wyrm. "We've got to get out."

I was grabbing at her frantically, smearing her clean leather armor with gore and pus. "We promised we'd heal him. Asher needs to—"

She took hold of my arms and stopped me. "He's dead."

That didn't make any sense. "No… no… I just saw him up in the tunnel, he's—"

"The wyrm." She sighed. "He's done. We're done. It's over."

Victory!
Potency increased to 57
Piety increased to 15
Climbing: 4/10
Resonant Dominion: 10/10
380 Experience Gained

Denial is a hell of a drug. "We're going to save him. We're going to heal him. We're going to fix this, and then he'll be super grateful, and we'll go on dragon rides, and he'll help us fight the Voidgod, and—"

She slapped me in the face. "Dude. He's dead. Stop being crazy."

It felt like the floor beneath me had given out. It hadn't, but the wyrm on top of it definitely did. We plunged down through the rapidly decaying corpse to land in the heap of bones that was all that remained of Tsangaanax. "I didn't… I didn't mean to…"

Mercy took hold of my hands. "He was trying to kill us. He was suffering. You made that stop."

"I didn't want to…" Tears were prickling at my eyes. I'd just had a massive awesome dragon fight and saved the world. Why was I so sad?

She slapped me again, although this time I was pretty sure it was just because she was having a good time slapping me. "Sometimes all we can do is make the bad stuff stop."

I turned the useless Restoration I'd been holding onto back on myself and regrew my fingers. "Okay."

It took some time to pick our way over to what was left of the White Prophet. Just one more set of bones amidst so many more. The decay that the power of the shards had been inflicting and holding at bay in equal measure had swept through the gargantuan wyrm so quickly that it was hard to believe he had been alive only a few moments ago.

The Prophet's annihilation had not been so clean. There were still scales draped over his corpse, rotting threads of flesh clinging across the black-streaked tangle of bones beneath. What Tsangaanax had been trying to do to me, he had successfully done to his most loyal servant—the one who saw his master suffering and moved heaven and earth to find a way to make it stop. I would never get to find out if he was happy with the result of his labors. I told the crumbling body, "It's done."

Asher was making his way down to us, slipping and scrabbling for purchase on the angled bones he was trying to use as a ramp. I had to jog over and catch him when he inevitably slipped and came tumbling down.

"My thanks to you."

I managed a smile. "Any time."

Asher looked as shell-shocked as me now that he was down here amidst the death, gawking and hissing at each fresh horror he passed by. There were bones riddled with decay, pocked and withered. The scales had turned to powder entirely once the great wyrm lost cohesion. The whole chamber was painted white with the dust, overlayed here and there with a black splatter of decay. It crunched underfoot like fresh snowfall.

Mercy clapped her hands together, startling us both out of our reverie. "Alright. Let's do it."

"I'm still a bit hung up on my dead girlfriend, but I'm sure Asher would be happy to…"

Asher was frantically shaking his head.

"I will cut your dick off!" Mercy snapped. "I mean the sword, the shards, the blade. Reforging. Let's get it done."

I let out a shaky laugh. "You don't want to take a minute?"

"I want this whole thing over with." She kicked me in the ass—but playfully instead of viciously. "I want the Voidgod to pop up, get his ass kicked, and then we can all get back to having a good time. So come on, let's do it. Get busy. Do your divine blacksmith stuff."

I got all of the pieces of the Rusted Blade out of their respective pockets and lined them all up on the floor. The metal that I had wrapped around the Lucis to make it into a great-sword slunk away to lie in a heap beside me, providing any material I needed for patching gaps.

The Lucis itself was resistant to my Artifice, so I had to reach out with my bare hands and surge Potency to snap the blade off cleanly. From there it was more awkward work, prying the shard free of the Artifact that had been its home for so long. I kept the handle of the Lucis aside. That would serve as the Rusted Blade's new home too.

I set all the pieces down in front of me on the bare and dusty stone. This was it, what we'd been waiting for all this time, what we'd been working for since we first arrived on Amaranth. It was finally done. We were finished.

"Are you just going to stare at it?" Mercy kicked me again. "Come on!"

Asher gawked at her. "This is a momentous occasion!"

"There have been way too many momentous occasions lately." Mercy didn't even bother to face him. "Let's just get this over with."

I stretched out my hands over the assembled shards, and I closed my eyes. Artifice swept out from me. The bones all around us cried out to be made into something. The only thing that felt real in this whole cavern of Void-blighted stone. I ignored them, and I turned the weight of my attention onto the shards.

The moment my consciousness brushed against them, the Voidgod was there.

Araphel stood just beyond the shards, towering over me as I crouched there. When Leofric had wanted you to feel a certain way, he could force his feelings on you. When Koschei had wanted a thought in your head, he could push it in. Araphel did neither, but the weight of his unbridled fury washed over me all the same. *Do not dare.*

All of this time, I'd been bearing the burden of these chats with the Voidgod by myself, but not anymore. The secret was out. "Araphel says we shouldn't make the sword, guys. Do you think we should listen to him?"

Mercy laughed out loud, and Asher, still the more respectful of us even after watching one of his own gods being reduced to bones, merely shook his head.

I shrugged at the Voidgod. "Sorry, man, I took a vote, and the three of us said yes to making the sword that can kill you. And you don't get a vote. Because you're a ghost."

The first two shards slotted together perfectly, a jigsaw perfect match, and all it took was a tiny push of Artifice to make the steel merge into one piece.

"*Do you know what an enemy you are making? Before I had a whole world arrayed against me and it was too weak a foe, and now you would make yourself my sole target? Why do you crave death so?*"

The joined pieces slotted neatly into the Lucis handle, with just a little extra iron added in to fuse the blade to the tang of metal running the length of the grip. "I've got to tell you, Araphel, you're sounding kind of scared right now."

"*Cease this pointless exercise, and I shall reward you. On my return, I shall raise you up. You shall be first among my generals. The whole of Amaranth will be ours to claim.*"

I added on the next shard up—the one that we'd retrieved from the land of the dead, and it sealed onto the blade seamlessly. There was still rust and ruin engraved into every piece of metal, but there was no denying that it was a sword now. "Amaranth isn't yours to give away."

"*Power is the only truth in this life, and there is no power greater than mine.*" He crept in closer until the featureless expanse of his face filled up my vision with darkness. "*Your gods are cripples, unable to even walk this world. Your own powers are so insignificant that it is comical to behold.*"

With all your might, you could not scratch me. Sword or no sword."

"Yeah, that's why you're so scared." I gave him my best sneer, even if I could feel my hands trembling at his presence. "Because this isn't going to kill your ass."

He reared back from me as if I'd hit him, and in that moment of distraction, I forged another fragment into the blade. The harmonies between the pieces were no longer there. All shards were one shard All shards were this one blade. In the place of the humming there was a hunger. It was so close to done now. Just two more pieces and my life's work to date was over. The quest that had driven us from the first moment we stepped foot on Amaranth. Mercy put her hand on my shoulder, and a glance showed me the smile on her face. Asher still looked nervous, presumably because I was picking a fight with the Voidgod, but what was I meant to do? Not fight him? He was the bad guy. The baddest of all bad guys.

Araphel stood over me once more, amidst the swirl of dust that had kicked up as I used my Artifice. *Do not do this. Name your price. Do you want me to return your little wench? Do you want dominion over all this world? Over your old world—whichever it was? I can give you it all. I have the power.*"

"If you're so powerful, why do you need to beg?" I slotted another shard into place. Only the Alvaren piece was left—the very tip of the blade.

"*Is it my debasement that you seek? If I fall to my knees and proclaim you my master, will that be enough to sate you?*" Araphel's voice had gone from booming to a hiss. He actually did it. He bent down onto his knees, held up his wickedly clawed hands, and he begged. *"Do not do this. Please, do not do this.*"

I was so surprised that I actually stopped. "Uh, guys, he's on his knees, begging me to stop."

Mercy snorted in disdain. "Don't stop."

"That's what she said." I chuckled back.

Asher groaned. "Now at the moment of our great victory, you must pause to declare your innuendos? I beg you too, please just let it be done."

"Do not forge the blade. Do not fight me." Araphel's voice, usually so grating and grim, sounded almost soft as he pleaded with me. *"Whatever you desire is yours. Whatever it is within my power to give is yours. All that you need do is stop."*

Staring up into the total darkness of his face, I didn't have to think twice about my answer. "No."

I slipped the last piece into place.

Quest: Return of the Voidgod
   Reforge the Rusted Blade: 1/1 Complete
   400 Glory Gained

The sword, in all of its glory, did not look very impressive. It was a longsword, once upon a time, and the rust had long since taken any edge off it. The Lucis handle was the only part of it that looked fit to touch, but still, it was the sword that had killed the Voidgod before. That had to count for something.

I reached out a hand to take it, and it exploded.

The Void leapt out of the blade and washed over us—a concussion of absolute darkness that blinded all my other senses and made my Deathsense shriek as it was overwhelmed. Even with the protections of being a Void Eternal, the force of it was enough to launch me into the distant wall of the cavern.

Mercy and Asher had been right by my side, and they had none of that protection. Asher hung, impaled right through his middle from one of Tsangaanax's ribs. Mercy had been even less lucky. Half of her body was just gone, and half her face melted away, her skull shining out. I crawled over to lay my hands on her and pour out Restoration, but it was like everything else that the Void blighted, it couldn't touch her. "No. No. No."

She was panting, still impossibly alive. One eye was all she had left, and tears of terror and agony were flowing freely from it.

I had to kill her. If the Void killed her, then she might never come back. That lethal energy that let me slay Eternals was the same thing as had struck her. But my sword was gone, the leftover metal I'd been using had been wiped away from my senses with the explosion. All I had was my bare hands. "I'm sorry. I'm so sorry."

I closed my hands around her neck, and I twisted. I could see the fear on what was left of her face. I could see the moment of pain when I turned her neck too far, and the bone began to give. Her lips were moving, but no sound came out. Her body was too damaged to puff out the air. "I'm sorry."

Her neck broke, her body vanished, and I willed with all I had that she'd end up whole and healthy back in her shrine at Talon's Keep.

I turned to look to Asher, and then I saw him.

Araphel stood proudly in the crater where the Rusted Blade had been, blacker than night. Black as the space between the stars. Hazy, as the little light that there was around him died as it came close.

"Oh, I beg you, mighty godling, pretty please." His laughter made my stomach turn. Like nails on the chalkboard of my brain. *"Oh, please don't put the blade that my soul was trapped in back together again. Don't undo what your desperate predecessor did to keep me from being reborn the very moment he struck me down."*

My brain still couldn't make sense of what my eyes were seeing. "Araphel…"

With one clawed hand he reached up towards Asher and disintegrated the skeleton of the Wyrm. Asher fell boneless and useless to the dust, the spear through his chest now gone and the blood flowing freely. *"You cannot imagine my delight when I realized what an imbecile you were. That you would be so easy to trick."*

When I tried to rise, I felt like all the strength had been knocked out of me. I had to grab onto bones that were already crumbling away, just to force myself to my feet so I could face him. If I was dying, I was dying standing. "You played me?"

I knew the answer. It was blindingly obvious. But I needed him to go on talking. I needed his gloating to fill up the time it took me to force my body forward. It was like walking against the tide. The power pouring out from him in waves almost tipped me right back over again as I closed the distance.

Araphel's laugh dug in like broken glass. *"The girl, she had wit enough to concern me, her suspicions were well grounded, if misplaced, but somehow you managed to make her believe that you were harmless. You made a shield of your own ignorance, and it protected me so very well. I suppose that I should thank you, though you did not know I was the one that you served."*

Getting closer to him was a bad idea on so many levels. My soul seemed to be trying to crawl out the back of my body. Looking right at him hurt my eyes. Just being in his presence hurt. It got so much worse once he was inside my Sphere of Influence. The static buzz that had marked all that he had touched was turned up to eleven, not just numbing my senses but making them screech in agony. I had to fight every instinct to come closer, to put my hand into that metaphorical fire, even though I knew it was going to burn.

"Have you come now to give obeisance." Every grinding word he spoke hit me like a hammer. My skin peeled away on the surface closest to him. More pain. Just another drop in the ocean. *"To admit defeat and hope that I will be merciful?"*

It took everything I had to say, "No."

"What then?" His giggles were the worst thing I'd ever experienced, and I've been dissolved from the inside out with acid. *"You cannot*

mean to fight me."

I guessed that was as close as I was getting. I flung out my arms and let Artifice wash out.

The wyrm's bones were shattered and ruined by the Voidgod's return, the surface levels of them invisible to my Artifice, but they were old and huge, and even the passive touch of a god didn't reach all the way through them. There was still workable bone somewhere inside. I pulled it all out, and I flung it with all my might.

Whatever bones weren't already crumbling to dust around us exploded into shards now, the razor fragments of them sharpening into darts as they flew. Araphel's laughter was deafening. He didn't even raise a shield against my attack. Everywhere a bone struck him, it simply vanished into the darkness like it was falling into the black hole of his body.

"Pathetic."

As an attack on him, yeah, it was pretty useless. But the problem with being all-powerful and worshipped and all that jazz, is that you tend to forget that you aren't actually the center of the universe. The shards that had struck Asher had hammered home, and I willed his spirit away to Talon's Keep just a moment before his body blinked out of sight.

Needless to say, Araphel wasn't happy to lose one of his new toys, and a wave of destruction ripped out of him. All the bones, all the dust, everything in the cavern was obliterated. Only me and the Voidgod remained at the center of a perfect sphere in the stone when he regained his composure. *"It matters little. He shall be destroyed just as all this world shall be destroyed. You have bought him time. Perhaps long enough for him to make peace with those he worships before the end. Was that the kindness you meant to do him?"*

The bare cavern was dead to me. I had nothing to work with. No way to forge a weapon and off myself before Araphel did it for me.

I did not want him to decide where my spirit went. It would not be somewhere pleasant, and he certainly wouldn't be keeping me around on Amaranth to fight him.

Araphel strode towards me in the sudden silence of the empty chamber, and I'm not too proud to admit that I fell to my knees. It wasn't about bowing down to him, and it wasn't about admitting defeat, my body just couldn't hold up against the strain of being so close to him. I tried to think back to the gods I'd met before, if any of them had this effect on me, and I honestly couldn't think of anything like it. Not even Chernghast had this raw power.

"Will you weep now, little godling? Will you cry because you have doomed the world? It would be just for you to know sorrow, when you have unleashed the end of all things with your folly."

Until he'd said that I had been feeling a bit like crying, but that snarky little comment brought the old rage in my guts boiling up. I wasn't evil because I'd been tricked. He was evil for tricking me. That cold anger, more than anything else, helped me to rise back up.

"Perhaps fair recompense would be to let you feel what I have felt these past millennia." He reached out to me with his clawed hands, tail lashing behind him, and I felt the power that had been washing harmlessly around me until now crystalize into a jagged pain in the middle of my chest. *"Let me rend your soul apart and spread it throughout the universe. Let me scatter all that you are, so that you feel you will never be whole again. So that you feel the loss of your entirety, ever aching across the fathoms."*

The power of the void pressed into me, blood blossomed from my chest, and ribs snapped and sprung out as he drove that force of pure destruction deeper and deeper. Araphel was taking his time, savoring the first kill since he was reborn.

Even through the pain, the screaming of my Deathsense was still overpowering. All of the destructive energy of the Void swirled through Araphel, projecting out into the point that pressed into my flesh. So much raw power than any other time, I could have seized control of and used in a twin-strike to slay my enemies. It was not mine to command. Araphel had total mastery over the void. The powers of destruction that I had barely started toying with were his to wield with a thought.

In a moment I was going to die, and while I know that I keep on saying death is not the end, that one probably would have been. How do you recover from having your soul torn to pieces and scattered throughout the universe if you aren't a god that had plans to spend the next few millennia tricking schmucks into putting you together again? You don't. This was as final a death as ever there was.

Blood bubbled up to my lips as I whispered, "Araphel."

He leaned in close, smug despite the absence of any face to be smug with. "*Yes?*"

Spirit Strike leapt out from my forehead to plough into his. That perfect nude shot I'd shown to Leo echoed into the mind of the Void-god, and like that other pompous arrogant prick, it threw him. "*What?*"

A moment of indecision was all that I needed. I strained every pillar of divinity together, and powers that were never meant to mix collided. Artifice and Slaughter.

The blade already buried in my chest was all that I needed, and the mind that was driving it had just lost its grip. It might have been forged from death instead of steel, but the blade in my chest was a sword. All swords were one sword. In the moment that that blade was mine, I set off a Twin Strike. The echo of the void-blade leapt through me, shredding me from the inside out, the pure destruction rolling out through my body and obliterating every inch of flesh that remained.

Nothing but pain was left in my mind. Pain and a desperate wish to go home.

Then there was darkness.

CHAPTER 31

I hung shapeless and still in the darkness for so long that I was convinced that I'd failed. That Araphel had seized control of my soul's destination and thrown me into the Void. I saw nothing, heard nothing, felt nothing. It was as peaceful a moment as I'd ever experienced—apart from the rage still churning inside me.

As soon as I was resurrected, relief washed through and that strength fled me. I stood for just a moment, grasping at myself to check if I was all there or if Araphel had managed to claw some pieces back. My body seemed to be intact, but my soul would take a bit more careful study. As for my mind, I was pretty sure it was damaged beyond repair.

Mercy caught me as I fell. Her white hair was missing on the injured side, and her face was a spiderwebbed mass of scars where the Void had touched her. She had a shard tied to her soul, the same as me. Maybe that was what had helped her to survive.

We leaned against each other, swaying as the exhaustion of it all washed over us. The helplessness. "You saved us. You got us out."

Asher was not a big cuddler as far as emotional displays went, but right now, I think we all needed something to hold onto. He wrapped his arms around the both of us, as much to keep us standing as to give us comfort. I don't think I'd ever seen Mercy crying before that day. I don't think any of us had ever felt so helpless.

The dvergar came pouring out of their fresh-built town to welcome us home, all smiles and certainty that no matter what the world threw their way, they were going to be safe now. We hadn't just ruined our own lives, we'd doomed all of them too. The whole world of Amaranth was going to be destroyed. We had nothing that could stand up to

Araphel. No magic sword… no special powers… nothing.

Asher was the one to say what we'd all been thinking. "What have we done?"

Mercy shook within our embrace, not with sobs but with anger. "We didn't know. How could we have known?"

There was no answer to that—and no need for one. I looked out across the gathered Dvergar. I could see the fear mounting on their faces. I could feel that same dread in my chest. This wasn't a game, this wasn't a story, the Voidgod was here, now. He was coming. If he wasn't stopped, this whole world would die. The universe that was an echo of Amaranth would follow after.

Asher's voice hissed out behind me. "What… do we do?"

That was a question that needed a reply, and even as fear fought to strangle me, I said what I knew I had to say. The only thing that you could say in the face of something evil coming to destroy everything you know and love.

"We fight."

To be concluded in
Savage Dominion: *Voidgod*

Thank You All! Please Read!

Hi everyone! Thank you so much for taking the time to read *Savage Dominion: Wyrmshard* and continuing along with us on this awesome LitRPG adventure! We both hope that you all had a blast and are excited to see what happens to Maulkin and the others in the last and final book of the series! It's only because of all of your support and excitement that we're able to work on these stories and continue to improve.

On that subject, a few notes:

First: **Please, *please*, consider rating and reviewing *Wyrmshard* on Amazon, Audible, Goodreads, as well as any of your other favorite book sites**. Many people don't know that there are thousands of books published every day, most of those in the USA alone. Over the course of a year, a quarter of a million authors will vie for a small place in the massive world of print and publishing. We fight to get even the tiniest traction, fight to climb upward one inch at a time towards the bright light of bestsellers, publishing contracts, and busy book signings.

Thing is, we need all the help we can get, and that's where wonderful readers like you come in!

Second: If you want to join our growing community, be sure to join Wraithmarked Creative's private readers' group on Facebook! Both of us are active participants in the group, so tag us with any questions, check out all the other awesome books Wraithmarked is publishing in the coming months, and chat with those authors as well!

Regardless of whether or not you choose to review, reach out, or support us elsewhere, thank you again for taking the time to read *Savage Dominion: Wyrmshard,* and we will see you in the final book - ***Voidgod!***

Thank you all so so much,
Luke & GD